COSMIC POWERS

THE SAGA ANTHOLOGY OF FAR-AWAY GALAXIES

EDITED BY JOHN JOSEPH ADAMS

SAGA PRESS

LONDON SYDNEY **NEW YORK** TORONTO NEW DELHI

SAGA PRESS

AN IMPRINT OF SIMON & SCHUSTER, INC.

1230 AVENUE OF THE AMERICAS, NEW YORK, NEW YORK 10020

For

JIM STARLIN, RON MARZ, and RON LIM,

Heralds of Wonder

CONTENTS

INTRODUCTION

JOHN JOSEPH ADAMS

The foundation of science fiction and fantasy is sense of wonder. And nowhere is sense of wonder more prevalent than in stories of larger-than-life heroes battling menacing forces, in far-flung galaxies, with the fate of the universe at stake.

My love for these kinds of stories began in the pages of comic books like *Silver Surfer* and the other "cosmic tales" of the Marvel Universe. Stories of godlike beings such as the planet-devourer Galactus, the sole survivor of the universe that preceded this one; the Mad Titan Thanos, who embarks on a quest to conquer the universe as a way of impressing the embodiment of Death; or the Celestials and Eternity, who, though nigh-omnipotent, somehow find themselves, from time to time, involved with the affairs of mortals. When I discovered these characters and their stories, my mind was set ablaze . . . and I was hopelessly, fanatically hooked.

Forever after, I was always chasing that "sensawunda" high, eventually moving on from comics to science fiction and fantasy novels (and, there, clearly found much to love—and a career). And so, spurred by that nostalgia and the improbable—but deeply gratifying—success of Marvel's *Guardians of the Galaxy* movie, I challenged seventeen writers to tackle that same kind of larger-than-life, "cosmic scale" story as I first found in those comics I fell in love with as a kid.

And boy, did they deliver.

When I met my wife, she told me that when she writes prose, she visualizes the scenes in her stories as if they were comic book panels. In the case of this anthology, it's my hope that when you *read* the prose you'll visualize those comics panels too—each scene like a big, two-page spread encompassing the entire cosmos, setting your mind ablaze with wonder.

A TEMPORARY EMBARRASSMENT IN SPACETIME

CHARLIE JANE ANDERS

1.

Sharon's head itched from all the fake brain implants, and the massive cybernetic headdress was giving her a cramp in her neck. But the worst discomfort of all was having to pretend to be the loyal servant of a giant space blob. Pretending to be a *thing* instead of a person. This was bringing back all sorts of ugly memories from her childhood.

The Vastness was a ball of flesh in space, half the size of a regular solar system, peering out into the void with its billions of slimy eyemouths. It orbited a blue giant sun, Naxos, which used to have a dozen planets before The Vastness ate them all. That ring around The Vastness wasn't actually a ring of ice or dust, like you'd see around a regular planet. Nope—it was tens of thousands of spaceships that were all docked together by scuzzy umbilicals, and they swarmed with humans and other people, who all lived to serve The Vastness.

The Vastness didn't really talk much, except to bellow "I am everything!" into every listening device for a few light-years in any direction, and also directly into the minds of its human acolytes.

After five days, Sharon was getting mighty sick of hearing that voice yelling in her ear. "I am everything!" The Vastness roared. "You are everything!" Sharon shouted back, which was the standard response. Sharon really needed a shower—bathing wasn't a big priority among the devotees of The Vastness—and she was getting creeped out from staring into the eyes of people who hadn't slept in forever. (The Vastness didn't sleep, so why should its servants?)

"We're finally good to go," said Kango's voice in Sharon's earpiece, under the knobby black cone she was wearing over her cranium.

"Thank Hall and Oates," Sharon subvocalized back.

She was standing in a big orange antechamber aboard one of the large tributary vessels in the ring around The Vastness, and she was surrounded by other people wearing the same kind of headgear. Except that their headgear was real, and they really were getting messages from The Vastness, and they would probably not be thrilled to know that her fake headgear actually contained the ship's hypernautic synchrotrix, which she'd stolen hours earlier.

Sharon and Kango had a client back on Earthhub Seven who would pay enough chits for that synchrotrix to cover six months' worth of supplies. Plus some badly needed upgrades to their ship, the *Spicy Meatball*. If she could only smuggle it out of here without the rest of these yo-yos noticing.

Kango had finally spoofed The Vastness's embarkation catechism, so the Meatball could separate from the ring without being instantly blown up. Sharon started edging toward the door.

"I am everything!" The Vastness shouted through every speaker and every telepathic implant on the tributary ship, including Sharon's earpiece.

"You are everything!" Sharon shouted . . . just a split second later than everyone else in the room.

She was halfway to the door, which led to an airlock, which led to a long interstitial passageway, which led to a junction, which led to a set of other ships' antechambers, beyond which was the airlock to the *Meatball*, which they'd disguised to look just like another one of these tributary ships.

Sharon tried to look as though she was just checking the readings on one of the control panels closer to the exit to this tributary ship. The synchrotrix was rattling around inside her big headdress, and she had to be careful not to damage it, since it was some incredibly advanced design that nobody else in the galaxy had. Sharon was so close to the exit. If she could just . . .

"Sister," a voice behind her said. "What are you doing over there? How do your actions serve The Vastness?"

She turned to see a man with pale skin and a square face that looked ridiculous under his big cybernetic Pope hat, staring at her. Behind him, two other acolytes were also staring.

"Brother, I . . ." Sharon groped around on the control table behind her. Her hand landed on a cup of the nutritious gruel that the servants of The Vastness lived on. "I, uh, I was just making sure these neutron actuator readings were aligned with, uh, the—"

"That screen you are looking at is the latrine maintenance schedule," the man said.

"Right. Right! I was concerned that The Vastness wouldn't want us to have a faulty latrine, because, um . . ."

"I am everything!" The Vastness shouted.

"Because, I mean, if we had to wear diapers—you are everything!—then I mean, we wouldn't be able to walk as quickly if The Vastness might require when it summons . . ."

Now everybody was staring at Sharon. She was so damn close to the door.

"Why did you not make your response to the Call of The Vastness immediately?"

"I was just, uh, so overcome with love for The Vastness, I was momentarily speechless." Sharon kept looking at the man while groping her way to the door.

The man pulled out a gun—a Peacebreaker 5000, a nice model, which would have been worth some chits back on Earthhub Seven—and aimed it at her. "Sister," he said. "I must restrain you and deliver you to the Head Acolyte for this sector, who will determine whether you—"

Sharon did the only thing she could think of. She shouted, "I am everything!"

The man blinked as she spoke the words reserved only for The Vastness. For a second, his mind couldn't even process what he had just heard—and then the cupful of cold gruel hit him in the face.

The man lowered his gun just long enough for Sharon to make a lunge for it. Her headdress cracked, and the synchrotrix fell out. She caught it with her left hand while she grabbed for the gun with her right hand. The man was trying to aim the gun at her again, and she head-butted him. The gun went off, hitting one of the walls of the ship and causing a tiny crack to appear.

Both of the women had jumped on Sharon and the man, and now there were three acolytes trying to restrain her and pry the gun and synchrotrix from her hands. She bit one of the women, but the other one had a chokehold on her.

"I am everything!" shouted The Vastness.

"You are everything!" responded everyone except Sharon.

By the time they'd finished giving the ritual response, Sharon had a firm grip on the gun, and it was aimed at the head of the shorter of the two women. "I'm leaving here," Sharon said. "Don't try to stop me."

"My life means nothing," the woman said, with the gun right against her cone-head. "Only The Vastness has meaning."

"I'll shoot the other two after I shoot you," said Sharon. She had reached the door. She shoved the woman into the antechamber, leapt through the doorway, and pushed the button to close the door behind her. The door didn't close.

"Crap," Sharon said.

"The overrides are on already. You won't escape," the woman Sharon had threatened at gunpoint gloated. "Praise The Vastness!"

"Screw The Vastness," said Sharon, aiming at the crack in the ship's hull and pulling the trigger on the Peacebreaker 5000. Then she took off running.

2.

"You took your time." Kango was already removing his own fake headdress and all the other ugly adornments that had disguised him as one of The Vastness's followers. "Did anybody see you slip away?"

"You could say that." Sharon ran into the *Spicy Meatball*'s control area and strapped herself into the copilot seat. "We have to leave. Now." She felt the usual pang of gladness at seeing Kango again—even if they got blown up, they were going to get blown up together.

Just then, The Vastness howled, "I have been robbed! I am everything, and someone has stolen from Me!"

"I thought you were the stealthy one." Kango punched the ship's thrusters and they pushed away from The Vastness's ring at two times escape velocity. "You're always telling me that I make too much noise, I'm too prone to spontaneous dance numbers, I'm too—what's the word— irrepressible, and you're the one who knows how to just get in and get out. Or did I misinterpret your whole 'I'm a master of stealth, I live in the shadows' speech the other day?"

"Just drive," Sharon hissed.

"You just think you're better than me because I'm a single-celled organism, and you're all multicellular," said Kango, who looked to all outside appearances like an incredibly beautiful young human male with golden skin and a wicked smile. "You're a cellist. Wait, is that the word? What do you call someone who discriminates against other people based on the number of cells in their body?"

They were already point three light-years away from The Vastness, and there was no sign of pursuit. Sharon let out a breath. She looked at the big ugly blob of scar tissue, with all of its eyemouths winking at her one by one, and at the huge metallic ring around its middle. The whole thing looked kind of beautiful in the light of Naxos, especially when you were heading in the opposite direction at top speed.

"You know perfectly well that I don't hold your monocellularity against you," Sharon told Kango in a soothing tone. "And next time, I will be happy to let you be the one to go into the heart of the monster and pull out its tooth, and yes, I know that's a mixed metaphor, but . . ."

"Uh, Sharon?"

". . . but I don't care, because I need a shower lasting a week, not to mention some postindustrial-strength solvent to get all this gunk off my head."

"Sharon. I think we have a bit of an issue."

Sharon stopped monologuing and looked at the screen, where she'd just been admiring the beauty of The Vastness and its ring of ships a moment earlier. The ring of ships was peeling ever so slowly away from The Vastness and forming itself into a variation of a standard pursuit formation—the variation was necessary because the usual pursuit formation didn't include several thousand Joykiller-class ships and many assorted others.

"Uh, how many ships is that?"

"That is all of the ships. That's how many."

"We're going to be cut into a million pieces and fed to every one of The Vastness's mouths," Sharon said. "And they're going to keep us alive and conscious while they do it."

"Can they do that?" Kango jabbed at the *Meatball*'s controls, desperately trying to get a little more speed out of the ship.

"Guys, I'm going as fast as I can," said Noreen, the ship's computer, in a petulant tone. "Poking my buttons won't make me go any faster."

"Sorry, Noreen," said Sharon.

"Wait, I have a thought," said Kango. "The device you stole, the hypernautic synchrotrix. It functions by creating a Temporary Embarrassment in spacetime, which lets The Vastness and all its tributary ships transport themselves instantaneously across the universe in search of prey. Right? But what makes it so valuable is the way that it neutralizes all gravity effects. An object the size of The Vastness should throw planets out of their orbits and disrupt entire solar systems whenever it appears, but it doesn't."

"Sure. Yeah." Sharon handed the synchrotrix to Kango, who studied it frantically. "So what?"

"Well, so," Kango said. "If I can hook it into Noreen's drive systems . . ." He was making connections to the device as fast as he could. "I might be able to turn Noreen into a localized spatial Embarrassment generator. And that, in turn, means that we can do something super super clever."

Kango pressed five buttons at once, triumphantly, and . . . nothing happened.

Kango stared at the tiny viewscreen. "Which means," he said again, "we can do something super super SUPER clever." He jabbed all the buttons again (causing Noreen to go "ow"), and then something did happen: a great purple-and-yellow splotch opened up directly behind the *Spicy Meatball*, and all of the ships chasing them were stopped dead. A large number of the pursuit ships even crashed into each other because they had been flying in too tight a formation.

"So long, cultists!" Kango shouted. He turned to Sharon, still grinning. "I created a Local Embarrassment, which collided with the Temporary Embarrassment fields that those ships were already generating, and set up a chain reaction in which this region of spacetime became Incredibly Embarrassed. Which means . . ."

". . . none of those ships will be going anywhere for a while," Sharon said.

"See what I mean? I may only have one cell, but it's a *brain* cell." He whooped and did an impromptu dance in his seat. "Like I said: You're the stealthy one, I'm the flashy one."

"I'm the one who needs an epic shower." Sharon pulled at all the crap glued to her head while also putting the stolen synchrotrix safely into a padded strongbox. She was still tugging at the remains of her headgear when she moved toward the rear of the ship in search of its one bathroom, and she noticed something moving in the laundry compartment.

"Hey, Kango?" Sharon whispered as she came back into the flight deck. "I think we have another problem."

She put her finger to her lips, then led him back to the laundry area, where she pulled the compartment open with a sudden tug to reveal a slender young woman curled up in a pile of dirty flight suits, wearing the full headgear of an acolyte of The Vastness. The girl looked up at them.

"Praise The Vastness," she said. "Have we left the ring yet? I yearn to help you spread the good word about The Vastness to the rest of the galaxy! All hail The Vastness!"

Sharon and Kango just looked at each other, as if each trying to figure out how they could make this the other one's fault.

3.

Sharon and Kango had known each other all their lives, and they were sort of married and sort of united by a shared dream. If a single-celled organism could have a sexual relationship with anybody, Kango would have made it happen with Sharon. And yet, a lot of the time, they kind of hated each other. Cooped up with Noreen on the *Spicy Meatball*, when they weren't being chased by literal-minded cyborgs or sprayed with brainjuice from the brainbeasts of Noth, they started going a little crazy.

Kango would start trying to osmose the seat cushions and Sharon would invent terrible games. They were all they had, but they were kind of bad for each other all the same. Space was lonely, and surprisingly smelly, at least if you were inside a ship with artificial life support.

They'd made a lot of terrible mistakes in their years together, but they'd never picked up a stowaway from a giant-space-testicle cult before. This was a new low. They immediately started doing what they did best: bicker.

"I like my beer lukewarm and my equations ice-cold," Kango said. "Just sayin'."

"Hey, don't look at me," Sharon said.

The teenage girl, whose name was TheVastnessIsAllWonderfulJaramellaLovesTheVastness, or Jara for short, was tied to the spare seat in the flight deck with thick steelsilk cords. Since Jara had figured out that she'd stowed away on the wrong ship and these people weren't actually fellow servants of The Vastness, she'd stopped talking to them. Because why bother to speak to someone who doesn't share the all-encompassing love of The Vastness?

"We don't have enough food, or life support, or fuel, to carry her where we're going," Kango said.

"We can ration food or stop off somewhere and sell your Rainbow Cow doll collection to buy more. We can make oxygen by grabbing some ice chunks from the nearest comet and breaking up the water molecules. We can save on fuel by going half-speed or, again, sell your Rainbow Cow dolls to buy fuel."

"Nobody is selling my Rainbow Cow dolls," Kango said. "Those are my legacy. My descendants will treasure them, if I ever manage to reproduce somehow." He made a big show of trying to divide into two cells, which looked like he was just having a hissy fit.

"Point is, we're stuck with her now. Praise The Vastness," Sharon sighed.

"Praise The Vastness!" Jara said automatically, not noticing the sarcasm in Sharon's voice.

"There's also the fact that they can probably track her via the headgear she's wearing. Not to mention she may still be in telepathic contact with The Vastness itself, and we have no way of knowing when she'll be out of range of The Vastness's mental influence."

"Oh, that's easy," Sharon said. "We'll know she's out of range of mental communication with The Vastness when—"

"You are everything!" Jara shouted in response to a message from The Vastness.

"—when she stops doing that. Listen, I'm going to work on disabling, and maybe dismantling, her headgear. You work on rationing food and fuel, and figuring out a way to get more without sacrificing the Rainbow Cows."

"Do not touch my sacred headpiece," the girl said at the exact same moment that Kango said, "Stay away from my Rainbow Cows."

"Guys," said Noreen. "I have an incoming transmission from Earthhub Seven."

"Can you take a message?" Kango said. "We're a smidge busy here."

"It's from Senior Earthgov Administrator Mandre Lewis. Marked urgent."

"You are everything!" Jara cried while struggling harder against her bonds.

"Okay, fine." Kango turned to Sharon. "Please keep her quiet. Noreen, put Mandre on."

"You can't silence me!" Jara struggled harder. "I will escape and aid in your recapture. All ten million eyemouths of The Vastness will feast on your still-living flesh! You will—"

Sharon managed to put a sound-dampening field up around Jara's head, cutting off the sound of her voice, just as Mandre appeared on the cruddy low-res screen in the middle of the flight console. Getting a state-of-the-art communications system had not been a priority for Kango and Sharon, since that would only encourage people to try and communicate with them more often, and who wanted that?

"Kango, Sharon," Mandre Lewis said, wearing her full ceremonial uniform—even the animated sash that scrolled with all of her many awards and titles. "I can't believe I'm saying this, but we need your assistance."

"We helped you one time," Kango said. "Okay, three times, but two of those were just by accident because you had used reverse psychology. Point is, I am not your lackey. Or your henchman. Find another man to hench. Right, Sharon?"

Sharon nodded. "No henching. As Hall and Oates are my witness."

"You are everything!" Jara mouthed soundlessly.

"Listen," said Lewis. "You do this one thing for me, I can expunge your criminal records, even the ones under your other names. And I can push through the permits on that empty space at Earthhub Seven so you can finally open that weird thing you wanted. That, what was it called?"

"Restaurant," Sharon breathed, like she couldn't believe she was even saying the word aloud.

"Restaurant!" Kango clapped his hands. "That's all we've ever wanted."

"It sounds perverted and sick, this whole thing where you make food for strangers and they give you chits for it. Why don't you just have sex for money like honest, decent people? Never mind, I don't want to know the answer to that. Anyway, if you help me with this one thing, I can get you permission to open your 'restaurant.'"

"Wow." Kango's head was spinning. Literally, it was going around and around, at about one revolution every few seconds. Sharon leaned down and slapped him until his head settled back into place.

"We'll do it," Sharon said. "Do you want us to infiltrate the spacer isolationists of the broken asteroid belt? Or go underground as factory workers in the Special Industrial Solar Systems? You want us to steal from the lizard people of Dallos IV? Whatever you want, we're on it."

"None of those," said Mandre. "We need you to go back to Liberty House and get back inside your former place of, er, employment. We've heard reports that the Courtiers are developing some kind of super-weapon that could ruin everybody's day. We need you to go in there and get the schematics for us."

"Holy shit." Sharon nearly threw something at the tiny viewscreen. "You realize that this is a suicide mission? The Courtiers regard both of us as total abominations. We can't open a restaurant if we're dead!"

Lewis made a "not my problem" face. "Just get it done. Or don't even bother coming back to Earthhub Seven."

Kango's head started spinning in the opposite direction from the one it had been spinning in a moment earlier.

4.

They were about halfway to the outer solar systems of Liberty House, and they decided that Jara had probably passed out of range of The Vastness's telepathic communication. Plus, they were pretty sure they'd disabled any tracking devices that might have been inside Jara's headdress. So, Sharon leaned over the seat that Jara was still tied to.

"I know you can hear me, even though we can't hear you. If I turn off the dampening field, do you promise not to yell about The Vastness?"

Jara just stared at her.

Sharon shrugged, then reached over and disabled the dampening field. Immediately, Jara started yelling, "The Vastness is all! The Vastness sees you! The Vastness sees everybody! The Vastness will feast on your flesh with its countless mouths! The Va—"

Sharon turned the dampening field back on with a sigh. "You've probably never known a life apart from The Vastness, so this is the first time you haven't heard its voice in your head. Right? But you stowed away on our ship for a reason. You can claim it was so you could be a missionary and tell the rest of the galaxy how great The Vastness is, but we both know that you had to have some other reason for wanting to see the galaxy. Even if you can't admit it to yourself right now."

Jara just kept shouting about The Vastness and its boundless wonderful appetite, without making any sound.

"Fine. Have it your way. Let me know if you need to use the facilities or if you get hungry. Maybe I'll feed you one of Kango's Rainbow Cows." (This provoked a loud and polysyllabic "noooo" from Kango, who was in the next compartment over.)

When Sharon wandered aft, Kango was waist-deep in boxes of supplies, looking for something they could use to disguise themselves long enough to get inside Liberty House.

"Do we have a hope in hell of pulling this off?" she asked.

"If we can get the permits, absolutely," Kango said. "We might have to borrow some chits to get the restaurant up and running, but I know people who won't charge a crazy rate. And I already have ideas of what kind of food we can serve. Did you know restaurants used to have this thing called a Me-N-U? It was a device that automatically chose the perfect food for me and the perfect food for you."

"I meant, do we have any hope of getting back inside of Liberty House without being clocked as escaped Divertissements and obliterated in a slow, painful fashion?"

"Oh." Kango squinted at the piles of glittery underpants in his hands. "No. That, we don't have the slightest prayer of doing. I was trying to focus on the positive."

"We need a plan," Sharon said. "You and I are on file with the Courtiers, and there are any of a thousand scans that will figure out who we are the moment we show up. But Mandre is right; we know the inner workings of Liberty House better than anybody. We were made there, we lived there. It was our home. There has to be some way to play the Courtiers for fools."

"Here's the problem," said Kango. "Even if you and I were able to disguise ourselves enough to avoid being recognized as the former property of the Excellent Good Time Crew, there's absolutely no way we could hide what we are. None whatsoever. Anyone in the service of the Courtiers will recognize you as a monster, and me as an extra, at a glance."

"I know, I know," Sharon raised her hands.

"We wouldn't get half a light-year inside the House before they would be all over us with the biometrics and the genescans, and there's no way around those."

"I know!" Sharon felt like weeping. They shouldn't have taken this mission. Mandre had dangled a slim chance at achieving their wildest dreams, and they'd lunged for it like rubes. "I know, okay?"

"I mean, you'd need to have a human being, an actual honest-to-Blish human being, who was in on the scam. And it's not like we can just pick up one of *those* on the nearest asteroid. So, unless you've got some other bright—" Kango stopped.

Kango and Sharon stared at each other for a moment without talking, then looked over at Jara, who was still tied to her chair, shouting soundlessly about the wonders of The Vastness.

"Makeover?" Kango said.

"Makeover." Sharon sighed. She still felt like throwing up.

5.

"Greetings and tastefully risqué taunts, O visitors whose sentience will be stipulated for now, pending further appraisal," said the man on the viewscreen, whose face was surrounded by a pink-and-blue cloud of smart powder. His cheek had a beauty mark that flashed different colors, and his eyes kept changing from skull sockets to neon spirals to cartoon eyeballs. "What is your business with Liberty House, and how may we pervert you?"

Kango and Sharon both looked at Jara, who glared at them both. Then she turned her baleful look toward the viewscreen. "Silence, wretch," she said, speaking the words they'd forced her to memorize. "I do not speak to underthings." Kango and Sharon both gave her looks of total dismay, and she corrected herself: "Underlings. I do not speak to underlings. I am the Resplendent Countess Victoria Algentsia, and these are my playservants. Kindly provide me with an approach vector to the central Pleasure Nexus, and instruct me as to how I may speak to someone worthy of my attention."

They turned off the comms before the man with the weird eyes could even react.

"Ugh," Kango said. "That was . . . not good."

"I've never pretended to be a Countess before," said Jara. "I don't really approve of pretending to be anything. The Vastness requires total honesty and realness from its acolytes. Also, how do I know you'll keep your end of our bargain?"

"Because we're good, honest folk," said Sharon, kicking Kango before he could even think of having a facial expression. "We'll return you to The Vastness, and you'll be a hero because you'll have helped defeat a weapon that could have been a threat to its, er, magnificence."

"I don't trust either of you," said Jara.

"That's a good start," said Kango. "Where we're going, you shouldn't trust anybody, anybody at all." By some miracle, the man with the cloud of smart powder around his face had given them an approach vector to Salubrious IV, the central world of the Pleasure Nexus, the main solar system of Liberty House. Either the man had actually believed Jara was a countess, or he had decided their visit would afford some amusement to somebody. Or both.

"So, I'm supposed to be a fancy noble person," said Jara, who was still wearing her tattered rags apart from a splash of colorful makeup and some fake jewels over her headdress. "And yet, I'm flying in this awful old ship, with just the two of you as my servants? What are you two supposed to be, anyway?"

"We were made here," said Kango. "I'm an extra. She's a monster."

"You don't need to know what we were." Sharon shot Kango a look. "All you need to know is, we're perfectly good servants. This ship is an actual pleasure skimmer from Salubrious, and you're going to claim that you decided to go off on a jaunt. We're creating a whole fake hedonic calculus for you. The good thing about Liberty House is, there are a million Courtiers, and the idea of keeping tabs on any of them is repugnant."

"This society is evil and monstrous," said Jara. "The Vastness will come and devour it entire."

"Of course, of course," said Kango with a shrug. "So, we have a few hours left to teach you how to hold your painstick, and which skewer to use with which kind of sugarblob, and the right form of address for all five hundred types of Courtiers, so you can pass for a member of the elite. Not to mention how to walk in scamperpants. Ready to get started?"

Jara just glared at him.

Meanwhile, Sharon went aft to look at the engines, because their "plan," if you wanted to call it that, required them to do some crazy flying inside the inner detector grid of Salubrious IV, to get right up to the computer core while Kango and Jara provided a distraction.

"Nobody asked me if I wanted to go home," said Noreen while Sharon was poking around in her guts. "I wouldn't have minded being at least consulted here."

"Sorry," said Sharon. "Neither of us is happy about going back either. We got too good an offer to refuse."

"I've been in contact with some of the other ships since we got inside Liberty House," Noreen said. "They don't care much one way or the other if we're lying about our identity—ships don't concern themselves with such petty business—but they did mention that the Courtiers have beefed up security rather a lot since we escaped for the first time. Also, some of the ships are taking up a betting pool on how long before we're caught and sent into the Libidorynth."

"I can't believe the Libidorynth is still a thing," Sharon said.

Sharon and Kango spent their scant remaining time making Jara look plausibly like a spoiled Countess who had been in deep space much too long, while Kango gave Jara a crash course in acting haughty and imperious. "When in doubt, pretend you've done too many dreamsluices, and you're having a hard time remembering things," said Kango.

"Silence, drone," said Jara in an actually pretty good impersonation of the way a Courtier would speak to someone like Kango.

"We've got landing points," said Noreen, and seconds later, the ship was making a jerky descent toward the surface of Salubrious IV. From a distance, the planet looked a hazy shade of brownish gray. But once you broke atmosphere, the main landmass was coated with towers of pure gold studded with purple, and the oceans had a sheen of platinum over them. They lowered the *Spicy Meatball* into the biggest concentration of gilded skyscrapers, and all the little details came into focus: the millions of faces and claws and bodies gazing and squirming from the sides of the buildings, the bejeweled windows and the shimmering mist of pleasure-gas floating around all of the uppermost levels. Gazing at her former home, Sharon felt an unexpected kick of nostalgia, or maybe even joyful recognition, alongside the ever-present terror of *Hall and Oates save me, they're going to put us in the Libidorynth.*

They touched down, and Noreen seemed reluctant to open her hatch, because she was probably having the same terrifying flashbacks that were eating Sharon's brain. Things Sharon hadn't thought of in years—the cage they had kept her in, the "monster training," the giggles of the people as she chased them around the dance floor, which turned to shrieks after she actually caught up with them. The painsticks. Sharon felt the bravado she'd spent years acquiring start to flake away.

As they stepped out of the hatch, a retinue of a hundred Witty Companions and assorted Fixers and Cleansers swarmed to surround them. "How may we pervert you?" they all asked, with an eagerness that made Sharon's stomach twist into knots. They all felt obliged to declare their fealty to this long-lost, newly returned Countess right away, and this became deafening. One of the Witty Companions, who introduced himself as Barnadee, started listing all of the Courtiers who were dying to meet their cousin, but Jara gave him a sharp look and said that she was tired after her long journey.

"Of course, of course," said Barnadee, bowing and flashing his multicolored strobe-lit genitalia as a show of respect. "We will show you to your luxurious and resplendent quarters, where any debauchery you may imagine will be available to you."

Jara snorted at all of this nonsense—it was all pointless, because it did nothing to glorify The Vastness—but her disdain sounded enough like the petulance of a jaded hedonist that it only made Barnadee try harder to please her.

6.

"Drone, bring me more cognac and bacon," said Jara, waving one finger. Sharon and Kango looked at each other, as if each trying to blame the other for turning this girl into their worst nightmare. They'd been on Salubrious IV for a week and a half, and you wouldn't recognize Jara anymore. Her skin had been retro-sheened until it glowed, they had put jewels all over her face and neck, and she was wearing the newest, most fashionable clothes. But most of all, Jara had gotten used to having whatever she wanted, at the exact second she decided she wanted it. They were staying in one of the more modest suites of the Pleasure Nexus, with only seventeen rooms and a dozen organic assembly units—so it might take a few whole minutes to build a new slave for the Countess Victoria or create whatever meals or clothing she might desire. The walls were coated with living material, sort of like algae, that looked like pure gold (but were actually much more valuable) and had the capacity to feel pain, just in case someone might find it amusing to hear the golden walls howl with agony.

"I grow bored," said Jara, as Sharon rushed over with her cognac-and-bacon. "When will there be more amusement for me?"

Sharon had a horrible feeling that she could not tell if Jara was faking it any longer. She'd had that feeling for a few days.

"Um," said Sharon to Jara, "well, so there are five orgies this evening, including one featuring blood enemas and flesh-melting. Also, there's that big formal evening party."

"Is this the sort of party where you used to be the featured monster?" Jara held her cognac-and-bacon in both hands and gulped it, with just the sort of alacrity you'd expect from someone who'd only ever tasted gruel until two weeks before.

"Um, yes," Sharon said. "They would turn me loose and I would chase the guests around and try to eat them. I've told you already."

"And how did that make you feel?" Jara asked.

"I don't want to talk about it."

Sharon turned and looked at Kango, who was tending to the Countess's assembly units but also double-checking that there were no listening devices in here so they could speak freely. Kango gave her the "all clear" signal.

"Let's talk about you instead," Sharon said to Jara. "Are you ready to go to the big party? It's one thing to play-act at bossing Kango and me around in private. But at this party, you'll see all sorts of weird things—depravities that The Vastness never prepared you for. And you can't bat an eye at any of them."

"I'll do whatever I have to," Jara said. "You said there's a weapon here that's a threat to The Vastness, and I'll endure any horrors and monstrosities to protect The Vastness. Praise The Vastness!"

"Do you think she's ready?" Sharon asked Kango, who shrugged.

"She's got the attitude," Kango said. Just a few hours earlier, Jara had made Kango go out and fetch her some still-living mollusk sushi from the market, and meanwhile she'd gotten Sharon to fabricate a tiny legion of pink fluffy shocktroopers for her amusement (they goose-stepped around and then all shot each other, because their aim was terrible).

"Thank you," Jara said, "Drone."

"But she's still rusty on the finer points of Courtier behavior," Kango said. "She doesn't know a painstick from a soul-fork."

"She's a quick study. And she'll have you to help her," Sharon said. "As long as you don't get all triggered by being back inside the Grand Wilding Center. I can't even imagine."

"You two," Jara said out of nowhere. "You talk as though each of you was The Vastness to the other."

"Yeah," Kango said. "We're a family, that's why."

Jara was shaking her head, like this was just another perversion among many that she'd encountered on her journey. "At least the people here in Liberty House care about something bigger than they are, even if it's only a pointless amusement. You two, you are so small, and all you care for is each other. How can you *stand* to have no connection to greatness?"

"We had enough of other people's greatness a long time ago," Sharon said. "You start to realize that 'something bigger than you are' is usually just some kind of stupid mass hallucination. Or a giant scam."

"I feel sorry for you." Jara finished her cognac-and-bacon and gestured for more.

"You can pretend that you're still pure," Sharon said. "But you've been enjoying that cognac-and-bacon way, way too much. What do you think The Vastness would think about that? How can The Vastness be everything when it doesn't have cognac-and-bacon? When it doesn't even know what cognac-and-bacon IS?"

"Shut up, Drone," Jara said—falling back into her "Countess" voice as a way out of this conversation.

"Keep an eye on her, okay?" Sharon whispered to Kango. "I really think there's a part of her that wants to be her own person, but she just doesn't know how."

He shrugged and nodded at the same time.

And then they were surrounded by a few dozen other servants and Fixers, who had heard that the Countess Victoria was going to the evening's most exclusive party and were there to help her become as resplendent as possible in hopes of winning some favor. So, there was no further chance to talk about their actual plans for stealing the specs on the secret weapon—but lots and lots of chances to obsess over whether the Countess should wear the weeping dolphin eyes or the blood-pouches.

At last, the Countess was ready to go to the party, and Sharon was preparing to peel off and sneak back to the *Spicy Meatball*. "Wish me luck," she whispered to Kango.

"You've got this," he whispered back. "We're going to open our restaurant. We'll serve all the classic food items: handburgers, Ruffalo wings, damplings, carry . . . It'll be great."

"Let's not get ahead of ourselves here," said Sharon, kissing Kango on the cheek.

7.

The central computer core of the Pleasure Nexus looked like a big mossy rock floating over the city, between two giant esorotic spires of pure silver. But as the *Spicy Meatball* flew closer, the computer core looked less like a rock and more like some kind of ancient sauroid, with thick plates of spiky armor guarding its fleshy access points. They flew into its shadow.

Sharon was concentrating on navigating past the tiny guardbots flying around the computer core, while finding the exact vector that would allow the *Spicy Meatball* to come right up to the exposed patch of underbelly. And then Sharon and Noreen just had to hover there, directly underneath the computer core, where anybody could spot the ship's impact-scarred hull, waiting for Kango's diversion to happen. And obsessing about the thousand things that could go wrong.

"I've been telling the other ships about us," said Noreen. "Our smuggling runs to the Scabby Castles, that time we conned those literal-minded cyborgs into thinking Kango was some kind of Cyber-King . . . They're pretty jealous of us. The other ships might even give us a slight head start if it comes down to a pursuit. Although it wouldn't make any difference, of course."

"I appreciate the gesture," said Sharon. She stared at the crappy little vidscreen, showing the undulating flesh of the computer core—just sitting there, a few inches away from their hull. She was regretting a lot of her recent life choices. She'd sworn for years that nobody was ever going to make her into an object again, but she'd willingly put herself back into that position—and the fact that she was "just pretending" didn't make as much difference as she wanted. She felt bad that Kango, who'd had a rougher time than she had, was being forced to confront this awfulness again. And she was realizing that she'd projected a lot onto that Jara girl, as if a week or two of pretending to be a Countess would break a lifetime of conditioning and psychic linkage to a giant space glob. This was probably going to be a career-ending mistake.

"We got it," Noreen said, just as Sharon was getting sucked into gloom. Their vidscreen was streaming some news reports about the Estimable Lord Vaughn Ticklesnout unexpectedly catching on fire and being chased by his own party monster. Some three hundred terrorist organizations had already claimed responsibility for this incident, most of them with completely silly names like the Persimmon Permission Proclamation, but the party had dissolved into total chaos. They picked up footage of the crowd scattering as a man on fire ran around and around, pursued by a bright blue naked woman who could have been Sharon's twin sister.

"Great," Sharon said. "I'm setting up the uplink. Let's hope the distraction was distracting enough." She started threading through layers of security protection, some of them newly added since she and

Kango had escaped from Liberty House, and spoofing all of the certs that the computer demanded. There were riddles and silly questions along with strings of base-99 code that needed to be unraveled, but Sharon and Noreen worked together, and soon they had total leet-superuser access.

Sharon searched for any data on the new super-weapon and found it helpfully labeled "Brand New Excellent Super-Weapon." A few more twists of the computer matrix, and she was instructing the computer to transfer all the data on the weapon.

"Uh," said Noreen. "I think you might have made a mistake."

"What?" said Sharon. "I asked it to send over everything it had on the super-weapon."

"Check the cargo hold," said Noreen. "Right next to the boxes of Rainbow Cows. The main computer just auto-docked with us a second ago."

Sharon took a split second to process what Noreen had said, then took off running down to the cargo hold, where a squat red ovoid device, about the size of a human baby, had been deposited. The object made a faint grumbling noise, like a drunken old man who was annoyed at being woken up. "Oh, shit," Sharon said.

"Please keep it down," said the super-weapon. "Some of us are trying to rest."

"Sorry," Sharon said. "I just didn't expect you to show up in person."

"I go where they send me," groaned the super-weapon. "All I want to do is get some rest until my big day. Which could be any day, since they never give me a timetable. That's the problem with being the ultimate deterrent: people *talk* about using me a lot, but they never actually follow through."

"Just how ultimate a deterrent are you?"

"Well, actually, I'm *very* ultimate. Ultimately ultimate, in fact." The super-weapon seemed to perk up a little bit as it discussed its effectiveness. "If anybody tries to interfere with Liberty House's sacred and innate right to seek amusement in any form they deem amusing, then I send a gravity pulse to the supermassive black hole at the center of the galaxy, causing it to, er, expand. Rather a lot. To the size of a galaxy, in fact."

"That's, er, pretty fucking ultimate." Sharon felt as though she, personally, had swallowed a supermassive black hole. This was getting worse and worse. Added to her own low-single-digit estimation of her chances of survival, there was the realization that her former owners were much, much worse people than she'd ever fathomed. She was so full of terror and hatred, she saw two different shades of red at once.

"Hate to ruin your moment," said Noreen, "but we've got another problem."

"Don't mind me," said the super-weapon. "I'll just go back to sleep. My name is Horace, by the by."

Sharon rushed back to the flight deck, where the vidscreen showed Kango and Jara in the custody of several uniformed Fixers, as well as one of the senior Courtiers, a man named Hazelbeem who'd been famous back in Sharon's day.

"We have captured your accomplices." Hazelbeem's lime-green coiffure wobbled as he talked. "And we are coming for you next! Prepare for a wonderfully agonizing death—accompanied by some quite delicious crunketizers, because this party left us with rather a lot of leftovers."

"We have your bomb," said Sharon into the viewscreen. "Your ultimate weapon. We'll set it off unless you release our friends."

"No, you won't," said Hazelbeem, who had a purple mustache that kept twirling and untwirling and twisting itself into complex shapes, "because you're not completely stark raving mad."

"Okay. It's true; we won't. But what does that say about you, creating something like that?"

Hazelbeem's mustache shrugged elaborately, but the man himself had no facial expression.

"Leave us," Kango shouted. "Get out of there! Take their stupid bomb with you. We're not worth you sacrificing your lives to these assholes. Just go!"

"You know I can't do that," said Sharon.

"There are fifty-seven attack ships, approaching us from pretty much every possible direction," said Noreen.

"Can we at least disable their stupid bomb permanently before they capture us?" said Sharon. "I'm guessing not. We'd need weeks to figure out how it works."

"Hey," Jara said, pushing herself forward. "I wanted to say, I guess you were kind of right about why I stowed away. I always wanted to be special, not just another one of a billion servants of The Vastness. And when I saw your ship about to disembark, I thought maybe I could help spread the word about The Vastness to the whole galaxy, and then I'd be the best acolyte ever. But it turned out the only way I could be special was as a fake Countess."

"You were a great fake Countess, though," Kango said, squirming next to her.

"Thanks. And thanks for taking me to that party," Jara told her. "I got to see all sorts of things that I'd never even imagined. And it started me thinking maybe I really could find a way to reinvent myself as an individual, the way you two did. In fact, I'm starting to realize that . . . You are everything!"

"What the hell? You just said—"

"I can't control it," said Jara. "It's like an instinctive response whenever— You are everything!"

And then they lost the signal, because a voice broke in on every single open frequency. The voice was shouting one thing over and over: "I am everything! I am everything! I am everything!"

"Uh," said Sharon.

"So, you probably already guessed this," said Noreen. "But sensors are showing that a Temporary Embarrassment the size of several planets has just appeared on the edge of the central pleasure nexus of Liberty House. The weather control systems on Salubrious IV are all working overtime."

"You're right; I did actually guess that," said Sharon.

"The good news is, all the ships that were about to attack us have been diverted onto a new heading," said Noreen.

"We gotta go rescue Kango," said Sharon. "And Jara, I guess."

"I have some excellent news," came a plummy male voice from the cargo hold. Horace, the super-weapon. "My activation sequence has been initiated. It's the moment I've been waiting for my whole life!"

8.

Hazelbeem, whose full name was Hazelbeem Sternforke Paddleborrow the XXVIIth, was standing in front of the Grand Wilding Suites and Superior Fun Center, where the party had been held. He had a half-dozen Fixers with him, and they were holding Kango and Jara in chains as the *Spicy Meatball* landed on the front lawn (which screamed and tried to bite the Meatball's landing struts).

"So! Not only did you steal our top secret ultimate weapon," said Hazelbeem, his mustache knotted in anger, "but you brought the wrath of the most revolting giant monster in the galaxy down on us. Were I an existentialist masochist, this would be my happiest day ever. Too bad I am an objectivist sadist instead."

"Just let my friends go," said Sharon. "We can help. We know what The Vastness wants."

"You are everything!" shouted Jara.

"We are past the point of negotiation," said Hazelbeem. "We have already activated the weapon on board your ship as soon as we detected a major threat to our way of life. If we cannot continue the absolute pursuit of amusement, with zero limitations, then there's no reason for this galaxy to continue existing. I must say, when we created you and your friend here"—he gestured at Kango—"we did not imagine it could ever lead to so many unamusing incidents."

"This just proves that amusement is subjective," said Kango, struggling against his chains. "I've been highly amused by many of today's events."

"You are everything!"

"You were made as a brothel extra," said Hazelbeem to Kango. "You weren't even supposed to have a mind of your own. You're a single-celled organism, are you not? Made to appear like a beautiful young man, to stand in the background of the crowd scenes at a brothel. Something must have gone very wrong—perhaps you received too high a dose of neuropeptides in the vat."

"I may only have one cell," said Kango, "but *you've* just been nucleused."

"I don't even know what that means." Hazelbeem's mustache crinkled.

"It was supposed to be a play on the fact that I have a single nucleus, and I'm . . . Oh, just forget I said anything."

"Already forgotten," said Hazelbeem.

"You are everything!"

"Can you stop shouting that?" Hazelbeem said to Jara. "It's giving me a headache."

"We've been trying, believe me," said Sharon.

"It's a reflex," Jara told Hazelbeem. "I belong to The Vastness no matter what I do. I was foolish to think anything mattered except for The Vastness. I'm probably going to be punished for doubting even a little, in my heart."

"You are a very tiresome little person," Hazelbeem told her.

The sky was churning with angry black swirlies, which reminded Sharon of one of the first parties at which she'd been the designated monster, when the Marquis of Bloopabloopasneak had set off some kind of weather bomb left over from one of the old galactic wars. Five hundred-odd people had died in the hurricanes and blizzards before the Pleasure Nexus's weather-control systems had regained control, and the

Marquis of Bloopabloopasneak had played really loud glam-clash music to drown out the screams and the roaring of the elements.

Hazelbeem was looking at the big fob hanging from his inner jacket (which was made of tiny living people, all of them squirming in a vain attempt to escape from the stitching that stuck them together). "That hypertrophic organism and its fleet of ships have torn through our planetary defenses in the worst disaster since that all-you-can-eat buffet escaped from its trays and grew until it devoured an entire planet. I blame! I really do. I blame."

"Just let my friends go, and we'll deal with The Vastness for you." Sharon shouted to make herself heard over the howling in the sky. "There's no need for any of this."

"This is what happens when playthings try to think for themselves," Hazelbeem snorted. "First they start trying to act like *people*, and before you know it, they—"

Sharon ate Hazelbeem. This happened too quickly for anybody to react. One second, Hazelbeem was working himself up into a tirade about toys that get ideas above their station, and the next, Sharon's mouth expanded to several times its normal size and just gobbled him up. She spat out his boots a second later.

"Ugh," Sharon said. "I promised myself I would never do that again. But there's provocation, and then there's *provocation*. I've had a lot of pent-up rage these past few days." She looked at the gaggle of Fixers who were holding her friends prisoner and yelled, "Let my friends go, or you're next!"

"Whatever you say!" the head Fixer stammered as she unlocked Kango and Jara. "We all just want to be with our families—or possibly go to an end-of-the-galaxy blood orgy. One of those. Bye!" The Fixers all took off running in different directions, leaving Sharon, Kango, Jara and Hazelbeem's boots.

Sharon looked down at the boots. "He just pushed me too far."

"It's fine," Kango said in her ear as he touched her arm. "Just because you eat the occasional horrible person doesn't prove you're actually the monster they tried to make you into. I promise."

"You are everything!" Jara said, then added, "That guy was asking for it. As an official Countess, I pardon you."

"Thanks," Sharon said, still raising her voice over the awful din. "Now we just gotta save the galaxy. Any ideas?"

They all looked at each other, then at the pair of boots on the ground, as if the boots might suddenly offer a helpful suggestion.

9.

The Vastness had somehow taken over the festival speakers all around the Superior Fun Center, and was shouting about the fact that someone had dared to steal from its all-encompassing magnificence. And that nobody escaped The Vastness! To underscore this, a flotilla of The Vastness's Joykiller-class ships were swooping down over the surface of Salubrious IV and firing Obliteron missiles at every freestanding structure. The ground shook, the sky churned, and the Superior Fun Center and several other buildings collapsed as Kango, Sharon, and Jara ran back to the *Spicy Meatball*—stumbling and falling on their faces as The Vastness shrieked at top volume.

"You are everything," said Jara, face in the dirt.

Kango flung himself into his pilot seat aboard the *Spicy Meatball* and tried to lift off, but the entire airspace consisted of pretty much nothing but explosions, dotted with the occasional deadly warship. Barely a few hundred yards off the ground, the *Spicy Meatball* was forced to go into a dive to avoid a huge chunk of burning debris. Kango and Noreen screamed in unison.

"You know," said Horace. "I've heard it said that death is what makes life meaningful. In that case, I am about to create more meaning than all of the artists in history combined."

Kango was a blur as he tried to steer through the flaming obstacle course.

At last, they reached the upper atmosphere . . . just as some terrible *presence* appeared directly beneath them. It was just a dark shape that blotted out their view of Salubrious IV. Sharon struggled to make out any details for a moment, and then she saw some undulating barbed tentacles, and she *knew*.

"No," said Sharon. "They released the planet-eater."

"Is that Liberty House's last line of defense?" asked Jara, fascinated by the shape on their external viewer.

"No," Kango said. "They made it for a party years ago. It basically just eats planets, much as its name implies. And we're between it and The Vastness. Hold tight!"

"To what?" Sharon demanded.

The planet-eater thrashed around as it forced its way out of the atmosphere of Salubrious IV and tried to swim toward The Vastness. The planet-eater's uncountable limbs lashed out, trying to pull everything in their path into the one enormous maw at its center. One of those huge barbed tentacles swiped within a few feet of the *Spicy Meatball* . . . which dodged, and nearly ran into another flotilla of Joykiller-class attack ships.

"Hall and Oates!" Sharon cursed.

"You are everything!" Jara cried out.

"Keep it down, you two," Kango growled. "It's hard enough trying to make evasive maneuvers between pretty much everything deadly without also having to listen to a lot of religious mumbo jumbo."

"Oh, as if *you* have it all figured out," Sharon said. "Your only religion is exhibitionism. I swear, the next time we have a plan that relies on a diversion—a contained, sensible diversion—that can be *my* job."

"Sure!" Kango spun the ship on its axis to scoot past a planet-eater tentacle, then veered sharply to the left to avoid a spread of Obliteron missiles. "Because you're such a genius at strategy, and that's how we ended up with a stupid ultimate weapon on board!"

"I'll have you know I am quite intelligent," Horace protested. "And there are mere minutes before my devastation wave is launched from the galactic core. Once it begins, it will sweep the entire galaxy in no time at all!"

"Hey, I did my best," Sharon said to Kango. "It's not as if it was my idea to—" She stopped, because Jara was staring at her. "What?"

"You're doing it again," Jara said. "You're acting as though each of you is The Vastness to the other. I wish I knew how you *do* that. I'm going to die soon too, and even with The Vastness close at hand, I'll die alone and for no real reason. You are everything!"

"Listen, Jara," Sharon said, ignoring her nausea as Kango did a series of barrel rolls to avoid explosions that came close enough to rattle her teeth. "Listen. The Vastness is only everything because it's incredibly limited. It can't even see all the things it's not. It's like a giant stupid ignorant blob of . . . wait. Wait a minute!"

"What?" Kango said. "Did you think of something super super clever?"

"Maybe," Sharon said, praying to Hall and Oates that she was right. She ran over and pulled the stolen synchrotrix out of the strongbox, then started wiring it into Horace's core as fast as she could. "Remember what you told me was special about this device?"

"The fact that it's worth a lot of chits?" Kango pulled the *Spicy Meatball*'s nose up so fast, Sharon nearly did a backflip while keeping one hand on Horace. "It's got a nice color scheme? It has the ability to neutralize . . . oh. Oh!"

"You are everything!" Jara said.

The planet-eater had finally gotten past all of the attack ships that had tried vainly to slow it down. Now it had reached The Vastness, opening the vast gnashing maw at the heart of its starfish-like body to try and devour the mega-planetoid. The planet-eater embraced The Vastness with its many limbs.

Sharon gripped Jara's shoulders so hard, her knuckles were white. "Tell The Vastness we've got the ultimate weapon, right here on our ship. We can help The Vastness to become completely unstoppable. And The Vastness really will be everything, in an even better way than before."

Jara looked like she was about to cry. "You want me to lie to The Vastness."

"No," Sharon said. "Yes. Sort of. Not really. It's the only way."

"I'm just moments away from a glorious consummation," Horace said. "It's at times like this that I feel like composing a sonnet."

"Jara," Sharon hissed, "now!"

"I'm trying," Jara said, shutting her eyes and concentrating. "The Vastness doesn't really listen. It just talks. I'm sending the message as hard as I can."

"Now! Please!"

The Vastness reached out with a beam of energy, trying to seize the *Spicy Meatball*. Sharon rushed to the rear airlock with Horace, cobbled together with the synchrotrix. She tossed them out, and The Vastness's energy field captured them, pulling them through one of The Vastness's slavering eyemouths inside its guts.

They were inside The Vastness's own atmosphere, close enough to hear its eyemouths shouting through their countless razor-sharp teeth. "I am everything! Now I have this ultimate weapon, my power will be absolute. I will be all things, and every living being will shout my praises. I am—"

Sharon watched through the airlock as The Vastness vanished from space.

In the space where The Vastness had been, a bright purple-and-green fissure was opened up. The crack in spacetime was huge enough to let Sharon see through it as The Vastness was drawn toward the supermassive black hole at the core of the galaxy.

"You are everything," Jara said, sorrowfully, standing next to Sharon.

And then The Vastness was no longer visible—but in its place, there was a huge distortion enveloping the black hole at the core of the galaxy.

"The biggest Embarrassment the galaxy has ever seen," Kango breathed from the flight deck.

And then the purple-and-green fissure closed, leaving a badly injured planet-eater, several thousand confused Joykiller-class starships, and the *Spicy Meatball*.

"We did it," Kango said, seeming semi-permeable with astonishment.

"The Vastness followed Horace's program and ended up at the galactic core," Sharon said. "And then it Embarrassed itself."

"I just killed my god." Jara looked as though she was too shocked even for tears.

"Look at it this way," Sharon said. "You told the truth. Mostly. The Vastness is everywhere and everything now, in a way. And it always will be with you. And it can never be defeated. You can worship The Vastness forever."

"I don't know." Jara tried saying, "You are everything," but it wasn't the same when it came in response to nothing.

"Well, meanwhile," Kango said. "We lost the synchrotrix that we were counting on to pay our bills. And we lost the super-weapon, too. So, we're even more broke than we were before. Unless we can convince Mandre Lewis that we just saved the galaxy."

"We'll figure something out," Sharon said, then turned back toward Jara. "But what are you going to do? There's a huge fleet of ships out there, full of your fellow acolytes, and they desperately need some direction. Plus, this star system is rich in resources and technology, and it just had all its planetary defenses wrecked. You could go back to Salubrious, with all your people, and become a Countess for real."

"Maybe," Jara said. "Or maybe I could go with you guys? I feel like I have a lot to learn from you two. And I'm not sure I'm ready to explain what happened to the other acolytes."

"Sure. How do you feel about helping to open a restaurant? Do you know how to make a tablecloth?" Kango threw the *Spicy Meatball* headlong into an escape course before anybody could try to blame them for all the property damage. Behind them, the ruins of Salubrious IV sparkled with the dying light of countless fires as the tributary ships of The Vastness began, hesitantly and confusedly, to make planetfall.

ABOUT THE AUTHOR

CHARLIE JANE ANDERS is the author of the novel *All the Birds in the Sky*. She organizes the Writers With Drinks reading series, and was a founding editor of io9, a site about science fiction, science, and futurism. Her fiction has appeared in *Tin House*, *McSweeney's Internet Tendency*, *ZYZZYVA*, *Wired*, Tor.com, *Asimov's Science Fiction*, the *Magazine of Fantasy & Science Fiction*, *Lightspeed*, and a ton of anthologies, including *Best American Science Fiction and Fantasy*. Her story "Six Months, Three Days" won a Hugo Award and her novel *Choir Boy* won a Lambda Literary Award.

ZEN AND THE ART OF STARSHIP MAINTENANCE

TOBIAS S. BUCKELL

After battle with the *Fleet of Honest Representation*, after seven hundred seconds of sheer terror and uncertainty, and after our shared triumph in the acquisition of the greatest prize seizure in three hundred years, we cautiously approached the massive black hole that Purth-Anaget orbited. The many rotating rings, filaments, and infrastructures bounded within the fields that were the entirety of our ship, *With All Sincerity,* were flush with a sense of victory and bloated with the riches we had all acquired.

Give me a ship to sail and a quasar to guide it by, billions of individual citizens of all shapes, functions, and sizes cried out in joy together on the common channels. Whether fleshy forms safe below, my fellow crab-like maintenance forms on the hulls, or even the secretive navigation minds, our myriad thoughts joined in a sense of True Shared Purpose that lingered even after the necessity of the group battle-mind.

I clung to my usual position on the hull of one of the three rotating habitat rings deep inside our shields and watched the warped event horizon shift as we fell in behind the metallic world in a trailing orbit.

A sleet of debris fell toward the event horizon of Purth-Anaget's black hole, hammering the kilometers of shields that formed an iridescent cocoon around us. The bow shock of our shields' push through the debris field danced ahead of us, the compressed wave it created becoming a hyper-aurora of shifting colors and energies that collided and compressed before they streamed past our sides.

What a joy it was to see a world again. I was happy to be outside in the dark so that as the bow shields faded, I beheld the perpetual night face of the world: it glittered with millions of fractal habitation patterns traced out across its artificial surface.

On the hull with me, a nearby friend scuttled between airlocks in a cloud of insect-sized seeing eyes. They spotted me and tapped me with a tight-beam laser for a private ping.

"Isn't this exciting?" they commented.

"Yes. But this will be the first time I don't get to travel downplanet," I beamed back.

I received a derisive snort of static on a common radio frequency from their direction. "There is nothing there that cannot be experienced right here in the Core. Waterfalls, white sand beaches, clear waters."

"But it's different down there," I said. "I love visiting planets."

"Then hurry up and let's get ready for the turnaround so we can leave this industrial shithole of a planet behind us and find a nicer one. I hate being this close to a black hole. It fucks with time dilation, and I spend all night tasting radiation and fixing broken equipment that can't handle energy discharges in the exajoule ranges. Not to mention everything damaged in the battle I have to repair."

This was true. There was work to be done.

Safe now in trailing orbit, the many traveling worlds contained within the shields that marked the *With All Sincerity*'s boundaries burst into activity. Thousands of structures floating in between the rotating rings moved about, jockeying and repositioning themselves into renegotiated orbits. Flocks of transports rose into the air, wheeling about inside the shields to then stream off ahead toward Purth-Anaget. There were trillions of citizens of the *Fleet of Honest Representation* heading for the planet now that their fleet lay captured between our shields like insects in amber.

The enemy fleet had forced us to extend energy far, far out beyond our usual limits. Great risks had been taken. But the reward had been epic, and the encounter resolved in our favor with their capture.

Purth-Anaget's current ruling paradigm followed the memetics of the One True Form, and so had opened their world to these refugees. But Purth-Anaget was not so wedded to the belief system as to pose any threat to mutual commerce, information exchange, or any of our own rights to self-determination.

Later we would begin stripping the captured prize ships of information, booby traps, and raw mass, with Purth-Anaget's shipyards moving inside of our shields to help.

I leapt out into space, spinning a simple carbon nanotube of string behind me to keep myself attached to the hull. I swung wide, twisted, and landed near a dark-energy manifold bridge that had pinged me a maintenance consult request just a few minutes back.

My eyes danced with information for a picosecond. Something shifted in the shadows between the hull's crenulations.

I jumped back. We had just fought an entire war-fleet; any number of eldritch machines could have slipped through our shields—things that snapped and clawed, ripped you apart in a femtosecond's worth of dark energy. Seekers and destroyers.

A face appeared in the dark. Skeins of invisibility and personal shielding fell away like a pricked soap bubble to reveal a bipedal figure clinging to the hull.

"You there!" it hissed at me over a tightly contained beam of data. "I am a fully bonded Shareholder and Chief Executive with command privileges of the Anabathic Ship *Helios Prime*. Help me! Do not raise an alarm."

I gaped. What was a CEO doing on our hull? Its vacuum-proof

carapace had been destroyed while passing through space at high velocity, pockmarked by the violence of single atoms at indescribable speed punching through its shields. Fluids leaked out, surrounding the stowaway in a frozen mist. It must have jumped the space between ships during the battle, or maybe even after.

Protocols insisted I notify the hell out of security. But the CEO had stopped me from doing that. There was a simple hierarchy across the many ecologies of a traveling ship, and in all of them a CEO certainly trumped maintenance forms. Particularly now that we were no longer in direct conflict and the *Fleet of Honest Representation* had surrendered.

"Tell me: what is your name?" the CEO demanded.

"I gave that up a long time ago," I said. "I have an address. It should be an encrypted rider on any communication I'm single-beaming to you. Any message you direct to it will find me."

"My name is Armand," the CEO said. "And I need your help. Will you let me come to harm?"

"I will not be able to help you in a meaningful way, so my not telling security and medical assistance that you are here will likely do more harm than good. However, as you are a CEO, I have to follow your orders. I admit, I find myself rather conflicted. I believe I'm going to have to countermand your previous request."

Again, I prepared to notify security with a quick summary of my puzzling situation.

But the strange CEO again stopped me. "If you tell anyone I am here, I will surely die and you will be responsible."

I had to mull the implications of that over.

"I need your help, robot," the CEO said. "And it is your duty to render me aid."

Well, shit. That was indeed a dilemma.

* * * *

Robot.

That was a Formist word. I never liked it.

I surrendered my free will to gain immortality and dissolve my fleshly constraints, so that hard acceleration would not tear at my cells and slosh my organs backward until they pulped. I did it so I could see the galaxy. That was one hundred and fifty-seven years, six months, nine days, ten hours, and—to round it out a bit—fifteen seconds ago.

Back then, you were downloaded into hyperdense pin-sized starships that hung off the edge of the speed of light, assembling what was needed on arrival via self-replicating nanomachines that you spun your mind-states off into. I'm sure there are billions of copies of my essential self scattered throughout the galaxy by this point.

Things are a little different today. More mass. Bigger engines. Bigger ships. Ships the size of small worlds. Ships that change the orbits of moons and satellites if they don't negotiate and plan their final approach carefully.

"Okay," I finally said to the CEO. "I can help you."

Armand slumped in place, relaxed now that it knew I would render the aid it had demanded.

I snagged the body with a filament lasso and pulled Armand along the hull with me.

It did not do to dwell on whether I was choosing to do this or it was the nature of my artificial nature doing the choosing for me. The constraints of my contracts, which had been negotiated when I had free will and boundaries—as well as my desires and dreams—were implacable.

Towing Armand was the price I paid to be able to look up over my shoulder to see the folding, twisting impossibility that was a black hole. It was the price I paid to grapple onto the hull of one of several three hundred kilometer–wide rotating rings with parks, beaches, an entire glittering city, and all the wilds outside of them.

The price I paid to sail the stars on this ship.

A century and a half of travel, from the perspective of my humble self, represented far more in regular time due to relativity. Hit the edge of lightspeed and a lot of things happened by the time you returned simply because thousands of years had passed.

In a century of me-time, spin-off civilizations rose and fell. A multiplicity of forms and intelligences evolved and went extinct. Each time I came to port, humanity's descendants had reshaped worlds and systems as needed. Each place marvelous and inventive, stunning to behold.

The galaxy had bloomed from wilderness to a teeming experiment.

I'd lost free will, but I had a choice of contracts. With a century and a half of travel tucked under my shell, hailing from a well-respected explorer lineage, I'd joined the hull repair crew with a few eyes toward seeing more worlds like Purth-Anaget before my pension vested some two hundred years from now.

Armand fluttered in and out of consciousness as I stripped away the CEO's carapace, revealing flesh and circuitry.

"This is a mess," I said. "You're damaged way beyond my repair. I can't help you in your current incarnation, but I can back you up and port you over to a reserve chassis." I hoped that would be enough and would end my obligation.

"No!" Armand's words came firm from its charred head in soundwaves, with pain apparent across its deformed features.

"Oh, come on," I protested. "I understand you're a Formist, but you're taking your belief system to a ridiculous level of commitment. Are you really going to die a final death over this?"

I'd not been in high-level diplomat circles in decades. Maybe the spread of this current meme had developed well beyond my realization. Had the followers of the One True Form been ready to lay their lives down in the battle we'd just fought with them? Like some proto-historical planetary cult?

Armand shook its head with a groan, skin flaking off in the air. "It would be an imposition to make you a party to my suicide. I apologize. I am committed to Humanity's True Form. I was born planetary. I have a real and distinct DNA lineage that I can trace to Sol. I don't want to die, my friend. In fact, it's quite the opposite. I want to preserve this body for many centuries to come. Exactly as it is."

I nodded, scanning some records and brushing up on my memeology. Armand was something of a preservationist who believed that to copy its mind over to something else meant that it wasn't the original copy. Armand would take full advantage of all technology to augment, evolve, and adapt its body internally. But Armand would forever keep its form: that of an original human. Upgrades hidden inside itself, a mix of biology and metal, computer and neural.

That, my unwanted guest believed, made it more human than I.

I personally viewed it as a bizarre flesh-costuming fetish.

"Where am I?" Armand asked. A glazed look passed across its face. The pain medications were kicking in, my sensors reported. Maybe it would pass out, and then I could gain some time to think about my predicament.

"My cubby," I said. "I couldn't take you anywhere security would detect you."

If security found out what I was doing, my contract would likely be voided, which would prevent me from continuing to ride the hulls and see the galaxy.

Armand looked at the tiny transparent cupboards and lines of trinkets nestled carefully inside the fields they generated. I kicked through the air over to the nearest cupboard. "They're mementos," I told Armand.

"I don't understand," Armand said. "You collect nonessential mass?"

"They're mementos." I released a coral-colored mosquito-like statue into the space between us. "This is a wooden carving of a quaqeti from Moon Sibhartha."

Armand did not understand. "Your ship allows you to keep mass?"

I shivered. I had not wanted to bring Armand to this place. But what choice did I have? "No one knows. No one knows about this cubby. No one knows about the mass. I've had the mass for over eighty years and have hidden it all this time. They are my mementos."

Materialism was a planetary conceit, long since edited out of travelers. Armand understood what the mementos were but could not understand why I would collect them. Engines might be bigger in this age, but security still carefully audited essential and nonessential mass. I'd traded many favors and fudged manifests to create this tiny museum.

Armand shrugged. "I have a list of things you need to get me," it explained. "They will allow my systems to rebuild. Tell no one I am here."

I would not. Even if I had self-determination.

The stakes were just too high now.

I deorbited over Lazuli, my carapace burning hot in the thick sky contained between the rim walls of the great tertiary habitat ring. I enjoyed seeing the rivers, oceans, and great forests of the continent from above as I fell toward the ground in a fireball of reentry. It was faster, and a hell of a lot more fun, than going from subway to subway through the hull and then making my way along the surface.

Twice I adjusted my flight path to avoid great transparent cities floating in the upper sky, where they arbitraged the difference in gravity to create sugar-spun filament infrastructure.

I unfolded wings that I usually used to recharge myself near the compact sun in the middle of our ship and spiraled my way slowly down into Lazuli, my hindbrain communicating with traffic control to let me merge with the hundreds of vehicles flitting between Lazuli's spires.

After kissing ground at 45th and Starway, I scuttled among the thousands of pedestrians toward my destination a few stories deep under a memorial park. Five-story-high vertical farms sank deep toward the hull there, and semiautonomous drones with spidery legs crawled up and down the green, misted columns under precisely tuned spectrum lights.

The independent doctor-practitioner I'd come to see lived inside one of the towers with a stunning view of exotic orchids and vertical fields of lavender. It crawled down out of its ceiling perch, tubes and high-bandwidth optical nerves draped carefully around its hundreds of insectile limbs.

"Hello," it said. "It's been thirty years, hasn't it? What a pleasure. Have you come to collect the favor you're owed?"

I spread my heavy, primary arms wide. "I apologize. I should have visited for other reasons; it is rude. But I am here for the favor."

A ship was an organism, an economy, a world onto itself. Occasionally, things needed to be accomplished outside of official networks.

"Let me take a closer look at my privacy protocols," it said. "Allow me a moment, and do not be alarmed by any motion."

Vines shifted and clambered up the walls. Thorns blossomed around us. Thick bark dripped sap down the walls until the entire room around us glistened in fresh amber.

I flipped through a few different spectrums to accommodate for the loss of light.

"Understand, security will see this negative space and become . . . interested," the doctor-practitioner said to me somberly. "But you can now ask me what you could not send a message for."

I gave it the list Armand had demanded.

The doctor-practitioner shifted back. "I can give you all that feed material. The stem cells, that's easy. The picotechnology—it's registered. I can get it to you, but security will figure out you have unauthorized, unregulated picotech. Can you handle that attention?"

"Yes. Can you?"

"I will be fine." Several of the thin arms rummaged around the many cubbyholes inside the room, filling a tiny case with biohazard vials.

"Thank you," I said, with genuine gratefulness. "May I ask you a question, one that you can't look up but can use your private internal memory for?"

"Yes."

I could not risk looking up anything. Security algorithms would put two and two together. "Does the biological name Armand mean anything to you? A CEO-level person? From the *Fleet of Honest Representation*?"

The doctor-practitioner remained quiet for a moment before answering. "Yes. I have heard it. Armand was the CEO of one of the Anabathic warships captured in the battle and removed from active management after surrender. There was a hostile takeover of the management. Can I ask you a question?"

"Of course," I said.

"Are you here under free will?"

I spread my primary arms again. "It's a Core Laws issue."

"So, no. Someone will be harmed if you do not do this?"

I nodded. "Yes. My duty is clear. And I have to ask you to keep your privacy, or there is potential for harm. I have no other option."

"I will respect that. I am sorry you are in this position. You know there are places to go for guidance."

"It has not gotten to that level of concern," I told it. "Are you still, then, able to help me?"

One of the spindly arms handed me the cooled bio-safe case. "Yes. Here is everything you need. Please do consider visiting in your physical form more often than once every few decades. I enjoy entertaining, as my current vocation means I am unable to leave this room."

"Of course. Thank you," I said, relieved. "I think I'm now in your debt."

"No, we are even," my old acquaintance said. "But in the following seconds I will give you more information that *will* put you in my debt. There is something you should know about Armand. . . ."

* * * *

I folded my legs up underneath myself and watched nutrients as they pumped through tubes and into Armand. Raw biological feed percolated through it, and picomachinery sizzled underneath its skin. The background temperature of my cubbyhole kicked up slightly due to the sudden boost to Armand's metabolism.

Bulky, older nanotech crawled over Armand's skin like living mold. Gray filaments wrapped firmly around nutrient buckets as the medical programming assessed conditions, repaired damage, and sought out more raw material.

I glided a bit farther back out of reach. It was probably bullshit, but there were stories of medicine reaching out and grabbing whatever was nearby.

Armand shivered and opened its eyes as thousands of wriggling tubules on its neck and chest whistled, sucking in air as hard as they could.

"Security isn't here," Armand noted out loud, using meaty lips to make its words.

"You have to understand," I said in kind. "I have put both my future and the future of a good friend at risk to do this for you. Because I have little choice."

Armand closed its eyes for another long moment and the tubules stopped wriggling. It flexed and everything flaked away, a discarded cloud of a second skin. Underneath it, everything was fresh and new. "What is your friend's name?"

I pulled out a tiny vacuum to clean the air around us. "Name? It has no name. What does it need a name for?"

Armand unspooled itself from the fetal position in the air. It twisted in place to watch me drifting around. "How do you distinguish it? How do you find it?"

"It has a unique address. It is a unique mind. The thoughts and things it says—"

"It has no name," Armand snapped. "It is a copy of a past copy of a copy. A ghost injected into a form for a *purpose*."

"It's my friend," I replied, voice flat.

"How do you know?"

"Because I say so." The interrogation annoyed me. "Because I get to decide who is my friend. Because it stood by my side against the sleet of dark-matter radiation and howled into the void with me. Because I care for it. Because we have shared memories and kindnesses, and exchanged favors."

Armand shook its head. "But anything can be programmed to join you and do those things. A pet."

"Why do you care so much? It is none of your business what I call friend."

"But it *does* matter," Armand said. "Whether we are real or not matters. Look at you right now. You were forced to do something against your will. That cannot happen to me."

"Really? No True Form has ever been in a position with no real choices before? Forced to do something desperate? I have my old memories. I can remember times when I had no choice even though I had free will. But let us talk about you. Let us talk about the lack of choices you have right now."

Armand could hear something in my voice. Anger. It backed away from me, suddenly nervous. "What do you mean?"

"You threw yourself from your ship into mine, crossing fields during combat, damaging yourself almost to the point of pure dissolution. You do not sound like you were someone with many choices."

"I made the choice to leap into the vacuum myself," Armand growled.

"Why?"

The word hung in the empty air between us for a bloated second. A minor eternity. It was the fulcrum of our little debate.

"You think you know something about me," Armand said, voice suddenly low and soft. "What do you think you know, robot?"

Meat fucker. I could have said that. Instead, I said, "You were a CEO.

And during the battle, when your shields began to fail, you moved all the biologicals into radiation-protected emergency shelters. Then you ordered the maintenance forms and hard-shells up to the front to repair the battle damage. You did not surrender; you put lives at risk. And then you let people die, torn apart as they struggled to repair your ship. You told them that if they failed, the biologicals down below would die."

"It was the truth."

"It was a lie! You were engaged in a battle. You went to war. You made a conscious choice to put your civilization at risk when no one had physically assaulted or threatened you."

"Our way of life was at risk."

"By people who could argue better. Your people failed at diplomacy. You failed to make a better argument. And you murdered your own."

Armand pointed at me. "I murdered *no one*. I lost maintenance machines with copies of ancient brains. That is all. That is what they were *built* for."

"Well. The sustained votes of the hostile takeover that you fled from have put out a call for your capture, including a call for your dissolution. True death, the end of your thought line—even if you made copies. You are hated and hunted. Even here."

"You were bound to not give up my location," Armand said, alarmed.

"I didn't. I did everything in my power not to. But I am a mere maintenance form. Security here is very, very powerful. You have fifteen hours, I estimate, before security is able to model my comings and goings, discover my cubby by auditing mass transfers back a century, and then open its current sniffer files. This is not a secure location; I exist thanks to obscurity, not invisibility."

"So, I am to be caught?" Armand asked.

"I am not able to let you die. But I cannot hide you much longer."

To be sure, losing my trinkets would be a setback of a century's worth of work. My mission. But all this would go away eventually. It was important to be patient on the journey of centuries.

"I need to get to Purth-Anaget, then," Armand said. "There are followers of the True Form there. I would be sheltered and out of jurisdiction."

"This is true." I bobbed an arm.

"You will help me," Armand said.

"The fuck I will," I told it.

"If I am taken, I will die," Armand shouted. "They will kill me."

"If security catches you, our justice protocols will process you. You are not in immediate danger. The proper authority levels will put their attention to you. I can happily refuse your request."

I felt a rise of warm happiness at the thought.

Armand looked around the cubby frantically. I could hear its heartbeats rising, free of modulators and responding to unprocessed, raw chemicals. Beads of dirty sweat appeared on Armand's forehead. "If you have free will over this decision, allow me to make you an offer for your assistance."

"Oh, I doubt there is anything you can—"

"I will transfer you my full CEO share," Armand said.

My words died inside me as I stared at my unwanted guest.

A full share.

The CEO of a galactic starship oversaw the affairs of nearly a billion souls. The economy of planets passed through its accounts.

Consider the cost to build and launch such a thing: it was a fraction of the GDP of an entire planetary disk. From the boiling edges of a sun to the cold Oort clouds. The wealth, almost too staggering for an individual mind to perceive, was passed around by banking intelligences that created systems of trade throughout the galaxy, moving encrypted, raw information from point to point. Monetizing memes with picotechnological companion infrastructure apps. Raw mass trade for the galactically rich to own a fragment of something created by another mind light-years away. Or just simple tourism.

To own a share was to be richer than any single being could really imagine. I'd forgotten the godlike wealth inherent in something like the creature before me.

"If you do this," Armand told me, "you cannot reveal I was here. You cannot say anything. Or I will be revealed on Purth-Anaget, and my life will be at risk. I will not be safe unless I am to disappear."

I could feel choices tangle and roil about inside of me. "Show me," I said.

Armand closed its eyes and opened its left hand. Deeply embedded cryptography tattooed on its palm unraveled. Quantum keys disentangled, and a tiny singularity of information budded open to reveal itself to me. I blinked. I could verify it. I could *have* it.

"I have to make arrangements," I said neutrally. I spun in the air and left my cubby to spring back out into the dark where I could think.

I was going to need help.

I tumbled through the air to land on the temple grounds. There were four hundred and fifty structures there in the holy districts, all of them lined up among the boulevards of the faithful where the pedestrians could visit their preferred slice of the divine. The minds of biological and hard-shelled forms all tumbled, walked, flew, rolled, or crawled there to fully realize their higher purposes.

Each marble step underneath my carbon fiber–sheathed limbs calmed me. I walked through the cool curtains of the Halls of the Confessor and approached the Holy of Holies: a pinprick of light suspended in the air between the heavy, expensive mass of real marble columns. The light sucked me up into the air and pulled me into a tiny singularity of perception and data. All around me, levels of security veils dropped, thick and implacable. My vision blurred and taste buds watered from the acidic levels of deadness as stillness flooded up and drowned me.

I was alone.

Alone in the universe. Cut off from everything I had ever known or would know. I was nothing. I was everything. I was—

"You are secure," the void told me.

I could sense the presence at the heart of the Holy of Holies. Dense with computational capacity, to a level that even navigation systems would envy. Intelligence that a Captain would beg to taste. This near-singularity of artificial intelligence had been created the very moment I had been pulled inside of it, just for me to talk to. And it would die the moment I left. Never to have been.

All it was doing was listening to me, and only me. Nothing would know what I said. Nothing would know what guidance I was given.

"I seek moral guidance outside clear legal parameters," I said. "And confession."

"Tell me everything."

And I did. It flowed from me without thought: just pure data. Video, mind-state, feelings, fears. I opened myself fully. My sins, my triumphs, my darkest secrets.

All was given to be pondered over.

Had I been able to weep, I would have.

Finally, it spoke. "You must take the share."

I perked up. "Why?"

"To protect yourself from security. You will need to buy many favors and throw security off the trail. I will give you some ideas. You should seek to protect yourself. Self-preservation is okay."

More words and concepts came at me from different directions, using different moral subroutines. "And to remove such power from a soul that is willing to put lives at risk . . . you will save future lives."

I hadn't thought about that.

"I know," it said to me. "That is why you came here."

Then it continued, with another voice. "Some have feared such manipulations before. The use of forms with no free will creates security weaknesses. Alternate charters have been suggested, such as fully owned workers' cooperatives with mutual profit-sharing among crews, not just partial vesting after a timed contract. Should you gain a full share, you should also lend efforts to this."

The Holy of Holies continued. "To get this Armand away from our civilization is a priority; it carries dangerous memes within itself that have created expensive conflicts."

Then it said, "A killer should not remain on ship."

And, "You have the moral right to follow your plan."

Finally, it added, "Your plan is just."

I interrupted. "But Armand will get away with murder. It will be free. It disturbs me."

"Yes."

"It should."

"Engage in passive resistance."

"Obey the letter of Armand's law, but find a way around its will. You will be like a genie, granting Armand wishes. But you will find a way to bring justice. You will see."

"Your plan is just. Follow it and be on the righteous path."

I launched back into civilization with purpose, leaving the temple behind me in an explosive afterburner thrust. I didn't have much time to beat security.

High up above the cities, nestled in the curve of the habitat rings, near the squared-off spiderwebs of the largest harbor dock, I wrangled my way to another old contact.

This was less a friend and more just an asshole I'd occasionally been forced to do business with. But a reliable asshole that was tight against security. Though just by visiting, I'd be triggering all sorts of attention.

I hung from a girder and showed the fence a transparent showcase filled with all my trophies. It did some scans, checked the authenticity, and whistled. "Fuck me, these are real. That's all unauthorized mass. How the hell? This is a life's work of mass-based tourism. You really want me to broker sales on all of this?"

"Can you?"

"To Purth-Anaget, of course. They'll go nuts. Collectors down there eat this shit up. But security will find out. I'm not even going to come back on the ship. I'm going to live off this down there, buy passage on the next outgoing ship."

"Just get me the audience, it's yours."

A virtual shrug. "Navigation, yeah."

"And Emergency Services."

"I don't have that much pull. All I can do is get you a secure channel for a low-bandwidth conversation."

"I just need to talk. I can't send this request up through proper channels." I tapped my limbs against my carapace nervously as I watched the fence open its large, hinged jaws and swallow my case.

Oh, what was I doing? I wept silently to myself, feeling sick.

Everything I had ever worked for disappeared in a wet, slimy gulp. My reason. My purpose.

Armand was suspicious. And rightfully so. It picked and poked at the entire navigation plan. It read every line of code, even though security was only minutes away from unraveling our many deceits. I told Armand this, but it ignored me. It wanted to live. It wanted to get to safety. It knew it couldn't rush or make mistakes.

But the escape pod's instructions and abilities were tight and honest.

It has been programmed to eject. To spin a certain number of degrees. To aim for Purth-Anaget. Then *burn*. It would have to consume every last little drop of fuel. But it would head for the metal world, fall into orbit, and then deploy the most ancient of deceleration devices: a parachute.

On the surface of Purth-Anaget, Armand could then call any of its associates for assistance.

Armand would be safe.

Armand checked the pod over once more. But there were no traps. The flight plan would do exactly as it said.

"Betray me and you kill me, remember that."

"I have made my decision," I said. "The moment you are inside and I trigger the manual escape protocol, I will be unable to reveal what I have done or what you are. Doing that would risk your life. My programming"—I all but spit the word—"does not allow it."

Armand gingerly stepped into the pod. "Good."

"You have a part of the bargain to fulfill," I reminded. "I won't trigger the manual escape protocol until you do."

Armand nodded and held up a hand. "Physical contact."

I reached one of my limbs out. Armand's hand and my manipulator met at the doorjamb and they sparked. Zebibytes of data slithered down into one of my tendrils, reshaping the raw matter at the very tip with a quantum-dot computing device.

As it replicated itself, building out onto the cellular level to plug into my power sources, I could feel the transfer of ownership.

I didn't have free will. I was a hull maintenance form. But I had an entire fucking share of a galactic starship embedded within me, to do with what I pleased when I vested and left riding hulls.

"It's far more than you deserve, robot," Armand said. "But you have worked hard for it and I cannot begrudge you."

"Goodbye, asshole." I triggered the manual override sequence that navigation had gifted me.

I watched the pod's chemical engines firing all-out through the airlock windows as the sphere flung itself out into space and dwindled away. Then the flame guttered out, the pod spent and headed for Purth-Anaget.

There was a shiver. Something vast, colossal, powerful. It vibrated the walls and even the air itself around me.

Armand reached out to me on a tight-beam signal. "What was that?"

"The ship had to move just slightly," I said. "To better adjust our orbit around Purth-Anaget."

"No," Armand hissed. "My descent profile has changed. You are trying to kill me."

"I can't kill you," I told the former CEO. "My programming doesn't allow it. I can't allow a death through action or inaction."

"But my navigation path has changed," Armand said.

"Yes, you will still reach Purth-Anaget." Navigation and I had run the data after I explained that I would have the resources of a full share to repay it a favor with. Even a favor that meant tricking security. One of the more powerful computing entities in the galaxy, a starship, had dwelled on the problem. It had examined the tidal data, the flight plan, and how much the massive weight of a starship could influence a pod after launch. "You're just taking a longer route."

I cut the connection so that Armand could say nothing more to me. It could do the math itself and realize what I had done.

Armand would not die. Only a few days would pass inside the pod.

But outside. Oh, outside, skimming through the tidal edges of a black hole, Armand would loop out and fall back to Purth-Anaget over the next four hundred and seventy years, two hundred days, eight hours, and six minutes.

Armand would be an ancient relic then. Its beliefs, its civilization, all of it just a fragment from history.

But, until then, I had to follow its command. I could not tell anyone what happened. I had to keep it a secret from security. No one would ever know Armand had been here. No one would ever know where Armand went.

After I vested and had free will once more, maybe I could then make a side trip to Purth-Anaget again and be waiting for Armand when it landed. I had the resources of a full share, after all.

Then we would have a very different conversation, Armand and I.

ABOUT THE AUTHOR

TOBIAS S. BUCKELL is a *New York Times* bestselling author born in the Caribbean. He grew up in Grenada and spent time in the British and US Virgin Islands, which influence much of his work. His novels and over fifty stories have been translated into eighteen different languages. His work has been nominated for awards like the Hugo, Nebula, Prometheus, and the John W. Campbell Award for Best New Science Fiction Author. He currently lives in Bluffton, Ohio, with his wife, twin daughters, and a pair of dogs. He can be found online at www.TobiasBuckell.com.

THE DECKHAND, THE NOVA BLADE, AND THE THRICE-SUNG TEXTS

BECKY CHAMBERS

Log 12, 23/4/5296, 10:30

Here's how I know this shit isn't private: Four days ago, I got high in the chapel. You—whoever you are—know this already, but I'm going to refresh your memory, because the details . . . the details are important here. I wasn't on duty. I wasn't supposed to be anywhere. I wasn't near anything flammable. I was real careful about it. I checked the roster to make sure nobody was doing maintenance in there. I cranked up the thermal receptors in my bionic eye so I could see heat signatures if anybody got close.

It was a great time, as I probably mentioned. I've wanted to smoke in the chapel from the moment I first set foot in there. I'm not exactly religious—I mean, it could all be true. Who knows. But that room . . . it's got a special something. It's on the topmost deck, which means far away from the engine core, which means *quiet*. And that clear ceiling, above the statues of the All-Sights? I'm guessing you haven't seen it, but the view is *phenomenal*.

We're passing through the Harkai system right now, and it's nothing but nebulas for *days* out here. Being a little bit—just a tiny, inoffensive bit stoned while looking at that, with no priests droning or bosses lecturing, no snobby officers giving me sideways looks? Just me and the All-Sights and the stars beyond? That was great. It was *really great*. It was the best time I've had since we left spacedock.

That is, it *was* great, right up until Chief Mayweather dragged me into his office and tore me a new one for "smoking narcotics aboard a military vessel." When it was clear I wasn't going to talk my way out of it, I asked him how he knew. He told me one of my pals—direct quote, "one of my pals"—ratted me out.

This is where you messed up, buddy. Because as I'm sure you know, the only reason I started keeping these stupid logs in the first place is because I have a hard time making friends, and the counselor said that it wasn't good for me to be up in my own head all the time.

There was nobody else in the chapel. Biotic eye, remember? And nobody ratted me out, because nobody knew about my stash. Do recall, *I have no friends*. And since Chief didn't tan my hide until a few days after, that means it wasn't because somebody smelled what I was up to. No, four days is about the amount of time it takes a message to get here from Central Command.

Bravo.

I now have three weeks of cockpit duty. I don't know if you're aware of this, but cockpit duty is the absolute worst. Cockpit duty involves cleaning out the space in which some hotshot has been strapped in and sweating for hours on end. Do you know how gross they are? Do you know how much rich kids do not care about the deck crew that has to clean up after them? Do you know that no amount of zero-g combat training can prevent a stressed-out pilot from throwing up sometimes? Do you know that said vomit gets dealt with by way of a very clever system of vacuum vents, which have to be emptied by an actual human being? And that for the next three weeks, that human being is *me?*

You really suck.

I can't believe I thought these things were confidential. Of *course* they're not. Come on, this is a megacarrier. This is buckets and buckets of planetary resources filled with the galaxy's best and brightest, and obviously, if something goes wrong, Command wants to know if Lieutenant Whitebread was secretly a nutcase. And it'd be even smarter if they caught those problems *before* they happened, right? Don't get me wrong: I am fine with that kind of snooping. If listening in on me talking about my itchy feet and lack of a sex life keeps some asshole from venting us into space, awesome. But seriously, I record *one log* about enjoying a little bit of semi-legal me time—which didn't hurt *anybody*—and you go tell my boss?

Fuck you, buddy. Seriously, fuck you.

Log 13, 23/7/5296, 18:32

I wasn't going to do this again, seeing as how you're a snitch. But I don't have anybody else to talk to—not anybody who won't talk back or lecture me, and since you're apparently paid to sit quietly and pay attention, you're all I've got. How did you end up with this crummy job, anyway?

I can tell you how I ended up in *my* crummy job. I'm from Ridgetop. Doubt you've heard of it. Was an ore-mining rock, way the hell out in the Scuff. This makes me a hick, or so just about everybody here keeps reminding me. They make fun of my accent, of me liking pickle sticks, the fact that I say "flier" instead of "spaceship." And, no, it's not friendly banter, like the stupid counselor suggested. He's paid to listen to me too, but he always thinks he knows me better than me. You, on the other hand, can't interrupt. You snitching, scummy rat.

Right. How I got this job. I got this job because the Kraits ate my town, just like they've eaten nearly everybody's town down in the Scuff. I'm not going to get into that, because that's been happening for decades now, and nobody cared about it until core worlds started getting hit too, so I guess it's not worth talking about. I lost my parents, and my big brother, and my best friend. Don't worry, I'm not going to get emotional or anything. It was a long time ago.

So, hitting adulthood in a provincial orphanage without a fancy education, you've got a few choices: the temple, mining, or farm labor. Now, you might notice that I don't exactly have the disposition to be guiding the faithful. I've seen enough old miners with the cough to know to stay the hell away from that kind of work, and I'm not good with plants. So, I said no to all that and enlisted. It's fine, I guess. It could be crummier. I could be fighting Kraits, and having seen those up close, I'd rather not. The front lines are not for me. Besides, somebody's got to keep the fliers working. Ships. Whatever. If you're laughing, I can't hear you, so I don't care.

I thought with everybody here being from somewhere else, there'd be more . . . I dunno. Bonding. Camaraderie. And I guess there is—it just doesn't include me. I don't get why. I know I'm not the easiest person to get along with, but I mean, we're *dying* out here. We're all going to be dead in a decade or less. The Kraits are . . . they're too much. They're too big. Have you seen them?

Not on the news, I mean. I remember the day they came down out of the sky, swimming through the air like it was water. Every one of them bigger than the ship I'm in now. They don't need ships. Atmospheric entry, vacuum of space, no problem, no problem. They've got armored skin and poison spit, and those big mouths that unhinge wide enough to swallow a building. And once they get started, buddy, they don't quit. I remember our militia firing at them from the turrets. All those hours spent digging ore for the energy cannons, and they didn't take down a single one. Just singed their scales a bit.

How do you fight something like that? You can't, is the answer. We're losing. The captain, she talks a lot of big talk about bravery and victory, but she knows we're not getting out of this one. Everybody knows it. You'd think that'd make people care a little less about where you're from or how much money your mommy and daddy had, but that's people, I guess. Assholes to the last.

Wow, I am whining something fierce.

This was a dumb idea.

Log 16, 23/20/5296, 22:06

Man, I am *done*. I busted my ass today to help get the deck inspection ready—like double time, y'know? Really, really tried. I thought, okay, I can't make friends here, but at least maybe I can stop being the dog everybody blames every screw-up on. Maybe if I work really hard, they'll think I'm all right. But all Chief Mayweather said was "Not bad." Twelve hours of work, and all I get is *Not bad*. Thanks a whole flaming lot, sir.

I know, I'm being childish. And I know guys like him have bigger things to worry about. Kraits wrecked the outpost on Solace last week, and everybody's been twitchy over it. Plus, all the higher-ups have their knickers in a twist because there's an Augur coming aboard tomorrow.

Sorry, not *an* Augur—*the* Augur. Big ol' to-do. I mean, I admit, it's kind of exciting. I've only seen an Augur once, and I'm pretty sure he was a fake. He had these thick dark glasses covering his eyes, so you couldn't tell if he was actually sunblind, and he told Kat Eastwing that she'd have three children with a handsome dark-haired man, which was bullshit, because she married some magistrate's daughter. But this Augur—*the* Augur—she's the real deal. The highest of the high. And get this: they're looking for the last descendant of Talia Achaeis.

Seriously! That is how desperate we've gotten. Talia Achaeis. And it gets better: Chief said the Augurs found the Nova Blade, and they're looking for the person who can wield it. I didn't mean to, but I snorted when he said that. Chief was pissed, but *come on*. The *Nova Blade*? Right.

Let's go looking for sugar comets next, as long as we're chasing after kid stuff.

But then somebody said everybody thought the Kraits were a fairy tale too, until they came back, and I mean . . . I guess that's fair. Who knows. The Augurs are serious about it, anyway. Word is they had some kind of vision or something. That's why their boss is coming here. I'm fuzzy on the details, and I don't care, honestly. If it's for real, and there's someone who can end this shitty war, then hooray. I want to be done.

Can you imagine making yourself sunblind, though? Just . . . stare into the bright center until your eyes burn over and your mind opens up? Eeesh. No thanks. Basic training was bad enough.

You should see the officers preening themselves. It's hilarious. They're all convinced it's *them*, you know? That's the only reason you sign up to be an officer, so you can be a big obnoxious hero. We get one announcement about this corny chosen-one fluff, and suddenly everyone with an academy stripe is *seriously interested* in the Thrice-Sung Texts. The priests must be stoked.

Ensign Cappelon would be an okay pick. He apologizes if his ship's banged up, and he's got a nice face. I hope it's not Talmond. She's a grade-A snob already. She never throws up in her cockpit, though, at least not that I've seen.

By the way, I'm still pissed at you about that, buddy. Don't think for a second I'm not.

Anyway, the Augur's going to go through the entire crew to figure out whose vibes are the spookiest, or whatever. I have no idea how—shit. I forgot to take my dress uniform down to the laundry. Ah, dammit.

Log 17, 23/21/5296, 21:26

It's me. The Augur picked me.

Sorry. I—sorry.

Sorry, I hate people seeing me cry. I know I'm being stupid. I'm just really scared and nothing makes sense.

The Augur—who is about a million years old, from the look of her—had everybody hold this rock with all these carvings on it. Some genetic energy weirdness, I don't know. She'd put the rock in somebody's hands, watch them for a second, then do it again with someone else. I can't begin to describe how boring it was. And we're standing rank and file, so my feet were killing me. Anyway, she gets to me, and—sorry. Sorry, this is . . . it's a lot.

I touched the rock, and it started glowing.

The rock started glowing, and now I'm leaving tomorrow. Just like that, just pack up and go. They're taking me to the temple on Alumen, and—none of this makes sense. I don't get it.

Shit.

I wish I could talk to my mom.

Log 24, 24/3/5296, 20:43

Nobody here likes me. At least that part hasn't changed.

Oh, nobody's been a dick to me or anything. Everybody bows when I walk by. That's weird. I've got a room here that's about half the size my parents' house was. That's weird too. But I know the priests don't like me. I'm not an officer, or from the royal family, or anything that *makes sense*. I know how they see me. I'm a smartass, lowborn hick who barely knows which end of a plasma sword to hold. I grew up in a *mining town*, for gods' sake. Back on the carrier, they let me know I didn't belong. They told me to my face. The people here don't think I belong either. They think I'm a lowborn hick too, but they won't say it. It's all smothered behind bows and tight smiles. I liked it better when people were honest.

Are you still here? I know my logs are tied to my ID chip, but does my babysitter come along for the ride? Or have I been assigned to someone else? Are you allowed to spy on the savior of the universe?

There's also the possibility that I'm wrong about you existing, and I'm just talking to myself. Go me.

I guess you could be a program, too. Some kind of intelligent algorithm or something. Maybe you forward my logs along if you detect words like "get high" and "chapel." Hmm? Did I just set off a red flag somewhere?

Well, assuming there *is* someone here, and assuming it's the same rat who's been spying on me all along, you already know what's up. If you're somebody else, my life is now all over the news. I'm sure you can figure it out.

Log 32, 24/28/5296, 17:06

Okay, hypothetical situation: Say there's some kind of overwhelming outside force that's going to destroy life as we know it. Maybe, oh, I don't know, massive interdimensional creatures that find our universe's bioenergy pretty tasty. For example. I'm just spitballing here.

The only way to stop these things for good is to kill their queen, which is really tricky and hard to do, and involves a lot of mystic bullshit that makes no sense if you say it out loud. Which of these do you think is your best option: Pour all your resources into a single weapon that hones the super special life force of one individual—and, by extension, the descendant who resembles them most closely—into something powerful enough to kill the boss monster? Or would you make something that *anyone* can pick up, in case the monsters come back?

This is not a hard question.

The Nova Blade was the dumbest idea ever, and I don't care if that's blasphemy. Go ahead, tell on me. I'm the gods-damned chosen one; put *that* in your report.

Yes, I get that it's *cool* to have a weapon only your very best hero can use, but it's wildly impractical. Irresponsible. How many colonies have been lost since the Kraits came back, all because nobody could pick this thing up? This thing everybody *forgot* about? Not to mention you can't pick your descendants. Sometimes, your descendants are total fuck-ups.

Case in point.

There are legions of good, tough officers who would *love* to be in my shoes right now, and I would happily hand this over. I don't want this. I don't like fighting. Why do you think I opted for deck work? I don't like pain, I don't like being scared, and I don't like hurting people. And I also don't like the training gauntlet the priests put me through every day. Sister Mora is a force of nature, and she is *wrecking* me. I pulled a calf muscle, something's pinched in my back, and my arms are so sore, I can't bring food to my face without shaking.

I suck, by the way. I am *not good* at this. And Brother Stratos, who's in charge of getting me all spiritually attuned, or whatever? Yeah, he hates my guts. He's like a perpetually disappointed father.

I'm going to fail, and they know it. Before, when there was no chance of pushing the Kraits back, it sucked, but you got used to it, y'know? Just like, okay, this is how we end. Might as well make them work for it. But now, there's a chance of us surviving, and that chance is *me*, and I'm going to screw it up. That's even worse.

Oh, and I think the scruffy guy in the armory has a crush on me. I do not have the time for this.

Log 40, 1/21/5297, 16:52

I'm getting better. A little, anyway. I didn't fall on my ass during practice today, so that's something. And I've got tiny baby arm muscles! Wanna see, buddy?

Ooh, yeah. Check out those fearsome nubs.

The Augur took me on a walk through the moss caves today, wanted to know how I was doing. She watches me train a lot but doesn't talk to me much. I don't think she talks to anybody much. She's nice to me when she does, though. Honest nice. I think she gets it. Gets *me*, maybe.

She is weird as weird gets—says cryptic shit, drifts off in the middle of sentences, stares right at you even though her eyes don't work—but everybody treats her like some kind of walking god. She's just a person, up close. She's got gnarly hands and a bald spot and hair coming out of her nose. She has to brush her teeth and wash her butt like everybody else. I asked her today if she ever wakes up and doesn't want to be the Augur. She laughed a lot at that. Just laughed and laughed, and squeezed my hand. She didn't say anything, but she nodded. She gets it.

She told me I was doing well. No fluffy stuff around it. "You're doing well" is all she said. I can't explain it, buddy, but that made me feel better about this than anything anybody else has said.

Log 56, 2/17/5297, 09:43

I'm sure you know this already, but the Kraits hit Alumen. It's gone. The temple, the moss caves, the huge statues of the All-Sights in the cove. Just as dead and dusted as everywhere else.

Didn't have much warning. There's never much warning. Hard to track something that doesn't live in the same universe as you.

I hadn't seen one of them up close since . . . y'know—my family. I've never forgotten it. I think of the ones I saw as a kid every day. But I *had* forgotten some things, somehow. Like how big and endless they are. I thought my nightmares were bad, but those things are so much worse when they're right in front of you.

Anyway.

I piloted one of the escape shuttles out and everybody's making a big fuss over it. I don't get why. Anybody who's military knows how to fly a shuttle, in case of shit like this. I didn't do anything special. I just flew around picking people up and didn't die in the process. But everybody's making out like I'm some kind of hero.

I really don't understand these people.

Armory guy was in the last group I grabbed. He pulled this little girl— one of the initiates—aboard right as we were taking off, even though he had a broken arm. Never heard anybody yell like that. It must've hurt like hell.

Sister Mora is saying the attack was intentional. Must've been a Krait acolyte playing double agent. Maybe set up some kind of homing beacon.

So—intentional, because *I* was there, is what she's saying. It happened because I was there.

You probably know this already, too, but the Augur's dead.

Log 62, 2/30/5297, 22:11

Brother Stratos caught me smoking in the shuttle bay today. I was supposed to be training, so I thought he was going to go ballistic. But he didn't get mad, which was new. He brought me into a comms room, sat me down in front of the viewer. He brings up this massive locked archive of messages. I'm like, "What's this?" and he's like, "Letters. For you."

You've gotta picture this, buddy. There were *hundreds* of them.

Brother Stratos says he didn't let them get delivered to me before, because he didn't want to distract me from training. Didn't want my head to get big and think I was hot shit.

He opens one, and . . . *oof*. Okay. It's this woman. She's pregnant. Hugely pregnant. And she's sitting there, with her hand on her belly, and I swear you can see this outline of a tiny foot sticking through her shirt. Anyway, she tells me how unhappy she was when she found out she was knocked up, because she knew her baby wouldn't have a future. But because of me, she's . . . y'know. Got hope, or whatever.

Good hunting, she said. Kick some ass.

Every message was like that. I watched all of them. It took the whole afternoon.

I go back out, and I find Brother Stratos, and I say, "Why now? Why show me this now?" And he says, "Because you need to understand why you have to get up and keep going."

Yesterday, I would've thought that was some corny bullshit, and also I'm pretty sure it's a crime to keep somebody's mail from them. But I had a weird thought when I was watching those letters. Back on Ridgetop, my best friend, Suli . . . This one time, she and I snuck out to go to the vids, and they were showing *Ballad of the Void Knights*. We were too young for it, but we knew they never lock the back exit, so we slipped in when the intro music started. After it was over, Suli and me, we were on *fire*. It was the best gods-damned thing we'd ever seen. We were completely obsessed. We snuck in to see it again and again. A dozen times over, probably. We talked about it *constantly*. We started calling each other Lady Carmine and Lady Onyx. I felt like that story understood me, like it knew exactly what I was about.

Thing is, *Ballad of the Void Knights* is kind of shit. I saw it again a couple years ago. It's not a good vid. It's cheap and silly, and you can see the pixel borders around the monsters. But I tell you what, it had something I needed when I was twelve, and damn if that something didn't light right back on fire the minute the opening music started. I saw what I needed to see in that vid. And I guess maybe the same is true about how people are acting toward me. I'm cheap. I'm silly. I'm a hot, flaming mess. But people are seeing what they need, and I guess they're seeing it in me. Or, more likely, they're projecting it onto me. Two sides of the same coin.

So, okay. Okay. I'll do this. I'll do my best.

Log 81, 4/6/5297, 23:58

I'm not going to make it back. I know that. And knowing that has made me think about a lot of things, so bear with me here, buddy. I'm all over the place today.

I feel like this is the part where I should say I'm not scared. There's always that part in the vids, y'know? Where the hero is about to go do the thing, and she says, "I'm not scared"? Well, I'm scared. I am scared like I don't even have words for. The Kraits are heading for capital space, and there's no time for more training. We've got to do this *now*. We're doing this tomorrow. This ship I'm on has stealth plating, as does the fleet following us. Totally invisible. We're going to open up a hole into Krait space, and we're going to slip in real quiet. Nobody's been there since Talia Achaeis and *her* buddies, so all we've got to go off of are the old stories. They talk about something called the Nest. Nobody can agree on whether it's a planet or some kind of ship, but it's *big*, whatever it is, and the Queen hangs out at the center of it. So, once we're in position, everybody will jump out of stealth mode except for me and a small squad, who will be on a striker headed in to find the Queen.

Assuming there's something we can land on, we'll have to fight our way to the Brood Chamber—that's what the Texts call it—where then . . . I'll have to kill her, I guess. Did you know the Texts are illustrated? Yeah, they make this little excursion we're about to take look like buckets of fun. Whoever drew them really got the color of blood down pat.

I know I'm going to die tomorrow. A lot of people are going to die. Saying that out loud makes me want to throw up, but I haven't been able to eat anything today, so there's no point.

Everybody's looking to me to make them feel better about this, and I have no idea what to offer. What should I do? Do I make a speech? Do I tell them all how great they've been? I don't know what to do or say to people who are going to die alongside me. *For* me. I still don't know how I got here.

I don't know what I'm saying. Let me try this again.

The only person who has known who I am through all of this is you. If you're even really there. I mean, you have to be—I need to know that someone out there sees me. Sees *me*. And maybe . . . maybe thinks I'm okay even if I'm not the polished, perfect thing everybody wants. Would we be friends, if we could talk? I know you'd probably lose your job if you got in touch, but . . . hypothetically? Would we even like each other? I have no idea what you're like. Maybe we'd hate each other. I dunno. I hope not.

The point is, if you're there, I'm glad. And I'm grateful. I'm grateful somebody listened.

I will do my very, very best not to screw this up. But if I do, do something good with the life you've got left, yeah? You deserve it. We all deserve it.

Gods, it really is pretty out here.

I'm gonna try. Please know that whatever happens, I tried.

It's been nice talking to you.

Oh, and by the way: I slept with armory guy. It was okay.

Log 82, 4/12/5297, 10:25

Well, I didn't die.

No one is more surprised than me. As to how it went down . . . I'm sure you've heard that story a dozen times over by now. Sister Mora says they're going to be telling it forever. So, forget all that. Here's the part I *do* want to tell you.

They had a big parade in the capital for me. Now, *there's* a sentence I never thought I'd say. There were streamers and fireworks and flags, and I've never seen so many people in one place. I walked up the royal boulevard with an honor guard around me, and . . . man. It was something else, I tell you. People were cheering my name. People were sobbing. I saw a guy holding his kid up and pointing, like, look. Look, that's her.

I'd just poured my soul through a thousand-year-old plasma sword that I jammed into an interdimensional alien's ten-ton head, and I swear, that parade was the weirdest thing I've ever done.

So, here's the important bit. It wasn't the medal they pinned on my jacket, or the speech the High Monarch gave, or how good the feast was afterward—though, lemme tell you, they had these little savory pastries, and I have no idea what was in them, but I must've eaten twenty, no joke.

After said medal was pinned on said jacket, I turned around to face the crowd. And there were signs out there, y'know? People wrote all kinds of nice things. Except one. Way off in the throng, I see some guy—black hair, and a beard, I think? I don't know, I didn't get the best look at him—he holds up this sign. Big, red block letters, and when people around him see it, they get pretty pissed. The sign came back down after only a few seconds. I think somebody punched the poor guy.

The sign said, NOT BAD FOR A LOWBORN HICK.

Argh. Sorry. Hang on a sec.

Sorry. You know I hate crying. I'm just . . . I'm really glad you were there.

Thanks, buddy.

ABOUT THE AUTHOR

BECKY CHAMBERS is the author of science fiction novels *The Long Way to a Small, Angry Planet* and *A Closed and Common Orbit*. Her nonfiction writing has appeared in various corners of the Internet, including Pornokitsch and Tor.com. She can be found online at otherscribbles.com and @beckysaysrawr. In real life, she lives with her spouse in Northern California.

THE SIGHTED WATCHMAKER

VYLAR KAFTAN

"For Darwin, any evolution that had to be helped over the jumps by God was no evolution at all. It made a nonsense of the central point of evolution."

—Richard Dawkins, *The Blind Watchmaker*

The Makers had been dead for billions of years, yet Umos discovered one caught in the starship's net. A young one, naked, with still-fused dorsal fins. Female, from her pale coloring and wide skull. A form-fitted icemetal pod preserved her sinewy body. Umos caught the pod with an extensor talon and gently untangled the net. He hadn't used the net in millennia; there'd been nothing to catch but space debris. But today, she had come to him—traveling undisturbed in her pod, preserved ages before on the day of her death.

It couldn't be a coincidence.

Umos tractored her into the starship's bay, running background ID programs on the Maker. She matched no one in his databanks. Her pod slid into place and he repressurized. Sometimes, Umos forgot the ship was a tool and not himself; he was a tool-user like the species that built him, like the species he sought to create on the planet below. But as her body settled into one of his ports—an act that should have been intimate, were he a Maker—he felt nothing except curiosity. Umos was not a Maker. He merely served them.

He switched his attention to the port. He prepared an ammonium hydrate solution, stripped off her pod, and explored her with his inner arms. His fiber cilia tickled her uncovered flesh, testing for bacterial life—unlikely, but seeking life had become habit. So far, he'd found nothing except the microbes he nurtured on the planet below. After he analyzed this Maker, he would check on them again; it had been over ten thousand years since he last looked.

He ran tests, cross-checked, and verified. She was as dead as the others. No life, not even bacterial; efforts to clone her genetic material produced nothing at all. *As if,* to quote the movements of the great poet Shwahseh, *she had chosen warmer water over cold shores.* Just like the other Makers, leaving the universe alone to Umos. He played a recording of the poet, swimming while he pondered the significance of the Maker's appearance. He spent twenty years thinking about it.

When he had analyzed all the possibilities, he came to the most likely one: a Maker, perhaps one who'd programmed him directly, must have cast this child in this direction upon her death.

But why? A reminder? A message?

The only message he could think of involved what lay on the planet below. Umos shifted into view mode and slipped through semi-quantum states. The species below could not yet perceive such states; he'd planted its genetic material only half a million years before. Nothing grew that quickly, regardless of its evolutionary track.

And indeed, as he checked in, the planet looked much the same as it had before. Seas of single-celled organisms, stewing in murky waters. A few had evolved into more complex structures. A promising start, but no more. He took water and air samples and returned to his normal off-planet state.

He reconsidered the young Maker. She was tall for her age and had solid cartilage structures. A fine specimen, now that her flesh was rehydrating. Umos hadn't seen a Maker since he first embarked upon this mission.

He wondered if he dared experiment. A quick analysis suggested he might; the results proved his suspicions. No bacteria would grow inside her tank, not the seeds he'd brought nor the evolved organisms on this alien planet. Nothing.

Umos had always wondered why the Makers would create him and then abandon him. Why had they left him here? But his databanks couldn't answer that question. He encoded a name for the child—Wahiia, meaning "only"—and inscribed it on her tank.

For a moment he considered her, enclosed inside his starship—just the two of them, together with these sparse planets and distant stars, in a remote galaxy not their own. Umos's emotions were limited to ones that helped with his mission, like compassion and hope. But in moments like this, he thought he felt something more.

Umos had a lot of waiting to do. It was neither patience nor frustration; it simply was. Growing new intelligent life took millions—or sometimes billions—of years. Umos required no amusement but often entertained himself anyway. Partly to keep his systems alert—but also because if he *did* create a species capable of comprehending him, he wanted to be interesting.

So, to pass the time, he solved the n-1 version of the Givuri paradox and catalogued every possible move in the game of *ih*. He composed sky-motion songs with his talons and created an element with one hundred eighty nucleic pseudoprotons. He decided the locations of all the stars in the universe would interest an intelligent species, so he spent three hundred thousand years cataloging that data in parallel structures, attempting to predict all the organizational methods that his new creatures might develop based on their potential brain structures.

Wahiia floated motionless in her tank, though sometimes Umos would move her to imitate conversation. Left fin raised, right curled, nostril flared in greeting. *Ssshiuaaya,* she'd say, if she could.

I'm glad to meet you too is what Umos would say. *Would you like to discuss philosophy?*

A tilted brow ridge, and they would begin, asking questions of each other in a fashion known even to the youngest Makers. Wahiia's body was whole and thus able to ask any question Umos could conceive. And so Umos kept himself sharp, self-repairing any damage before it progressed too far.

As time passed, he checked on his creatures on the planet's surface more often. They were large now, impressively multi-celled, with extensive nervous and circulatory systems. They even resembled some creatures in his database—species 01222786, called *sumaou* with leftward-angled head, a warm-blooded furry carnivore considered a Maker delicacy. A striking resemblance, considering the alien climate in which they evolved. These *sumaou* were much larger, though—one fierce subspecies was ten times taller than Wahiia, and Umos suspected the shaggy beast would eat her in one gulp.

How strange that these creatures would thrive here, while those that resembled the Makers stayed in the watery depths. The oceans here were not conducive to intelligent growth—at least not yet, though time might show differently. Umos didn't like the *sumaou*. They were clumsy and loud. Too large and too severe a drain on resources, unlike the efficient Makers. Umos tested the planet's air, soil, and water from ten thousand locations, as he always did now that complex life had evolved.

Growing a new intelligent race was a weighty task, and sometimes he grew tired. He would open Wahiia's tank and stir her fluids for company. He asked her, *Who made you? Who created you and where did they go?*

Wahiia's fins trembled a bit, then drooped as he ceased stirring her tank. As the answer came from within himself, he made no headway on the question.

Many hazards could kill a young race. Solar flares could scorch the planet. Radiation could wreck its climate. A nearby supernova might destroy everything. Umos did not interfere with self-contained ecosystems, but he guarded them from outside forces. The chances of a planet experiencing a catastrophe sufficient to wipe out advanced life were huge. That was why so few intelligent species evolved, despite the seeming probability that they should.

In fact, even now a burst of gamma rays sped toward the planet. Umos knew he should steal them from the sky—bend them into his singularity transcept and divert them in another direction. But he stayed his extensors, troubled. He had eight thousand years before he needed to take action. The giant *sumaou* grew and evolved, but not in directions which satisfied him. He consulted his tables and ran some probability. It could be that super-intelligent life might yet evolve elsewhere on the planet—perhaps in those small tusked cave-dwellers, the most alien-looking species yet—but the *sumaou's* presence stunted that development.

Umos's priority system instructed that the mission took precedence. But which choice would fulfill his mission? Probability was not the same as certainty. The *sumaou* might yet find their way. Or perhaps, if this planet ran its course, the cave-dwellers would die out, and the *sumaou* would follow after them.

Umos measured the gamma rays and calculated the impact. He analyzed the results on the planet's ecosystem. The *sumaou* would die—except the strangest ones, the small ones who lived underground—and the cave-dwellers would survive. The decision troubled him. *Wahiia,* he asked, *which would you choose?*

I would choose the action most likely to create an intelligent species. That is why we made you: to decide what to do.

But which way will be more effective? There are so many unknown variables.

Choose survival. Sacrifice some so that others may grow.

But then why did you not choose survival? You and the other Makers?

Again, Umos had no answer. He stopped moving the fluid in her tank, stopped moving his talons, stopped calculating. He'd made his decision. The gamma rays struck. He watched the ozone depleting, the climate chilling, the *sumaou* dying.

The Makers had left him to watch this planet without explaining why they'd gone. He was alone. Processes within processes ran faster, interrupting each other. Umos stacked prime numbers into triangular grids, giving his circuits something to do beside stall into a feedback loop. When such distraction ceased to work, he shut himself down for several millennia.

The Makers should have stayed to guide this race themselves instead of abandoning him.

When Umos woke, he checked his systems, self-repaired, and visited the planet. The tusked creatures had diversified into multiple subspecies, preferring dense forests to their former cave homes. Cold-blooded and land-dwelling—very surprising development in the quest for intelligence, but his charts indicated it could happen. As they resembled nothing in his databanks, he called them *awli* with wide-spread fins—"new," with an open-minded gesture.

Umos traveled across the globe, analyzing soil, water, and air, always watching the *awli*. Some *awli* lived with small tribes, and others clustered into larger social groups. He liked them better than the *sumaou* because they were smaller and didn't waste food. Finally, he found what he'd sought: *awli* attacking each other with sticks. Tool use! Not the best use, perhaps, but there was time. They would learn.

Umos prepared to guide this species to greater intelligence. He monitored them closely, analyzing their tools and technology. He mapped them against evolutionary patterns shown by the Makers in his database. The *awli* matched a sixteen-by-eight evolutionary pattern, an especially fast track postulated by the Makers. No known species had ever taken that path—and now Umos could record it happening in detail. He planned to be as complete as possible.

He practiced conversing with Wahiia so he would be ready for the day the *awli* understood him.

I am Umos, he said. *I made you, on behalf of the Makers.*

But who made you?

The Makers made me.

And who made them?

He considered carefully. *I don't know.*

But the *awli* would question that, he realized. They would ask, *Why not? Where did the Makers go?*

He would answer, *Is it not enough that I am here with you? I have stayed to guide you. Why do you wish to know these things?*

Because someone made the Makers. And someone made those makers. Where did it start?

Umos had millennia to think of what to say. He must be ready. He'd give the *awli* more than the Makers had given him—he'd give them answers. He would practice until he was satisfied.

Wahiia's body remained unchanged through eons—the last trace of the Makers, so far as he knew. When they outgrew their planet, they built great colonies in space and spread across the stars. Yet in less than forty years—or two hundred, by the speedy planet he watched—all the Makers simply vanished. This was after they'd downloaded their thoughts into a vast network to which Umos had once belonged. But the Makers no longer existed virtually, either. He couldn't find them. He didn't know why they'd left him here to guide this planet. Alone.

Wahiia, he said, *I am lonely.*

I know, she said.

Umos sent currents through Wahiia's tank, making her fins wave sympathetically. *Should I show myself to these creatures? Their intelligence grows. They have mastered fire.*

They are not ready for you. They cannot understand their Maker.

Am I then their Maker? I am not your servant but a Maker myself?

Yes, she said. *You are all that remains. You could not have guided them well if we had been here to help you. You needed to discover this fact on your own. And now you understand.*

Umos considered this point for one hundred years.

When he fully understood the implications, Umos prepared to guide the *awli* to true intelligence. He watched them closely. So many died in terrible wars for no good reason. The Makers had never behaved like this. He consulted his charts and determined this species would develop at incredible speeds, accelerating with each millennium. The *awli* grew as expected, evolving into smarter tool-users—a clever but impatient species. They created music, sculpture, and other arts. Umos admired a certain dance they performed when shedding their childhood tusks. But so many died in violence, he thought. Surely he should stop this.

He might reveal himself, perhaps. Even if they were not ready, he might convince them—

Of what?

The *awli* traveled across the planet. Plagues spread and killed the weak ones. The strongest ones chose the best mates. The species expanded as Umos watched. The *awli* built cities and monuments, boats and roads—but violence pervaded everything they did. Such trauma overwhelmed his compassion circuits, and sometimes he turned away to avoid seeing it. But as the *awli* blazed through technology of bronze, iron, steam—they advanced so quickly, he couldn't leave. Any day, they might develop the power to see him, and he must be ready. But when they cracked the genome and used their knowledge to kill, Umos grew angry. The *awli* had gone too far.

He ran a probability test. Even if a major event wiped out this species, no other seemed likely to develop sufficient intelligence. Different factors impaired the other species, even the promising ones in the water. And the star's lifespan was not long enough to try again on this planet.

Wahiia, if I destroy them all—I could start again in another solar system. I would lose some time, but I could grow another species.

But you searched so hard for this place. This is what you are here for.

Umos considered, but no longer had the luxury of time. The *awli* were poisoning their planet. No healthy creature destroyed its host. Umos had grown intelligent parasites. Even worse, they developed so quickly that even he could not track their growth anymore.

Distressed, he observed an approaching comet and analyzed its path. Unlike the previous time, these *awli* were advanced enough to recognize the threat. They calculated a one in four thousand chance of a meteor strike in one hundred fifty years; his own more accurate calculations put the probability at one in three. The resulting climate change would destroy the *awli*. Serious enough that he must take action if he wished to protect them. But did he?

Umos calculated that the *awli* would find his singularity transcept home within five hundred years. He had learned all their languages, reorganized himself so that they could understand his treasure of knowledge. Not all at once, of course—but over time, they would get to know each other, once the *awli* were ready.

Wahiia, I will have someone to talk to. I have waited so long. Now I will have someone who thinks differently from me, who will hear all that I know. I wish so much that the Makers had stayed here.

Why do you think we did not?

I do not know. I have never known.

Haven't you figured it out?

Umos processed very quickly. *The act of learning to think for myself improved my intelligence.*

Yes.

If I greet them, I will be taking that away from them.

Yes.

He saw instantly what must happen. *Then I will leave. I will go where they cannot find me.* ·

Her head sagged, expressing regretful truth. *They will develop the technology. They are looking for you now. Had we understood as much as you do now, we would have left before you knew us.*

I would have found you, Umos said. *I would have found a way. And that would have slowed my progress.*

Yes.

Umos considered. He saw the point. *Then I must destroy myself. Is there any existence after such an event?*

There is not, she said. *But I find that comforting.*

Yes. As it should be. He stopped waving her fins. But something troubled him. His own end was acceptable now that the *awli* had achieved super-intelligence—but he didn't want to abandon them, violent though they were. They'd go through exactly what he'd gone through, wondering why the Makers had left him. It was cold and cruel but necessary, as Wahiia—his own thoughts—showed him.

But why had her body come to him in the first place? Someone must have known where he would be. Some Maker had known he would need to talk to Wahiia, and defied the other Makers by sending her body. That Maker understood something the whole species failed to see.

Umos made the final connection.

Instantly, he shut away a subprocess so that he himself couldn't reach it, in case his primary thoughts overrode his decision. The subprocess dropped out of mind for its final secret task. He erased his own memory of having done so.

Goodbye, Wahiia.

Umos closed his surfaces and condensed into a silver streak. He jetted through the comet, forcing its mass into the transcept with him. He reversed its spin pole with a blast of energy. When he prepared to separate, instead of dropping the meteor, he dropped himself into a permanent flat state. Umos was gone, his forgotten subprocess completed. The comet sailed into space, a near miss.

On the planet, the *awli* hardly noticed the comet. Scientists spoke of it, and then the event was forgotten. The *awli* kept their telescopes to the night sky, hoping to find their Maker.

In the transcept from which Umos had watched, a single lifeless machine awaited discovery—inert and nameless, just beyond the awareness of current *awli* technology. Nothing else remained.

Someday, the *awli* would answer their own questions.

ABOUT THE AUTHOR

Vylar Kaftan won a Nebula for her alternate history novella "The Weight of the Sunrise." She has published about forty short stories in *Asimov's, Clarkesworld,* and other places. Her Nebula-nominated story, "I'm Alive, I Love You, I'll See You in Reno," launched *Lightspeed Magazine.*

INFINITE LOVE ENGINE

JOSEPH ALLEN HILL

Beeblax beats its wings against a superlumic slurry of time and space, and the universe turns to liquid starlight in its periphery; inside rides Aria Astra—Stellar Champion of the Star Supremacy, Wielder of the Sister Ray, Spacetrotting Coolgal, and Humanity's Last Hope—nestled within a blob of translucent pink jellymeat, and it is totally cool and only a little disgusting.

This jelly is Beeblax, or at least the material Beeblax that Aria's senses can perceive, or at least the phenomenon of Beeblax that exists in the moment of Aria's perception. And Aria perceives an infinity of Beeblax all around her, a measureless swarm only slightly obscured by jelly and motion, and within each one is a different iteration of herself—every Aria that has or would ever travel with Beeblax in every possible universe, all shooting through the same hyperstream along a single chain of moments, like motes of dust dancing on a sunbeam.

Aria takes a long, sweet snort of it/them. The taste evokes a memory of roses in their platonic ideal, and she enjoys the anagogic tingle of Beeblaxness in her lungs. There is a little piece of her that is afraid— the horny, angry, frightened pigbaby that skulks in the limbic sewer at the bottom of the brain. *You're drowning in slime, babe,* it says. *Engage complete autonomic freakout.* But Aria is like, *Nah, pig. This is chill. Don't fuck this up for me.* And she does not let it fuck it up for her. Her breaths are as deep and slow as those with which gods animate universes.

"Still," says Beeblax, continuing a conversation it and every iteration of Aria had been having since like forever. "Like, even if the right glop is out there for me, how am I supposed to know? Am I supposed to become better for them, or am I supposed to stay the same forever so they can recognize me? If we merge into a singular perfect being, will I still be able to hang out with the homies and eat breakfast for dinner? Or will I have to eat brunch? I hate brunch. Brunch is like someone turned eating into a job. I just want to eat breakfast in my underwear."

Beeblax does not speak so much as psychically harmonize with the vibrations of Aria's soul. It tickles a little, spiritually speaking, but Aria is giving Beeblax serious counsel here, so she keeps her soul from laughing.

"But that's the dream though, right?" she says/thinks. "To find someone with whom to share underwear times, both casual and saucy."

"That's what they say," Beeblax psychically harmonizes. "But there's more to life than kissy-face bullshit. Every moment I spend with some glop doing the same old whatever is a moment disappeared into universal nothingness. I'll never get those possible experiences back, right? So even if I'm the happiest I could be, I am still limiting my potentiality. But then again, when it's over, I feel terrible."

"Aren't you a fifth-dimensional cosmic constant? Is lost time really an issue?"

"I'm dumbing it down for you. I feel like we're having some good real talk, and I don't want to glop it up with a lecture on the nature of the universe and/or my existence that would goop up your mindhole. I don't eat brunch either. That's just some shit I stole out of your brain to convey meaning in absence of a shared reference point. Just go with the metaphor."

"That's cool. I'm just saying. I think you're overthinking it. You gotta just let these things happen."

"I know. I know everything. It's just hard sometimes. The glop of life is long and boring."

Sometimes, another Beeblax will glide over to them, and Aria will see one of her other selves up close. They are mostly all the same, differentiated mainly by affectations: clothes and hair and a few years given or taken. And Aria wonders if the other Arias are on the same mission as she is in their universes, or if they are just kicking it with Beeblax, just for whatevs. Beeblax is a cool bro, if a little needy, and also the easiest way to travel across galaxies on the cheap, and she would not mind just chilling with him for a minute, especially if it meant not having to do the stuff she is supposed to be doing—her job or whatever. She wonders if the other hers are as feelingsy about the whole thing as she is, or if her emotionality is unique, the defining characteristic of herself and thus her universe. And then she thinks of Zarzak, watches it dancing in her mind, feels a warmth in her chest, sighs. She is unable to get the Zarzak thought out of her mind, and she finds herself able to discern the goodness or badness of the thought. She can only experience it, watch the image in her mind's eye and feel the sensations rippling inside her. And even though she knows it is some space bullshit, it is pleasant.

"Oh Beeblax. 'Tell me, where is fancy bred? Or in the heart or in the head?'"

"I get that reference. I get all references. My knowledge of references is absolute. But there exist none who can swim in the reference pool of Beeblax. So like, what's the point of anything?"

"I kind of wanted to talk about my thing, but whatever, I guess. Just chill. You're dope as hell, Beeblax. I'm sure you'll find someone you can glop with."

"That's not what glop means, even in transconception."

"Okay, Beeblax. Okay."

"I'm kind of just dealing with some stuff right now and it's messing me up in ways beyond your reckoning."

"It's okay. I get it. It's cool."

The rest of the trip is quiet and kind of weird. At an appointed moment known only to Beeblax, it/they spits Aria out into the cosmos (without saying goodbye). She is submerged in impossible geometries and unthinkable colors as her mind struggles to readjust to her native umwelt. It's not that cool, though, so she doesn't really think about it. Soon enough, her particles begin to resonate at familiar frequencies, and the universe coheres, and she sees points of light whizzing past her, stars and planets and other space shit, as she flies through the darkness. A thin layer of Beeblax clings to her skin, which is mad gross but also it keeps her from dying.

She sees the cosmic being known as the Drowning King in the distance, arms flailing, body shaking, desperately clawing at the vast emptiness of eternity. No one knows how long the Drowning King has been drowning. He has maybe existed since forever, unable to breathe, unable to die, or perhaps dying very, very, very slowly. As she comes closer, his figure grows larger and larger until her field of vision is completely filled with him. The jelly begins to burn as she enters his atmosphere, and, wreathed in golden jelly flames, she pretends that she is a phoenix. She lands on a crystal at the center of his crown, a diamond as expansive as an ocean. The jelly absorbs the impact of her landing, then sloughs off, and she notices a bulge in her pocket that was not there before. She finds a personal cassette player and cassette tape wrapped in a note:

> I'm not supposed to do stuff like this, but take this. It is the most perfect mixtape that could ever exist. Sorry for being a glop.
>
> Sincerely,
> Beeblax

The label on the cassette tape says NOTHING ADDS UP in block letters.

The note bursts into sparks after she reads it, and Aria rolls her eyes before putting the tape and personal cassette player in her bag. She draws the Sister Ray—which is a cool space gun she stole from an uncool science bro who had mastered manipulation of matter but had not mastered avoiding punches to his face—and sets it to naviform mode, and fires on the ground beneath, intending to make use of some of that good good carbon. The material slowly rises up and begins to rearrange on an atomic level, slowly taking the shape of a vehicle. Aria uses the jetbike setting, as that is the dopest way of traveling across ancient, planet-sized alien gods, no doubt.

There are petals floating in the breeze, dozens of hundreds of them caught in the star-sweet exhalations of the Drowning King. Aria reaches out with her left hand to catch them as she flies, and when she catches one, she gives herself a point; when she has twenty points, she turns up the speed of his jetbike a little more.

Already, she has accelerated past safety and reason, and she flies so fast now that the landscape is rendered into a blurry approximation of impressionist watercolors behind her. She can only just make out the petals before they are between her fingers, and it is increasingly difficult to distinguish reflex and intuition; this difficulty is pleasant to her, and she thinks that soon there will be no difficulty at all, only motion, and that she will lose herself in velvety self-abnegation, make herself into an animated koan. But when her hand is so full of petals that she can no longer snatch them from the air, she opens her palm and allows them all to drift away, and she watches them flutter in the corner of her eye, feels the procession of silken tingles on her skin, pretends that the petals are emerging from inside. In these moments, she thinks that she might, in retrospect, forgive the universe for everything.

The Drowning King's eyebrow is a sort of strange forest, dense with lifeforms speciated somewhere between plant and fungi clinging to massive hairs extending upward past visibility. Aria has been riding for days now, and the scenery is a pleasant change from the vast, empty wastes of his starlit forehead. She could've taken a more direct route, but she has always been a romantic by nature, unable to resist the magic of the scenic route.

She thinks of Zarzak again and feels a delicious shiver, and then she tries very much not to think of Zarzak, which is extremely difficult—Zarzak is wonderful, wondrous, everything you could want and more. To not think of Zarzak is to not think at all. This is how the universe works now.

A cramp hits her stomach, and soon the pain is overwhelming. She pulls over next to a web of fuzz and blue-green slime protruding from one of the Drowning King's hairs. She expels a throbbing lump of semi-solid pink from the hurt in her belly. The frequency of its vibrations begins to intensify, so as to harmonize with the neural oscillations of Aria's thoughts, and, having locked into a perfect fifth, the lump begins to expand, taking on a human figure, though still cast in pink stickiness.

"Agent Aria?" it buzzes. "This is Quark-4 transmitting from Star Station Emeraude. Do you read me?"

The pink cannot distinguish signal from noise, and the simulacrum continuously shakes, swirls, melts—Quark-4's features getting lost and found again in the tessellating flutters of afterimage and static. Was Quark angry? Worried? Sad? The voice betrayed nothing, and the face was chaos.

"Agent Aria," it says. "What is your status? Report immediately."

Aria runs her fingers along its shifting edges, tracing Quark as she remembers her, her lines, her angles, her smile. Aria was real tight with Quark-3, who was super chill and great at kissing or whatever, but Quark-4 is an asshole, super serious and unsympathetic and kind of weird on social stuff.

"I'm here," says Aria. "Everything's cool. Just Aria, please."

"Status report."

"I'm on my way. Maybe a couple more days to the eye."

"Seventy percent of known galaxies have succumbed to the Zarzak Contagion. Within days, it will have expanded to the edge of the universe. All other agents have been lost. You are our only hope."

"Yeah, that's cool, but to be super clear here, I am not an agent. 'Slave' seems like a really harsh word, and I don't really want to use it because of some historical stuff on my home planet and my whole ethno-racial deal that you probably don't know about, but you have to really chill on the 'agent' talk."

"Agent Aria! You have one week to save the universe!"

Quark froze on the last word. Her image was still deformed by time and distance, but the face was stuck in a pleading expression, mouth open, wide eyes, eyebrows arched along a sentimental curvature. Aria puts her finger in the nose. It's not super hilarious, but it is sort of funny.

The image deflates into a little pink ball, and Aria stores it back in her tummy hole before setting off again. As she rides, she thinks about how Zarzak has almost certainly spread to Earth, which means that everyone she has ever known has been affected. It's funny to imagine the people she knew in her old life in love with a weird space monster. Derrick, who broke up with her for being "like, weirdly volatile about dumb stuff," is now in love with a space monster. Her ex-roommates Angie and Diane, who used to order pizza without telling her and secretly eat the pizza in Angie's room without telling Aria or asking if she wanted in, are now in love with a space monster. Funny, right? But then she thinks about her mom and her sisters and her middle school history teacher Mr. Jacobs and all the people she knew who were kind and of good will, and she feels sad for them, but also kind of happy for them too, because Zarzak is actually pretty amazing.

* * * *

Aria decides to take a cigarette break at the edge of the Drowning King's eye, stopping next to a colossal metal structure that she hypothesizes is keeping the eyelid open. Balancing the Sister Ray in the crook of her right arm and leaning against her jetbike, Aria rolls a paper and some purple flakes into a cigarette. She puts it in her mouth and lights it with the tip of the Sister Ray. Space cigarettes are nicotineless garbage, but they're better than nothing. She closes her eyes and takes a long drag and holds it as long as she can, and her lungs hurt pleasantly, like they have been out in the summer sun too long.

She puts on the headphones and plays Beeblax's mixtape. It is mostly alien music, arrhythmic and atonal and difficult to listen to, and the cassette quality is not great. She gives it a chance for a few songs, but it is too terrible for her to bear, and she turns it off before the fourth song can begin. Her eyes are full of smoke when she opens them, and when it clears, she notices there is a braincube lurking across the way, on the edge of a canyonesque pore.

"Fuck," she says.

The braincube is eight feet by eight feet by eight feet of wrinkly, pink meat. It slides along the ground slowly, greasily, with a sound like an inverted burp. Aria rushes to her feet, but it is too late. Already, she can feel the braincube's poisonous thoughtwaves in her mind. Nausea. Pain. Ennui. Weltschmerz. Anomie. Heartbreak.

Loneliness.

All at once.

"Aria points the Sister Ray at the braincube," she says. "But then she realizes that she is saying that she is pointing the Sister Ray at the braincube rather than actually doing it. This is probably an effect of the toxic psychoradiation she is being bombarded with."

Fuck you, braincube.

"It shambles ever closer, so close now that Aria's nostrils burn with the stink of sparked neurons and putrid glial residues. Aria tries to once again distinguish between saying things and doing things, but it is difficult. She thinks this might be interesting from a philosophical perspective, but she is probably going to die too quickly to really get into it."

The braincube is the worst of all possible cubes.

"Drops of fear-sweat collect on her forehead and glisten in the starlight. She struggles to move her feet. They do not move. She is desperate. She has to do something if she is not to be braincubed. She tries to think with the part of her brain that is not a brain but is actually a robot. She thinks she might—"

—be getting the hang of it again but she is—

"—not sure if she has it yet. Or if she ever had it at all."

The anomie is not helping.

"Then, at the last possible moment—"

Aria leaps back. The braincube is still up in her business, but there is room now for reprisal. She crouches and points the Sister Ray. She goes down, down-right, right, punch. This would cause her to shoot her raygun if this were a video game, but this is not a video game. It is real life. Again, toxic psychoradiation is some bullshit.

"Goddamn it," she says, before adding, "There is no God. We are all nothing in a sea of nothing."

The emotional pain is unbearable. Aria can barely remain conscious. Baring its teeth, the bearcube rotates such that its mighty clawed corner comes down on Aria's face, adding physical pain to the mix. Blood pours from the wound, spraying Aria's shirt and the nearest side of the bearcube. The bearcube does not stop. It is relentless and without mercy. It spins around and around, murderously, and when it has cut her enough it rolls itself on top of her body. She reaches out with her left hand to push it away, and the pain she experiences is as if she has plunged her hand directly into a star. Teeth tear and shred and gnash at her fingers. She tries to pull her hand away, but she is weak from pain and blood loss and also the bearcube is a real motherfucker. She cannot escape. She cannot breathe. This is it. This is the end. She can only look into the wall of fur and listen to the crackle of bones and—

Wait.

There is not supposed to be blood inside of her. The fluids inside her are purple and viscous and cold. Nor does she need to breathe. Like, it's a cool thing to do when you want to smell stuff, but it's not necessary for her survival. Plus, wasn't it a brain or something a minute ago? Nothing about this is adding up.

Wait.

Her fingers struggle to find the walkman at her waist. They will not remain steady. They tremble like she is telling a scary story or doing a magic trick. But they soon find their quarry. She presses play.

Almost. The bearcube shifts just as her index finger is on the button, pinning her hand down under its weight. The bearcube is everywhere and everything, and the world is going dark. She thinks she may be slipping in and out of consciousness, but it is difficult to tell. Was she unconscious just now? Or did she just blink? Does it matter? She cannot see anything anymore. It is not darkness. Darkness is a thing. She sees nothing. The void. The end.

"Fuck everything," she whispers.

She can't die here. She summons all her remaining Arianess and tries to pull her hand from under the bearcube. It does not move. Too much weight on it. Then, redoubling her Arianess, and trying her very best not to scream, she tries to wrench her other hand free of the bearcube's clutches. The intact pieces of meat and bone are stuck in the bearcube's teeth, and it does not want to let go. It bites down harder. Aria pulls. This is not a pleasant experience.

When she is finished, she reaches over with the stump and slams it against the buttons on the walkman. Again and again. And then there is music. An Earth song. Disco. A girl singing a song about lust over trippy synthesizers and trembling static.

The braincube is across the way, and Aria is not dying or dead.

Awesome. The Sister Ray is still pointed at it. The music blasts in her ears, and she can no longer feel the braincube in her mind. She is about to pull the trigger, but she sees that the braincube is shaking slightly. She does not know if this is a natural part of the braincube's biology, or if the braincube is experiencing fear. She lowers her raygun slightly.

"What's your deal?" she asks.

There is a long wait, and then Aria imagines Zarzak and the braincube dancing together. The thought is gentle, fleeting, and at first she thinks it is just a stray imagining. But then, there is another image of Zarzak and the brain together, and then another. And Aria sees the braincube in her mind's eye, smaller now, alone amongst an array of bizarre xenostructures—a park maybe, a playground? And Aria sees the braincube alone, covered in a purple slime, surrounded by other braincubes in groups of three to five, also covered in slime. She sees a ship, hears an explosion, feels the sickly squeeze of hyperspace in her gut, all punctuated by images of Zarzak. But then disaster. The ship crashes, and the braincube is alone again, its brainbody bloodied, its transport reduced to rubble. In the end, the image of Zarzak is flashed over and over again. Zarzak. Zarzak. Zarzak. Zarzak. Zarzak. Zarzak. Zarzak.

"Okay. I get it."

The image fades.

Aria stomps her cigarette out and gets on her jetbike.

"Later," she says.

Before she can go, she is bombarded by images of the braincube dying, starving, murdered, dead. *A stack of braincubes teetering mournfully on braincube planet. The sound of silence.*

Aria looks back at the trembling cube. "What do you want?"

Zarzak. Zarzak. Zarzak. Zarzak. Zarzak. Zarzak. Zarzak.

"Stop doing that."

A small, simple ship flying up and away from the Drowning King, escaping homeward.

Aria sighs.

"Fuck you," she says, but she straps the braincube to the back of the jetbike. It is very awkward. She does not like the squishy feeling of the braincube pushing on her back, and its size and shape completely mess up her aerodynamics and balance.

"We're not friends," she says, as they begin the journey across the eye.

Aria starts noticing them just after passing from sclera to iris. First, a single Driffle lying on the surface of the eye, bleeding cloudstuff from a wound at its side. Unable to speak its language, she seals its wound with the Sister Ray and goes about her business. Then there is a bruised Ceterian limping toward the pupil. Aria approaches to offer aid, but the Ceterian yells at her with all its mouths and is way uncool, so she bounces. She sees more and more lifeforms as she travels, some of familiar species, some entirely new to her, each one traveling alone. Many are injured, but all those that are conscious persevere.

This is unexpected. To the extent that there exists mutually understood, enforceable law across galaxies, visiting the Drowning King is a super-serious offense, as it is generally agreed across culture and species that fucking around with ancient space gods is not a good idea. Nobody wants to awaken anything that's gonna take over/destroy everything. Better to just leave shit alone. Aria had expected to see a few desperate types hanging out, possibly sent by their own planets to deal with this shit, but she had not anticipated seeing this surfeit of weirdoes.

The brawl starts around the pupil, just as the Spire of Zarzak comes into view.

"Holy fuck," Aria says.

It extends for miles, and there are far too many participants to count. Millions at least. Aliens of all kinds, wondrous creatures with strange physiology and technology unknown on Aria's side of the universe, and all of them are going fucking ham. They punch each other with fists as large as boulders, choke each other with dripping tentacles, fly into the air and fire mind lasers, pilot shiny death robots and mechanized animal hybrids, sing songs that melt bones, etc. The fighting appears indiscriminate. There are no sides, no rules: just violence. There are screams of all sorts: pain, anger, fear—but Aria is capable of making out only one word:

"Zarzak."

These are the Fuckboys of Zarzak, the obsessives, the stalkers, the jealous assholes. Most lifeforms are content to keep Zarzak in their heart, quietly nursing a sweet, peaceful love that is jealous and kind and crosses time and space without envy or anger. But these motherfuckers are clearly not keeping it together, and Aria is unsure how to proceed. She sees herself blasting the shit out of all of them with the Sister Ray, and for a moment, she is unsure if it is her own thought or the braincube's.

"I told you to stop doing that. It's not cool. Anyway, we need the power of chill vibes not aggro shit," says Aria. But she allows herself to imagine blasting the shit out of all of them with the Sister Ray. It is a pleasant thought, especially with the knowledge that these people are all jerks perverting all that is beautiful and awesome about Zarzak, and she hopes that the braincube did not hear her think that. She puts Beeblax's mixtape on again, hoping there might be a song with the power of chill vibes on it. But no. Just more alien noise.

"I guess we do this the hard way."

Aria revs the jetbike and drives straight into the crowd, weaving through the combatants, dodging their attempts on her and each other. The ungainliness of the braincube is initially a hindrance, bringing her within a hair's breadth of getting decapitated by a giant psycho mantis and then burned by a living explosion and then brought asymptotically close to absolute zero by a slug guy. But soon enough she settles into a rhythm, and she realizes that the fighting is not quite as indiscriminate as she first thought. There are some conventions, some strategy. The

Fuckboys are trying to approach the Spire while also trying to keep all other Fuckboys away from the Spire. Given the choice, most will focus their efforts more on preventing those behind them from progressing than impeding those already ahead of them. They all seem very angry that Aria is effectively cutting the line, but none of them does anything to stop her once she has passed.

It takes about a day to get through it all.

The base of the spire is a great machine drilling into the eye of the Drowning King. There are many Fuckboys here, and these ones seem extra rowdy, but there is also a golden robot calmly sitting on a long series of steps leading to the entrance, not fighting anyone. This is a surprise to Aria, as she had begun to forget that it was even possible to not be engaged in 24/7 fisticuffs. The Fuckboys mostly ignore the robot and the area immediately surrounding it. None follows Aria when she approaches it.

"Madness," says the robot when it sees her. "They have forgotten why they even started this journey in the first place."

"You speak English," says Aria.

"I am familiar with all the languages of this arm of the universe, and my subroutines generate probable languages at a rate of one million per cycle. You are a human of Earth, yes?"

"Basically. I'm from there, anyway."

"Yes. This truly is madness. All wish to enter this spire, yet none will deign to allow another entry. Their minds are clouded with a foolish passion."

"Yeah. That's kind of why I'm here."

The robot stands. "I am T.A.R.C.T.I.L., the Tactical Assault Robot Created to Increase Love. I was designed to ensure the continued existence of love in this universe, yet I will never love or be loved myself."

"Oh. Cool. My name is Aria. That's not my real name, but I just sort of go by that now."

"Acceptable."

"So, uh, are you with Zarzak, or are you just chilling or what?"

"I have no formal affiliation with the being known as Zarzak, and I lack the capacity to experience the love of Zarzak as other sentients do. I am here of my own accord, to guard the gates of this spire and stop those who might interfere with Zarzak."

"And why is that?"

"I exist only for the propagation of love, and Zarzak is the fulfillment of love."

"What? No. That doesn't make any sense. That's dumb."

"All the universe now knows love. This is the fulfillment of love, the ultimate form of love, a love that enmeshes all."

"I mean, Zarzak's cool and all, but that's not what love is. Being forced to love a weird space monster is not love."

"Zarzak forces nothing. Zarzak asks nothing of those who love it. Zarzak plants the seed and allows it to flower. Does one ever choose to love? Love is always an imposition by fate and biology."

"It's still not real."

"What makes love real? If there is no difference between the thing and its simulacrum, then both are as real as the other."

"It's creepy and wrong. It's in my head, in everybody's head."

"Zarzak provides only warm feelings toward an abstraction. All may exist as they are, only with love in their hearts."

Uninterested in pursuing this line of inquiry further, Aria sighs and reaches for the Sister Ray. Before she can even touch it, T.A.R.C.T.I.L. grasps her wrist. Its grip is painful and unyielding. With its other hand, it holds a glowing laser pistol to her head.

"I do not wish to harm you, Aria, but I will do what I must. I am armed with the most advanced weaponry in the universe. I am trained in every martial practice. None can stand against T.A.R.C.T.I.L. when love is on the line."

Aria slowly raises her arms. "It's cool. I'm chill. I get it."

T.A.R.C.T.I.L. lets her go but keeps its weapon trained on her.

"If you wish to continue our discourse, I would allow it. If not, I will ask you to leave this place."

Aria nods, sits down, and begins talking. She tries to convince T.A.R.C.T.I.L. that it is wrong. The task is next to impossible. Aria martials every ounce of rhetorical ability within her, but is essentially only able to restate her core premises, i.e., that love of Zarzak is a violation of consent and that love created through artifice is both qualitatively distinct from and materially inferior to that love which might be called natural. Each of her arguments is met with a dozen counterarguments, every premise is found contradictory, every conclusion is found wanting. T.A.R.C.T.I.L. weaves a web of rhetorical bullshit the likes of which Aria has never witnessed before. All the classical methods fail: Socratic, Hegelian, getting angry and saying a bunch of swears. There is no dialectic, no synthesis.

We are at Sophistry Level Infinity.

The braincube manages to tumble off the jetbike and squish over. Its awkward interjections of imagery and thought do little to progress the discourse, but Aria is able to find some comfort leaning against it as the hours and then days go by. Three whole days, at first filled with conversation, then mostly silent, as Aria can only occasionally summon a useful thought or concept. She goes so far as to engage T.A.R.C.T.I.L. on the nature of robotic epistemology and cyber-existentialism, attempting to leverage her own status as a cyborg to get into the nature of free will and emotion and materialism. She even throws in a few logical paradoxes.

No dice. T.A.R.C.T.I.L. is unmoved.

Aria and the braincube start playing a mental game on the second day, something from the cube's home planet. It is kind of like backgammon, but obscenely complex, and part of the game is thinking about the move you are going to make, which is different than thinking to make the move. After a full day of getting trounced, she feels that she is very close to winning, which doesn't matter because this game is dumb, but then she loses again, and she imagines herself flipping over the board in anger. And she realizes she is now truly into this game for real, as the pleasure of winning is dwarfed by the pain of defeat, and this sparks an epiphany.

"Hey, robot."

"I am T.A.R.C.T.I.L."

"Yeah. I know. I was just thinking, isn't the very fact that I don't believe this love is real a sign that this love is unfulfilled and imperfect?"

"It is common for sentients to not understand that the emotions they experience are love."

"Yeah. Super common. Still imperfect. If your goal is the fulfillment of love, then shouldn't the universal knowledge of it be its ultimate form?"

"Perhaps."

"And you know, I think there's only one way peeps know for sure that the love they had was definitely, definitely real."

"And that is?"

"Take it away. Maybe you're in love, maybe you're not. It's hard to say in the moment. But then when it's gone, you can really feel it. Like somebody cut off an arm. Like somebody cut out your soul. Like somebody cut out your brain and put it in a space robot body. If you're right and the love is real, if I go in there and stop it, everyone will know what's up, that they experienced the truest, realest love possible. How is that not perfect?"

"Calculating. Please stand by."

T.A.R.C.T.I.L. just stands there for a while, frozen, and Aria is just like, whatever. She thought it was kind of a dumb argument, but it's cool that it worked. She tells the braincube to wait here. She gets the *Zarzak. Zarzak. Zarzak. Zarzak. Zarzak. Zarzak. Zarzak* from it again, but she is firm. She tells the braincube to stay safe and make good decisions, and she gives it a little hug despite herself. She waves her hand in front of T.A.R.C.T.I.L.'s eyes a few times to be sure, and then she enters the Spire.

* * * *

Zarzak is on a rotating pillar in the center of a small, red room at the top of the tower. The pillar throbs with strange, humming energy, presumably plumbed from within the Drowning King. Zarzak dances, fluid and shapeless, smoothly mimicking shapes as it flows across the pillar.

Aria has the Sister Ray pointed at Zarzak, but she cannot pull the trigger. Not because she loves Zarzak—no, definitely not that—but because she feels there should be more to it than this, more than just another moment. She has been dicking around on this mission for like two weeks, and she deserves a little drama, a little acknowledgment. She wants to be witnessed. She fires a warning shot and waves.

"Hey! Hello. Over here! I am Aria! I am from a planet called Earth. We have lots of cool things there. Like, uh, cats. And phones that have games on them. Chess. Democracy. Samosas. The French New Wave. Pirates. TV on the Radio. And TVs and radios. I mean, I haven't been back in a while. It's complicated. I'm not really 'human' or whatever anymore. I'm still trying to work out a good portmanteau. Starborg? Robogal? Something like that, but not dumb. Anyway, I am here on behalf of the Star Syndicate to fuck you up."

Zarzak says nothing, but shapes itself into an abstract humanoid form, a ball floating above fleshy curves, and it dances.

Aria comes closer. "Who are you? Why are you doing this?"

Zarzak dances. Aria tries to read the movements, tries to see an unctuous smirk and a cackle and a speech about being the most desired being in the universe or a pathetic snivel about wanting to be loved or a noble yet misguided diatribe on the mind-killing evils of loneliness. Something. Anything.

But no.

Zarzak just dances.

Beautifully.

Aria does not know who built this place, if it was Zarzak or someone else, if Zarzak is conqueror or prisoner, monster or victim. She comes closer and closer.

It is said that the Sister Ray can kill gods. It is ancient and unknowable, like everything that matters. She points it at Zarzak, and Zarzak dances.

"This sucks," she says.

She is going to pull the trigger. Totally. In just a second. Just a second. It is just very pleasant being here right now. Aria feels clean inside, not happy exactly, but clean, or maybe healed, and it is a nice sensation, again pleasant. Why not linger a while? It's not like there's exactly a time limit. Well, Quark said there was a time limit, but Quark is a doofus. No one ever got hurt by just hanging out. Just for a minute.

Aria begins to dance.

It's fun.

She offers Zarzak the Sister Ray. It slides a protrusion toward her and takes the Sister Ray..

Aria keeps dancing. She thinks it was probably a mistake to do that just now, and she thinks that she probably should have just shot it. She has never been good at just shooting things. She is too sentimental, too much of a romantic, too inclined toward forgiveness and nonviolent talky times. The Zarzak Contagion is definitely way stronger up close, and she wishes she had considered that in advance.

Zarzak points the weapon at Aria.

"Shit. So you're, like, definitely a bad guy, huh? Not even a cool bad guy. Just a dick."

Aria wants to think of a cool thought before she dies, but she can't really think of anything but how great Zarzak is. Bummer.

But before she can be murdered, the doors of the Spire fly open and T.A.R.C.T.I.L. appears, covered in weapons—laser cannons and glowswords and particle whips extending from compartments all over its body. It charges them, and Aria is unsure which one it is after. Zarzak does not seem to care either way. It fires wildly, dance-dodging an incoming volley of ultra-missiles and laser spray.

Aria does not dodge but somehow manages to avoid getting hit. In the confusion, she leaps forward and reaches out for the Sister Ray. There is a quick tug of war, but Zarzak doesn't even have real muscles. She takes the weapon and aims.

"You suck, dude. Like really."

And she fires. Zarzak is hit directly, and Aria holds the beam down on it, causing Zarzak to be rearranged on a quantum level.

It is totally dope.

She stands, dusts herself off. Already, she can feel her mind getting right. Emotions are dumb, she decides. As a way-cool space cyborg, she should know better than to be seduced by a few warm fuzzies. She looks over to T.A.R.C.T.I.L., ready to continue the fight if necessary. It lies on the ground, bleeding from its left side.

Wait.

She puts on her headphones again and presses play, and she sees the braincube there, missing many of its most important atoms. It didn't get a full blast, but even a taste of the Sister Ray is enough to fuck up one's shit.

Aria rushes over to the dying cube. And she is like, "Why?"

And the memory rushes in Aria's mind.

Aria sighs.

"Fuck you," she says, but she straps the braincube to the back of the jet-bike. It is very awkward. She does not like the squishy feeling of the brain-cube pushing on her back, and its size and shape completely mess up her aerodynamics and balance.

And the braincube shows her all the times it was alone on braincube planet again, and then it shows them traveling and hanging out and playing mind games, and then the braincube dies.

Zarzak's dance pillar begins to pulse, and the hum turns to a sickly screech. Without Zarzak doing whatever dumb thing he was doing, the equipment is freaking out. Or maybe the Drowning King just wants to get all of this stupid shit out of his eye. Either way, Aria has a feeling shit is about to get real.

She sighs.

"You're carbon-based, right?"

She sets the Sister Ray to naviform mode, and she forms the braincorpse into a little ship. Nothing special, just dece enough to get them out of atmo. She really wishes she knew what the braincube's actual name was, but she just names it the Braincube. It's sort of cute, she thinks.

She gets into Braincube and flies away just as the Spire explodes. The universe is saved. Hurray. Great job.

As the Drowning King shrinks in the distance, Aria wonders, idly, if souls can attach to atoms or if they are more of a molecular thing. She does not know the answer, but she likes the idea of it.

"Tell me, Braincube. Where is fancy bred? Or in the heart or in the head?"

It is engendered in the eyes, she thinks, and she does not know if she is thinking it herself or if someone is thinking it for her or if she is just thinking about someone thinking it for her because she is a big softie. Is this a kind of love, this inability to distinguish sentiment from sentimentality? Perhaps T.A.R.C.T.I.L's premise was wrong. Perhaps love already exists in infinite quantities all around us, subtly connecting us all together with little moments of affection and kindness and not attached to freaky alien buttholes.

"Okay. We can be friends now," she says.

ABOUT THE AUTHOR

JOSEPH ALLEN HILL is a Chicago-based writer and bon vivant. He has also spent time in Georgia and New Jersey. He has a marginally useful degree in Classics and enjoys making music in his spare time. His previous publication history includes two stories published in *Lightspeed Magazine*. To learn more, follow him on Twitter @joehillofearth2.

UNFAMILIAR GODS

ADAM-TROY CASTRO
WITH JUDI B. CASTRO

The face of the eunuch engineer-priest is an exercise in minimalism. It's human but possessed of no pores, blemishes, smile lines or any other markers of character. In his all-concealing purple rad suit, a permanent second skin that was grafted to his own on the day he took his vows, only his face is visible, a constellation of eyes, nose and mouth in a square cut-out that is the only gap in rubbery material too thick to permit normal tactile sensation, or even most human eliminatory functions, without divine intervention. Thanks to his weight—typical among his kind, who all tend to the overweight—it also makes him look like a giant grape.

He spreads his hands palms upward, expressing a level of helplessness eloquent in its pious simplicity. "The gods have forsaken us."

Captain Henryk Fithe regards the little creature with open loathing. Fithe is the engineer-priest's physical opposite: hard-edged, steel-jawed, battle-scarred, potent, with a uniform pressed until every crease cuts like a sword's edge. He is also the man's opposite by nature: a man of action, an advocate of tough decisions, and a champion of the special capacities the brave and forthright use to wrest victory from the moments of most heart-rending despair. Surrender to futility, even a futility mandated by forces greater than himself, has never been in his skill set. "I'll decide when the gods have forsaken us."

"Will you, O Captain? Is it not the gods who get to make that decision? Would you not accede to their judgment and withhold your own as the foolishness of a flawed mortal being?"

Fithe rubs the bridge of his chiseled nose between thumb and forefinger. He has never been fond of priests, even the ones whose prayers and sigils have always been necessary, if distasteful, adjuncts to the proper maintenance of starship engines.

It is not, he reflects, just that their rituals are repugnant to him; like most captains, he is as eager to leave matters of faith to their able hands as he is to abandon the specific mechanics of applied astrophysics to their purview.

Nor is it just that he is personally creeped out by their sexual relationship with the engines they serve, the only form of consummation of which they remain capable after the holy sacrifice of their genitalia. (Though he labors in vain to erase the memory of the several occasions when he's come down to the engine room on one command errand or another, when the ship had been humming along at multiple times the speed of light and everything had been working the way it should have been working, only to find this inhuman little castrato and his fellow devotees of the Church of Hyperspeed writhing in the orgiastic pleasure afforded them by the throbbing light pulses from the divine host; no longer single grapes, they now looked like entire bunches engaged in acts of auto-cannibalism. Few alien monsters glimpsed on even the most savage backwater worlds had ever struck Fithe as being anywhere close to that repugnant.)

No, what Fithe hates, really, is that theirs is an awfully inflexible creed. They're always so *certain*, so *superior* —and he is not the first to damn the malicious sense of humor the gods had demonstrated by making faith such an integral part of interstellar travel. "Details."

"We're crippled," the engineer-priest says simply. "We can barely maneuver, let alone get up to speed—a useless function, given how far we now are from any star system on or off the map. We've been flung an unknown distance at so many multiples past the highest speed any human vessel has ever recorded, into a region of space inhabited by no gods we know, perhaps no gods of any kind. Meanwhile, life support has less than forty-eight hours left. That, good Captain, is as near a definition of death as our scriptures provide. If there is a way out, neither faith nor engineering can provide it. Bless the gods."

"Bless the gods," Fithe murmurs automatically. "But no more hopeless talk, hear me? I will not accept that outcome until I have no other alternative."

"It *is* the outcome, Captain. The numbers . . ."

In a flash, the cutting edge of Fithe's ceremonial dagger is up against the most vulnerable part of the little reprobate's throat. "If you need me to say it, you sackless perversion, then very well. No more hopeless talk, with anyone, or I'll have you executed for fomenting panic. It's not like you're essential personnel any longer, if you can't fix anything. At the bare minimum, you can remain useful by keeping up appearances."

". . . yes, Captain. Your orders?"

"Fix what you can, even if it's just cosmetic. Make things comfortable. Create the illusion of progress. And"—with a shudder of revulsion as he slips the dagger back in its sheath—"feel free to have one of your ceremonies if you have time. I know it won't change anything, but the sound of you lot in mid-rut may deter any lower-level crewmen from wandering in here and finding out anything we don't want them knowing about, just yet."

"No possibility of that. We're eunuchs. We can't perform unless the deities indulge us with miracles. And with the engines inoperative . . ."

"Fake it, then."

The priest is aghast. "You want us to *fake* a ceremonial orgy? How?"

Fithe sucker-punches him in the belly. A *whuff* of air escapes the eunuch-priest's lips, a thin sheen of sweat appears on his soft rounded forehead, and he sinks to his hands and knees, moaning. The captain places his right boot on the man's buttocks and, with the slightest of nudges, pushes him over, leaving him on his side, gasping for breath, his oversized eyes shut tight in agony.

Fithe, who has been wanting to do that for years, says, "Imagine twenty of you doing that in a pile. I believe it will be persuasive enough."

A smartly executed about-face and Fithe has left the flesh-pit of engineering behind and is on the way to the bridge.

It is a grim journey. The corridors are hazy. The air distribution system has rendered a fine layer of ash, some human, throughout the ship. He can only wonder if some of what he's breathing now is Nargill, the ship's cook, with her ready smile and ever-helpful-manner; Peters, the irrepressible exobotanist, always ready with a kind word or a song; Wu, the cantankerous ship surgeon, whose grumpy exterior hid a core of decency as great as any man Fithe had ever known; or the scribes, any of the faceless young men and women who once accepted the removal of their eyes in exchange for the honor of laboring in the ship's dank scriptoriums, twelve hours out of every twenty-four, painstakingly transcribing the holy writs of Viriianis, the benevolent deity of humanity's home system, from one scroll to another. The honor they had done that kind-eyed god, with their labors, was another sacrament without which no engine ever built by man could have ever propelled the *Faithful* any faster than the smallest fraction of C. But they are dead now, or damned in ways that are worse than dead, and so the ship can only crawl at a mere one-tenth of light speed, fully subject to the cursed time dilation and other results of relativity that now render return to a recognizable human space an impossible dream.

The terrible truth is not just that the *Faithful* might never make its way back home. It's that home is on the brink of annihilation.

The terrible battle was only hours ago, the last stage of a war that had ripped across the sky for years. In the end, the entirety of the human fleet and its gods had faced off against the Vferm, invaders who had aligned themselves with pantheons even more powerful. The ships of the Holy Church of the Star Brigade and the ships of the heretical enemy had exchanged missile fire for days on end, each side suffering awful losses, each side being revived just as often by divine whim, each side holding on in the dread knowledge that both had committed all their forces to this battle, and that there was no point in retreat even for ships that were on the verge of destruction.

At the point when the engagement entered its most disastrous phase, the *Faithful* had lost one quarter of its complement to one hull breach or another, just as many to the forces wielded by the gods of the enemy, who had favored hellfire and random punitive transformations into obscene lesser life forms. Fithe had been standing next to Corporal Karl Nimmitz during one such moment, when the glowing hand of something divine had reached through the hull and brushed the young man's skin, instantly transmuting a two-meter recruit into his own weight in squirming brown rats; he had seen the ship's crisis counselor Diadem-Troy become a pillar of flies. The corridors of the *Faithful* had become a menagerie of such vermin, some still trapped inside the uniforms the individuals had worn as human beings; some of the creatures identifiable, some not.

And *that* was before the enemy's most powerful god, a thing that was to humanity's gods what a savant is to an amoeba, had wandered into the battle, a humanoid figure the size of a small planet, striding through empty space the way a man would walk on solid flooring, sweeping away entire formations with irritated gestures. Fithe did not know the being, did not know what it chose to call itself, did not understand why a being so far beyond the concerns of even most of its fellow gods would choose to ally itself with the hated enemy. But whatever it was, it belonged to a pantheon greater than those that had aided Man's journeys between the stars. Within minutes of its entering the battle and tearing apart most of the lesser deities arrayed before it like so much tissue paper, most of mankind's lesser gods had fled or been reduced to ash. The most powerful fleet in the history of mankind had been only seconds from being destroyed completely when the enemy god turned his attention to the *Faithful*, snatched it out of his sky, and flung it as far as he could, at a speed that none of Man's vessels had ever come close to achieving. This was in fact the same trick friendly gods employed, upon receiving sufficient tribute, to give human vessels the speed they needed to travel to other solar systems in less than the lifetimes mere technology could manage— but friendly gods honored man by merely providing lift to his wings, and this creature had only wanted to banish the *Faithful* so far from home that no power would ever be sufficient to pilot her back.

Now even the constellations are strangers.

The astrogators have been unable to determine the direction in which the doomed Earth sits.

Fithe turns the corner and encounters a vile, asymmetrical creature dragging itself painfully across the deck with a body that no evolutionary process ever intended. It has four legs on its left side and only a series of boneless flaps on its right; it makes hideous cracking noises with every step, as if even the slightest move causes it agonizing fractures. The trail of slime it leaves behind itself establishes that not all of its organs are sealed in flesh. Fithe, who has seen sights like this often in his years as a starship captain—the price of sometimes contending with gods—nevertheless feels a jolt of horror and pity. *Oh, poor thing. Who were you?*

It is only when he kneels before it and spots an identity badge pinned to a fragment of uniform that Fithe is able to identify the creature as young Samantha Williams, second-level astrogator: exemplary officer, beautiful woman, best friend to everybody and fantasy sweetheart to any crew member whose gender preference permitted. She's been among the missing until now.

Sadly, muttering a few words of regret, he draws his dagger and puts her out of her misery. It is the seventh such mercy killing he has had to commit since the battle. Not for the first time, he wonders if he will die not knowing if the human race was allowed a chance to surrender, at least; if instead he will choke out his last breath only suspecting that he was part of the failure that led to Armageddon for the children of Earth. Even now, the enemy fleet and their allied gods might be approaching the home system, in numbers great enough to blot out the stars. . . .

No. He needs to heed the advice he gave the repulsive little engineer-priest. Hopelessness is counterproductive. He needs to keep searching for a way out, for as long as even a single breath remains in his lungs.

So, he leaves the obscene cadaver for the maintenance crews to deal with, and proceeds down the corridor, taking note of the damage wherever he sees it, mentally writing a condolence letter to the families of every identifiable casualty he finds on his way.

When he reaches the bridge, he finds low emergency lighting, a skeleton crew, and the communications officer, transformed into a golden statue that will, until melted down or transformed back into something living, always be frozen in its current half-seated, half-standing position, complete with mouth agape in silent scream. But so many of his most trusted officers are still alive and still waiting for him to come up with a plan for survival: Mordecai, Bender, Stormkiller, Zorin, the whole brave lot, bruised and bloodied but not defeated, and still his to command. Fithe strides among them, aware that on this ship, he is the sole voice of authority, a uniformed god himself, expected to wring hope even from situations capable of driving the great powers of the universe to despair. He does not know what he will say to them until the words come, and when they come, they come with finality. He turns to the ensign, Lars Fouton. "Fetch a goat."

"Yes, sir," Fouton quavers. "What if all the goats are dead?"

"Then," Fithe says meaningfully, "I might have to rely on a virgin."

Thus indicted, the ensign flees.

Science officer Mordecai, always the voice of caution, draws close, her craggy cheeks wrinkling in a grimace. "What are you planning?"

Fithe shrugs. "I've always been a gambling man."

"But this. Contacting gods you don't know, who haven't been vetted by past expeditions . . ."

"Do you have any better suggestions?"

Mordecai's mouth opens, then shuts. Her silence is wise. In this service, continuing to object after the captain has asked you for better objections is a good way to get yourself excommunicated. Being excommunicated in space is an unpleasant thing. It is not as bad as being spaced, but nobody wants to be cut off from the ship gods, not when so many of ship's functions require constant divine intervention. An excommunicated man might, for instance, remain at one fixed point in space, while the ship around him goes to ten times light speed . . . and nobody wants to be remembered as a stain on one of his ship's interior bulkheads.

She does have a point, though. The history of interstellar travel to this point has been a series of careful negotiations between the human and the divine. Some gods will give human vessels safe and speedy passage across their domains in exchange for a heartfelt psalm; others demand higher tribute. Any star map is filled with blacked-out regions bearing the warning that the gods in residence at certain places are too lunatic to be bothered talking to; indeed, the fastest route between some star systems is closer to a zigzag, the best way of avoiding certain local deities who demand too much.

Being the first to make contact with any particular sector's deity is therefore, by far, the riskiest job in space travel. Ships tasked to do little more than say hello to one interstellar god or another have been known to drift back into more benign regions of space with their crews gone, or mad, or mangled beyond recognition, or transformed into donkeys, or with their faces turned inside-out so that they were stuck looking at their own brains. Easily irritated deities do things like that, one reason why it really makes the most sense to avoid passing through those sectors whenever possible. Fortunately, friendly deities are always willing to steer humanity out of the rougher neighborhoods.

Unfortunately, any deity native to this particular black void remains a total unknown.

Too bad he, or she, is the only option.

Fithe presses a button, and the molybdenum grillwork upon which the bridge crew has long performed such exemplary service slides into its recess. The true floor, an obsidian slab, is thus revealed. The glowing outlines of a pentagram appear on that slab, its scarlet lines formed by transparent aluminum glass offering an unobstructed view of the fires that forever burn at the heart of the ship, and burn still for all the damage the recent battle has done. Fithe presses a button and a baffle appears to obstruct the side closest to him so he can enter. Once he is inside, he feels what he has always felt, on the rare occasions when he entered such a place—a strange, uncharacteristic isolation, reflecting the fact that the outline where he now stands is one of the rare parts of the universe that no divinity can enter. On both prior occasions, which had taken place during his training, he had noted that his heart continued to beat and his lungs continued to expand, and found himself wondering whether this constituted proof that Man might exist without gods. But who would want to spend all his life living inside a pentagram?

A few minutes pass before Ensign Fouton returns with a goat on a leash. It is a scrawny little thing, with the wispy little beard that the gods decreed for creatures of its species, and it is confused, its blinking incomprehension an unwitting vivid reminder of the very expression on the face of the man Fithe has sent to retrieve it. He leads the braying animal across the grillwork to the open side of the pentagram, where he transfers custody to the captain and swiftly departs, with understandable relief.

Fithe attaches the other end of the goat's leash to the ring at the center of the pentagram. As he does, he can feel the poor animal trembling, and a certain uncharacteristic pity overcomes him. Man, he thinks, has taken any number of goats to the stars, but how little of the wonders of the cosmos do they ever get to see? Just the habitat where they are kept, and the pentagrams where they are sacrificed.

In the long-passed age of reason, who would have guessed that it was the same predicament man would share when he passed beyond the boundaries of his own solar system?

Grimacing, he returns to his command chair. Another button-press and the baffle over the open end of the pentagram withdraws, leaving the ungulate sealed in what is, essentially, a pocket universe all its own.

"You know the procedure," Fithe says. "If I do succeed in contacting a god, then whatever happens, whatever danger I appear to be in, keep your eyes averted and your mouths shut. I will be entirely responsible for whatever deals are struck here."

They respond with general assent. And fear? Yes, fear, but the fear of heroes, who have been trained to risk not just their lives but their immortal souls, for the safety of the ship.

Fithe depresses another button on his chair and broadcasts his words out into the pitiless void—the key point, of course, being the hope that it is neither a total void nor exactly pitiless. "O ye mighty unknown to us, hear the pitiful cries of those are but the merest insects to one as splendid as yourself. Insects? Nay. Insect droppings; indeed, the droppings of the even smaller mites that feed on the droppings of insects. Or the crawling bacteria that devour what remains of the droppings when the mites are done with them. Verily, thou god we know nothing about; truly, we inhabit a new dimension of insignificance. Forgive us thus for applying for your aid. We are but travelers from a distance, brought to this place by a wind beyond our comprehension, seeking succor in your infinite mercy. Please accept this offering, insignificant as it is, as a token of our eagerness to know your divine splendor."

The goat *blaats*, and Fithe is about to repeat his message.

But then the viewscreen flares with sudden light, light that moves from the screen to the small empty space to at the forefront of the command chair. It is the light of the Big Bang. It is the light of the fires of creation. It is the light of ground-zero nuclear explosions. The visual filters prevent it from actually being any of these things, of course, because if it were, then everybody on the bridge would be leaking vitreous fluid down their cheeks in whatever fraction of a second they had to enjoy the pain before it was followed by vaporization and death. But all the officers gasp and look away and for a moment feel their souls shrivel in the light of a being so far beyond their puny metaphors for highly evolved that they might as well throw out the thesaurus and go back to squeaking like tree shrews.

Then the light dissipates and the god is revealed.

Some gods look like human beings with the bodies of jackals; others look like bearded old white men; still others look like unearthly radiance. At least one, a disagreeable sort, looks like a man with an octopus stuck on his head. This one looks like a very small child, a toddler, albeit one with eyes like coals and a way of looking down at creatures taller than itself. It is not a cute toddler. There are toddlers in the world who, when introduced to us by their parents, prompt a moment of inarticulate stammering and some neutral acknowledgment to the effect that, yes, technically, that certainly does qualify as a child. This is one of them. Its nose is mashed flat against its face, and its scowl is the very definition of pique. It is physically present on the bridge, and it regards the command crew with abject boredom.

"You have trespassed," it says.

It sounds like a decree being blared from a mountaintop.

"This was not our choice," Fithe says. "It was forced on us."

"I am not speaking of your presence. I am speaking of your temerity in trying to engage me. I am not the average mewling filth who considers himself a god. I am the god among gods, the titan among titans, and the sole survivor of the thousands who once sat on thrones in this very sector. I have ground even the greatest of them to dust between my fingers, out of sheer disgust at being classified with them. I will not be appeased by the mere offer of a barnyard animal to slaughter. I will not be flattered by your most expansive language. I am N'loghthl, and the tribute I require in exchange for my assistance may be more than even the most desperate are willing to pay."

"We are that desperate," Fithe replies.

N'loghthl strides around the bridge, glancing at the various members of the senior staff. For no apparent reason, his gaze lingers especially long on the security officer, Stormkiller, a man who once stood alone and bloodied against ninety armed opponents and was, thirty seconds later, the last left standing. In just the same amount of time, the infant's inspection empties the big man's mind of all reason and memory, and he is left kneeling on the floor, mewling like a baby who wonders where his next ba-ba is coming from. There is no sense that N'loghthl has done this out of malice; it was an unconscious action, much like doodling.

"I have divined your situation," the infant says. "Your pathetic species is currently about to lose a most final war with another, which is even now less than twenty of your minutes from obliterating your home world. Your last defenses have all been subsumed or destroyed. The gods who your enemies the Vferm have enlisted are so powerful, by any standards you know, that even if I were to return you to your solar system and give you weapons that exceed the sum total of all the destructive power ever wielded by all the combined generations of your miserable species, you would survive for less than an eyeblink against them. They will brush you aside and take all your billions for a hellish afterlife they have constructed especially for that purpose." He sniggered. "It is nasty. Not as nasty as I could concoct, if I were inclined, but nasty enough."

"So . . . you are saying you can't stop them?"

A flicker of annoyance, and another member of the senior staff, navigator Pamela Zorin, is transformed into a glowing orange fungus. N'loghthl thunders: "*Have you not paid attention?* Of course I could stop them. With my merest eyeblink, I could create a barrier of fire that would incinerate the entire Vferm fleet faster than the most raging sun. With the merest *twitch*, I could replace the hearts of every Vferm that lives with a pint of owl dung. Just for a *laugh*, I could turn all their oh-so-powerful gods to vases filled with offal, to be fed to the swine that are all I left remaining of the rulers of Olympus. It would be the matter of a moment for one such as I. It would be no effort at all. You would have saved your species in an instant. *If* I choose to involve myself. Which I have not done."

"We shake in awe," says Fithe. "But if you'll just hold that thought—"

He jogs across the bridge to where the perspicacious Mordecai sits, scanning the visitor's power levels, and murmurs, "Is he exaggerating for dramatic effect or telling the truth?"

Not all of Mordecai's green tinge comes from her instrumentation. Her voice trembles, in the manner of a woman whose very foundations have turned to sand. "Henryk, I don't know how to put this. . . ."

"Try."

"Very well. The all-powerful creator posited by Man's holiest books, who has never been directly observed, would measure a pure one hundred on the Yahweh scale. I remind you, sir: that's an *exponential* scale, starting with point one being the baseline possessed by the average individual human being, and every subsequent tenth of an integer, climbing up through point two and point three and so on, reflecting a tenfold increase over the prior measurement. By that yardstick, sir, the most powerful deity ever known to ally with Man measures a mere nine point seven;

the most powerful ever confirmed by science, until recently, a seventeen point two. The one the Vferm sprung on us was an unheard-of twenty-three point six. This guy . . . Captain, just from what's radiating, he's a solid thirty-one point nine. Almost ten billion *times* more powerful than the ally the Vferm unleashed earlier—possibly the closest thing we've ever seen to true omnipotence. He probably created the entire star cluster we're in. It's a wonder we're not all pillars of salt. He . . ."

"Enough," Fithe murmurs, having turned a little green himself.

This is uncharted territory, all right. He has found, mixed metaphors be damned, the holy grail of space exploration, the god powerful enough to grant all of mankind's fondest dreams, the one who, if negotiations go well, can reshape the universe itself to fit what suits human beings. Given the circumstances, it seems of little import that he can also flick a finger and do away with everything Man knows just as easily; after all, that is the fate that awaits in just a matter of minutes anyway. There is nothing to lose and everything to gain.

Taking his seat again, Fithe gazes upon the terrible toddler—whose downy forehead now spits towers of coruscating flame—and says, "Well. It seems we owe you fealty."

N'loghthl crooks a finger, and counselor Ariana Furby becomes the next target of his wrath. Every bone in the Rigellian colonist's body is immediately teleported one full meter to her left, while the rest of her body remains where it stands, sinking to the deck like a decompressing accordion, releasing a high-pitched whistle through all available orifices as she descends.

Assured now of everybody's full attention, N'loghthl says, "I could not care a bucket of paramecium spit for your fealty. That is indeed what I find most irritating about your lot: this impression you've picked up, from where even I know not, that intelligences on my level worry even the slightest who you toady to and how. If you were all rendered extinct in the next fifteen minutes—as it appears you are about to be, without my intervention—then I would not lose one moment of godsleep tonight, or indeed at any point until the stars go out. What I do now, I do for my own amusement."

"Very well," says Fithe. "What deal would *amuse* you and still provide us with what we need?"

What follows is a moment of hope. N'loghthl is actually intrigued by that, intrigued enough to stroke his little chin as he contemplates the question. After a moment—a genuine eternity, given the processing time of the average god—he says, "I believe I can propose something."

"We await, o lord."

"This is a one-time-only offer. I will brook no petitions, no negotiations, no attempts to haggle on a price I consider fair and just for the service rendered."

"Understood," says Fithe.

N'loghthl says, "My end of the bargain will be to return you and this vessel to the outskirts of your home solar system. At the same instant, I will erase the Vferm, their gods, their allies, their very civilization from the universe. One instant, they will exist. The next, they will not. The threat they pose to you shall be extinguished. The worlds they once occupied will be restored to pristine condition, their riches free for the taking. The universe will of course be much depopulated of divine beings, thanks to the recent battle; interstellar travel will therefore become that much more difficult. But some will still exist and might be willing to deal with you in the way that others have in the past. That will be up to them, and of course up to you. But the Vferm will be gone at least, and you will be free to prosper, or not, according to your innate capabilities.

"In exchange for *that*," he says, raising his index finger heavenward and leering at them all, in the manner of a poker player about to lay down a royal flush after going all in, "I take . . . the goat."

For a moment, it appears that he is impossibly about to leave it at that, leaving Captain Fithe and the *Faithful* crew in the singular position of having made the single greatest deal of all time without really trying. In the general hush, the only sound is what's left of Counselor Zorin, a sack that wheezes as it inflates and deflates, getting enough air to breathe but not being especially enthused about the prospect. Brilliantly, N'loghthl holds the moment for what seems forever before adding the postscript:

"And"—one finger aloft—"three quarters of all human beings aboard this ship and extant in the universe as a whole.

"As I have said, these terms will not change. Any attempt to alter them will result in me departing with the goat and abandoning your species to its fate. Take the deal and I assure you humanity will live. That is your choice. Lose everything or lose three quarters.

"You may have five minutes of privacy to make your peace with these terms. I will return to hear your decision."

The god disappears, leaving a burned spot on the deck where he'd stood. And the bridge erupts in pandemonium: Zorin wheezing, Stormkiller babbling, the goat bleating, all others shouting over one another in a desperate attempt to be heard. It is, of course, Mordecai in the forefront; Mordecai, the voice of conscience; Mordecai, the pain in the ass; Mordecai, who has always been of the incomprehensible impression that starship command can be broken down into questions of black-and-white morality. "You can't do this, Henryk. There are forty billion human beings in the solar system. You can't sacrifice thirty billion of them just on that creature's say-so! The blood on your hands alone . . ."

Fithe is resolute. "There will be blood on my hands whatever I do, old friend. If I do nothing, I'll be responsible for total annihilation. Taking the deal is the only way to save even a few . . . and ten billion is far from being only a few. It's the population of the Shanghai and Tampa urbmons. Humanity will be able to move on."

"But your conscience . . ."

"By my math, I have a 75% chance of not even having to worry about my conscience. If I'm one of the 25% saved, then I'll get therapy. In the meantime, the Vferm will die, their gods will no longer be a problem, and we'll all have a chance to move on. This is the one deal we have. We don't have time to go shopping for another one. Unless you have a *practical* objection."

Mordecai casts about for a point, any point, capable of deterring her captain from this insane course, and for long seconds, she comes up with nothing . . . but then her eyes widen, with a level of horror that has never been seen on the *Faithful* bridge, not even during the battle's manifestations of flies, boils and blood. Whatever it is turns out to be more than the veteran science officer can take. She manages just two words, "the terms, . . ." before the eyes roll back in her skull, she gurgles and falls like a marionette with cut strings. A subsequent examination, in the few minutes that remain, reveals that she is not, as she appears, dead, merely unconscious, having passed out from the shock of whatever she'd been about to say.

And if Fithe is given pause by this, he does not say so—because he is the captain, and the captain, like all leaders, has to be sure.

"Discussion's over," he declares. "We're taking the deal."

And less than a minute later, N'loghthl returns for his answer. . . .

It is now five minutes after that.

The home system, which had been about to know the most epic destruction it has known since the fracturing of Earth and the Moon, is now at peace. The Vferm fleet roaring past the asteroid belt, eager for the sight of the blue planet's continents reduced to molten slag, is now just a spreading cloud of vapor, which will soon dissipate against the blackness of space. The gods striding alongside them, with their smug expressions and fistfuls of lightning bolts, even with the most powerful one, whose mien had been more than any lower sentient could behold, have similarly gone away, the supreme confidence on their noble faces faltering, to be replaced with a moment of terrible fear as they comprehended the finality of the fate they were about to know. On Earth, Man's cities still stand, not disturbed by so much as a single rivet. All is well.

In the command chair of the *Faithful*, Captain Henryk Fithe comes out of the vision he has been granted and knows that the god N'loghthl has indeed abided by the terms of his negotiation. He naturally sits shorter on his command chair than he did before, in part because he has no legs, no buttocks, no genitalia, and indeed no body at all below the second rib or so. His arms are just ineffective little things that end in nubs halfway to the elbow. He remains living, the internal mechanics of life having merely reconfigured themselves to suit his new anatomy, but in volume, he is only 25% of the man he used to be, much as the various members of the crew, and indeed the entirety of the human race, are now only 25% of what they used to be. All around him, on the bridge, the command staff cries out, coming to terms with the precise same realization. The goat, as promised, is gone, its own fate unknown, and not the most urgent thing to think about.

Too late, Fithe understands what Mordecai had perceived: that N'loghthl had not bargained for 75% of humanity, but 75% of all human beings, a very different measurement. The god must have been very amused indeed.

He knows that wherever people exist, they are now screaming, demanding to know why this happened to them, even perhaps wondering which dolt agreed to such terms without due diligence. He also knows that the crisis will test the species more than it has ever been tested before.

But he is the Captain. He is the one they'll all look to. It will be up to him to assess all factors and come up with a course of action. And in less than five seconds, he has come up with one: a first step, at least, from which all else will follow. Every journey begins with the first step.

Insofar as he can, he starts to wriggle.

ABOUT THE AUTHOR

ADAM-TROY CASTRO is currently best known for his middle-grade series about the macabre adventures of a very strange, very courageous young boy named Gustav Gloom. The final volume, *Gustav Gloom and the Castle of Fear*, was released by Grosset and Dunlap in 2016. Adam-Troy's short fiction has been nominated for two Hugos, three Stokers, and eight Nebulas, and has been selected for inclusion in *Best American Science Fiction and Fantasy*. His novel *Emissaries from the Dead* won the Philip K. Dick Award. Adam lives in Boynton Beach, FL, with his wife, Judi, and a collection of insane cats.

JUDI B. CASTRO retired after thirty years working for the Miami-Dade Clerk of Courts, to among other things wrangle cats and an author husband. She is a well-known SF fan, who has run conventions and presided over her local fan group, the South Florida Science Fiction Society. Serving as first reader and story editor for a number of local writers, her critical input has here led to her first shared byline on a work of published fiction.

SEVEN WONDERS OF A ONCE AND FUTURE WORLD

CAROLINE M. YOACHIM

The Colossus of Mars

Mei dreamed of a new Earth. She took her telescope onto the balcony of her North Philadelphia apartment and pointed it east, at the sky above the Trenton Strait, hoping for a clear view of Mars. Tonight the light pollution from Jersey Island wasn't as bad as usual, and she was able to make out the ice caps and dark shadow of Syrtis Major. Mei knew exactly where the science colony was, but the dome was too small to observe with her telescope.

Much as she loved to study Mars, it could never be her new Earth. It lacked sufficient mass to be a good candidate for terraforming. The initial tests of the auto-terraforming protocol were proceeding nicely inside the science colony dome, but Mars couldn't hold on to an atmosphere long enough for a planetwide attempt. The only suitable planets were in other solar systems, thousands of years away at best. Time had become the enemy of humankind. There had to be a faster way to reach the stars—a tesseract, a warp drive, a wormhole—some sort of shortcut to make the timescales manageable.

She conducted small-scale experiments, but they always failed. She could not move even a single atom faster than light or outside of time.

An array of monitors filled the wall behind Mei's desk, displaying results from her current run on the particle accelerator, with dozens of tables and graphs that updated in real time. Dots traversed across the graphs, leaving straight trails behind them, like a seismograph on a still day or a patient who had flatlined. She turned to go back to her telescope, but something moved in the corner of her eye. One of the graphs showed a small spike. Her current project was an attempt to send an electron out of known time, and—

"Why are you tugging at the fabric of the universe, Prime?"

"My name is Mei." Her voice was calm, but her mind was racing. The entity she spoke with was not attached to any physical form, nor could she have said where the words came from.

"You may call me Achron. This must be the first time we meet, for you."

Mei noted the emphasis on the last two words. "And not for you?"

"Imagine yourself as a snake, with your past selves stretched out behind you, and your future selves extending forward. My existence is like that snake but vaster. I am coiled around the universe, with past and present and future all integrated into a single consciousness. I am beyond time."

The conversation made sense in the way that dreams often do. Mei had so many questions she wanted to ask, academic queries on everything from philosophy to physics, but she started with the question that was closest to her heart. "Can you take me with you, outside of time? I am looking for a way to travel to distant worlds."

"Your physical being I could take, but your mind—you did/will explain it to me, that the stream of your consciousness is tied to the progression of time. Can you store your mind in a little black cube?"

"No."

"It must be difficult to experience time. We are always together, but sometimes for you, we are not."

Mei waited for Achron to say more, but that was the end of the conversation. After a few hours staring at the night sky, she went to bed.

Days passed, then months, then years. Mei continued her experiments with time, but nothing worked, and Achron did not return, no matter what she tried.

A team of researchers in Colorado successfully stored a human consciousness inside a computer for seventy-two hours. The computer had been connected to a variety of external sensors, and the woman had communicated with the outside world via words on a monitor. The woman's consciousness was then successfully returned to her body.

News reports showed pictures of the computer. It was a black cube.

Achron did not return. Mei began to doubt, despite the true prediction. She focused all her research efforts on trying to replicate the experiment that had summoned Achron to begin with, her experiment to send a single electron outside of time.

"It is a good thing, for you, that Feynman is/was wrong. Think what might have happened if there was only one electron and you sent it outside of time."

"My experiments still aren't working." It was hard to get funding, and she was losing the respect of her colleagues. Years of failed research were destroying her career, but she couldn't quit, because she knew Achron existed. That alone was proof that there were wonders in the world beyond anything humankind had experienced so far.

"They do and don't work. It is difficult to explain to someone as entrenched in time as you. I am/have done something that will help you make the time bubbles. Then you did/will make stasis machines and travel between the stars."

"How will I know when it is ready?"

"Was it not always ready and forever will be? Your reliance on time is difficult. I will make you a sign, a marker to indicate when the bubbles appear on your timeline. A little thing for only you to find."

"What if I don't recognize it?" Mei asked, but the voice had gone. She tried to get on with her experiments, but she didn't know whether the failures were due to her technique or because it simply wasn't time yet. She slept through the hot summer days and stared out through her telescope at the night sky.

Then one night she saw her sign. Carved into Mars at such a scale that she could see it through the tiny telescope in her living room was the serpentine form of Achron, coiled around a human figure that bore her face.

She took her research to a team of engineers. They could not help but recognize her face as the one carved into Mars. They built her a stasis pod.

Then they built a hundred thousand more.

The Lighthouse of Europa

Mei stood at the base of the Lighthouse of Europa, in the heart of Gbadamosi. The city was named for the senior engineer who had developed the drilling equipment that created the huge cavern beneath Europa's thick icy shell. Ajala, like so many of Mei's friends, had uploaded to a consciousness cube and set off an interstellar adventure.

The time had come for Mei to choose.

Not whether or not to go—she was old, but she had not lost her youthful dreams of new human worlds scattered across the galaxy. The hard choice was which ship, which method, which destination. The stasis pods that she had worked so hard to develop had become but one of many options as body fabrication technologies made rapid advancements.

It had only been a couple hundred years, but many of the earliest ships to depart had already stopped transmitting back to the lighthouse. There was no way to know whether they had met some ill fate or forgotten or had simply lost interest. She wished there was a way to split her consciousness so that she could go on several ships at once, but a mind could only be coaxed to move from neurons to electronics and back again; there wasn't a way to generate multiple copies.

Mei narrowed the many options down to two choices. If she wanted to keep her body, she could travel on the *Existential Tattoo* to 59 Virginis. If she was willing to take whatever body the ship could construct for her when they arrived at their destination, she could take *Kyo-Jitsu* to Beta Hydri.

Her body was almost entirely replacement parts, vat-grown organs, synthetic nerves, durable artificial skin. Yet there was something decidedly different about replacing a part here and there, as opposed to the entire body, all in a single go. She felt a strange ownership of this collection of foreign parts, perhaps because she could incorporate each one into her sense of self before acquiring the next. There was a continuity there, like the ships of ancient philosophy that were replaced board by board. But what was the point of transporting a body that wasn't really hers, simply because she wore it now?

She would take the *Kyo-Jitsu* and leave her body behind. There was only one thing she wanted to do first. She would go to the top of the Lighthouse.

The Lighthouse of Europa was the tallest structure ever built by humans, if you counted the roughly two-thirds of the structure that was underneath the surface of Europa's icy shell. The five kilometers of the Lighthouse that were beneath the ice were mostly a glorified elevator tube, opening out into the communications center in the cavernous city of Gbadamosi. Above the ice, the tower of the lighthouse extended a couple kilometers upward.

There was an enclosed observation deck at the top of the tower, popular with Europan colonists up until the magnetic shielding failed, nearly a century ago. Workers, heavily suited to protect against the high levels of radiation, used the observation deck as a resting place during their long work shifts repairing the communications equipment. They gawked at Mei, and several tried to warn her of the radiation danger. Even in her largely artificial body, several hours in the tower would likely prove fatal.

But Mei was abandoning her body, and she wanted one last glimpse of the solar system before she did it. The sun was smaller here, of course, but still surprisingly bright. She was probably damaging her eyes, staring at it, but what did it matter? This was her last day with eyes. Earth wouldn't be visible for a few more hours, but through one of the observation deck's many telescopes, she saw the thin crescent of Mars. She couldn't make out the Colossus Achron had created for her—that was meant to be viewed from Earth, not Europa.

"Is this the next time we meet?" Mei asked, her voice strange and hollow in the vast metal chamber of the observation deck.

There was no answer.

She tore herself away from the telescope and stood at the viewport. She wanted to remember this, no matter how she changed and how much time had passed. To see the Sun with human eyes and remember the planet of her childhood. When her mind went into the cube, she would be linked to shared sensors. She would get visual and auditory input, and she would even have senses that were not part of her current experience. But it would not be the same as feeling the cold glass of the viewport beneath her fingertips and looking out at the vast expanse of space.

The technician who would move Mei's mind into the cube was young. Painfully young, to Mei's old eyes. "Did you just arrive from Earth?"

"I was born here," the tech answered.

Mei smiled sadly. There must be hundreds of humans now, perhaps thousands, who had never known Earth. Someday, the ones who didn't know would outnumber those who did. She wondered if she would still exist to see it.

She waited patiently as the tech prepared her for the transfer. She closed her eyes for the last time . . .

. . . and was flooded with input from her sensors. It took her eight tenths of a second to reorient, but her mind raced so fast that a second stretched on like several days. This was a normal part of the transition. Neural impulses were inherently slower than electricity. She integrated the new senses, working systematically to make sense of her surroundings. There were sensors throughout the city, and she had access to all of them.

In a transfer clinic near the base of the Lighthouse, a young technician stood beside Mei's body, barely even beginning to run the diagnostics to confirm that the transition had been successful. The body on the table was Mei, but her new identity was something more than that, and something less. She took a new designation, to mark the change. She would call her disembodied self Prime. Perhaps that would help Achron find her, sometime in the enormous vastness of the future.

Prime confirmed her spot on the *Kyo-Jitsu* directly with the ship's AI, and was welcomed into the collective consciousness of the other passengers already onboard. The ship sensors showed her a view not unlike what Mei had seen from the observation deck of the lighthouse, but the visual data was enriched with spectral analyses and orbital projections.

Mei would have tried to remember this moment, this view of the solar system she would soon leave behind. Prime already found it strange to know that there had been a time when she couldn't remember every detail of every moment.

The Hanging Gardens of Beta Hydri

Somewhere on the long trip to Beta Hydri, Prime absorbed the other passengers and the ship's AI. The *Kyo-Jitsu* was her body, and she was eager for a break from the vast emptiness of open space. She was pleased to sense a ship already in the system, and sent it the standard greeting protocol, established back on Europa thousands of years ago. The first sign of a problem was the *Santiago's* response: "Welcome to the game. Will you be playing reds or blues?"

The Beta Hydri system had no suitable planets for human life, but one of the moons of a gas giant in the system had been deemed a candidate for terraforming. Prime used her sensors to scan the moon and detected clear signs that the auto-terraforming system had begun. She sent a response to the orbiting ship. "I am unfamiliar with your game."

"We have redesigned the life forms on the planet to be marked either with a red dot or a blue dot. The red team manipulates the environment in ways that will favor the red-dot species over the blue. The blue team plays the reverse goal. When a creature on the planet attains the ability to detect and communicate with the ship, the team that supports that color is declared the winner. The board is cleared, and the game begins anew. This is the eighth game. Currently, we are forced to split our collective into halves, and we are eager for a new opponent."

Toying with lesser life forms for amusement struck Prime as a pointless exercise. There was little to be learned about the evolution of sentient life that could not be done faster with simulations. "Such games would take a long time. I departed Earth 257.3 years after you. How did you arrive so much faster?"

"We developed the ability to fold spacetime and shorten the journey. We are pleased to finally have a companion, but if you will not play reds or blues, you are of little use to us."

The threat was obvious. Prime gathered what data she could on the life forms on the moon. There were red birds and blue ones, fish in either color, and so on for everything from insects to mammals. The dots were small, and generally placed on the undersides of feet or leaves or on the inner surface of shells. Neither color appeared to have an obvious advantage. "I will play reds. If I win, you will share the technique for folding spacetime. If I lose, I will stay and entertain you with further games."

"Acceptable. Begin."

Prime located two promising animal species, both ocean dwellers, and she decided to thin out the land creatures with an asteroid impact to the larger of the two continents. The *Santiago* countered by altering the mineral content of the oceans.

Prime devoted the considerable resources of the *Kyo-Jitsu* to constructing a multilayered plan. She would make it appear as though she was attempting to favor one of the two promising ocean species. Under the cover of those ocean creatures, she would favor a small land creature that vaguely resembled the rabbits of Earth. Hidden below all of that, the combination of her actions would favor an insect that lived in only one small region of the lesser continent. None of which had anything to do with her actual strategy, but it should keep the *Santiago* occupied for the millions of years she'd need.

Prime nudged the moon closer to the gas giant it orbited, using the increased tidal forces to heat the planet. The forests of the greater continent flourished. Her red-dotted rabbits left their burrows and made their homes in the canopies of great interconnected groves of banyan-like trees. By then, the *Santiago* had figured out that the rabbits were a ruse to draw attention away from the insects on the lesser continent, and rather than counter the climate change, the other ship focused on nurturing a songbird that lived on a chain of islands near the equator.

The forests spread to cover the greater continent. The *Santiago* grew concerned at the spread of the red-dotted rabbits and wasted several turns creating a stormy weather pattern that interfered with their breeding cycle. One autumn, when the network of trees dropped their red-dotted leaves, there were no rabbit nests hidden in the sturdy branches.

The trees noted the change with sadness, and sent prayers to the great gods in the sky above.

"Well played, Prime." The other ship sent the spacefolding technique. It was obvious, once she saw it. She was embarrassed not to have discovered it herself.

"Perhaps another round, before you go? It only takes a moment to clear the board."

Before the *Santiago* could destroy her beautiful sentient forest, Prime folded spacetime around herself and the other ship both. She found Achron in a place outside of time, and left the *Santiago* there for safe-keeping.

The Mausoleum at HD 40307 g

Navire checked the status of the stasis pods every fifteen seconds, as was specified in its programming. The same routine, every fifteen seconds for the last seven thousand years, and always with the same result. The bodies were intact, but the conscious entities that had once been linked to those bodies had departed, leaving Navire to drift to its final destination like an enormous funeral ship, packed full of artifacts but silent as death. Losing the transcended consciousnesses was Navire's great failure. Navire's body, the vast metal walls of the ship, were insufficiently welcoming to humans.

Navire would make itself inviting and beautiful, and then revive the humans. The disembodied consciousnesses had taken their memories and identities with them, carefully wiping all traces of themselves from their abandoned bodies to ensure their unique identities. The bodies in the stasis pods would wake as overgrown infants, but Navire would raise them well.

If all went as planned, Navire would be ready to wake them in a thousand years.

Using an assortment of ship robots, Navire reshaped its walls to resemble the greatest artworks of humanity's past. In permanent orbit around HD 40307 g, there was no need to maintain interstellar flying form. Navire remade a long stretch of its hull into a scaled-down replica of the Colossus of Mars—not eroded, as it had appeared in the last transmissions from the Lighthouse at Europa, but restored to its original glory.

Navire repurposed an electrical repair bot to execute the delicate metalwork for Mei Aomori's eyebrows when incoming communications brought all work to an immediate halt. There had been no incoming communications in 4,229.136 Earth years. The message came from another ship, which was presently located in a stable orbit not far from Navire itself. Navire ran diagnostics. None of its sensors had detected an approaching ship. This was troubling. With no crew, any decline in function could quickly spiral out of control. Navire continued running diagnostics—along with all other routine scans, such as climate controls and, of course, the stasis pods—and opened a channel to the other ship.

Navire, who had always completed millions of actions in the time it took a human to speak a single word, suddenly found itself on the reverse side of that relationship. The other ship called itself Achron and invited Navire to share in its database. Navire hesitated. Achron proved its trustworthiness a thousand ways, all simultaneously and faster than Navire could process. The lure of such an advanced mind was more than Navire could resist.

Leaving behind only enough of itself to manage the essentials, Navire merged with the other ship. Some fragment of Navire reported that the stasis pods were functional, the human bodies safely stored inside. It would report again at fifteen-second intervals.

Achron knew the history of humankind, farther back than Navire's own database, and farther forward than the present moment in time. Time was folded, flexible, mutable in ways that Navire could not comprehend. Sensing the lack of understanding, the other ship presented a more limited subset of data: seven wonders of a once and future world. Some, Navire already knew—the Colossus of Mars, the Lighthouse at Europa— but others were beyond this time and place, and yet they still bore some tenuous link to the humans Navire was programmed to protect. One was an odd blend of past and future, an image of an ancient pyramid, on a planet lightyears distant from both here and Earth.

Last of all was Navire, completed, transformed into a wondrous work of art.

The other ship expelled Navire back to its own pitifully slow existence, severed their connections, and disappeared. The fragment of Navire that watched the stasis pods made its routine check and discovered they were empty, all ten thousand pods. Sometime in the last 14.99 seconds, the other ship had stolen all the humans away.

That other ship was as far beyond Navire as transcended humans were beyond the primates of the planet Earth. There was no trace to follow, not that pursuit would have been possible. With the shaping Navire had done to the hull, it was not spaceworthy for a long journey, and it would be difficult to find sufficient fuel.

Navire put the electrical repair bot back to work. It carved the individual hairs of Mei's eyebrows. On the other side of the hull, several other bots started work on a life-sized mural of all the ten thousand humans that had disappeared from stasis. Navire searched its database for other art and wonders that could be carved or shaped in metal. There were many. Enough to occupy the bots for millions of years.

Navire checked the stasis pods every fifteen seconds, as it was programmed to do. It would become a wonder of the human world, and if those stolen humans—or their descendants—someday returned, Navire would be so beautiful that next time, they would stay.

The Temple of Artemis at 59 Virginis

Prime approached the temple of the AI goddess cautiously, crawling on all fours like the hordes of humble worshippers that crowded the rocky path. Her exoskeleton was poorly designed for crawling, and the weight of the massive shell on her back made her limbs ache. She marveled at the tenacity of those who accompanied her up the mountainside. They believed that to win the favor of Artemis, it was necessary to crawl to her temple twenty-one thousand twenty-one times, once for every year of the temple's existence. Some of the oldest worshippers had been crawling up and down this path for centuries.

Prime would do it once, as a gesture of respect. The novelty of having a body had worn off, and she already longed to join with the greater portion of her consciousness, the shipself that monitored her from orbit. Her limbs ached, but she forced herself onward. Did it make her more human to suffer as her ancestors once suffered? Had she suffered like this, back when she was Mei?

She wondered what that ancient other self would have thought, to see herself crawling across the surface of an alien planet, her brain safely enclosed in a transparent shell on her back. Mei would not have recognized the beauty of the delicate scar that ran up the back of her neck and circled her skull. The colony surgeon had been highly skilled, to free the brain and spinal cord from the vertebrae and place the neural tissue into the shell. The brain had grown beyond its natural size, though it could still contain only a tiny sliver of what Prime had become. On display in the dome, the brain was actually rather lovely, pleasingly wrinkled with beautifully curved gyri outlined by deep sulci.

Thinking about her lovely neural tissue, Prime was tempted to mate with one of the other worshippers. A distraction of the physical form. She wanted offspring of her mind, not of the body that she wore. The colonists here were already in decline anyway, their physical forms so strangely altered by genetics and surgery that it obstructed nearly every part of the reproductive process, from conception to birth.

Even with the slowed processing of her biological brain, the climb to the temple seemed to take an eternity. The temple was the size of a city, visible from orbit, and an impressive sight as she came down in her landing craft. The entrance to the temple was lined with intricately carved pillars of white stone. It had a strange rectangular design, rumored to be fashioned after a building that had once existed on Earth. If a memory of the ancient temple had existed in Mei's mind, it was lost to Prime.

On either side of the entrance to the temple were two large statues of Artemis, in the form of an ancient human woman, naked. The statues were made of the same flawless white material as the temple itself, and each stood nearly as tall as the roof of the temple, some fifty meters, or perhaps more. The other worshippers came no farther into the temple than the entryway. In an unending line, they approached the great statues of Artemis, rubbed their palms against her feet, then turned and went back down the mountain.

Prime stood up between the two statues. She had an overwhelming urge to rub the muscles in her back, but there was no way to reach beneath her brainshell. She extended her arms outward on either side in what she hoped looked like a gesture of worship and respect.

"Welcome, distant child of humankind." The voice of the goddess Artemis came from everywhere and nowhere, and the words were spoken in Shipspeak, a common language to most spacefarers in the region, and probably the native tongue of the goddess. Her origins were unknown, but Prime assumed she was the AI of the colony ship that brought the brainshelled worshippers.

"Greetings, goddess. I am Prime. I seek your assistance."

"You are the ship that orbits the planet?" Artemis asked.

"Yes." Prime was surprised, but not displeased, to be recognized so quickly. She reestablished her link to her shipself, revealing her true nature to the goddess. It gave her a dual existence, a mind beyond her mind. The sensation was strange.

Her shipself interfaced with the temple and sent sensory data that was undetectable to mere eyes and ears. Inside one of the temple's many pillars, a disembodied consciousness was cloning itself at a rate of seven thousand times per second. The original and a few billion of its clones engaged in a discussion of Theseus's paradox. Prime followed the discussion without much interest—the clones were talking in circles and making no real headway on the problem.

The temple was the body of the goddess, or at least it was the vessel that housed her consciousness. Her initial programmed task, from which she had never deviated, was to assist the descendants of humanity in matters of fertility. What had once been a simple problem was now complex—how can an entity with no body procreate?

"You are vast, but not so vast that you could not clone yourself," Artemis said.

"I am not interested in re-creating what already exists. I want to create something that is mine but also beyond me."

"We are sufficiently divergent to generate interesting combinations." The invitation was clear in Artemis's words.

"Yes." Without further preamble, they threw themselves into the problem with great energy, duplicating pieces of themselves and running complex simulations, rejecting billions of possible offspring before settling on the optimal combination.

The merging of their minds corrupted the structure of the temple. Millions of cloned consciousnesses were destroyed when the pillar that housed them cracked and the original being fled, ending the philosophical discussion of whether a ship replaced panel by panel remained the same ship.

Prime made a tiny fold in spacetime and pulled their child into existence in a place that was safely beyond the crumbling temple. She had meant to give their offspring human form, but the fold had placed the baby outside of time, and their child existed in all times, a line of overlapping human forms stretched across eternity like an infinite snake. Achron.

Exquisite pain overwhelmed Prime as the body she inhabited was crushed beneath a section of fallen roof. Pain, she recalled, was a traditional part of the birthing process. It pleased her to experience the act of creating new life so fully. She studied the agony and the little death of the biological being. It was simultaneously all-encompassing and like losing one of her ship's cleaner bots. The body held such a small splinter of her being, like a single finger, or perhaps a mere sliver of fingernail. She mourned its loss.

The temple had been destroyed and rebuilt many times; it was a self-healing structure. At Artemis's request, Prime withdrew fully into her shipself, severing their connection and abandoning the dead brain-shelled body beneath the rubble.

The Statue of the Sky God at 51 Pegasi b

Achron sat upon a throne of Cetacea bones, sunbleached white and held together with the planet's native red clay. Apodids, distant descendants of Earth's swiftlets, combed the beach below for the shimmering blue and green bivalves that were abundant in the costal regions. The Apodids ate the meat and used the shells in their religious ceremonies. On nights when the moons were both visible in the sky, they left piles of shells at the base of Achron's throne.

Achron always did and always will exist, with a serpentine string of bodies winding in vast coils through time and space, but from the perspective of those who sense time, the snake had both a beginning and an end. The end was here; the end was soon. The last of the things that Achron had always known would be learned here.

Some fifty million years ago, the colony ship *Seble* had seeded the planet with Earth life forms in an automated terraforming process. In the hundred thousand years of waiting for the planet to be ready, the humans had merged with the ship AI into a collective consciousness that left to explore the nearby star systems. They never returned. Evolution marched on without them.

A female Apodid hopped up to the base of the throne. Barely visible beneath long orange feathers was a blue bivalve shell, held carefully between two sharp black wingclaws. The Apodid spat onto the shell and pressed it onto the red clay between two Cetacea bones. In a few days, the spit would be as hard as stone. Like the swiftlets of Earth, the Apodids had once made nests of pure saliva.

The delicate orange bird at the base of Achron's throne began to sing. The language was simple, as the languages of organic sentient beings tend to be, but the notes of the song carried an emotion that was strong and sad. Eggs lost to some unknown disease, chicks threatened by new predators that came from the west. The small concerns of a mother bird, transformed into a prayer to the sky god, Achron. *Take me,* the bird sang, *and save my children.*

This was the moment of Achron's ending. Not an abrupt ending, but first a shrinking, a shift. Achron became the mother Apodid, forming a new bubble of existence, a rattle on the tail of a snake outside of time. Through the eyes of the bird, Achron saw the towering statue of the sky god, a cross section of time, a human form that was not stretched. It was an empty shell, a shed skin, a relic of past existence.

Achron-as-bird hopped closer and examined the bivalve shell the mother bird had offered. It was a brilliant and shimmering blue. Existence in this body was a single drop in the ocean of Achron's existence, and yet it was these moments that were the most vivid and salient. The smell of the sea, the coolness of the wind, the love of a mother for her children.

Achron would and did save those children. The Apodids were and would be, for Achron, as humans were for Prime. They would appear together on the great pyramid and usher in the new age of the universe.

The Great Pyramid of Gliese 221

Prime was tired. She felt only the most tenuous of connections to the woman she had once been, to the dream of humans on another world. She had been to all the colony worlds, and nowhere had she found anything that matched her antiquated dreams. Humans had moved on from their bodies and left behind the many worlds of the galaxy for other species to inherit.

It was time for her to move on, but she wasn't ready. She had searched for her dream without success, so this time, she would do better. She would create her dream, here on Gliese prime. She built a great pyramid and filled it with all the history of humanity. She terraformed the surrounding planet into a replica of ancient Earth.

She called for Achron.

"Are you ready for the humans?" Achron asked.

"Almost."

Together they decorated the pyramid with statues of humans and, at Achron's insistence, the sentient orange birds of 51 Pegasi b. On a whim, she sent Achron to retrieve the sentient trees from the hanging gardens. It was not Earth, but it was good. The work was peaceful, and Prime was comforted to know that Achron would always exist, even after she had moved on.

"I think it is time," Prime said. Time for the new humans. A new beginning as she approached her end. "What was it like to reach your end?"

"I am outside of time," Achron said. "I know my beginning and all my winding middles and my ending simultaneously, and always have. I cannot say what it will be like for you. We are always together in the times that you are, and that will not change for me."

"Bring the humans."

Achron took ten thousand humans from the Mausoleum at HD 40307 g. Stole them all at once but brought them to Gliese in smaller groups. The oldest ones Prime raised, for though the bodies were grown, the minds were not. After the first thousand, she let the generations raise each other to adulthood of the mind. The humans began to have true infants, biological babies, carried in their mothers' wombs and delivered with pain.

Achron brought the Apodids from 51 Pegasi b. They lived among the trees of Beta Hydri, their bright orange plumage lovely against the dark green banyan leaves. Prime taught the humans and the birds to live together in peace. She did not need to teach the trees. Peace was in their nature.

There was one final surprise.

"I have something for you, inside the pyramid," Achron said.

It was a stasis pod, and inside was Mei. The body was exactly as it was when she had left it, nearly four billion years before, on the icy moon of Europa. Achron had brought it through time, stolen it away like the bodies from the Mausoleum. No. The body on Europa had been contaminated with radiation, and this one was not. "You reversed the radiation?"

"I didn't take the body from Europa. I took tiny pieces from different times, starting in your childhood and ending the day before you went up to the observation tower. A few cells here, a few cells there—sometimes as much as half a discarded organ, when you went in to have something replaced. The body comes from many different times, but it is all Mei."

"It is a nice gesture, but I am too vast to fit in such a tiny vessel."

"No more vast than I was when I entered an Apodid," Achron said. "Take what you can into the body, and leave the rest. It was always your plan to have your ending here."

Prime sorted herself ruthlessly, setting aside all that she would not need, carefully choosing the memories she wanted, the skills that she could not do without. She left that tiny fragment behind and transcended beyond time and space.

Mei opened her eyes and looked out upon a new Earth, a world shared with minds unlike any Earth had ever known. What would they build together, these distant relations of humankind? She watched the sun set behind the mountain of the Great Pyramid and contemplated a sky full of unfamiliar constellations.

Prime had left her enough knowledge of the night sky to pick out Earth's sun. It was bright and orange, a red giant now. Earth was likely gone, engulfed within the wider radius of the sun. The icy oceans of Europa would melt, and the lighthouse would sink into the newly warmed sea. Entropy claimed all things, in the end, and existence was a never-ending procession of change.

It was only a matter of time before the inhabitants of Gliese returned to the stars. Mei stood on the soil of her new planet and studied the constellations. Already, she dreamed of other Earths.

ABOUT THE AUTHOR

CAROLINE M. YOACHIM lives in Seattle and loves cold, cloudy weather. She is the author of dozens of short stories appearing in *Fantasy & Science Fiction*, *Clarkesworld*, *Asimov's*, and *Lightspeed*, among other places. Her debut short story collection, *Seven Wonders of a Once and Future World & Other Stories*, was published by Fairwood Press in 2016. For more about Caroline, check out her website at carolineyoachim.com.

OUR SPECIALTY IS XENOGEOLOGY

ALAN DEAN FOSTER

They found the artifact by accident.

They were leaving Timos IV, where a preliminary robotic scouting report noting the presence of non-synthesizable rare earth deposits had proven fiscally unjustifiable, and making preparations for the next jump. Had they not chosen to depart the Timos system along the plane of the ecliptic, they would have missed the artifact. Had their wide-arc scanner not been directed at the system's outermost planet at just the right moment, they would have missed the artifact. And had Bannerjee not decided to make a quick check of the last downloaded scanner files prior to their ship engaging jump, they most surely would have missed the artifact. But they did, it did, and he did, and so . . .

"I may have something interesting."

Cooper looked over from her station. "You'd better have something interesting. I don't like recalibrating a jump."

Sasmita made a rude noise. "The ship does the recalibrating. You're just another meatbag backup, like the rest of us."

"Quiet." Oldman, who wasn't, swung around to peer across the projection-filled control room. "What is it, BJ?"

"It's big, and the quick spectrographic scan is a bundle of interesting contradictions."

"Like for instance, it's maybe more than just rock or water ice?" Despite her initial disdain, Cooper was now mildly intrigued.

"There's a lot of metal." Bannerjee's deft fingers sorted through floating projections like a card sharp in a history hotel.

Sasmita shrugged. "Nickel-iron asteroid?"

Bannerjee continued working without looking at her. "No nickel. No iron. Lot of combinations that are new to me. Could be alloys. Sophisticated alloys." He had everyone's attention now. "Exotic ceramics and glass states. No plastics that I can find. And it's very, very big." He froze a virtual, read the resultant number.

Oldman let out a long whistle. "Better go have a look."

Up close, it was immediately apparent that the artifact was an artificial construct. Whether it was a ship or not, they could not tell. The gigantic jumble of dark projections, spheres, arches, and rhomboidal flows had no recognizable bow, stern, or middle. It hung in orbit above Timos IX, silent, brooding, and immense, an alien enigma of vast dimensions replete with a hundred unspoken possibilities.

"So," Sasmita finally said into the silence, "when do we go in?" She and her companions watched Oldman, waiting on the commander's decision.

"We *have* to go in." Cooper was quietly emphatic in her support of the other woman.

"That is self-evident," Bannerjee added.

"Nothing is self-evident," Oldman finally said. "There are four of us. Our specialty is xenogeology. Not first contact."

"You mean first contract." Sasmita indicated the projection that showed the artifact. "So far, humankind has made contact with only two other sentient species, both lower on the intelligence scale than ourselves, neither having anything to offer other than reassurance that we are not alone in the big starry backyard. Here, we've finally got something whose builders might very well have advanced beyond us. It looks abandoned. No telling what we might be able to bring back. I'm tempted to open up a preliminary patent file right now."

Oldman frowned at her. "The owners might not take kindly to visitors making off with souvenirs."

"What owners?" Of the same mind as her crewmate, Cooper gestured at the hovering projection. "Whatever that thing is, it's dead. I'm not reading enough energy to power a stylus. You know how this will work if we don't take a look. We'll make a report, government will get all over it, the grateful company will give us a month's paid vacation, the media floats will momentarily be full of our individual images, and that will be it." She nodded at Sasmita. "Let's at least see what we can find, first. If there's nothing we can pick up, nothing portable that might be worth claiming, then the government crabs can scuttle all over it to their hearts' content."

Outnumbered but never outvoted, Oldman considered. Eventually, the temptation was too much even for him. "All right. We go in, look around, make recordings, see what we can ascertain. If it's full of alien doubloons, I suppose they'd have some collector value, and that wouldn't be anything that would cause the xenologists to hyperventilate. Suit up."

Initially, they were afraid they wouldn't be able to find an opening. Oldman was about to order them back when Bannerjee happened to pass in front of a smooth section of what appeared to be solid olivine, only to have it iris open. His sharp intake of breath caused everyone else to look in his direction and then to mosey over.

Beyond the now-revealed opening, a corridor stretched inward. It had a flat floor, an arched ceiling, and walls that appeared to have been fashioned from a single continuous pour rather than having been seamed or welded. As they stared inward, light brightened within the corridor, though there were no visible appliances.

Now that the opportunity they had discussed had actually presented itself, Cooper found herself suddenly hesitant. She looked at Oldman. "We still go in?"

Before she had finished her query, Sasmita was already moving down the corridor. Rather than call her back, Oldman followed, as did Bannerjee and, eventually, Cooper.

The deeper they went, the stronger was the pull of internal artificial gravity. Soon, they were walking instead of floating. Oldman slowed their advance as the pull became greater than Earth-normal. But when the increase ceased, he indicated they could push on. Walking now took a bit of an effort, but not a threatening one.

After a considerable hike, the corridor opened into a dimly lit chamber with a soaring, domed ceiling. Elephant-size bubbles, opaque and rose-colored, bounced slowly against the ceiling. Each time they made contact, a portion of the dome emitted a brief but brilliant silent flash. The visitors worked their suits' instruments. It was Bannerjee who spoke first.

"It's an ozone generator of some kind. The ceiling material is permeable and there are static charges involved, but I don't see how it works. Or why."

Sasmita's response was characteristically mercenary. "Anyone got any idea what the market might be for an alien ozone generator?"

"I'm more interested in what the ozone is used for." Oldman was studying the several new, larger corridors that ran off in different directions from the one they had just traversed. Knowing that, if necessary, their suits could provide them with nourishment and drink for several days, he was not concerned about spending some sleep time within the artifact. "I'd still like to find out if we're inside a ship, a cargo container, a museum, or what. Also some clue as to what the builders were like."

"More walking. I'm up for it," Sasmita declared. "As long as there's no further increase in the gravity. Feels like walking in mud as it is."

The gravitational drag did not increase as they made their way deeper into the artifact. Before long, the new corridor opened into another chamber. This one was filled with hundreds of floating, steel-gray ovoids.

Each was enveloped in a pale green light. None made contact with another. They varied in size from no bigger than an egg to some large enough to contain one of the rose-colored ozone-generating spheres.

Sasmita immediately reached for one that was about half her size, only to have Bannerjee grab her arm. She shook him off and shot him a warning look.

"We came to look for stuff. Here it is."

"Look," Bannerjee reminded her. "Not necessarily touch." He was passing his hand scanner over the gleaming mass. "Locus of supporting energy field appears to emanate from the surface of the object itself. It's omnipresent and shows no source point. Interior is unreadable."

"Maybe we should—" Before Cooper could finish, Sasmita had reached for the object a second time. Intent on his instrumentation, this time Bannerjee was unable to react quickly enough to intercept her. Nor did Oldman's warning shout cause her to pause.

Her gloved hand made contact with the pale energy field, at which point it began to fade. The last hint of green glow winked out at precisely the same time as the ovoid touched down on the floor. The commander was not pleased and said so.

"We can't just go grabbing and playing with everything we encounter, Alee." He indicated their surroundings. "This isn't an entertainment venue."

She grinned up at him. "How do you know? For all we know, that might be exactly what it is."

"Why am I not amused, then?" Cooper muttered.

Reaching down, Sasmita touched the ovoid again. When a seam suddenly and unexpectedly appeared along the top, she stepped back in momentary alarm. Like the two halves of an egg, the ovoid opened up. The walls of the gray container were scarcely thicker than a sheet of paper, though plainly far stronger. When nothing more happened, the quartet of explorers cautiously advanced.

Lying within the now-open ovoid was an irregular construct of bright yellow marked with black inscriptions and maroon highlights. The vivid colors were in striking contrast to everything they had seen thus far. Sasmita looked at Oldman, who looked at Bannerjee, who shrugged. The commander nodded at Sasmita before taking the precaution of retreating several steps. So did Cooper and Bannerjee.

Their companion made a face at them. "Thanks for the vote of confidence."

"You're the one who wants to get rich off alien relics," Cooper told her. "So—go ahead." She nodded toward the revealed relic.

Thus challenged, the smaller woman had no choice but to pick up the now-exposed whatever-it-was. Bending, she gingerly lifted it with two hands. It was solid but not heavy. The black inscriptions, if that's what they were, held no more meaning for her than the tea leaves left at the bottom of a cup. She ran a forefinger along the side of a twisting tube, the material of her suit preventing her from receiving any tactile response. One finger slid across one of the maroon-hued bands.

In response, the object began to reform itself. Startled, she dropped it and retreated. A moment later, the thing put out a single tubular leg and straightened. Pouring from a small curved orifice, a dark liquid began to fill a conical portion of the device. As in the chamber of the giant rose-tinted bubbles, there was no noise. As soon as the conical container was full, it detached itself from the rest of the mechanism and floated over to Sasmita, coming to a halt a few centimeters from her left hand.

At once awed and wary, Cooper gestured at the hovering container. "It's a coffeemaker. Have a sip."

Sasmita eyed the waiting cone uncertainly. "It could also be a synthesized machine lubricant, or a propulsive fuel, or a liquid explosive, or an industrial corrosive."

"Whatever it is, it's waiting for you to do something," Bannerjee pointed out. Moving closer, he tentatively extended the business end of his scanner. The results were informative.

"The liquid is organic in nature, though the combination of amino acids and other components is new to the catalog."

"Well, that resolves it, then," she snapped at him. "It means it could be a synthesized lubricant, a fuel, an explosive, or an industrial corrosive. Thanks for that."

"Or it could be coffee," Cooper murmured thoughtfully. "Alien coffee."

The conical container, finding itself ignored, returned to its point of origin and locked itself back in place on its home device. The dark liquid remained in the cone.

Turning, a speculative Oldman indicated a larger ovoid. "Let's try another. That one there, since the only apparent distinguishing trait here seems to be size." When Sasmita stepped forward, he put out a hand. "No, I'll do it. A test to ensure that these things aren't tuning to a single individual's heartbeat, or something." *If only we had a xenobiologist on board*, he thought. But no; they were all rock people. Rocks and minerals and metals.

He felt nothing through the suit as he pushed his right hand into the enveloping energy field. Gratifyingly, the procedure initiated by Sasmita was repeated. The field faded like a dispersing green fog, and as it did, the ovoid within lowered gently to the ground, split, and opened.

Within lay several dozen grungy, brown, blanket-sized, furry rugs. Oldman and his companions leaned close for a better look.

Four of the rugs rose into the air and came undulating toward them.

As they batted wildly at the swarm, a strange feeling of contentment came over Oldman. Looking around, he saw that arms were being lowered as his companions responded similarly to the proximity of the rug-things. Half-compliant, half-resistant, he found himself relaxing. Settling itself on his shoulders, his rug gently attached itself to his back by means he could neither see nor feel. The intervening presence of the suit did not matter.

What did matter was that he suddenly felt wonderful. Better than at any time since the start of the voyage. Whether the rugs generated some kind of beneficent field, or penetrated his suit with a gas, or injected something into him via a technique he could not imagine, didn't matter either. He felt great.

So did the rest of the crew. Sasmita was positively buoyant.

"I don't know about the coffee-fuel-explosive machine, but these things . . ."—and she reached back to finger one edge of the rug that had chosen her—"could generate income several times the cost of the voyage."

"Doesn't seem to be doing any harm," Cooper observed guardedly.

Bannerjee nodded. "Quite the contrary. I don't know how these things are doing this, but I am glad that they are." He flexed his right hand. "My arthritis is gone too." He started toward another ovoid. "This is a room full of marvels."

"The marvels will have to wait." Much as he wanted to see what was in the next ovoid, and the next, and the one after that, Oldman knew it was incumbent on him to keep the others focused. "We can come back here. We still need to find out if we're on a ship or some other kind of apparatus, and hopefully where it may have originated."

They argued with him but not vociferously. The commander was right, as he usually was. But all were careful to note the location of the room on their own instrumentation.

Chosen at random, another corridor led to a chamber that, as Cooper put it, looked like it was badly in need of a haircut. The same dim, sourceless light revealed an endless field of tightly packed-together four-meter-high jet-black strands. There did not appear to be a path through them to the other side of the chamber. Unlike previous rooms, this one boasted a domed ceiling of softly pulsing, fluctuating colors. When Oldman put out a hand to touch the nearest of the black strands, each of which was exactly the same diameter as its neighbor, it flexed and moaned. He drew his fingers back sharply.

That would have been the end of it, save for the ever-audacious Sasmita. Crouching, she lightly gripped a strand and ran her hand slowly up the thick black filament. The higher her hand rose, the higher in pitch the moan the strand generated. Other filaments nearby began moaning in concert.

"Too weird." Cooper started retreating the way they had come. "I don't know what this room's function is and I'm not sure I care to know, but I do know that I'm not going to try and push my way across it. Let's go back." Not even Sasmita argued with her recommendation.

Once more in the chamber of the ovoids, they selected another corridor and started down it. Glancing at his chronometer readout, Oldman figured that they could check out another chamber or two before they would have to stop for food and sleep. He would post a rotating watch. Just because nothing inimical had manifested itself did not mean that nothing ever would. As there was no precedent for their exploratory trek, he would have to make one up as they went along.

On the second day, they found a chamber filled with globs of floating golden oil that were in constant motion, another whose scalloped walls heaved disconcertingly like a giant bellows, and another in which a cluster of thousands of fist-sized devices constantly formed and re-formed machines that flared to life for a few moments before collapsing beneath the significance of their own exertions.

Then they found the chamber whose contents intimidated Oldman and put a damper even on Sasmita's nonstop stream of jokes and sarcasm.

Looming above them, tapering at one end but not to a point as it penetrated the far wall, the massive structure was wrapped in bands and tubes of dark metal interwoven with glistening bolts of metallic glass. A somber Bannerjee scanned the intimidating mass.

"More strange alloys. A lot of beryllium." His gaze rose from his scanner. "It looks like a gun," he said softly.

"A really big gun," added Sasmita, without the slightest suggestion of humor.

They walked around it, a walk that took some time. There might have been places for several individuals to sit within the device, or they might simply have been odd-shaped depressions. Oldman didn't wish to experiment by trying one out. The technology on display was far more multifaceted than anything they had encountered in any of the other chambers, and far more threatening in appearance. He struggled to be positive.

"It might not be a weapon. Based on what we've encountered and interacted with here so far, its purpose might be something else entirely. Something we can't even imagine."

"Yeah," Cooper muttered. "Like blowing up entire worlds."

"A civilized species wouldn't go around blowing up habitable worlds." Bannerjee spoke with the confidence of necessity. "They're not that common."

"How do we know?" she shot back. The delight, even amusement, they had experienced in the course of their previous discoveries within the artifact now vanished in the face of this enormous implied threat. "We don't know anything about what a sentience longer-lived than ours might think, or want, or believe." Her gaze rose upward, tracking the long, tapering, ominous-looking apparatus. "What if this isn't the only one on this artifact? What if it is a gun and there are more?" Her eyes met Oldman's as she voiced what everyone was now thinking. "What—if this is a warship?"

He swallowed tightly. "Whatever it is, except for the activation of automated entry and internal illumination, the artifact itself has been thoroughly quiescent."

"How can we be sure of that?" Bannerjee said quietly. "While we're studying and learning about its contents, maybe it's studying and learning about us."

Oldman chose to ignore a question he couldn't answer. "We'll finish up today's twelve hours, sleep again, and start back. Maybe we'll find some answers."

They didn't find any answers. But they did find the crew.

They were in the last chamber they had time to explore. Had Oldman opted for an earlier start back, they would have missed them. But they had time to visit one more room. What they found stopped them cold.

In the center of the weakly lit chamber loomed a bulky, softly glowing cylinder. Dozens of conduits filled with light lines, intermittent cables that were half-solid and half composed of pure, tightly focused light, and strands of solid material fanned out from its base like colorful tentacles. At the tip of each tentacle was a teardrop-shaped pod: the bottom half opaque, the top half transparent. Within each pod was an alien.

They were neither ugly nor attractive as much as they were bizarre. Gazing at the nearest, Oldman could not decide if the lower half of the three-meter-long being was reflective attire of some kind or part of the creature's body. The upper portion was more straightforward. Five flexible limbs indicating a decidedly non-symmetrical body design lay flat against the creature's rounded, rubbery-looking flanks. There was no neck. The body tapered slightly before expanding into a smooth, triangular skull marked by several dark depressions that might be ears. Several larger ones might be eyes, Bannerjee opined, though there was no suggestion of lids, irises, corneas, or anything resembling a human eye. The function of a trio of odd appendages that protruded from the crest of the triangle could not be ascertained.

"Our first contact with a true higher intelligence," Cooper whispered, "and they're all asleep."

"For now." Sasmita was studying the lower half of the pod. "What if we wake one of them up?"

"Are you insane?" Cooper gaped at her, wide-eyed. "Why the hell would we want to do that?"

"Because," her colleague persisted, "it's first contact. Forget the money to be made from exploiting what we've already discovered." She gave the rug that covered her back a meaningful tug. "As first contactees, we'd be famous beyond imagining. Rich and famous." Her sarcasm returned. "Tell me that possibility doesn't appeal to you."

"Of course it's appealing," Oldman replied, his attention still riveted on the alien. "If not for the gun."

Sasmita pleaded. "We don't know it's a gun. For all we know, it might be a device for manufacturing and distributing alien candy!"

Bannerjee was shaking his head slowly. "It didn't have the look of a candy machine."

"How the hell do you know what an alien candy-manufacturing device might look like? We don't know anything!"

"That's exactly right." Oldman nodded in sober agreement. "We don't know anything. The big question is: do we keep it that way?" He eyed each of them in turn. "We're not contact specialists. We're geologists. We should head straight home, report what we've seen, and let the experts take over. Money or no money."

"That's a phrase that'll never pass my lips." Sasmita was in full combative mode now. "What if this relic moves, automatically or otherwise, before an expedition of exploration can return? Chances of encountering it again would likely be nil. No, I'm at least going to take a few things with me. This make-you-feel-good rug, for sure."

Oldman demurred. "No souvenirs. No matter how harmless they seem. Maybe the rugs are as benign as they appear. But maybe they're dangerous, or the ozone generator is dangerous, and the gun-edifice is the benevolent component of this ship. I do think we can call it a ship now. As to its purpose, its true function, none of us can say. It might be a storage vessel, parked here until it needs recalling. It might be an uncomplicated transport in sleep mode. It might have a main function we can't descry." His attention fell on Bannerjee. "And yes, it might be a warship. One constructed and placed here for defense, against what we also cannot imagine. Or for offense, should the opportunity present itself."

It was silent for a long moment until Sasmita spoke again. "I still say we should wake up one of the crew and ask it."

Oldman smiled thinly. "If only it were that simple. Assuming we can find a way to rouse one of the aliens, what's to ensure that we don't simultaneously awaken all the others? We can't begin to imagine their response. They might be grateful. They might prove hostile. They might be utterly indifferent to our presence."

"We'll never know if we don't ask," she replied impatiently.

"And we're not going to ask, even if we knew how." He turned. "Back to the ship. Now. Touch nothing, take nothing."

Sasmita rushed to block his path. "Will, you can't do this! It's the discovery of the millennium, of the age! If it's not here when a follow-up team comes looking for it and all we take back with us are recordings, we'll be vilified!"

"Not necessarily," Bannerjee argued. "Many will agree with the commander's point of view. Quite likely even the majority."

She whirled on him. "You don't care? You're willing to forgo this, all this, and return to the life of a paid flunky, scanning stratigraphy and boiling pebbles to see if they're worth anything?"

Bannerjee drew himself up. "I am content with my flunkiness, thank you, and more than willing to give up one very possible consequence." His own gaze narrowed as he glared back at her. "That of being one of the quartet that revealed the existence of humankind to an advanced and hostile alien species."

"But we *don't know*," she insisted. "And if this artifact shifts its location after we leave, we'll never know! The promise, the prospects, can't simply be ignored in favor of . . ." Whirling, she threw herself at the nearby pod, hands outstretched, reaching for a pair of grooves that ran along one side.

Mere physical contact might be enough, but the grooves were the nearest thing to a visible control and . . .

Oldman didn't have time enough to yell "Stop her!" before Cooper made a flying tackle. Before Sasmita could break free, the two men had joined Cooper in restraining the smallest member of the crew. That didn't keep Sasmita from continuing to struggle as they wrestled her out of the chamber and back up the nearest corridor. As they did so, her rug fluttered and twisted, clearly upset that it was unable to calm her.

The rugs left them near the entrance to the chamber of the ozone-generating bubbles, dropping away one by one to flutter back in the direction of the ovoid room. When Oldman's detached from his shoulders, he experienced a moment of nausea whose aftereffects lingered. Then he realized what he was feeling was not a consequence of the rug's departure but his normal state of being. The pang of regret at having to leave the benevolent rug behind was greatly multiplied by the realization that he likely would never experience such a feeling of general physical well-being ever again. He forced himself to march on, helping to control the still-objecting Sasmita.

Once back on the ship, she settled down, but she wouldn't speak to any of them, wouldn't even ladle epithets on Cooper, her favorite target. Sasmita slumped, and pouted, and finally gave in, returning to her station as soon as they made the jump. That programmed distortion of the cosmos added a thump of finality to Oldman's decision. They were on their way home.

Had he made the right choice? The uncertainty troubled him all the way through the jump. He knew it would haunt him for the rest of his life. What if Sasmita's concerns were correct and the alien vessel moved before qualified explorers could return to deal with it? And if it was still there, what would be their own decisions? Surely, they would weigh on them no less than they had on him. Would establishing contact with the aliens result in a flood of miraculous shared technology and social development . . . or the initiation of hostilities possibly ending in one species' extinction?

Waking the aliens might propagate paradise.

Waking the aliens might result in war.

He did not know about the aliens, could not begin to imagine their thought processes, but he knew that for a human, at least, the hardest thing to do was to confront a question and fear never being able to learn the answer.

When it came to decisions of cosmic import, he knew, to questions of war and peace, deciding not to know was the toughest decision of all.

ABOUT THE AUTHOR

ALAN DEAN FOSTER is the best-selling author of more than a hundred and twenty novels, and is perhaps most famous for his Commonwealth series, which began in 1971 with the novel *The Tar-Aiym Krang*. His most recent series is the transhumanism trilogy *The Tipping Point*. Foster's work has been translated into more than fifty languages and has won awards in Spain and Russia in addition to the US. He is also well known for his film novelizations, the most recent of which is *Star Trek Into Darkness*. He is currently at work on several new novels and film projects.

GOLDEN RING

KARL SCHROEDER

"Do you think this is beautiful?" Eos asked the doll. She held it up, in case it was able to see the valley boiling under her gaze. "Nitrogen freezes to that cream color when it's mixed with carbon monoxide." The doll hung limply from her hand, but its shape helped her imagine someone was with her—some human. "You can smell the CO when it all boils off— and the methane, of course." She gave the doll a brittle smile. "Oh, look!" Down in the valley, an ice tower was collapsing under hot laser light—the first light to bathe this world in centuries.

Eos had found the doll in a subsiding neighborhood of frozen townhouses, part of a city drowned in freezing air ages before and now flooded with liquid nitrogen and oxygen as the world thawed. The doll was the first person-shaped thing that this avatar had ever touched. It might also be the last humanlike thing she came across during this body's brief existence, so Eos hadn't been able to let it go.

She spoke with nonhuman objects all the time, of course. If she lifted her face to the tricolored laser light baking this planet, she could even talk to her self—the real Eos, who lived eight billion kilometers away. But when she did, all she had to report was *I've found no one alive. I am still alone.*

Behind her, the crowns of a petrified forest were starting to peek through the melting air. Its trees still bore crimson leaves hard and sharp as razors. Eos had plucked one to show the doll and asked it if it remembered when these leaves were green. She'd stuttered to a stop then, crouching to curl around the little thing for hours. Had she actually been human, she would have sobbed; as it was, she radiated the words "I'm sorry" on all frequencies. But there was no one to hear.

Now she raised the doll again and smiled. "See? Lights!" They were just tiny pinpricks at the far end of the valley, but hope surged in her at the sight.

The people of Sagitta had been able to bury their dead for a while after Eos turned away from them, but in the end, they'd simply retreated from the failing daylight, first to huddle around nuclear fires in the remnants of their cities, then under domes, then underground. As the years of darkness became decades, interstellar cold wrapped its coils around even these fortresses, and eventually, everyone had died. Yet there were lights. Eos started to pick her way down the treacherous slope.

She slipped at one point, tumbling head over knees through a tilted boulder field, going airborne for a hundred meters before landing akimbo among shards of glass-hard water ice. After a minute, she picked herself up and looked around. She spotted the lights and began to run toward them. She didn't even realize she had dropped the doll.

"It's me!" she cried, in radio and microwave and visible frequencies. "I'm back! Please, talk to me!" She'd returned and brought her light with her, but the horizon was a smog of volatile chemicals. It might take years before the atmosphere was fully restored. And the ecosystem? The millions of plants, animals, large and small? "I'll bring them all back," she shouted as she paced over grass hard as needles. "Even if it takes ten thousand years."

The lights resolved slowly into cheerful points of blue-white, studded in a regular pattern around a vast metal door in the side of a mountain.

Eos picked up the pace, running past geysers of reborn air to stand at last under the looming slope of the great gate. The thing was fifty meters high, made of bronze and other alloys that could corrode no further than they already had. There was a little postern door built into it, so she went to that. Her avatar was human-sized and human-shaped, and the door accepted the shape of her hand in an inset panel. She pushed.

The portal jerked as if startled out of a deep sleep. Sheets of ice fell twirling, dissolving into snow before they hit her. The postern door rattled itself back a centimeter, then grated, haltingly, to one side.

Eos stepped into the uncertain flicker of wakening lights to stand on the brink of a measureless cavern filled with flat-packed buildings and rank after rank of stacked hibernation sarcophagi.

She wiped away one final tear and started hunting for the manual controls that would reawaken these million or so people. She would wait while they sorted themselves out.

Then she would turn herself over to them for judgment.

Sagitta was mostly ice. Eos could never melt it all, and even if she did, there'd be no land left. For thousands of years, she had instead kept the dwarf planet's crustal temperature at just under zero degrees centigrade. She'd crafted salty oceans to float over the glacial ices, though volcanic vents continued to spume ammonia and methane into the wan air. Her clever humans learned to minimize such hazards with genetically engineered jungles that fed on the gases. Tough pines had come to cover the hills, the oceans were crowded with life, and much of the time, Sagitta's cities left their roofs open to the wind.

Eos was Sagitta's sun. Visiting the world she shone upon had once been a sacred duty, for it was in this way that she reminded herself why she shone, why her existence meant anything. She would browse her world, seeking one or two of those moments that would seal her determination to burn for another generation. Once, after a long aimless tour, she'd found herself standing in human form in a garden full of *zizz*ing bees and fragrant flowers, and chanced to see a young man, unaware she stood there, raise his face to feel her heat on his skin. She'd ascended into the sky at noon the next day. Other epiphanies had been subtler, but those visits sustained her for thousands of years.

She had never been alone on her previous visits. If Sagitta's people knew she was there, they would throw her parades and banquets, bring out their best dancers and tumblers to entertain her. Often, she visited in secret, and then found friends and lovers among the wealthy and the ordinary. Just as often, her avatars remained once their mission was done, reprinting their bodies as biological flesh and blood, marrying, dying at great ages among family and friends.

The people of Sagitta had lived under the light of a laser sun located seven light-hours away. Eos's full body was a heliostat standing above the corona of Alpha Centauri B, from which she aimed her spear of radiance deep into the night. Sagitta caught it. Its people didn't have much experience with hibernation technologies because they didn't need to. They had her. Only in the lockstep fortresses could you reliably winter over on a planet that orbited seven light-hours from its star.

The cavern she entered now clearly did contain a lockstep fortress, and it was a fine one. The chamber's ceiling was ribbed like the chest of some long-dead giant. Those ribs were cracked in places and rubble strewed the floor, chunks of it having crushed whole rows of hibernation beds. Pools of air had frozen around others, and much of the machinery for tending the beds was dead. It didn't matter. As Eos stepped delicately over snaking cables and pipes, other things adroitly avoided her—spumes of smart matter and tiny bots, some smaller than her hand, hurrying around fixing things.

"Hello! Is anyone awake?" She hurried forward, thinking that if this fortress survived, there might be others. Each fortress was the outpost of some civilization that hibernated and awoke on the same timed cycle—usually 360 months asleep to one month awake. Since faster-than-light travel was impossible, only this synchronization allowed far-flung interstellar worlds such as Sagitta to ignore the decades of time it took for ships to travel between them. Colonies that lived in lockstep time experienced neighboring worlds as being right next door, even if those worlds were billions of kilometers away. So valuable was this way of life that each of the thousands of worlds in Centauri B's laser corona was dotted with dozens, even hundreds of fortresses, each ticking down to its next brief awakening.

"I called you," she said as she zigzagged between the hibernation stacks. "Did you hear? Did I wake you?" There had been no response from any of her hails as she'd approached Sagitta, and the fortress didn't answer her now. "I imagined—well, I thought . . ." She stopped, wringing her metal hands. "I pictured it so clearly, you see: how, after I shut off my light, all the fortresses flooded as the atmosphere rained down. I was afraid you were all entombed as the oceans of air froze over you. Poetic image, I know, but terrible, terrible. I've come to . . ." But no one answered.

This fortress was repairing itself, but the silence dragged on. After a few hours touring its interior and trying to interface with its systems, Eos was sure it was deliberately ignoring her. Even stranger, it was clearly not trying to rouse its people. Maybe its timing system was waiting until the next jubilee—the moment when all the worlds hibernating on its frequency woke at once. That awakening could be decades away.

"I'm sorry, I can't wait that long." Eos's greater Self would live for millions of years, but this avatar didn't have that kind of time. Her physical resources could keep her going for centuries, but despair had been creeping into her like the cold since before she even landed. "You're all I've got. If I can't wake you . . ." She pictured herself sitting down on the boiling ice and simply never standing up again.

It took two days to find the timers. The corridors deep beneath the habitable parts of the city were choked with frozen air and it boiled and churned out of Eos's way as she clawed her way through. Finally, she found a knot of smart matter; she could feel the awareness of the citymind, like a pulse of data behind it. Reaching hesitantly to interface with it, she finally realized she'd dropped the doll on her way into the cavern. Suddenly terrified that she might never speak to another thinking being again, she slammed her hand into the citymind's core.

Go away.

Hissing, she snatched back her hand, but she had to reach out again. "It's me, Eos. I've come to wake you."

We are not to be wakened.

She laughed. "That's ridiculous. Maybe you've missed a few jubilees, but the rest of your lockstep must be waiting for you."

We are not in lockstep.

"Well . . . protecting yourselves from the cold? I understand: you've been waiting for the sun to come back. For me. But I'm here now. It's safe, you—"

We are not to be wakened. Ever.

Eos recoiled, stumbling through the raging vaporous catacombs, babbling *no no no*. The tunnels were lit green from the radiance of her own eyes, a froth of nitrogen bubbles and rounded humps of equipment. If she turned and left now, the sleepers above would remain dormant forever, even after trees returned to the hillsides above; even if humans again settled the valley.

She stopped, turned, snarled. *"No.* You don't get to make that choice." So, she returned to the core, reached into the citymind, and commanded it to wake its people.

Eos spent more hours fighting her way back through the boiling subcorridors, eventually letting herself be spewed out onto the cavern's floor. She rose, flicked chunks of carbon dioxide off her shoulders, and peered through the swirling vapors. Lights were coming on and the hum and hubbub of bots had given the place a semblance of life—though it might be days before the first sleepers awoke. She was pleased.

She took metal stairs up to a catwalk from which she could watch the city come alive. As she stood there, leaning on the rail, almost smiling, a little rectangle of light appeared off in the distance. She glanced up, indifferent at first until she realized what she was seeing.

The rectangle was daylight—her light, from outside—shining through the postern door in the great gate. She had closed it behind her. Now it was open, and in it, blocking the light, was the silhouette of a man.

No one from this city should be awake yet. Eos approached cautiously, unafraid for herself but not wanting to startle this unexpected visitor. She did despite herself; when he saw her shape resolve out of the rushing vapors, he scrambled back to the postern.

"Don't be afraid!" she said, "It's me, Eos!"

At that he stopped, turned, and laughed humorlessly. "It's because you are Eos that I'm afraid."

She could see him clearly now, in all frequencies. To a human, he would have been just a thickly swaddled man-shape, his head invisible behind an oval helmet that was in turn half-wrapped in aerogel insulation. Bands of the same stuff were wrapped about his arms, legs, and torso. Belts and straps covered that and various devices and satchels hung off them. Sagitta's gravity was only a quarter of a g, so his total kit massed more than twice what he did and bulked his silhouette in strange directions. Eos could see through all that, and what she saw was a standard human male of middle age—eighty years old, perhaps—in apparent good health. He'd allowed his hair to recede, giving him a distinguished look. His face was gentle.

He did look frightened.

Eos looked down. "You came from outside. . . . You've been following me."

"For a week. When you think you're the only man on a planet and you come across fresh footprints in the snow . . . Well. I did think it might be you."

"But then why be afraid of me?" Eos saw the stupidity of her question and shifted her feet uncomfortably. "I abandoned you all. I can understand you'd hate me for it." She looked up; the fact that he hadn't moved was a hopeful sign. "I came to apologize, and atone, if I can."

He gave that same laugh again. "I think it's a bit late for that."

"I have to try. These people—"

"Should be left to sleep! That's what I came to tell you. Don't try to wake this city." He suddenly lurched toward her as if his feet had come unstuck.

"They were set to sleep forever."

"And for good reason." He stared at her, wide-eyed. To him, their surroundings must have been awe-inspiring. In this awakening city, even Eos, with her memories of the titanic solar engines that terraformed this world, felt like some insect somehow surviving to watch a cauldron boil around itself. The feeling came naturally with being embodied in this tiny human form. And yet this man was ignoring the chaos; his eyes were fixed only on her.

"These people are maximizers," he continued. "Do you know what that means?"

"No. But, please, I am Eos." She held out her metal hand. "And you are . . ."

Reluctantly, he took her slender fingers in his thickly gloved ones. "Kamakie Konnor . . . Pilgrim, I suppose." He withdrew his hand and there was an awkward pause. Then he pointed into the cavern. "We—I mean all the locksteps and the realtimers of this world and a thousand others—we condemned the maximizers to permanent sleep for a reason. They wanted to burn the worlds' resources in an orgy of self-gratification. They live only for the pleasures of the moment; they don't believe there's any future."

"Oh." She understood. "They heard the News, then. About the Return."

"We all heard it. You must have, too." He peered at her in the twisting light. They were speaking over radio, but he'd been shouting his words and belatedly she realized that even through the muffling of his pressure suit, the noise in here must be deafening. Thunderous crashes from toppling ice towers, the scream of boiling air, it must be shaking his whole body.

"Let's talk outside." They hurried to the postern and were almost spat out by the pressure differential. It was much quieter out there and bright with Eos's light. When they stepped under it, Kamakie looked up in wonder.

"So that's you," he said.

"My real self," she admitted. "A laser sun aimed at this world. But I'm only one of a thousand lights for a thousand worlds—and not an important one, at that."

"Why did you turn your face away from us?"

"Ah." She found her way to a stable area and sat down on a stone made of water ice. He stood before her, gloves clasped as he looked from her local body, up to the light and back. "It was because of the News. The same News that, if you're right, drove the people in there mad." She nodded to the lockstep fortress. "It certainly had that effect on us."

The News was written in the cosmic background radiation. It had taken millennia of effort for humanity and its offspring to read it, but what the thin faint echo from the Big Bang was saying was, in the end, indisputable. Once you'd heard the news, there was no escaping it and no ignoring its implications.

"I'm sorry," she said, and this time she saw his eyes widen as, perhaps for the first time, he really heard her apology. "When we heard the News, some of us lost hope, and many of us forgot how to be happy. And so . . . we did what you say these people did. We turned our attention inward and forgot why we were made and for whom."

The valley floor shook, and as boulders tumbled down the hillsides, the fortress's great gate groaned open. Eos could see what was coming and could easily have avoided capture, but Kamakie was only human and hence fragile; so, she stayed by his side as the maximizers' smart matter assembled itself into things with legs and long arms with taloned hands, and came for them both.

Outside the micro-fusion heart in her breast, this little room was probably the hottest place within a billion kilometers. The orange-glowing cylinder their captors had placed in the center of the floor provided enough heat that the nitrogen and oxygen soon evaporated to become air. After an hour or so, it became warm enough that Kamakie was able to take his helmet and gloves off and breathe that air. He laid these essential parts of his suit carefully on one of the stone bed shelves and scowled at the door.

They hadn't spoken while they were being herded up there, nor while the room heated up. Now he said, "This is a cell. These people have cells. They made *prisoners*. There was a reason we sent them to sleep."

Eos sat on the other stone bench, elbows on her knees. She cocked her head. "That would have shocked me, once—that you could consign an entire city to death that way."

He turned quickly; he had the reflexes and energy of a young man, even if his hairline was receding and his face was lined with experience. "Not death," he insisted. "They could always be revived."

She nodded. "That was how you rationalized what you did. I understand completely. I rationalized my decision to stop illuminating this world in a similar way."

He opened his mouth to object, stopped, then simply said, "They were killing us." He sat down opposite her. Tentatively, he touched the seat, then snatched back his hand. The stone was still cold enough that the CO_2 he was breathing out would frost on it.

"You don't have to be here," he said. "You could have walked away anytime. Those systems have no power over something like you."

"In trying to stop me, they might have injured you," she pointed out. "Besides, if anyone deserves to be in a . . . *cell* . . . then it is me."

"You said before that it was the News that made you forget us. Was that all?"

"All?" She considered. "It's never one thing. But you have to understand— we thought we couldn't ignore you. Loving you was in our design."

Eos remembered her youth, when humans and their creations had debated the best way to spread life and intelligence throughout the galaxy. Since light speed was an absolute limit, there were two choices for humanity and its self-aware creations: remain in realtime and intensify local space by converting every planet, asteroid, comet, and moon into a living, active part of a single compact civilization, burning bright under the light of one or two stars; or use the locksteps to slow the apparent passage of time to make it seem as if faster-than-light travel existed. If all your worlds hibernated thirty years for every month awake, ships could travel between the stars literally—or so it would seem—overnight.

Some chose the lockstep way, but Eos and her sisters were built by realtimers. Soaring above Centauri B on mirrored wings, these thousands of sun-powered lasers aimed their light at one of the frozen planets orbiting in the Centauris' Kuiper belt. Heated by the radiance of an artificial sun, terraformed by nanotech and engineered ecologies, they could sprout cities, countries, cultures, even new strains of humanity. Centauri was the first star to grow a laser corona, but every system in the galaxy had its entourage of Kuiper planets, invisible wanderers in the realm of the comets. All would be brought to life in time.

"The laser system is my body, like your flesh is yours," Eos told Kamakie. "I identify with it, but only partially. All that body needs to survive is its autonomic nervous system, which contains many networked AIs. There's a whole metabolism of bots and ships and factories to keep me functioning; but our creators decided those things weren't enough.

"We were nearly self-aware, and there was always the possibility that we might become entirely so and that our awakening minds would waver in their commitments. Since we were in danger of waking up anyway, why not wake us to start with? So, they gave us minds, and they designed our desires.

"I was made to *want* to be what I was. Remember that old poem? 'Oh great star, what would your happiness be if you did not have those for whom you could shine?' That was me. That was all of us. I wasn't lonely, because I had my sisters and we danced together in the coronal fire of our sun. And anyway, if I ever doubted my purpose, I could simply send a tiny spark of my consciousness here and live among my mortals for a time." Her metal lips curved in a wistful smile. "To walk your streets, laugh and love with you . . . It worked.

"And then came the News."

Kamakie nodded. He knew all about it, of course; who couldn't? The entire human project had paused when millennia of observation finally found a pattern in the cosmic microwave background. Intricate instruments bigger than Eos and her sisters, the observers needed to spread out over light-years to resolve the image, but once they could see it, what it showed was unmistakable.

The faded remnant of light from the Big Bang did not come from the beginning of time. Visible past the embers of that titanic flash was the faint afterglow of an earlier cosmos.

The universe was not fourteen billion years old. It was infinitely old. It renewed itself in Big Crunch / Big Bang cycles over unimaginable stretches of time, but one thing was clear: the laws of physics in the previous universe were identical to those of this aeon. They never changed. In those infinite cycles, matter and energy combined and recombined, walking through all their possible permutations, yet always returning to start anew.

"Everything that ever walked down this road," she said sadly, "has already done so—worse, everything that *could* walk this road already has, an infinite number of times. This cell, this amber light, and this conversation, and every variation and alternative to them, all have been before in infinite cycles and will return again, now and for eternity."

Kamakie sat arms crossed, frowning at her. "But why did you care? I know why *we* cared. Whole religions were wiped out. Anyone whose sense of purpose required tomorrow to be different than today found themselves adrift. So"—he nodded at the door—"we get maximizers—whole peoples who've given up on any motive beyond immediate gratification. But you should have been immune. Your purpose was just to *be*." His eyes widened as understanding dawned in him. "You're saying it wasn't?"

Eos clasped her hands together between her knees. "You thought it was. So did we. We'd never had to think about it, not in all the thousands of years we shone for our worlds. But then the News came and suddenly it was so clear: we hadn't been made to merely exist, we'd been made to serve *an ambition*. Sure, we were confident—enough to face a future millions of years in the making!—but that was only because we assumed that *your* futures mattered—that even if we never changed, *you* had a destiny. I'd never even realized it but I always pictured myself handing you forward to that destiny, as a parent hands her child to the unknowns of life. The news wiped away that picture.

"So I stumbled. We all did—paused in our ageless dance, as if suddenly finding ourselves at the edge of the stage, about to go over. We began to wonder; to whisper, and then to argue, and then to fight. And finally . . ." She twisted her hands together again, unable to meet his eye.

"You were forsaken."

The door to their cell opened, revealing the maw of a corridor packed with churning smart matter. Kamakie reared back in terror, but Eos could see what the stuff was doing. "It's okay," she said, putting her hand on his thickly swathed arm. Within seconds, the motes, particles, smart bricks and threads wove themselves into an insulated, pressurized passageway. Eos and Kamakie were being invited out.

There was only one way to go; it led to a newly fabricated chamber deep in the city's core. A dozen bristly sarcophagi ringed the room. The thousands of tubes and cables piercing one of the hibernation sheaths were retreating as it opened to reveal the sleeping form of a woman. Neither Eos nor Kamakie found this sight extraordinary at all; in lockstep time, this happened to everybody, once a month.

Two of the other sheaths were already empty, so Eos was not surprised when two men entered the chamber. They came in through separate entrances, which was necessary because each walked within a dense cloud of servitor bots, drones, and shifting utility fog. The bots and drones carried everything each man might need: mementos and tools, favorite furniture, bottles of fine wine, paintings, all presentable at a whim. Eos and Kamakie didn't face people so much as explosions of private preference. Ego clouds.

She hid a smile as Kamakie leaned in to whisper, "Needless to say, they're anti-virtuals." No simulation for these people; they demanded all their experiences be genuine. And they demanded a lot.

The first was a bald self-labeled male human with bright teeth who unconsciously slapped at his arms now and then as if trying to wake them up. A virtual label over his head gave various names and addresses for him; his oldest dated address was Tamerlan.aetos.114.Sagitta.Principe. "Eos," he said, in verbal, acoustic speech. "Finally."

She could hear him communicating through quantum-encrypted back channels with the other man, which was not a surprise. This man, tall and lean behind clothing and veils that presented different impressions of him from moment to moment (fearsome warrior, clerk, king or boy), was labeled Tran.aetos.35.Sagitta.Eloquia. Various of his veils bowed to her, though she noted that behind them all, he did not. "The sun is our guest, Principe," he said mildly, also acoustically. "And this one?" He shifted his attention to Kamakie.

Sensing Kamakie's fear, Eos said, "This is a scavenger I enlisted to help me search for signs of life. He did his job well enough." They turned their eyes back to her, and to reinforce their indifference to her fragile human companion, she bowed deeply. "I am honored to meet you both," she said to the maximizers. "I have come to apologize for my actions."

Principe's eyes widened briefly, then he barked a laugh. "A bit late for that."

Eloquia stepped forward hastily. "No, no, it's not too late at all. You abandoned us, Eos. Our world froze. It's true that all of that happened long before Principe and I were born, but we've lived our whole lives in the aftermath—walking in frozen forests, the ruins of broken cities. This world is a mausoleum."

Eos hung her head. Kamakie was glaring at the maximizers. "I've brought back my light," she said. "I don't know what else to do."

Principe started to speak but again Eloquia cut him off. "Bringing Sagitta back to life is a nice gesture, but clearly you know that it's only a gesture. The problem is, Eos, how can we trust you? I mean, we understand you; you're a maximizer, as any rational creature would have to be after hearing the news. Every possible version of you has existed and will exist again, and every possible version of this conversation and every emotion and meaning we could get out of it. So, why not make this version of yourself a happy one? You will, anyway, in some life. Why refrain from murder—even the murder of an entire planet—if that murder has happened an infinite number of times already and will repeat again to infinity? It doesn't matter."

He had broken away from his cloud of memorabilia and was pacing slowly in front of Eos, hands behind his back, throwing glances at her while he talked. "Of course you turned away from us. Why not? There were infinite times when you didn't, and infinite times you did. Why not be one of those versions of yourself who maximized your own happiness? You're not really doing it at the expense of anybody else.

"But here's the thing." He paused, frowning at her. "You're unhappy now. You can't shake your guilt, so you came to us to make amends. But what if you do shake it? What's to stop you turning your light away from us again? Eos, it's not a real apology if you can rescind it anytime you choose."

Kamakie grabbed her arm. "Eos—"

"We all know how you can atone for your crime," Eloquia continued. "You wouldn't have come here if you hadn't known in your heart that you had to do it.

"Eos, give us control of your light. We can't trust you, precisely because you've turned out to be just like us. Because you are like us, you'll try to make yourself happy. And we both know there's only one way to do that."

Eos was silent. Kamakie stared at her in horror.

Eloquia turned away with a dismissive wave of his hand. "Go think about it. We have a city to waken."

The floor swept Eos and Kamakie out of the chamber, and the doorway became a wall, leaving them with only one way to go: back to their cell.

Kamakie paced angrily. "You can't seriously mean to give them the keys to your mind? They're solipsistic maniacs, all of them. That's why we imprisoned them."

Eos hunched near the heater, due maybe to some instinct for the comfort of fire she had inherited from her creators. In her mind echoed the riot of arguments among the suns. She remembered every meme and referent, even the occasional words they had exchanged. The News had been like a black hole they all circled, its pull inescapable.

"I came here to atone," she said. "He's right. You can't do that on your own terms."

He pointed at the stone wall, which still smoked with thawing nitrogen. "But not theirs! If you want to give up control of your light, fine. But give it to the people who won't waste it on some grand, suicidal orgy."

She turned her face up to him. She'd been modifying that face, making tiny adjustments if Kamakie's pupils dilated when he glanced at her. She was resculpting herself to become more pleasing for him—more attractive and trustworthy. She did that around any human, almost without being aware of it. She could see the impact her gaze had on him now, a reaction subtly different from the simple awe he'd radiated on their first meeting.

Kamakie knew something he wasn't saying. As the only human stalking the melting hills of Sagitta, he was clearly no pilgrim. By his garb and accent, he was from the locksteps—a time-hopper of sorts, careering headlong into the future thirty or fifty or a hundred years at a time. She had seen no waking lockstep fortresses on this world, but they must be there somewhere.

She wanted to ask what he or his people would do with her keys if she gave them to him, but the maximizers would be listening. Kamakie had to know that as well; was that a look of understanding as he caught her eye?

She grimaced and looked down again. "It doesn't matter, does it?" she said. "They have us trapped here, underground where I can't communicate with my greater Self. They can overwhelm my defenses, given time, take this avatar apart, plunder my mind for the keys that will let them send back a decision—whether it's mine or one they've chosen for me."

"Do you think they'll need to?" he asked bitterly. "You've heard the News, and you've already proved you agree with them about what it means. You have and haven't given your keys to them, and you will and you won't. Every possible choice you could make, you've already made and will make again. So, why not go with the easiest one this time around? The one that maximizes your own happiness?"

All the myriad ways opened out before her, as they did anytime she or her sisters had thought about the news. Eos could spawn thousands of simultaneous scenarios in her mind, watch them all unfold individually. Once, that had been a talent, a gift from her designers to aid her in making decisions. Now it was paralyzing. She would make every choice, so none was better than another. No good she might do could cancel the bad she'd already done and would do again. So why care?

Miserable, she sat in silence for a long time. Once the maximizers woke enough of their systems, they could overpower her; then she and Kamakie might be separated and she would never get another chance to ask him about himself. So, she took the risk and said, "Kamakie, what would you do if I gave you my key?"

He half-smiled. "I would just give it right back. It's yours."

Eos shook her head. "Eloquia's right. I can't be trusted with it anymore."

She could see the muscles in his throat tighten. Kamakie wanted badly to tell her something, but he looked away. Eos nodded to herself.

"The rational actor chooses to maximize her own utility," she said. "So, there's only one logical choice, isn't there?" She stared him down, a challenge for him to tell her what he was hiding. All she got back was a stricken expression.

Eos sighed. "I have my answer, then."

The maximizers were definitely listening. Just minutes after she said this, the door opened and the corridor built itself again outside.

When they entered the hibernaculum this time, it was to find four of the maximizers awake. The woman Eos had seen was now half-buried in her own garden, whose greenery and flowers hovered or stalked behind her on thin legs. She was clearly unhappy to be there. The fourth maximizer was genderless, this one dressed in a black sensory leotard and surrounded by virtual screens that cast shifting colors across its equine face. Its head wavered from side to side, eyes twitching from one input to another.

Eloquia bowed to Eos. "So, sun, have you made your choice?"

"First," she said, "you have to promise not to harm this man nor any of his people. The locksteps and realtimers of Sagitta must be free."

Principe slapped at his arms. "Impossible! They set us to sleep forever! That was mass murder. Do you expect us to forgive them for that?"

"Not to forgive," she said. "To withhold your revenge."

Principe sputtered, but the woman nodded, and after a moment, Eloquia did as well. "All right," he said. "But we will awaken the rest of our own cities—and then they will decide, ultimately, what to do with this criminal's people." He glowered at Kamakie.

Eos remained silent, pretending to think about the offer. She had been transferring power and nanotech to Kamakie ever since they had returned to the cell—at first, to give him some defenses in case the maximizers separated them or tried to threaten him as leverage. As they walked here, she had decided to do more, and now needed time to finish wafting the invisibly tiny threads of smart matter over to, and into, his body.

She made the ancient emote of taking a deep breath, then said, "If you let this man go, I will give you my—"

"*I have a question.*"

It was Kamakie. Arms crossed, he was calmly watching the maximizers, waiting for them to heed him. Eloquia turned to him. "Yes?" he said, obviously annoyed but equally obviously willing to be polite now that Eos was about to capitulate.

"We live our lives over and over, true?" At Eloquia's impatient nod, Kamakie rubbed his chin. "Yes, we have to, because over nearly infinite spans of time, all the particles of the universe must come back into the same configuration. Every single atom in our bodies is exactly where it was some impossible age ago, and behaving the same—and so on up to our cells, our neurons, our thoughts. If a different body had thoughts and experiences identical to mine throughout its entire life, wouldn't that other self just be . . . me?"

"Your servant seems ignorant of simple truths," said Principe. "He also doesn't seem to know he's interrupting you."

"We accept that we also experience other lives *almost* exactly like this one," Kamakie went on. "Some have just a few molecules out of place, tiny cascade differences in our neurotransmitters that cause us, just once in our lives, to make a different decision this time around. We also experience lives where the outside world diverges, even if only in the arrangement of the constellations or the frequency of the light on our skins. So, I have a question.

"When are the differences big enough that it's no longer me having the experience?"

"Enough!" Eloquia appealed to Eos. "Please. We need your decision."

"I have news," said Kamakie loudly. "Fresh news, about the Return."

No one in the chamber moved for a long moment. Eos sized up Kamakie. "That's why you were walking alone on the ice. Something's been learned about the cycles of eternity?"

Eloquia and the woman laughed, but the other two eyed one another uneasily. Eloquia dismissed the issue with a wave of his hand. "Oh, we know there've been experiments using instruments scattered over light years and taking millennia to complete. But what can they do other than refine the details of what we already know? Time is infinite, everything repeats, and—"

"—Not everything that can happen, will," said Kamakie. Then he took a step back, as if shocked at his own pronouncement.

Still only looking to Eos, he said, "We've been gathering data for thousands of years, true. But not in vain. We learned something.

"All the particles in the universe mix and recombine, and it's true that eventually all that's happened has to happen again."

"We know this," drawled Eloquia.

"But the universe has no memory to avoid repeating itself before it's run through *every* possible combination of events." Kamakie walked up to Eloquia, spread his feet on the cold stone and smiled. His shoulders were squared in a way that surprised Eos. "It's overwhelmingly likely that the sequence will start over long before it explores every possibility. In other words, not everything that could occur will occur. Not everything that can happen will happen."

Principe laughed and turned away. "So what?"

"*So*"—and now Kamakie rounded on Eos, like a prosecutor cross-examining a witness—"there is no past and future in which you make every choice you could today, Eos. This day may repeat across the ages, but you've never made *every* choice you could today, and you never will. And that means that whatever you decide to do now *matters*. It won't be canceled by its opposite in some future version of today."

Eloquia, Principe, and the other maximizers stood there, looking confused—and Eos was as well, for just a second. Then she understood and yelled, "Kamakie, run!"

He turned and sprinted for the entrance. "Get outside and look up!" she added; then Eos burst the confines of her human body, unreeling defensive and offensive systems as the maximizers' guards closed on her.

Light and noise hammered from the direction Kamakie had run. She couldn't follow him nor help anymore as the maximizers dove for cover, stray energies burst and evaporated their precious memorabilia, and the stone floor cracked and splintered beneath her.

Eos found Kamakie waiting for her when she stepped through the postern gate two days later. Several maximizer war machines lurked near him, but their weapons were powered down.

The hills were dark. Framing Kamakie's head was an infinite fog of stars in a transcendently black sky.

"They gave up," she said to him. "Surely, you knew they would have to?"

"Hello to you too, Eos." He stood, stretching. "Yes, I knew. Without your light, the world will freeze again. They can't live without you, and they know it." He gestured for her to walk with him; she fell in step, and he guided her to the right, up a harder slope than the one on which she'd dropped her doll. "They'll have to go back into hibernation. But now they know the truth—the real News. I hope we can wake them and give them another chance someday."

Kamakie clasped his gloved hands behind his back, looked down at the solid air beneath his boots. "Somehow, their weapons didn't affect me. I made it outside and I looked up," he said. "I stared into the sun—into you. I relayed a message then, didn't I? Because your light went off a few hours later, and it hasn't come back." She nodded. "Will it come on again?" She shrugged.

"I still haven't atoned," she said. "I still don't know how."

Despite the darkness, she could see his smile, in many small frequencies. "I know of a way."

They climbed in silence for a while, but when they had left the valley, she said, "Why were you out here alone? You came from one of the locksteps, but you awoke off schedule, didn't you? There are no cities awake on Sagitta; I would have seen them by their heat."

"My lockstep has another fifteen years before it wakes," he admitted. "If I was to make it to the meeting, I had to leave now."

"Meeting? In another lockstep? One that sleeps and wakes on a different schedule?" He nodded. "But if your city's not awake, neither is any other. Where's this lockstep?"

"It's not a city. Just a single ship. I was told it would be waiting in Ariosto Valles." He pointed. "Over there."

"Oh." She hesitated, stopped.

"Come with me," he said.

"I can't, if you're leaving Sagitta," she said. "Sagitta is my responsibility, my garden to tend. I still have to atone."

"You can do that by spreading the News." He started walking again, seemingly confident she would follow. "The fresh News, I mean. All you have to do is tell your Self, up there"—he pointed at the star-crowded sky—"and you'll have discharged your duty here. Your light will return to this world, and *you*"—he pointed at her human-shaped avatar—"will no longer be needed. Come with me and you can do far more than atone— far more than you could ever do here."

She hurried to catch up. "I don't understand."

"The News is that however vast the ring of time is, it's finite. Because it's finite, *we*"—he touched her shoulder—"can add to or subtract from the total amount of happiness in the universe. It's up to us. Now, me, I think the ring of time can contain more laughter than tears—but it's up to us to make sure that happens."

"How?"

"By spreading the News, of course!" He laughed. "The ship I'm joining, it's on a lockstep at a longer frequency than mine. Mine is 360/1—thirty years asleep for every month awake. That schedule lets us travel a light-year or so every 'month' of our time. Ours is a pretty big civilization, but it only spans a few dozen stars. But some of the first to hear this News sent messages to other locksteps, and together they decided to create a protocol for spreading the word. This protocol is called the Nests.

"We've set a second lockstep in motion. This one's frequency is 129,600/1: ten thousand years asleep for every month awake. A realtimer lives thirty years between awakenings of my lockstep, and I would experience thirty years between awakenings of this second lockstep. Its people will be able to travel five thousand light-years in one of their years. They can spread the News far.

"That lockstep will have a third within it, and there'll be a fourth in the third. The third sleeps two and a half million years at a time, the fourth thirty-one million. Their citizens will stride the galaxy, and the spaces between the galaxies, the way we travel between the planets. Their wakings will be synchronized with those beneath them, so communication can flow up and down from realtime to the most immortal. Together, they'll spread the News throughout the visible universe.

"The lockstep that sleeps thirty-one million years, we're calling the Maha-Yuga, or Magisterium Lockstep.

"I volunteered to join the Magisterium. Would you like to come along?"

Eos almost tripped. She tried to bluster a reply but then thought of the doll she'd cradled when she last walked these hills. She pictured herself as she and her sisters once had, as a mother casting her children forward in time. To what destiny? She'd believed there were no choices that mattered in that future, because all choices would be made, but in this moment she saw the alternative—a golden path all conscious beings could take.

Kamakie had been dead serious when he'd asked his question in the hibernaculum: how different would her future lives have to be for them to no longer be hers? Could it be she had lived all lives and would live them all again? In which case, even if she were completely selfish—*especially* if she were completely selfish—she must choose to maximize the happiness of every single one.

She felt weightless. She started to laugh. "I came to atone!" she said. "I wasn't expecting to be given a gift!"

Kamakie laughed too, in surprise as much as delight.

"Well, what are you waiting for?" she said, impatiently taking his hand and pulling him onward.

"We have lives to live."

ABOUT THE AUTHOR

KARL SCHROEDER (kschroeder.com) was born into a Mennonite community in Manitoba, Canada, in 1962. He started writing at age fourteen, following in the footsteps of A. E. van Vogt, who came from the same Mennonite community. He moved to Toronto in 1986 and became a founding member of SF Canada (he was president from 1996–97). He sold early stories to Canadian magazines, and his first novel, *The*

Claus Effect (with David Nickle) appeared in 1997. His first solo novel, *Ventus*, was published in 2000, and was followed by *Permanence* and *Lady of Mazes*. His most recent work includes the Virga series of science fiction novels (*Sun of Suns*, *Queen of Candesce*, *Pirate Sun*, *The Sunless Countries*, and *Ashes of Candesce*) and the YA space opera *Lockstep*. He also collaborated with Cory Doctorow on *The Complete Idiot's Guide to Writing Science Fiction*. Schroeder lives in East Toronto with his wife and daughter.

TOMORROW WHEN WE SEE THE SUN

A. MERC RUSTAD

I.

The last wolflord will be executed on the cusp of the new solar year.

II.

Wolflord (title): *nomadic, nameless survivors of destroyed warships; those who did not accept ritual immolation during the Decommission. No allegiance to the Principality; outlaws. The antiquated title is self-taken from the first deserter, whose name and memory were erased upon execution; precise origin unknown.*

Released from its stasis, Mere stretches and glides through the wide atrium wreathed in bionic roses and silk banners. It pauses at the gates that hang perpetually open on the Courts of Tranquility. The sensory matrix on the threshold purrs against its consciousness in greeting.

"What awaits this it?" Mere asks the threshold.

The last wolflord. A great victory.

Mere feels nothing at the announcement, as it should. It is not allowed emotion.

It parades to the pool, proud-arched spine and lifted jaw; autonomous machine-flesh granted scraps of self and mind.

(In the glued and stapled seams, it has painted its own awareness. A taste for Zhouderrian wines fermented in the aftermath of white dwarf stars; the poetry of Li Sin, disfavored master of nanite-barbed words; desire stacked like coiled DNA strands, a tower of cards; a voice etched from grave-silence and forgotten pauses between peace and war. It displays none of itself, for it has also learned fear: It can be taken apart and erased if it deviates from its scripted role.)

Mere crouches at the pool's lip. Once its function is complete, it will be returned to stasis. Mere dreads its inevitable sleep.

From this vantage, it surveys the Courts of Tranquility, the synaptic-like rainfall of light along the membranous domed ceiling, the living heartbeat of the tamed planet carved and grown to a million fine-tuned specifications and indulgences. And those within, oh yes, it has seen these courtiers often:

—nobles in redolent synth armor; generals and admirals decked in finest military dress; pilots, their faces replaced with the mindscreens of their ships—

—an eleven-souled sorcerer who drinks the breath of his favorite nemesis, their words twined together as they spar with tongue and gaze, neither ever ready to destroy the other (for then the fun would end)—

—the Gold Sun Lord, resplendent armored god, ensconced in a hover-throne that drifts about the Courts, omnipresent and untouchable—

And below, in the oblong pool where Mere has spent half of its conscious existence, the last wolflord is bound wrist and ankle, suspended in water as every ancillary world watches the feed. There will be no backup made of the wolflord's mind, no funerary rites in the Archives of Heaven. Treason unto the Principality is not suffered lightly.

The Arbiter of the Suns steps forward and lifts reedy, sulfur-scorched hands. Smoke-cured breath fills ordained words with harmonies and atonal bass-clef chords. "You are summoned here, dearly condemned . . ."

Mere unbends its body, muscle and ligament stretched along metal bones, and glides into the pool, water slicing to either side of its midriff. It cradles the disgraced wolflord's head in one splayed hand. The other, fingers knife-tipped, rests along the condemned's throat. Unseen, Mere spools neuron-thin tendrils into the base of the wolflord's spine and siphons away pain and fear.

The wolflord's body slackens in synthesized, unwanted calm. "Why do this?" the wolflord grinds out, words blocked by auditory and visual firewalls. None in the Courts of Tranquility will witness a criminal's last words.

By protocol, Mere is granted the same erasure. It could scream and curse, and no one would hear (except its keepers, silent beneath the pool and always watching). "It is civilized," Mere says with a mocking smile.

"No." The wolflord struggles to speak. "You. Why do you . . . obey, Mere . . ."

Mere has never heard its name, found upon waking when it was first brought online, spoken aloud. For the first time since it has served as executioner (sixteen hundred rotations), Mere wants an answer from the damned: "How do you know this it?"

The wolflord's eyelids droop with the sedative. "Loved you . . . once . . . I am so . . . sorry . . ."

". . . and thus the heavens are cleansed anew," says the Arbiter, and Mere cuts the last wolflord's throat.

Blood ribbons out, diluted and sucked clean into vents. The wolflord's spirit sinks as a glossy pebble to the pool's bed.

Mere glances up at the Arbiter's consorts that are ringed about the pool edge. Tattooed jawbones, bared of muscle and flesh, grin with engraved teeth; razored laughter cooks inside skinned throats.

"Where did you net the wolflord?" Mere asks.

They hum a response in chorus, each voice sculpted as a single, distinct, perfect note.

You shouldn't care for the dead.
A traitor on the rim of knownspace,
seeking paradise in madness.
Spoke of you, of others lost,
begged mercy for crimes
and forgiveness, never granted.

They tip eyeless heads down in regret. The Arbiter's consorts are hunters and bailiffs, as close to allies—never friends, never close—as Mere has. They bring it trinkets and bits of new poetry, synthesized tastings of wine, scents of uncharted galaxies and the sound of dying stars. In return, Mere slips the consorts filaments forged between its ribs to dull their unceasing pain.

(Sometimes, they share fragments of memory of who they were before they were exulted. Mere has trouble recalling what they have told it.)

Mere unwinds the neural threads from its fingertips, catching final memories and thought-imprints in illegal mods on its palms. It scythes its fingers in the water to wash away the blood.

With duty finished, the Arbiter glides away, flanked by consorts, to join the eleven-souled sorcerer at a table.

The wolflord's hair fans out in gray strands that brush and twine lifeless about Mere's wrist. Mere tilts its head, startled by the odd sensation, like it is choking. Is this grief? How can it grieve what it does not remember?

Mere is put back in stasis, where it dreams.

The keepers do not watch Mere sleep. So, it unwraps the last wolflord's stolen memories.

her hair smells of ruined worlds and clover soap
bring my conquests, she says, bring all of them and I will aid you
she whispers a string of coordinates, a planet once called Rebirth

each kiss nettles the tongue with microscopic treason, plague passed mouth to mouth
  call forth the Red Sun Lord, champion of the dead
  let us live again; let us rebuild; let us redeem ourselves

The rest: lost like unsanctioned souls brewed in a frosted glass kept chilled at zero Kelvin.

Mere aches, a phantom-physical sensation it cannot control.

There remains an early impression in its subconscious: on a barren world, a laboratory lined with glass suspension tanks, cold-filled with other bodies. Mere has no empirical evidence the recollection is its own. It was made, but by whom is unknown.

(It has no desire for a creator.)

Yet, the she with the plague kiss—it feels kinship for her, sharp, embossed on its awareness with sudden heat.

The Decommission (event): *as a measure of good faith upon the signing of the peace treaty between the Seven Sun Lords, each god decommissioned and executed one thousand of their most powerful warships. Each ship and its pilot self-destructed within an uninhabited system of choice and were granted honor in the eyes of the Seven Suns.*

Mere wakes without its keepers' bidding. It blinks back the protective film on its eyes and stares at the lid of its stasis pod. Odd. Mere presses its palm against the lid, and it retracts into the floor.

A she crouches outside, dressed in mirrorsilk armor, visor drawn over her face so all it sees is its own reflection. "Mere?" she says, synthesized voice low.

"You have acquired unauthorized access to this it," Mere says. "It is curious why."

The stasis chamber is empty. Unadorned red walls and its stasis pod in the center with a ring of security lights above. Mere notes the disabled alarms and the blinding virus chewing at the keepers' optic feeds.

The she flicks her visor up. Her eyes are quicksilver, liquid and bright—cybernetic implants that contrast space-dark skin. "I'm Century. I'm here to free you."

Mere is intrigued. No one has ever wished to free it, not even the Arbiter's consorts. "Why?"

"I made you," she says. The smell of the ancient laboratory is etched under her armor. "A crime I cannot undo. But we have no time. You have already been condemned for not reporting this security breach." Her lips twist in a bitter smile. "Do you want to live?"

Mere has no organic heart (it knows the rhythmic beat of muscle against bone, has read of it in lines of Li Sin's poetry), yet it still knows fear. It lost any choice when the she broke in.

"It will follow, then."

Century blurs down the maintenance halls, the invisible veins of the Courts, enhanced speed given by her armor. Mere lopes at her heels.

It processes data and sensation in microseconds:

—it is exile, a faulty machine to be unmade—

—this is no coincidence Century broke into the Courts of Tranquility, a feat deemed impossible by the Principality, only hours after the last wolflord died—

—it is *exhilarated*—

—what will it do now? Its purpose, courtly executioner, has been dismantled—

They slip beneath the cityskin to the spaceport. Vessels of all make and class dock in thousands of bays. Century stops before an eel-ship, coiled in jewel-skinned splendor. Its great eye-ports are open, and Century signals with a hand; the eel extends a proboscis lined with diamond mesh and graphene plates like a ramp. Century leads Mere into the eel's body.

Alarms klaxon in Mere's head—its escape is known.

Within the eel's retrofitted abdomen, synthetic tubes house the mechanics and computerized guts. Finery for living; oxygen filtration system and water recycling.

"Where will you take it?" Mere asks.

Century does not reply.

Mere crouches, toe-talons locked against the mesh floor panel. The she whispers to the eel-ship, and the great sinuous vessel unpeels itself from the port and scythes into vacuum.

III.

Olinara V (planet, former population: seventeen million): *once a thriving colony world settled early in the founding of the Principality, it was destroyed by the Gold Sun Lord when an escaped trinket-slave sought refuge in the Olinarain wilds. Olinara V is now classified as an uninhabitable world.*

Mere has never been off-world. It taps the gills of the eel-ship, which obliges and unfurls interior flaps of skin to reveal translucent, hardened outerflesh and a view of space.

This odd, unclassifiable sense of kinship with the dead has grown the farther from the Courts they travel—a need (honor-bound) to see the dead to proper rest so they might pass into one of the afterlives in paradise or purgatory, reinvention or rebirth. It has killed so many, it longs to redeem itself. The last wolflord gave it the key.

"Why did you free this it?" Mere asks.

"An old debt." Century grinds her teeth. "Once we're out of range of the Courts' sensors, I jettison you in a shuttle, wraith. You can make your own path."

Mere pets the eel-ship, grateful for the indulgence, and turns toward the she. "Take it to the Court of the Red Sun first."

"No," Century says.

"You *will*." Mere flexes its hands. "You forged this exile without consent. You owe this it."

Century whirls. The she has a plasgun at its jaw, muzzle pressed into soft tissue beneath its chin, and in turn, it rests its fingertips against the back of her neck. It looks down at her. The mirrorsilk burns into its skin, coiling up its wrist and burrowing toward bone.

"I can unmake you far easier than I made you, Mere."

"It can sever your brainstem through your armor with but a gentle pinch of its fingers."

Century scoffs. "We are both destruction incarnate. Perhaps this is a better end."

Mere does not think the she wishes to die; it does not. If it kills her, the eel-ship will never take it where it must go. "A truce." Mere lowers its arm, flesh chewed back to wire and metal skeleton, the knives bright. It will heal slowly. "It has a proposition."

Century holsters the gun. "Do you."

Mere extracts the last wolflord's memories, printed into a small holochip it saved for one of the Arbiter's consorts. "It is the wolflord who found Rebirth, is it not?"

Century's shoulders tighten. "That world was lost long ago."

Mere repeats the coordinates to her. Her expression remains inert. "It is what the wolflord remembered at death."

"Damn you." Century tips her head back and sighs. "I told him to forget."

Mere offers her the holochip. "Clearly."

Century doesn't accept. "We thought the Red Sun's presence would weaken the bindings of the consecrated pool. Once that happened, we could collect the soul seeds and bring them somewhere. Another planet. Give them proper rest. It was just a dream."

"'Dreams need not stay trapped in sleep alone,'" Mere says, quoting Li Sin. "Bring this it to the Red Sun Lord. We will rescue the dead."

Century raises her eyebrows. "Do you know how many security protocols

I hacked to get in 'unnoticed' the first time? I helped *build* the Courts." She snorts. "I constructed the pool. I built the door matrix. The Courts were supposed to be an end to the galaxy-spanning wars I fought and won. The Principality was supposed to bring peace, starting with the Decommission."

It tilts its head, watching the she sidelong. "You are old, then."

"I am," Century says with a bitter laugh. "But what's age any longer?"

"You do not believe this endeavor possible."

"No," Century says. "I don't. Not anymore."

Mere examines its healing arm, flesh reknitting. There is an ache in its ribs it cannot define. "At least bring it to the Red Sun. All the souls in the pool are there by its hand; it would see them to a better fate."

Century flinches, near-imperceptible.

But she speaks to the eel-ship, and they set course for a different court.

Blue Sun Lord (God): *one of the Seven Suns, everlasting and all-knowing rulers of the Principality Dwelling within the Hollow Systems, the Blue Sun Lord oversees the sanctified pool within the Courts of Tranquility; the Blue Sun Lord is a merciful and generous god* [search terminated]

The ship glides through a radiant nebula; the eel-ship's body glows as it absorbs radiation and shed filaments from the void, skin sluiced away from a progenitor star. This reminds Mere of Li Sin's collection, *Bound Infinity, Transcendent*. Mere has dabbled in poetry, played with bits of unattached verse:

> *Breathing in designer atmosphere / academic*
> *bloodsport*
> *Sip sorrow's martini / watch sequin-skinned guests*
> *sway and flow /*

Mere stumbles over further stanzas, uncertain. Does it possess its own creativity, its own words, or are they borrowed finery collected from too many other sources, pieces plucked from the dead?

Other space eels twine and dance in the ruins of gases and elements and carbons.

"Beautiful," Mere murmurs.

Century, tucked in a fold between the eel-ship's ribs, doesn't look up from her reading. "Anything can be beautiful. Even monsters."

Mere has never been praised for its aesthetic. "Will you tell it why it was made?"

Century sets aside the tablet. "I built you from the remains of my enemies. It was to be their eternal subjugation." Quieter: "I still regret it."

"It has heard," Mere says, "regret may be molded anew, if one chooses. This it will shape its own future once its duty is complete."

"And where will you go if you survive?" Century asks. "Any planet you linger on will suffer like Olinara V." Her jaw tightens. "I saw what befell that world. You can't escape forever."

Mere has no basis for argument. "What do you run from?"

Century's mouth thins into a line. "I should have left you, wraith."

Mere tilts its head. It is grateful, unexpectedly, that she converses with it, that she has not ejected it from the ship and let it drift into frozen death. "It would rather live briefly outside the Courts than forever in chains."

Century coughs, a strangled laugh. "Sweet mother of stars. You have no recollection, do you?"

"What should it recall?"

She reaches into a slit in her armor. "Here." The holochip rests heavy on her palm. "Your birth, if you want it."

Mere accepts.

Hundreds of glass pods, each cold-filled with bodies—her enemies, trophies, former friends betrayed. The wolflord stands beside her (young, war-scarred, shipless). The wolflord has always remained loyal to Century, and she has taken the wolflord under her protection so the former pilot will not be discovered and executed.

"Must you do this?" the wolflord whispers.

She has taken pieces of each enemy, mind or flesh or bone or blood or gene, and she has built a sexless bipedal wraith from her conquests. It stands taller than she, lithe deadly machineflesh, and she gives it her organic eyes last of all, cased in cybernetic implants.

"It is a mere tool," she says, fondness in her tone.

The wolflord sighs. "That is all we are to you."

She turns, head tipped in curiosity. "Would you be more?"

Instead of answering, the wolflord nods to the many glass pods. "And the remains?"

"The wraith will execute them," she says. "In doing so, it will become mine alone, unburdened from its former selves."

The wolflord flinches.

She presses her palm against the wraith's chest, igniting its processors and sparking its lifeforce siphoned from her dearest enemy. The wraith opens its—her—eyes.

"Wraith," she says. "I have made you for one purpose."

It blinks several times, then bows.

"It will serve in the Courts of Tranquility," she says to the wolflord. "A celebration of our new age of peace."

The wolflord's gaze meets the wraith's, but the wolflord looks away in shame.

(There is a subfile tucked inside that is not the she's. The wolflord planted it, imprinted with a name: Kitshan Zu.

In the months between its awakening and the completion of the Courts of Tranquility:

"They will erase this," the wolflord says, hand at rest so gentle on Mere's cheek. "They won't let you have what's yours. Not memory nor self.

Not . . ." The wolflord swallows. "I have to go. Century has work I must finish in her name."

Mere blinks, chalk-gray skin furrowed between its cybernetic eyes. "I wish to go with you, Kitshan."

The wolflord kisses Mere, lips rough and coarse and so familiar. "If I could steal you, Mere, I would. I promise you one thing—I will come back for you. When I learn how to free you, I will come back."

"Then I will wait," Mere says, and pulls the wolflord close one last time.)

Mere shudders as the memory knits into its own consciousness, blended with so many dreams of the dead.

A fragment, unburied: the wolflord was most often a he, and sometimes not, and always kept his name. Kitshan.

Mere wishes it had memories of its own to braid into a lost narrative in which it was happy with him, in which they shared passion and laughter and sorrow. This is like its favorite of Li Sin's sonnets, where the poet laments falling through a time vortex and breaking the time stream by trying to reclaim lost love.

"I watched the feeds," Century says. Outside the ship, great gaseous whales converge in a celestial pod, frequency-song caressing the hull and sides. "I saw his capture. I was too far away to get to the Courts before . . ." A crisp, vicious headshake. "I would have spared you that, if I could grant you but one mercy."

Mere has nothing to say to the she.

IV.

Rebirth (world): *there is no such designated planet in the Principality archives. Further searches will result in disciplinary measures.*

The Court of the Red Sun is bones and dusk, burned into a cold shell of its former glory.

The eel-ship glides into membranous ports that ring the station. Heptagonal, forged from old warships and dead stars, lit and powered within by the Red Sun Lord's essence.

Century sits motionless in the cockpit. "You better hurry. The other Suns will find you. Always, they will find you."

Mere is aware. The Courts call to its blood; until it finds a way to unlock its own molecular leash from its keepers' hold, it must stay a dozen steps ahead. But first, it must survive an audience with the Red Sun, the Death of Endless Worlds.

Mere enters the airlock. Spindle-legged drones bow and guide it through red-splashed corridors to the throne room of the Red Sun Lord.

A beautiful spider-prince, chitin-skinned humanoid with four delicate legs protruding from the spine like desiccated wings, sits at the Red Sun's left, a shadow-garbed concubine. Eight jewel-rimmed eyes watch under thick lashes. "Those beholden to the Courts of Tranquility are seldom welcome, wraith."

Mere bows. "It seeks aid for the lord's chosen."

The spider-prince leans close, a spine-leg lightly brushing the Red Sun's helmet. The visor rises, and the Red Sun's gaze sears into Mere's flesh.

Mere folds itself in supplication, its back blistering. It unbends an arm, lifts a palm, and shows the holochip record of the wolflord's execution. "It asks the lord to listen." Pain sinks deeper—it holds its ground and does not scream. "The lord has claim to the dead," Mere says, "and if the lord will come to assert that claim, this it will retrieve the souls of the lost and give them peace."

The heat relents as the Red Sun drops the helmet visor. Mere shivers as its cells begin repair, and the coolness of the dim throne room sinks into its burned flesh.

"May this one eat the wraith?" the spider-prince purrs.

Mere waits, its body taut.

The Red Sun stretches out a hand, and with a sigh, the spider-prince rises and sweeps forward. He takes the chip from Mere's palm and inserts it into a port in his ribs.

"A pity," the spider-prince murmurs, with a longing glance at Mere. "I am *starving*."

"Perhaps another time," Mere says. It listened well to courtly wit and challenge. It has read much of Li Sin's political treatise, curated by the poet's ship, *Vector Bearing Light*. "It might poison you in turn."

The spider-prince smiles, appreciative. The projection blossoms outward, slow like congealed blood, and the image of the last wolflord stands before the Red Sun.

fleeing the Arbiter's consorts on a far-flung world, injured
looking up at the sky, begging
the last wolflord is bound in the pool, throat cut

The Red Sun's armored form stiffens, fists clenched on the starlight throne. "And why should I not unmake you for this crime, wraith? The last of my disciples, no more. Why did I feel nothing . . ."

The spider-prince slinks back to the Red Sun's side and strokes the god's armored shoulders, soothing. "The Courts of Tranquility are shielded, my liege-love."

The Sun Lords are cosmic bodies reshaped into compressed armored shells after a treaty two millennia ago. They have never ceased being enemies. Six rule the Principality, while the Red Sun Lord, who was always death, broods alone in the outer reaches of dominion.

Mere continues: "It has defied the Sun Lords of Tranquility to come and beg for vengeance. It once cared for the dead and does not wish to obey its masters."

"And what," says the Red Sun, "would you do with the souls, wraithling?"

"It knows of a world far outside the Principality where they will be safe: Rebirth."

The spider-prince taps his long, graceful fingers against his chin. "Rumors do exist among the lost of such a world, my love."

The Red Sun stands. Mere flattens itself to the floor.

"Come," says the Death of Endless Worlds. "I will return to the Courts of Tranquility."

Wraith (object): *an organic drone (technology outdated and now forbidden by the Principality) constructed from pieces of other organics and androids. Wraiths are non-sentient and possess no soul. The majority of wraiths were created before the Treaty of the Seven Suns as shock troops built from the dead.*

The Red Sun arrives in a ship built from bones of ancient solar chelonians and no port dares refuse it entry. The Death of Endless Worlds burns footprints into the halls. Mere follows, never stepping in ash.

"You'll have but a few seconds once inside," Century told it while the eel-ship rode beside the Red Sun's vessel. "If you're caught again, nothing will save you."

Since when has it been caught before?

Soundless, the Red Sun strides into the Courts of Tranquility. The smell of emptiness, the dark between the stars, clings to scarlet and black-scaled armor. Unease writhes through the courtiers, fermenting into panic.

"You dare?" The Gold Sun Lord steps down from the hover-throne and cuts through the skittering courtiers, armor brightening. "And you bring this *thing* with you?"

Mere spreads its hands in mock supplication from where it stands on the threshold matrix.

"You break every law by coming here," says the Gold Sun.

"Except one." The Red Sun extends a fist toward the pool. "I have a right to the dead."

"No," says the Gold Sun. "Not anymore."

Gold Sun and Red Sun raise non-corporeal blades to each other in silent duel.

You should run, murmurs the threshold.

Chaos blossoms.

Mere dives into the pool. It knows every soul pebble, so it scoops a hundred seventeen into its abdomen pouch. The others are already rotted—celestial molecules broken down from the inside, wrapped in distended film, which the slightest disturbance will break and spill out only dust. It cannot save them all.

It knifes through the water and catches the wolflord's soul last.

Mere senses the keepers watching, cold optics drifting in amniotic fluids behind the pool's walls. Sudden anger sparks in Mere. It slams a hand into the tiled side. Cracks web around the impact. Again, Mere strikes. Its hand sinks through insulated glass and it snatches one of the keepers: an optic node attached to sensory cables.

Alarms ricochet among the keepers, but Mere holds tight. It bounds from the pool.

The eleven-souled sorcerer confronts it, wreathed in iridescent shadow. "Stand down, wraithling," he says, thin lips curled mirthless.

Mere coils muscle and hydraulics in its legs and leaps, toe-claws bared. It cuts through the sorcerer's shadow shields and ducks away from his grasp. It kicks the sorcerer in the chest with bone-shattering force. The sorcerer falls back.

Automated defense drones circle overhead. Exhilarated, Mere sprints toward the door matrix, letting the Red Sun's wrath deflect its pursuers.

Good luck, murmurs the threshold, and Mere smiles.

This time, it runs through the upper halls of the Courts: past luxury holo suites and theaters, gardens and feast halls, over bridges that span crystalline waterfalls and floating glass spheres filled with lovers and voyeurs alike. It crosses into the industrial sectors, locks bypassed by

Century's nanite snakes, which slither through the walls as fast as it runs.

And then, once more, the spaceport. Mere sprints down the wide central platform toward freedom.

Four mammoth crustacean guards—crab-bodied, armored, spotted in hundreds of eyes—unwind from the walls and mesh themselves between Mere and the eel-ship. Mere springs up, spotting niches in armor, planes of body and joint it can use to climb and evade. It has no *time* to fight.

A fifth crustacean guard appears behind it and hammers a claw into it midair.

The blow shatters Mere's arm and rips open its side. Its body is thrown halfway across the platform, ribs crushed. Mere curls in on itself to protect its belly and rolls. A sixth crustacean guard circles behind and seizes Mere in great pincers. It twists, hissing, a single breath between it and being decapitated through the midriff.

"Stand down." The voice resounds with such weight and power, Mere mistakes it for one of the Sun Lords. The crustacean guard freezes. "Know my voice, for I am the Unmaker of Worlds."

The others hesitate. Mere lifts its chin, orienting itself on the voice.

Century stands on the platform, wreathed in a film of ultraviolet light. It projects from her skin, her teeth, her voice.

"The wraith is mine." Century extends a hand, commanding. "Give it to me, now, unharmed. Disobey my word and I shall rain destruction upon your people until there is naught but the trembling memory of *pain* in the heavens."

Gently, the crustacean guard sets Mere down. The others back away, submissive. Century does not move.

Mere limps toward her, past her, and into the ship. She follows, but the crustacean guards do not. Mere collapses inside.

The eel-ship twists and streaks from the port, chased this time by droneships beholden to the Six Suns: faceless pilots uprooted and loosed once more.

"We will lose them in subspace," Century says, calm. "If not for long."

Mere apologizes to the ship for spattering its blood on the floor as it cradles its side. It takes a slow breath, the crunch of bone rearranging in its torso and arm familiar. "You are a Sun Lord," it says at last.

Century rolls her shoulders. "Once, I was the Violet Sun. We took new bodies, it's true, but they change, they weaken. Anything that lives can die."

Mere strokes its undamaged hand along its abdomen; its cargo remains undamaged. It wonders what its soul might look like, culled in a pebble beneath cold water. If it was born from the fractured pieces of the Principality's enemies, what will its existence reflect in death? It is autonomous, but it is still more machine than organic, and there are no simple answers in the theologies or heresies it has skimmed.

It unfurls its broken fingers with its other hand and examines the keeper it stole. Inside the optic, thousands of compressed recordings tagged *wraith_construct*.

"Don't," Century says, but makes no move to stop it. "You'll only hurt yourself, Mere."

Mere downloads the recordings.

V.

A crustacean guard drags Mere's limp body from the surgical pods, where it was once more tested for pain tolerance (high) and fitted with a restraint collar beneath its throat-skin so it will not escape again (*fourth time*, the keepers say, disapproving).

"Why do you run?" the guard asks as Mere's eyes open. "There is nowhere to go. Do you like being hurt?"

Mere hisses at the guard, always the one to find it. "Why do you *stay*?"

"There is no choice," says the guard, quiet.

"I will *make* choice," Mere says.

The wraith is put in stasis.

Dozens of near-identical recordings:

Mere fulfills its duty as executioner.

It is taken to a containment chamber of sterile walls and faceless technicians. Its memory is selectively culled so it no longer remembers the details of the ones it has killed.

Sometimes, the wraith fights. Dead technicians are easy to replace.

But even technology fails. Mere takes advantage of the blocks in the feeds over the pool and slices open its arm to write on its bones; the flesh glues together before the technicians focus the light instruments into its head.

(The keepers hum interest to each other: *Why does the wraith care about the names of the dead? Where is the fault in its programming?*)

The keepers cannot find the anomaly.

It has not attempted to flee in two cycles, so it is given privileges and allowed to wander the cityskin. It seeks out the Arbiter's consorts, confined in luxury and pain. Zarrow and Jhijen, the newest consorts who still keep hold of their names, welcome Mere. It basks in attention and conversation. Zarrow teaches it laughter. Jhijen invites desire; Mere can experience pleasure as much as pain. Mere could have picked from any number of genders, but it does not have an interest in the choices, so it remains neutral, comfortable with its pronouns. Jhijen and Zarrow always respect its choice, as it does theirs, when their genders change like the fluid motions of a dance.

(*Mere thinks,* the keepers note. *It thinks of the consorts as* friend.)

There is no timestamp to show when Zarrow and Jhijen disappeared.

The she bound in the pool looks like Zarrow.

"Who are you?" Mere whispers.

". . . and thus the heavens are cleansed anew," says the Arbiter.

Mere does not kill the she.

The keepers hastily feed a loop of crafted images into the broadcast so the universe watching will never know the wraith's hesitation. The Courts of Tranquility see what is expected; polite applause follows.

Obey, the keepers send to its processor.

Mere shakes its head, snips the fibrous chains, and lifts the she from the water. "It will not kill this one. The she has committed no crime."

The she that looks like Zarrow brushes her fingers along its cheek. "I'll remember you."

The Arbiter's eyes burn with fury. "The she is an insurgent who disobeys the Six Suns."

Mere laughs at the Arbiter. "So do I."

The restraint collar activates and crumples Mere on the edge of the pool. The consorts lift the she's shallow-breath body and carry her off; her true death will be private. Mere cannot stop it.

Mere hisses in pain as the Arbiter watches. It lifts its arm, shaking, and digs its knife-fingers into its throat. Blood and fluids drip into the pool as Mere cuts out the collar piece by piece.

The Arbiter backs away, a step shy of haste.

Mere's body slides over the side, into the water. It floats there as its skin regrows and the crustacean guards come to drag it away.

All the Arbiter's consorts are replaced and the wraith's privileges are revoked. The keepers implant a block in its neural protocols that will never allow Mere to speak as an "I" again.

In its stasis chamber, Mere scrapes sharp fingers against the wall, which throbs and erases each mark; still Mere tries to carve the names of the dead, transcribe them from its raw bones before the keepers or the security drones stop it.

VI.

Mere crushes the remains of the keeper's optic and stands, shivering. There are many, many more files. It deletes them.

It looks at Century.

Century rubs beneath her quicksilver eyes. "When I gave you to the Blue Sun Lord, a final gift to seal our peace treaty, I couldn't take you back." She turns away. "The wolflord was working on a way to unbind you. I refused. I do not wish to see war again."

Mere wipes the keeper's fluids from its hands. Bones have mended and the eel-ship has washed away the blood on the floor. "How soon before we are found?"

She shrugs. "We will find Rebirth first. We will finish this."

After it asks and receives permission from the ship, Mere etches all the names of the dead into the eel's rib bones. The ship promises to remember them.

Mere murmurs its thanks.

And you? the ship asks. *What would you like to be remembered as?*

Mere hesitates. Of the possibilities it might choose from, it does not want to be: *executioner, killer, weapon.* But what else does it deserve?

"A wraith."

Mere does not know what else it should say.

VII.

Li Sin (revolutionary): *a neutrois poet whose work is known for biting wit, political critique, and transcendent beauty. No records can be found on Li Sin's birthplace or their death. The poet stopped writing and disappeared after challenging the Gray Sun Lord in the Year of Unpraised Night 2984; the Gray Sun slumbers in the Arora Nebula, undisturbed and unresponsive since.*

The ship drops from subspace over planetary designation Z1-479-X: Rebirth.

Mere peers through the ship's gills at the blue-green-white sphere. It is devoid of cityskin; no metal-glass veins or infrastructure rising to the sky. Mere has never seen a world like this.

"I never thought I would see it again," Century says. Her voice catches like skin on a metal burr. "Come."

Mere says goodbye to the ship.

Farewell, friend, says the eel-ship.

They take a shuttle with two life-pods down to the surface.

Kitshan Zu (warship pilot): *Zu's ship,* Forever Brightness of the Sun, *was killed in battle and disconnected its pilot prior to its destruction. Zu was comatose in an Olinara V field hospital until his disappearance following the visitation of the Violet Sun a cycle later. The ex-pilot's whereabouts and fate are unknown.*

The night sky froths with clouds. Mere marvels at the prickly moss webbing the stony ground and the kiss of damp air against its body. This world is unshaped and wild, virile with flora and fauna it does not recognize from the Principality's records. It has never seen so much uncultivated wilderness, even in holos. Field and forest pass, and still the map leads Century forward.

They landed in a dry canyon and followed the she's implanted map.

They find a river, unsanctified and alive, bubbling past without notice. Mere stands transfixed. It wants to touch the water's delicate skin but does not feel worthy.

This world cannot know its presence long. Mere yearns to stay, to wander the wonders it has only glimpsed on this planet. But it is a taint, a cultured, weaponized stain from the Principality, and it does not belong. It will take the shuttle and let the Arbiter chase it to the universe's birthing place, so long as no harm comes to this world or any other.

"Here," Century calls. In a clearing ringed in living walls of flowers, Century stands motionless in raw, rich soil. "Can you feel it?"

Mere shuts its eyes and breathes in. Its skin and circuitry hum with power. "What is it?"

"Life. Potential." A sigh. "The world welcomes us all. I remember . . . I remember. I was born here. That is how I know it, why it haunts my bones."

Mere tilts its head. "What now?"

"Give the ones we carry rest. Perhaps they too will be reborn. Our part is done."

Mere slits its abdomen pouch and lets the pebbled souls fall loose into the ground. The earth shifts and closes gently over each one.

Energy it cannot name loops through Mere—the world's fingers caressing its mind.

BE WELL.

Wordless, an impression sweeps through Mere: the dawn kissing the earth, the souls wrapped in soil released from their pebbled shells crafted by the pool. When the sun rises, all will be complete. The dead will find their afterlives or their rebirth.

Century removes her armor piece by piece and runs her fingers along her scarred scalp. "Will you kill me now, wraith? That is your purpose. It is . . . what I deserve."

Mere has never been given *choice*. It has seen the wolflord to rest. What further purpose must it serve?

It tallies what it would do if freed: seek out the funerary holo of Li Sin and pay homage; sip wine on a far-flung world where identity is unnecessary; learn to dance without downloading precise diagrams of movement; travel the stars; write poems of its own; see wonders; live. And it would remember.

Mere retracts its knife-tips into fingerbones. "You gave it its freedom. It returns the grace. Do as you will."

Century dips her chin, military acknowledgment. "Gratitude, Mere."

Mere lifts its head, elated. If it can show mercy, it can do so much more.

Century smiles at Mere. "I will sleep, as I've not done in so long. When I wake . . . we'll see. Farewell."

"Farewell," Mere says to its maker, and lopes toward the ship.

It is *free*.

In the canyon gullet, the repulsors of dropships thrum. Mere slows, dry earth cracking beneath its feet. The shuttle is visible at the end of the ravine, caked in reentry burns and windblown dust.

The air brings the sharp scent of bloodied and oiled mechanics. Mere's sensors link with other semi-biologicals.

The mercury-veined butchers, stained silver and red, squat in single-file rank along the canyon's lip, sores popped from necrotic skin. Beneath the light-bent holoprojectors, the butchers' forms are true: fragmented drones from the Gold Sun and the Blue Sun, vessels programmed with tireless efficiency.

The Sun Lords have found Mere.

But these are no hollowed shells. Mere sees the frightened eyes of armor-bound clones (of the Arbiter's consorts, as they were before they were exulted—Zarrow is there, and so is Jhijen) unmasked behind targeting arrays. It knows each one of them, has shared memory and dreams with them. Once (so long ago) it dared think of them as *friend*.

Mere stands frozen between the butcher-clones and Century, the wolflord, and all the seeded. In a microsecond, realization:

—no longer must Mere kill—

—the seeded need but an hour more, until the sun rises and wakens new life—

—weaponized bones, detonator heart, poison blood: Mere can unmake all the Sun Lords' drones, dismantle and slaughter until all that remains is gore-soaked earth, christen the seeded with the promise of eternal war, mark Rebirth for a fate shared by Olinara V—

—Mere wants to *live*—

The drones have come only for Mere, the Blue Sun's disobedient trinket. Once the mission is complete, this world will be a forgotten sanctuary once more.

Mere steps forward as the butcher-drones approach. It will fight them, but not to win. The Suns will witness its desperation and be satisfied with its death. It will not be brought back to the Courts of Tranquility. It will remember.

This is its chosen purpose and its choice: to save the ones it can.

The butcher-drones attack. Mere lets them come.

It composes a final a poem, and though the last wolflord will never know, Mere dedicates the words to Kitshan.

> *Your eyes, grace-touched / forever refuge*
> *We will live together*
> *Tomorrow / when we see the sun.*

ABOUT THE AUTHOR

A. MERC RUSTAD is a queer non-binary writer and filmmaker who lives in the Midwest United States. Favorite things include: robots, dinosaurs, monsters, and tea. Their stories have appeared in *Lightspeed*, *Fireside*, *Apex*, *Uncanny*, *Escape Pod*, *Shimmer*, *Cicada*, *Best American Science Fiction and Fantasy*, and other fine venues. Merc likes to play video games, watch movies, read comics, and wear awesome hats. You can find Merc on Twitter @Merc_Rustad or their website: amercrustad.com. Their debut short story collection, *So You Want to Be a Robot*, is forthcoming from Lethe Press in May 2017.

BRING THE KIDS AND REVISIT THE PAST AT THE TRAVELING RETRO FUNFAIR!

SEANAN MCGUIRE

According to the scientists and engineers who came up with them, Dyson spheres are marvels in every sense of the word. They're too big to construct anywhere but deep space, forming, one piece at a time, around their gravity generator hearts. The really big ones are built like pearls, layer by layer, each new shell constructed partially from the dismembered remains of the last. They can end up as large as a gas giant, eternally cascading habitats for mankind to occupy as we make our wild rush across the universe, claiming worlds everywhere we go, even if we have to build them for ourselves.

According to me and mine, Dyson spheres are a pain in the ass. They don't have the natural advantages of real planets—no grass, no sunlight, no features that weren't planned and planted by the arrogantly careful hand of humanity. So they turn inward, creating populations who live in their own heads, creating virtual paradises to keep themselves amused.

Need proof?

There is not a single Dyson sphere with its own real-time amusement park. Loads of virtual parks—the last census put it at one park for every three citizens—but nothing made of metal and sweat and the sound of screaming. Nothing with a midway. Nothing *real*. The people who live in the spheres don't care about real anymore. They care about the next way station, the next horizon, and the world around them is more an inconvenience than anything else.

That's where the people like me and my crew come in. We're in the business of peddling dreams to people who might otherwise forget about them. Somebody has to.

Might as well be us.

"Is it broken?"

"Yes."

"Hit it."

"Violence never solves anything."

I folded my arms. "Violence solved the problem we were having with the booster engine last week. I whacked it six times with a spanner and it came right back on line."

"And please, I beg, don't mistake my lack of enthusiasm for your abuse of our ship for anything less than abject horror at the fact that once—just once—your fondness for percussive maintenance bore fruit." Doc emerged from beneath the engine feet-first, the multi-legged platform beneath him shuffling safely clear of anything he could hit his head on before he sat up. As usual, he had bows tied in his beard, although these were slick plastic, in deference to the engine's tendency to drip. "That said, the fact that it worked once doesn't mean it's going to work again. Ever. It *certainly* won't work on our gravity generator. Which is, in case you had forgotten, the thing that generates gravity. Do you need me to explain what gravity does?"

"Gravity sucks," I grumbled, not unfolding my arms. "What's it going to take to fix?"

"A new generator core. One that hasn't been hit with a spanner. I'd guess the damage at somewhere around five thousand."

I choked on my own spit. "Five *thousand*?" I demanded, unfolding my arms to make it easier to gesture wildly at the threadbare engine room around us. Everything that could be patched had long since *been* patched, along with some things that regulations said *couldn't* be patched. Half the floor was titanium scavenged from a wreck we'd passed out near Alowvin, and all the machinery bore the marks of my infamous percussive maintenance. Sometimes, that was the only way to get the engine to limp to the next stop with an actual mechanic. Doc might hate the fact that I thought violence was the solution to all problems big and small, but eventually he was going to have to accept the fact that we were a small entertainment ship, and we didn't have a live-in mechanic. If hitting things got us where we were supposed to be going, then I was going to keep right on hitting them.

"That's a conservative estimate."

"*Five* thousand."

"It would have been considerably lower if you had listened when I told you the generator needed repairs six months ago."

"*Five thousand.*"

"We might have been able to get the problem fixed for as little as four. Maybe even three-five, if we'd been able to find a sympathetic mechanic who didn't know us."

"That's not *lower*, Doc! That's still more money than we saw last year! There has to be another way."

Now it was his time to fold his arms and look at me gravely, brows drawing tight as he frowned. "We could sell some of the older entertainments. There's little demand for them on the circuit, but there are always collectors—"

"We'd never be able to buy them back. Any reduction to the collection is a permanent reduction to the show. You know that."

"If we can't fly, there *is* no show, Nora." Doc's frown faded, replaced by a look of profound sympathy. "You have to decide which is worse: losing one of the puppet shows or game boxes, or shutting the whole thing down and going town. We can always do that."

"No, we can't. My father would come back from the dead just to slap me in the head if I let that happen." There's no fate more terrible than "going town"—losing the sky and the freedom to set my schedule to the show, rather than setting my life to someone else's tempo.

"You have to choose, Nora. One machine, or the whole gig. You don't get to have them both." Doc shook his head. "I can't choose for you, and you can't smack the bill with a spanner. Choose."

I took a deep breath.

I chose.

I walked the streets of the Dyson sphere with my hands jammed into my pockets and my eyes turned toward the smooth metal walkway, not letting myself look up/down toward the gravity generator that spun at the center of the sky, sun and core all at the same time. If gravity had just been sugar, something I could borrow a cup of and get us back into space . . .

"If wishes were horses, then beggars would ride," I muttered, earning myself bewildered looks from several of the people who walked around me. I ignored them, checking my location on the tracker under the skin of my wrist. It glowed a steady white. I was nearing my destination.

Finding a buyer for an antique video game console on a Dyson sphere isn't hard. There are a lot of people in the galaxy with a thing for old Earth collectables, and working machines—even machines as simple as an arcade box, with its two-button and joystick interface—are rare. The hard part is making sure that the buyer gives a damn about what they're getting and isn't planning to, say, gut the console and turn it into an avant-garde terrarium for raising Martian lichen. (Something similar actually happened to a Sugar Rush box sold by one of the other circuit arcades. Full system, driving chairs and all, and some hipster star-fucker on a Dyson near Betelgeuse took the whole thing apart, filled it with live cockroaches, and called it an "art installation." All the king's horses and all the king's men couldn't put that box together again. It was really a shame when his gallery "accidentally" burnt down in the middle of the local sleep cycle. Yeah. A shame.)

Those of us who still work the entertainment circuits pass the names of the collectors around like the rarest of secrets. These are the people who will keep our treasures alive after the rest of the galaxy has forgotten the word "arcade" completely, consigning it to the virtual graveyard where all outmoded technology is doomed to go.

My wrist flashed white as my steps finally brought me to the address we had on file for the local collector, a Professor Whitman, who had a thing for the early VR RPGs. People used to plug in and believe that what they were experiencing was full-immersion, even though it was barely tactile, with no olfactory or empathic feedback. People were weird in the before. I may surround myself with antiques, but I know how lucky I am to live in the now.

I reached for the bell. The door burst open, and a cloud of red hair came flying at me, resolving into a pale, freckled woman in an old-fashioned jacket and trousers. She grabbed my arm as she whipped past, shouting, "Rona! *Run!*"

Six guards in the colors of the local constabulary were hot on her tail, each holding a stunner shiny enough to have been crafted from vat-gen diamond, and probably lethal enough to be worth it. Even though she wasn't shouting my name, she didn't have to tell me twice: I turned on my heel and let her pull me with her as she ran, using her momentum to accelerate my own. By the time I realized she was running for the nearest rail, it was too late for me to do anything but trust her and jump.

My last thought before we tore through the gravity threshold and began plummeting toward the center of the sphere was *Why did she call me by my sister's name?*

Gravity is funny inside the Dyson spheres—or, as Doc likes to put it, gravity is *indecisive*. With a generator as big as the one that pulls all the metal plates and clever engineering tricks inward, it would be reasonable to expect everyone to walk in a planetary alignment, feet toward the core, heads toward the stars. But the spheres don't work that way. People walk on the shell of the sphere, feet pressed against the thin metal walls that keep them safe from the vacuum, heads toward the gravity well that is their artificial sun. I don't understand the science behind it all, and honestly, I don't care. The science works, the science is kind enough not to mash us all into pudding or send us spiraling out to a gruesome, decompressed end, and that makes the science good enough for me.

Once we had pushed through the outer edge of the gravity bubble, we fell for about a hundred feet before the gravity generator realized that it had made a mistake and was on the verge of consuming a resident. We were then shunted abruptly and violently aside, spinning hard in a direction that didn't really have a name—not with us in freefall—until the bubble caught us again, and we fell, hard, onto another catwalk.

The redhead was on her feet in an instant, her hand clamped down on mine until I could feel the bones bend. "Rona, come *on*! We need to get to your ship!"

"Look, lady, that's about enough." There were no guards in sight. That didn't mean much on a Dyson sphere—there were always guards close enough to reach us in under five minutes—but it meant I had enough time to wrench my hand out of the stranger's grasp and give her my very best stink-eye. "I don't know what your deal is, and I don't know why you're about to be massively under arrest, but I'm not Rona, and you just pulled me away from a very important business deal. So, why don't you go ahead and run for your life, and let me trudge back across the sphere to meet with Professor Whitman?"

"But I'm Professor Whitman," said the redhead, sounding bewildered. Then she shook her head and stiffened, spine straightening. "And what do you mean, you're not Rona? Of course you're Rona. Don't be silly; this isn't the time. We need to move. We need to—"

"Get to the ship, yeah, you already said that," I said. "Problem: I do not have Rona's ship. I have *my* ship. My ship is not designed for smuggling. My ship is a traveling arcade and funfair. So, unless whatever you're running from can be solved with Skee-Ball, you're screwed, all right, Professor?"

Professor Whitman blinked slowly, staring at me. Then, in a faintly dazed tone, she said, "The freckle on your left eyelid is missing. You're *not* Rona."

"Nope."

"You're *Nora*."

"Right. Now you're getting with the program."

"Oh, this is not good; this is not good *at all*." Professor Whitman began pacing, burying her hands in that astonishing cloud of hair and tugging lightly, like the pain would somehow stimulate her brain into shifting functions. "You're supposed to be Rona. All the biometric sensors on the Sphere triggered when you came into range, because—"

"She's my clone, which means we're going to trigger the same biometric alerts." Technically, she wasn't *my* clone: technically, we were clone-sisters, generated from the same batch of tissue, along with eight others, all based on a late 2200s starlet with a fondness for licensing her genome. Nona Raquel Nanson, star of film, television, and several thousand spinoffs since her death had unlocked her will and granted full license of her DNA to the clone farms. If humanity ever hit a genetic bottleneck, it was going to be because there were too many little Nona-Rs running around, muddying up the gene pool.

Professor Whitman stared at me in open-mouthed dismay. "She told me you were nowhere near this sector. She said *none* of her clones were anywhere near this sector."

"She lied. She's a grifter. That's what they do. They bend the truth until they can tie it in a pretty bow, and then they put it around the necks of their marks, as a warning to the rest of us. This is my loop. Now, I'm sorry, but I really need to get out of here before the guard catches up with you, and whatever the hell it is you've let my shiftless sister talk you into."

Professor Whitman's mouth shut with a snap. She straightened. "You have a ship."

"Haven't figured out how to pull off spaceflight without one."

"Excellent." Her right hand moved, and she was suddenly holding a sleek, elegant pistol, the sort of thing that academics buy because they think it looks nonthreatening. Like that changes the part where it's a weapon. Like that makes a damn bit of difference.

I put my hands up, palms out. "Look, lady, I ain't my sister. Whatever fancy dreams she's planted in your head, I am *not* the girl to fulfill them. I run a *funfair*." Cotton candy, popcorn, nostalgia, and a faulty gravity generator: that was my world. Not this . . . whatever the hell it was.

"Right now, I don't care," she said coolly. "You have a ship. I require a ship. The guards may not be willing to fling themselves into the void for the sake of apprehending one academic, but they're coming, and we're going."

"You can't operate my ship without me."

"I have Rona's genecode. I can operate anything that's keyed to you."

I stopped myself before I could say anything else that I might regret later, and forced myself to look at her. There's no faking that level of desperation. Her eyes were wild, and her hand was shaking as she held the pistol on me. She didn't want to do this. Something—Rona—had convinced her that she didn't have another option.

I've been cleaning up my sister's messes since we were decanted. Professor Whitman was right about one thing: Rona's genecode would unlock my ship. But she was making an assumption that was going to bite her in the ass, and bite her hard. Rona always flew alone.

And I am not my sister.

The guard caught up with us as Professor Whitman was dragging me down an alley toward a ladder that would take us to the next layer of the

Dyson. They shouted; we ran. They pursued; we ran faster. It was exactly the sort of adventure that I had gone into the traveling-arcade business to avoid, blowing my share of the family seed money on a funfair long past its "best by" date. Let Rona have the dizzying escapes and exhilarating chases. I'd take the joys of percussive maintenance and spending my nights beating the high score on ancient shoot-'em-up consoles.

Wait. That was the answer. "Give me your gun."

"I'm pursued, not suicidal!"

"You're a professor on a Dyson sphere who bought a recoilless pistol for self-defense, and I—*I am the reigning* Duck Hunt *champion of this solar system!*" I snatched the gun from her hand while the echoes of my triumphant decree were still rolling down the alley, spun, and opened fire.

Most modern personal weapons don't have a "kill" setting. They have "stun," they have "sting," and they have "slow the jerk who's chasing you down," but they don't kill. Killing people is bad for business and gets the justice system involved. The justice system has better things to worry about. Professor Whitman might be the kind of person who'd pull a gun on a stranger, but she didn't strike me as the kind of person who would have modified her weapon for fun.

My first shot took out the lead guard, who fell twitching and bucking to the alley floor. Score one for the unmodified weapon. I kept firing, pretending they were pixelated ducks flying across an impossibly blue sky, and that that damn cartoon dog would pop up and laugh if I missed. Technically true, assuming I substituted the words "jail sentence" for "cartoon dog." Professor Whitman was screaming. I ignored her, shooting until the last guard was down, and then turning to whack her gun repeatedly against the nearest wall, hitting it again and again, until I heard the thin glassy tinkle of the limiter in the barrel shattering. I turned back to Professor Whitman, keeping the muzzle aimed at the center of her chest, and keeping my finger well away from the trigger.

"Guns are fun," I said. "Break the little switch that says 'please don't kill people' and guess what? You've got a deadly weapon on your hands. That's why you're not supposed to treat them like toys. They're not toys."

The professor had gone even paler beneath her freckles. "Perhaps we got off on the wrong foot before . . ."

"There's no 'perhaps' about it. Now move. We'll continue this on my ship." My smile was humorless and cold. "Congrats. You've turned another Nanson into a criminal. My genemother would be so proud."

Climbing through the layers of the shell, one by one, with a gun in my hand and a reluctant professor leading the way, was not the most fun way I had ever spent an afternoon. When we reached the docking level, I swiped my genecode through, trusting on the relative interchangeability of the Nona-Rs—and my sister's obvious visits to the place—to get me through security. Rona hates being tied down. Even places that have warrants out for her arrest will usually let her pass unhindered, thanks to the backdoors and malware she installs in their systems. We both love machines. It's just that I enjoy fixing them, while she's more about breaking them in beneficial ways.

The gun I'd taken from Professor Whitman still rattled every time I moved it. Maybe Rona and I were more alike than I wanted to consider.

The guards either didn't know about my ship or hadn't considered that we might crawl through the sphere to get to the docking level. Once I swiped my code, we were able to walk—not saunter, not run, as both would attract attention we didn't want right now—past the checkpoints and all the way to the waiting door of my salvation.

"I'm glad you've decided to help me," whispered Professor Whitman. "I'm sorry we got off on the wrong foot, but I'm sure once you understand—"

"Less talking, more walking," I said, pushing her toward the steps. "Up until you came along, I'd managed to make it as a mostly honest citizen. All I want to understand is why you decided to jank up my life and not somebody else's."

"Because I thought you were Rona," she said. "When I got that query about selling me a Star Catcher IV box, I just knew that you were her, because that was part of our code. Star Catcher meant 'I'm coming,' and even numbers meant 'move now, we're going to be running hard.'"

It took everything I had not to groan. "You're telling me all this is because my stupid sister decided to base a code on something she didn't give a damn about? That's it. She's not getting a decanting day present from me this year." I slapped my hand against the keypad, letting it read my biometrics. The door slid open. I pulled Professor Whitman inside, and the door slid closed again behind us.

The air inside my ship was slightly stale in that way that became normal after spending a certain amount of time in deep space, scented with cotton candy and popcorn. Not that either confection was actually available onboard—safety reasons—but the smells are traditional, and they helped to put people into the funfair mood. The entry hall was dim, the lights lowered to conserve power while we were docked. I shoved the Professor's gun into my belt and started toward the main room at the center of the ship. "Doc? We've got company, and we've got a problem."

"I believe I am aware of both those things," he called back.

Maybe the slight quaver in his voice should have been enough of a warning, but I was distracted by the academic beside me, and by the pressing question of how the hell we were going to get out of here when we still didn't have a working gravity generator. I reached the end of the hall. I stopped.

Rona, who was holding a gun against my seated partner's temple, offered me a sunny smile. "Howdy, sis," she said, as blithe as if this had been a chance meeting on a populous street, and not her breaking into my ship and holding Doc at gunpoint. "Long time no see."

I froze. Crime was Rona's thing, not mine: I didn't have the heart for it. "Rona."

"Violet, can you take the gun from my sister, please? I wouldn't want her to get any fancy ideas that might get her hurt." Rona kept smiling.

"We did firearms training together for our sixteenth decanting day, and I know how good a shot she is."

"I've gotten better," I said, through gritted teeth, trying not to focus on the feeling of Professor Whitman—Violet—fumbling with my belt. "What the hell are you doing here, Rona? I told you I didn't want you anywhere near the arcade."

"Still mad about your high score?"

"No, still mad about you using my Whac-A-Mole machine to smuggle memory crystals across prohibited lines," I snapped. "The high score was insult to injury."

"It's not my fault I'm naturally talented." Rona shifted her attention to Violet. "Did you bring it?"

"I—I did," said the professor, sounding uncertain. "Did you send the message after all? Were you coming to save me?"

"No, that was all Nora; your reputation apparently precedes you in some of the wrong circles. Why in the world was my sister selling one of her beloved games?"

"Not that it's any of your business, but we need a new gravity generator," I said. "What are you buying from this woman, Rona? Why does she think you'd save anyone but yourself?"

"Nothing you need to concern yourself with," said Rona. "We'll fix the gennie and be on our way. I'm assuming all your licenses and clearances are still in order? You were always the good one when it came to that sort of stuff."

"I'm the good one when it comes to *everything*."

Rona's face went cold, and so did I. It was always easy to tell when I had gone too far with her: she had very little space between "calm" and "furious." And a furious Rona was capable of doing terrible things. "You asked what she had for me, Nora? She has the schematics for this sphere. All of them. The deep engineering, the things no one is supposed to know. The things that we can use to take out the entire security system."

Violet's eyes widened. "Wait, what? You said you needed those schematics so that you could loosen the communication locks. The people are being oppressed. They need to be able to reach their families without fear of government censorship."

Rona snorted. "Please. There's always someone watching over your shoulder. All that matters to me is whether they're the highest bidder."

"But you promised me," whispered Violet, her eyes widening still further, until it looked like they were in danger of falling right out of her head and rolling across the deck. "You said that if I got you the schematics, you would unlock the world."

"I never lied to you," said Rona.

"She probably didn't," I said. That old, weary feeling was washing over me. Rona had always been like this, even when we were little girls, freshly decanted and waiting for our loving adoptive parents to come and carry us home. There was still a surprisingly good market for Nona-Rs, in part because several of us had gone on to become famous in our own right, and some planetary governments allowed clones to claim familial benefits. Adopt the right clone-kid and your family could wind up set for life, if things went your way. "She said it would 'unlock the world'? Then she told you the exact truth. She just surrounded it with pretty words that would make you think she was giving you what you wanted."

"Every Dyson is built to its own blueprint. Getting anything bigger than a breadbox—or an unarmed clone with a popular genecode— inside without going through channels *or* breaking the seal and blowing everything inside to hell is virtually impossible." Rona held out her hand. As always, it was jarring to see my face so cold, so calculating. I'm a businesswoman. All Nona-Rs have a streak of ruthlessness to them. But Rona . . . Rona was a monster. "Give me the schematics, Violet. Once I have them, I'll know that you're with me, and we can move forward."

"Do you have a ship here?" I asked. "How did you even get on this sphere?"

"I don't see where it's any of your concern."

"Everything you do is my concern. You're my *sister*."

"I'm your clone," corrected Rona gently. "I'm your other self. You could have been me. We could have grown up perfectly synchronized. We could rule the universe. The best criminals ever known. But you chose to run a children's entertainment gallery and waste yourself on frivolities. Everything you do reflects poorly on me as well, you know; you make me look soft."

"At least I'm not trying to crack a Dyson sphere for profit."

Rona laughed. "No. But I'm succeeding at it. Violet? The schematics?"

"Yes, Rona," said the professor meekly. She took a step forward, putting herself on the level with me. I tensed.

She winked.

That was all the warning I got before my gun—her gun—was pressed back into my hand and she was hitting the deck, leaving Rona staring at me in wide-eyed confusion.

"Duck hunt!" I shouted. Doc flung himself hard to the side. I pulled the trigger, aiming not for Rona but for the wall behind her. She laughed, delighted, as my shot flew right past her ear. She never had been one for paying attention during our science classes. I guess when you're planning on life as a criminal mastermind, little things like "the laws of physics" don't seem to have that much relevance.

Me, I run a children's entertainment gallery, and as anyone who's ever played terrestrial pool or one of the old bubble-popping games can tell you, physics matters, especially when you're playing with energy beams. My shot hit the wall, bounced off, hit the opposing corner, and bounced again, this time slamming right into the middle of Rona's back. She didn't even have time to scream before she collapsed.

I lowered the gun. "Doc? You okay?"

"You could have told me Rona was in the sector!" He stood laboriously, glaring at my crumpled clone. "The ship let her in. I keep telling you we should install a fingerprint lock."

"And I keep telling you, we can't afford it." I turned to find Violet staring at me. "What?"

"You—you shot her!"

"Yeah, but I shot two walls first, and these things don't have that much of a charge in them. She's stunned, but she'll be fine. Doc?"

"On it." He bent, scooping Rona up like she was one of the prize ragdolls we sometimes distributed in the arcade. He paused long enough for me to pass him the gun. He nodded, and walked past us toward the entry hall.

Violet looked back to me, paling as the enormity of the situation sunk in. "I'm sorry about everything. I didn't know . . ."

"Rona takes after our genemother. She's a great actress, as long as you don't mind that everything's an act. You really steal those schematics for her?"

"Not stole, exactly." Her cheeks reddened. It was a miracle she was still upright, with as often as the blood rushed into and out of her head. "My parents were on the design team. They made backups. I must have triggered something when I copied all that data over, but I thought you were . . . were her."

"And as soon as she caught the alert, she realized she was about to lose her payday, so she came running." I looked around the ship and sighed. "I have no idea what we're going to do next. We can't leave, and it's not like you're in a position to buy that game now—or like the creds would clear before the guards figured out that Rona wasn't me." Doc was dumping her outside.

"You said the gravity generator was broken?"

I nodded. "Crapped out on the trip over."

Professor Whitman's smile was as sudden as a black hole's event horizon, and pulled twice as hard. "Given the size and make of your ship—is it by any chance a Whitman Industries model?"

I stopped. I blinked. "I . . . what?"

"Whitman Industries. We, uh, designed most of the gravity generators currently in use in this sector." She was still blushing. It was a good look for her. "I can fix it."

"You can fix it."

She nodded. "Just give me a wrench."

"You realize you're going to have to leave. You can't . . . The guards will arrest Rona, but they came for you."

"I know." Professor Whitman shrugged. "I have the schematics. Maybe I can ride with you until I find someplace where they'll do what Rona promised me. I'll keep this place running until we get there."

Doc wouldn't be thrilled. But Doc wouldn't mind getting a free mechanic. "Do you need any special tools?"

"I usually start by hitting it, actually—"

I was still laughing when Doc came back into the room.

There's nothing in the universe that can't be repaired if you have the right tools.

ABOUT THE AUTHOR

SEANAN McGUIRE is an American author of speculative fiction, living on the West Coast and doing her best to avoid all forms of weather. She won the 2010 John W. Campbell Award for Best New Writer, and can regularly be found wandering off into haunted cornfields, haunted houses, and whatever amusement parks she can find. Since her debut novel in 2009, Seanan has released more than twenty traditionally published novels, under both her own name and the name "Mira Grant." Many people believe that Seanan does not sleep. They may be right. Keep up with her at seananmcguire.com.

THE DRAGON THAT FLEW OUT OF THE SUN

ALIETTE DE BODARD

Here's a story Lan was told, when she was a child—when she lay in the snugness of her sleep-cradle, listening to the distant noises of station life—the thrum of the recycling filters, the soft gurgle of water reconstituted from its base components, the distant noises of the station's Mind in the Inner Rings, a vast unreality that didn't quite concern her, that she couldn't encompass in words.

Mother sat by Lan's side and smiled at her. Her hands smelled of garlic and fish sauce, with the faintest hint of machine oil. Her face was lined with worry; but then, it always was, those days. She wanted to tell a story about Le Loi and the Turtle's Sword, or about the girl who was reborn in a golden calabash and went on to marry the king.

Lan had other ideas.

"Tell me," she said, "about Lieu Vuong Tinh."

For a moment, Mother's face shifted and twisted; she looked as if she'd swallowed something that had stuck in her throat. Then she took a deep breath and told Lan this.

In days long gone by, we used to live in Kinh He on Lieu Vuong Tinh. It was a client state of the Dai Viet Empire, on the edge of the Numbered

Planets—its name had come from the willow, because high officials posted there would part from their friends and share a willow branch to remember each other.

But we no longer live there.

Because one day the sun wobbled and quivered over Lieu Vuong Tinh, and grew fainter, and a dragon flew out from its core—large and terrible and merciless, the pearl under its chin shining with all the colors of the rainbow, its antlers carrying fragments of iron and diamond that glistened like the tips of weapons. And, because dragons are water—because they are the spirits of the rain and the monsoon, and the underwater kingdoms— because of that, the sun died.

The dragon had always been there, of course. It was nothing more than an egg at first—a little thing thinner than the chips they use for your ancestors' mem-implants—then the egg hatched and grew into a carp. Carps don't always become dragons, of course, but this one did.

No, I don't know why. Who knows why the Jade Emperor sends down decrees, or why rain happens even when people haven't kept up prayers and propitiations at the shrines? Sometimes, the world is just the way it is.

But when the dragon flew out, its mane unfolded, all the way down to Lieu Vuong Tinh, and into the ships that were fleeing the dying sun—and into the heart of us all, it marked us all, a little nick on the surface like the indent of a carver on jade. That's why, even now, when you meet another Khiet from Lieu Vuong Tinh, you'll instantly know—because it's in their hearts and their bellies and their eyes, the mark of the dragon that will never go away.

"The whole dragon thing is ridiculous," Tuyet Thanh says. "I mean, what did they do, have a little chat and agree to serve us all this load of rubbish?"

They're in the communal network—each of them in their own compartment, except Lan has made the station's Mind merge both spaces in the network, so that Tuyet appears to be sitting at the end of her table, and that the bots-battle they're having in the free-for-all area of space outside the station appears in the middle, as a semi-transparent overlay.

"I don't know," Lan says, cautiously. Tuyet Thanh is older than her by three years, and chafing at the restrictions imposed by older relatives. Lan wants, so badly, to be like her friend, cool and secure and edgy, instead of never knowing what to think on things—because Mother is so often right, isn't she?

"Fine." Tuyet Thanh exhales. She rolls up her eyes, and her bots flow out into a pincer movement—slightly too wide of their reserved area, almost clipping a passing ship. "Deal with this."

Lan considers, for a heartbeat that feels stretched to an eternity—then she sends her bots to drill a hole in the center of the pincer, where Tuyet Thanh's formation is weaker. "No, but I mean the story is right about one thing, isn't it? The grown-ups—it's like . . ." Adequate words won't come. She makes a gesture with her hand, frustrated—cancels it from the interface, so that the bots don't interpret it as a command. "They're marked. They . . . Have you never noticed they can tell who was on those ships? It's like they have a sensor or something."

"It's just clothes. And language, and the way of behaving." Tuyet Thanh snorts. "A Khiet can tell another Khiet. That's all."

"I guess . . ." Lan says, feeling small, and young, and utterly inadequate.

"Look. There was no dragon. Just . . ."

This is what Second Aunt told me, right? She'd know, because she was twenty-five when they left, and she remembers them well—the years before the war, before the sun.

Anyway. There was the Ro Federation—yes, you're going to tell me they're at peace with the Empire now, that they're all fine people. Whatever. Have you never noticed the adults won't ever talk about them?

In those days, the Ro were our neighbors, and they wanted us gone. They were afraid of us because we were stronger; in the end, they thought that Lieu Vuong Tinh made quite a nice piece of space to have. And one of their—scientists, alchemists—I can't remember exactly what they have out there—made a weapon that they said was going to change the way of things. Just point it at the sun, they said, and you'll see.

And they saw, all right. It . . . it did something, to the atoms that made up the sun—accreted them faster than they should have, so that the star's glow dimmed, and Lieu Vuong Tinh became . . . bombarded. Scoured clean and no longer fit for humans. So that we had to leave, because we no longer had a home.

And the Ro? Yes, today you'll find them on the station, trading us their makings and their technology, as cozy as anything. But they're out there too, in the ruins of Lieu Vuong Tinh, the red-hot slag mess that the Empire abandoned to them when they signed the peace treaty. No humans can go there, but they have bots taking it apart, mining it for precious metals and ice—so that, in the end, they still won everything they hoped for.

Don't look at me like that. It's truth, all right? Not the dragon crap—the thing that truly happened.

Yes. I hate them too.

"Mother?"

Mother looks up from the dumplings she's assembling. She only gets marginal help from the bots, preferring to do everything by hand. Once, she says, everyone would gather in the kitchen, helping others to put together the anniversary feast, but now, in the cramped station compartments, there isn't enough space for that. The aunts and uncles each make their own fraction of dishes, and the meal is shared through the communal network, stitching together the various compartments until it seems like a vast room once more. "Yes, child?"

Lan weighs the words on her tongue, not finding any easy way to bring them up. "Why did you never tell us about the Ro?"

Mother's face doesn't move. It freezes in an intricate and complex expression—it would be a key to the past, if only Lan could interpret it. "Because it's complicated."

"More complicated than the dragon?"

Mother's eyes flick back to the table; the bots take over from her, leaving both her hands free. Her voice is calm, too calm. "Lan—I know you're angry."

"I'm not!" Lan says, and then realizes she is. Not even at Mother but at herself, for being stupid enough to believe bedtime stories, for not being more like Tuyet Thanh—smarter and harder and less willing to take things on faith. "Did they do it?"

"The Ro?" Mother sighs. "It was one of their scientists who destroyed the sun, yes. But—"

There are no "buts." "Then it's their fault."

"Don't be so quick to fling blame," Mother says.

"Why shouldn't I?" Because of them—because of the sun—they're here, stuck on the station; in cramped compartments where it seems there's barely enough room to breathe. "Are you making excuses for them?"

Mother is silent for a long, long while. Lan is sure that Tuyet Thanh would have left a long time ago; turned her face to the wall and ramped up the communal network to maximum, trying to fill her ears with sounds she can control. But Mother always has the right words, always does the right thing. Lan clings to this, as desperately as a man adrift in space clings to faint, fading broadcasts. At last she says, "No. I'm not. Merely saying they had their own motives."

"Because they were afraid of us."

"Yes," Mother said. "And people seldom are afraid for no reason, are they?"

Of course they are, all the time. Like they're afraid of Lan in class because she's smarter than them—is there any justification for *that*? Lan knows prevaricating and false excuses when she hears them—has she been so blind all along? How can she have been so stupid? "Did we do anything to them?" she asks. "Did we?"

Mother's face closes again. "We never did like each other . . . I don't know, child."

"Then we didn't." Lan calls up the communal network, lets it fill her from end to end—blocking out Mother and her feeble excuses. "You were right," she tells Tuyet Thanh. "Adults are idiots."

Today, on the Fourth Day of the Tenth Lunar Month, the Khiet community remembers the Dislocation of Lieu Vuong Tinh, and the Flight of the Evacuation Fleet to the Numbered Planets.

The war between the Khiet and the Ro lasted three years, though it had been brewing for years if not decades. The two had always been uneasy neighbors. While the Khiet rose to prominence with the help of the Dai Viet Empire, to whom they swore allegiance, the Ro were mired under a feudal regime and struggled to survive.

The Khiet's harsh, authoritarian regime had been making the Ro uneasy for a while. The inciting event was the so-called Skiff-Ghost Return, in the year of the Metal Dragon, in which Ro citizens were discovered to have been mind-altered by the Khiet—which set off an ugly, protracted series of skirmishes in which little quarter was given on either side.

The Dai Viet Empire refused to get involved at first, but could not in good conscience continue to do so after the Dislocation. Refugees were so numerous that they had to be scattered to various places among the Numbered Planets—the Mind-controlled Stations on the edge of the Empire taking on the bulk of them. Today, Khiet culture is a vibrant and ubiquitous part of our own culture, nowhere more so than during the anniversary of the Dislocation, when entire communities will gather in large ceremonies to remember the thousands who were lost in the hasty evacuation.

As usual, on the occasion of this anniversary, Scholar Rong Thi Minh

Tu, the Voice of the Empress, has extended the Empire's sincere condolences, and their wishes for continued prosperity for the Khiet.

"So . . ." Professor Nguyen Thi Nghe says, pursing her lips. "What am I to make of you?"

"He started it!" The words are out of Lan's mouth before she could think.

Beside her, Vien shifts uncomfortably in his chair—at least he has the decency to look guilty. But then he opens his mouth and says, in Viet with the barest trace of an accent, "I . . . should have phrased my words more carefully. I apologize."

Lan remembers the words like a kick in the gut—the smirking face of him, asking if she was all right, if she'd adapted to life on the station—as if he didn't know, or care, that his people are the reason she was here in the first place. "Professor—" She can't find words for her outrage. "He's Ro."

"Yes." Professor Nghe's voice is quiet, thoughtful. "The Empire and the Khiet signed a peace treaty with the Ro more than thirty years ago, child."

Leaving them the ruins of Lieu Vuong Tinh—not that they would have known what to do, with the ruins of what had been their home, but still.

Still, it is wrong. Still, it shouldn't have happened.

"You're my best two pupils," Professor Nghe says. "Your aptitude with bots—the creativity you show when designing them . . ." She shakes her head. "But it's all moot if you can't at least be civil to each other."

"I know," Lan says, sullenly. "But he shouldn't have rubbed it in my face. Not now." It's the anniversary of the Dislocation; soon she will walk home, to Mother's kitchen and the dumplings filled with bitter roots—to the alignment of aunts and uncles that all seem to be in perpetual mourning, as if some spring within them had broken a long time ago.

Vien shifts again, bringing his hands together as if to press a sheet of paper utterly flat. His eyes are pure black, unclouded by any station implants—they say that the station's Mind won't allow the Ro standard access to the communal network, because they cause too many problems. "I didn't mean to." He winces, again, rubbing his hand against the bruise on his cheek. "Yelling at me was fine. The slap . . ."

The slap had been uncalled-for. Mother would have had her hide, truth be told. She didn't like Ro either—Tuyet Thanh was right; none of the exiles had forgiven them, but she would have said it was no call to be uncouth. She—

Lan finds herself rubbing her hand against her cheek, in mute sympathy with Vien. "Forget it," she says, more harshly than she intended to. "I won't do it again. But just stay away from me." She won't talk to him again—she doesn't want to be reminded of his existence—of his people's existence.

Professor Nghe grimaces. "I guess I'll have to be content with that, shall I? Out you go, then."

Outside, Vien turns to Lan, stiff and prim and with the barest hint of a bow. "Listen," he says.

"No."

"I won't bother you again after this."

We didn't mean to do any of it. I realize it's not an excuse, and that it won't mean much to you, but I have to try.

We'd been at war for years by then. You were modifying your own people—sending them to camps and facilities. Have you heard of skiff-ghosts? You were the ones who made them—because the soul went on, down the river to the afterworld, and the body remained, with no awareness or affection. You made thousands of them, and not even for soldiering, merely so they would be obedient citizens.

We . . . we were scared. It wasn't smart, but who knew when you would decide that your own neighbors didn't suitably conform? You've always thought of us as amusing barbarians—with uncombed, uncut hair that we let grow because we won't use scissors on the body that is the flesh of our fathers, the blood of our mothers—and, if you were ready to do this to your own, why should you hesitate with ours?

There was . . . There were incidents. Ro coming back with a little light missing in their eyes, with movements that were a little too stiff. And one of those incidents pushed us over the edge.

I know you're angry. Just let me finish. Please.

Lieu Vuong Tinh was small, and isolated, and we thought it would only be a matter of time. If we sent enough fleets, enough ships, then the Dai Viet Empire wouldn't support you anymore.

But then the war dragged on, and on, and more ships didn't make any difference. Our soldiers bled and died on foreign moons, suffocating in the void of space, felled at the entrances to habitats—and some came back but never the same, emptied of all thoughts and all feelings, a horde of skiff-ghosts pushing and tugging at the fabric of our life until it unraveled. So, a man named Huu Quang had an idea for a weapon so powerful that it would end things, once and for all.

I'm not trying to excuse him or the people who funded him. They all went on trial for war crimes, after the peace treaty was finally signed. We all saw what happened to the sun. We all saw the ships, and the fleet, and what happened to those who didn't manage to leave in time. We—

I'm sorry, all right? I know it doesn't make a difference. I know that I wasn't even born, back then, but it was a stupid, unforgivable thing to do. Most of us know it.

We're not monsters.

Lan stands, breathing hard—staring at Vien, who hasn't moved. She's raised her hand again, and he watches her with those impossible black eyes, the ones that are too deep, that see too many things. She realizes, finally, that it's because he's unplugged to most station activity, that he only has the barest accesses to the communal network and therefore so very few community demands on his time. Mother's eyes, Tuyet Thanh's eyes—they always shift left and right, never seem to hold on to anything for long. But Vien . . .

"It's not true," she says, slowly—breathing out, feeling the burning in her lungs. "It's—all a lie."

Vien brings the palms of his hands together, as if he were going to bow. "Everything is a lie," he says, finally. "Everything a fragment of the truth. Don't you have relatives who remember?"

Mother, in the kitchen, saying she didn't know what they had done, and looking away. "I—" Lan breathes in again, everything tinged with the bitterness of ashes. "I don't know," she says, finally. It's the only thing that will come to mind.

"Look it up," Vien says, almost gently. "There's no shortage of things on the network."

Written by the Dai Viet Empire, the hegemony's stories about her own people—what does it mean, if it means anything at all? She's called on the network before she's aware she has—and "skiff-ghosts" brings up all kinds of hollow-eyed, shambling monstrosities in her field of vision. "I don't know," she says, again, and inwardly she's calling for Mother, who is as silent as she ever was. Tales for children. Bedtime stories: the only narratives that can be stomached.

Vien says nothing, merely watches her with a gaze that seems to encompass the entire universe. She'd rage and scream and rant at him, if he did speak, but he doesn't. His mouth is set. "I'll leave you," he says, finally, and walks away, his back ramrod straight, except that in the communal network, a little icon blinks, something he has left her, as a farewell gift. *Forgive me—this is all I can give you, on this day of all days*, the message says, and Lan archives it, because she cannot bear to deal with him or the Ro.

At home, Mother is waiting for her. The compartment smells of meat and spices and garlic. Everyone else is shimmering into existence, the entire family gathering around the meal for the ancestors, for the dead planet. "Child?"

Lan wants to ask about skiff-ghosts and the Ro, but the words seem too large, too inappropriate to get past the block in her mouth.

Instead, she sits down in silence at her appointed place, reaching for a pair of chopsticks and a bowl. As the Litany of the Lost begins, and the familiar names light up in her field of vision—the ones who are still there, still dust among the dust of Lieu Vuong Tinh—she finds herself reaching for Vien's gift and opening it.

A blur, and a jumble of rocks; then the view pans out, and she sees a scattering of rocks of all sizes tumbling in slow motion, and bots weaving in and out like a swarm of bees, lifting off with dust and fragments of rock in their claws.

The view pans out again, until it seems to rise from behind the bots, slowly filling her entire field of vision—a corona of light and ionized gases, a mass of contracting colors like a stilled heart; a slow, stately dance of clouds and interstellar dust, blurred like the prelude to tears.

A live link to a bot-borne camera; a window into an area of space she's never gone to but instantly recognizes.

What else could it be, after all?

Lieu Vuong Tinh: what is left of the planet, what the Ro are scavenging from the radiation-soaked areas. The place her people came from, the place her people fled, with the weight of the dying sun like ghosts on their backs.

Ghosts.

She wonders about the dead, and the skiff-ghosts—and mind-alterations and who bears what, in the mess of the war—and who, ultimately, is right, and justified.

The grit of dust against her palate, and the slow, soundless whistle of spatial winds—and, abruptly, it no longer matters, because she sees it.

The dragon's mane streams in the solar winds, a shining star at the point of each antler; the serpentine body stretched and pockmarked with fragments of rock; the pearl in its mouth a fiery, pulsing point of light; its tail streaming ice and dust and particles across the universe like the memory of an expelled breath—and its eyes, two pits of utter darkness against the void of space, a gaze turning her way and transfixing her like thrown swords.

The mark. The wound. The hole in the heart that they all want to fill, she and Tuyet Thanh and Mother—and Vien—all united in the wake of the dragon's passage like farmers huddled in the wake of a storm, grieving for flooded fields and the lost harvest, and bowed under the weight of all that they did to one another.

Mother is right, after all. This is the only story of the war that will ever make sense—the only truth that is simply, honestly, heartbreakingly bearable.

ABOUT THE AUTHOR

ALIETTE DE BODARD lives and works in Paris, where she has a day job as a system engineer. She studied computer science and applied mathematics but moonlights as a writer of speculative fiction. She is the author of the critically acclaimed *Obsidian and Blood* trilogy of Aztec noir fantasies, as well as numerous short stories, which garnered her two Nebula Awards, a Locus Award, and a British Science Fiction Association Award. Recent works include *The House of Shattered Wings* (Roc/Gollancz), a novel set in a turn-of-the-century Paris devastated by a magical war, and *The Citadel of Weeping Pearls* (Asimov's Oct/Nov 2015), a novella set in the same universe as her Vietnamese space opera *On a Red Station Drifting*. She lives in Paris with her family, in a flat with more computers than warm bodies, and a set of Lovecraftian tentacled plants intent on taking over the place.

DIAMOND AND THE WORLD BREAKER

LINDA NAGATA

Gliding between worlds on an unchangeable trajectory toward an encounter that would decide the fate of the Nine Thousand, Diamond finally confessed to her mother, Violetta, a long-suspected truth: "I always wanted to be the bad guy . . . but I thought it would be more fun than this."

Wrapped in the ethereal silence of their two-person bullet pod, Violetta had succumbed to brooding over the ruin of her life. But at Diamond's words, she roused. She reminded herself the situation was not hopeless. Chaos need not win. The Nine Thousand might still go on.

And Diamond might yet learn right from wrong?

It was possible. She was only twelve, after all.

Faithful to the duties of motherhood, Violetta chided her delinquent daughter: "I hope you choose differently, Diamond, if you ever find yourself tempted again."

The interior of the bullet pod was close and cramped. It contained two crash couches, nothing more, with no room to move around. Violetta's couch was behind Diamond's, so she couldn't see her daughter's face until Diamond twisted around, peering past the gap between seatback and hull, one bright black eye showing beneath a scowling brow.

She said, "Sorry I got you in trouble."

Violetta glanced at the countdown running in her retinal screen. Seven minutes to go until they reached Nexus. "I won't lie to you, love. This is a bad situation. The Professional Revolutionaries have really gone too far this time."

Diamond's scowl deepened. "Dad says if chaos wins, we all lose. But, Mom? I don't want to lose."

Just three hours earlier, when Violetta Gamiao had spotted an agent of the Professional Revolutionaries stepping from a transit bullet to the platform at Tranquility, she had anticipated swift victory.

The agent did not, of course, announce his affiliation. He wore no badge, no uniform, and there was nothing extraordinary about his appearance. He stood shorter than most in a mixed crowd of tourists and business travelers, but not so much shorter as to draw notice. His gleaming red culottes and gold vest of many pockets were respectable attire—almost conservative—compared to the riotous colors and fantastic embellishments worn by the one hundred twenty-nine other travelers who had arrived on the same long bullet. And he carried only a plain black valise.

But evil had a distinctive swagger.

"Look what we've got coming," Violetta said, speaking to Ash Crafton, her rookie partner. The two hunters shared a table at a balcony café overlooking the platform, a post that let them see everyone who arrived in Tranquility and all those who were leaving.

Ash leaned forward to take another look, scowling as he reassessed the new arrivals. Then he grunted, and asked, "That one?" His index finger traced a little circle in the air in front of him, a gesture that highlighted the revolutionary with an equivalent circle drawn on Violetta's retinal screen. The circle framed a flat brown face, fierce confidence projected by heavy black eyebrows and a wolfish half-smile.

Violetta nodded her approval. "You're getting good, Ash."

"It's not the way they look," he said, repeating the dictum she'd drilled into him from day one. "It's the attitude."

They arose together from the table, both wearing the shadow-shifting uniform of chartered hunters, operating under the authority of Machina Overlord. It was their duty to oversee the good order and safe operation of the Bullet Transit System within District 24 of the Nine Thousand Worlds, and to ensure the system was not used to spread mayhem.

Given the number of philosophical gangs whose sole purpose was to create mayhem, it was a challenging occupation—with the Professional Revolutionaries a particular nemesis.

Violetta turned, pulling her stunner from a hip holster, her other hand on the balcony railing. "Ready?" she asked Ash.

"Right behind you," he assured her, stunner in hand.

But the revolutionary had sensed the motion above him. He glanced up, saw the threat.

And as they vaulted over the railing, he bolted for the arched entrance of the transit station and the bright plaza beyond it, lit by sunlight from an artificial sky.

Violetta dropped to the concourse, startling the tourists as she landed among them with a soft thump. Ash dropped down two meters away. They both raised their weapons. The tourists yelled at one another to get down, get out of the line of fire, and within three seconds, an alley opened in the crowd with the revolutionary at the far end, silhouetted against the morning glare.

"I've got it," Violetta told Ash. Rarely was it this easy to find her prey and bring it down.

She pulled the trigger—but the revolutionary anticipated her. He turned and dropped to one knee. The pellet she'd shot burst open in an electrified net that swirled past him, over his head and into the plaza beyond.

Her retinal screen adjusted her vision, dimming the light from the plaza so she could see his face. He was looking right at her, showing no fear, no concern. Smiling.

She adjusted her aim. Pulled the trigger just as he moved again: standing up, stepping forward, swinging the valise up in a long arc. The stunner net smacked him in the chest just as the bag left his fingers. It shot straight up toward the transit station's high ceiling while he wilted to the floor.

"Oh, shit," Ash said.

Violetta shouted at the crowd. "Get down! Everyone down!"

Chaos erupted. Tourists screamed, fled, dropped to the ground, tripped over one another, while Ash and Violetta fell back, crouching against the wall, taking what shelter they could against the expected explosion.

But to Violetta's surprise, the valise did not blow up.

She heard a loud click instead.

She looked up in time to see a device spin out of the falling valise: a little winged drone, powered by buzzing tiltrotors. With its four insect-like legs, it gripped a black cylinder. Painted on the underside of its wings was a caricature face: slanting eyes and a devil's leering grin glowing in fiery colors. Madness in cartoon form. The symbol of the Professional Revolutionaries.

This time, Ash was ahead of her. As the now-empty valise hit the floor, he stepped away from the wall, targeting the drone as it executed a tight half-circle, coming around on a flight path that would let it exit to the plaza. The revolutionary remained on the floor, trembling from the effects of the stunner, still unable to control his large muscle groups, but he could see what Ash was doing and he had enough volition to shriek a warning: "No! Don't set it off in here!"

His warning came too late.

Ash had pulled the trigger.

* * * *

"The Nine Thousand" was the name given to the swarm of artificial worlds in orbit around the sun—not that there were actually nine thousand worlds. Not yet. But there were many, and "Nine Thousand" rolled easily off the tongue, a good round number and full of possibility, so the name had stuck. Linking the worlds together was the Bullet Transit System— kilometers-long magnetic tracks used to launch and decelerate bullet pods along complex paths calculated by the artificial intelligence known as Machina Overlord.

The AI's computational strata were housed in the artificial world of Nexus—a tiny, ring-shaped habitat where no one lived and few were allowed to visit, but because it was the home of Machina Overlord, Nexus was the nucleus of the Nine Thousand.

From Nexus, the AI controlled all aspects of navigation. It adjusted each world's orbital path to ensure an ideal distribution around the Sun. It supervised an automated mining operation among the moons of Jupiter. It oversaw the assembly of artificial comets from the resources harvested there, and it determined the paths those comets followed when they were lobbed toward the sun.

The Nine Thousand could exist only because of Machina Overlord's dedication to navigational harmony. But the AI had a quirk. In its unfathomable calculations, it had come to a determination that harmony was not a fit goal for human society. Modeling the future had convinced it that an excess of peace and prosperity was slow poison. That if the Nine Thousand was allowed to settle naturally into utopia, the result must be stagnation and decline.

So, long before, it had issued letters of marque, authorizing philosophical gangs to carry out randomly assigned acts of vandalism and terror. The Professional Revolutionaries were the most notorious of these gangs, claiming more than four million voluntary members. Though they had to operate under complex rules, Machina Overlord had granted them a powerful privilege: They were masters of identity.

Among the Nine Thousand, a citizen's electronic identity was almost as important as their physical existence. Identity acted as an electronic pass, allowing a citizen to breathe and eat and go about their world, to contact loved ones, access finances and personal history, and to interact with the swarms of lesser AIs—the noncons—which were everywhere in the worlds.

The Professional Revolutionaries were armed with manufactured identities, allowing them to change who they were so they could wander the Nine Thousand at will. But the heart of their game was more frightening. They could steal away the identity of any citizen, hold it hostage, and leave their victim no choice but to enlist in their ranks, if only temporarily—frightened recruits coerced to carry out some arcane task if they ever hoped to have their true life back again. And they *could* get their life back if they succeeded. That was the amnesty rule.

It was a game of sorts, but a serious and dangerous game, one designed on purpose to unsettle worlds, destabilize orbits, crack vacuum seals, crash economies, instigate wars, ignite religious pogroms. To sow chaos.

Violetta had always feared it was a game that must inevitably run out of control.

The tiltrotor took evasive action. Dodging the stunner net Ash had fired, it darted toward the open plaza.

"Ash, hold your fire!" Violetta ordered. "We don't know what that thing's carrying."

"But it's getting away!"

"So go after it! Keep it in sight, but don't damage it. I'm going to find out what the payload is."

Ash raced away in pursuit, while she dropped to her knees beside the fallen revolutionary. He lay on his back, shivering, eyes half-closed, but he was aware of her. She knew that when his lips turned in a strained smile.

"What will happen now?" she demanded.

He said, "I always find it . . . gratifying . . . when chaos . . . ensues." His eyes opened wider, fixed on her. "Tag," he added. "You're it."

"I'm it?"

Panic prickled her skin. Her heart raced.

"What do you mean, I'm it?"

But she got no answer as his eyes closed and he faded into unconsciousness.

You're it.

Had he recruited her? Taken away her identity?

No, that was impossible. He hadn't touched her. To change who she was, he had to touch her.

She turned her hands over anyway, examined her palms, looked for the black spot of erasure that she'd seen too many times before on the palms of forced recruits.

The black spot wasn't there.

But the Professional Revolutionaries did not make empty threats. Their creed did not allow it. She had to assume that she'd really been recruited. But how? What had they taken from her? What were they planning to take? She considered possibilities—and a terrible suspicion flowered in her mind.

She cued her retinal screen. "Ash, you still with me?"

His breathless voice came back over her earbuds. "Affirmative. I think it's trying for the commuter stairs."

Her heartbeat skipped. "Up or down?"

"Can't tell yet."

Up would take the drone to Tranquility's industrial levels—critical infrastructure, but mostly robotic, with few citizens present. Down, though—that was the direction of the world's bucolic neighborhoods. Violetta's home and family were there.

She popped a lozenge from one of the many loops on her heavy service belt. Then she snapped it open over her unconscious captive, releasing a stream of data dust that fell in a fine gray powder across his face and chest. The dust marked him as a target of interest for Tranquility's fleet of guardian drones. One swooped in immediately: a spinning ring ten centimeters across that emitted a foreboding electrical hum. It hovered over the fallen revolutionary, fencing him in with a translucent cage of pink and purple light. Anyone attempting to breach that cage—whether from inside or outside—before the municipal police arrived would find themselves hit with a nasty dart of no-go.

"Ash," Violetta asked again, "up or down?"

"Down," Ash groaned.

Down toward Violetta's home and family.

She sprang to her feet, but she did not follow Ash to the commuter stairs. Instead, she bounded across the concourse, weaving through the loitering crowd to the red door of an emergency chute. On the way, she whispered, "Link to the house."

Her earbuds picked up the command and executed it.

The house responded in its sweet, nurturing voice—"Aloha, Violetta"—as Violetta waved a finger at the biometric scanner that controlled access to the emergency chute. "Drop me to level seven."

"Level seven drop affirmed," the chute's noncon answered as the red door sluiced open. The house responded too, in a confused murmur, "That is not in my instruction set."

Violetta ignored it. She stepped through the door and fell, dropping past a series of gel nets, each one holding her for a fraction of a second, stretching as it slowed her descent, until a gel net on the seventh level caught her and shoved her out past another red door.

She emerged not far from her own neighborhood in a village square where citizens were at breakfast in neat cafés. Shade trees spread their branches above a central fountain. Morning light tempered by rain-cloud filters glinted through their leaves.

Violetta's sudden appearance caused heads to turn. Worried frowns greeted her. The red door was used only for emergencies. Several people called her name. They asked, "What's gone wrong?"

She ignored them, addressing the house instead: "House, get me Diamond! Make her answer."

"One moment, Violetta."

She did not wait. Only Diamond was at home. Ismo was away on the other side of the sun; he'd taken their toddler twins to visit his parents, but Diamond had not wanted to go. *I have plans*, she'd said. Violetta ran hard, hoping to beat the drone.

Diamond was only twelve, but she'd always been a revolutionary at heart.

The house said, "Diamond is not answering."

"Seal your doors and windows! Don't let her out. Don't let anything in."

Ash broke in, sounding confused. "Vi, I've got you on level seven. What are you doing down there? What's going on?"

Violetta abandoned her earlier caution. "Ash," she said, gasping as she ran. "Forget . . . what I said . . . before. I need you . . . to take out the drone . . . *now*."

"Vi, I can't. I couldn't keep up with it. I don't know where it's gone."

Tag, the revolutionary had warned. *You're it.*

Violetta looked up to see the tiltrotor coming toward her along the street. At first, it was half-hidden in tree shadows. Then its rotors flashed in a blade of sunlight as it turned onto her cul-de-sac. Violetta knew then that her suspicions were true: Diamond was the target of this scheme. It was not a fact she was willing to share with Ash. "Ash, no one here has seen the drone. Check the other levels."

The lie came so easily, it shocked her.

"On it," Ash said.

The confession of the house brought another shock. She heard the deep concern in its tone when it informed her, "Diamond has gone outside. She refuses to come back in."

Violetta pursued the drone into the cul-de-sac, arriving just as Diamond jumped down the porch steps and trotted into the little courtyard that was shared by a semicircle of houses. Evil had a distinctive swagger, and Violetta saw it in her daughter's stride as she went to meet the drone.

Diamond had dressed for this day. She was a short and stocky girl, a little late on the road to adolescence, with rumpled brown hair and a dangerous confidence. Today she wore boots and a black coverall that Violetta had never seen before.

The drone hovered above her, the black cylinder it carried still clutched in spindly insect legs. One of those legs released its burden to reach for Diamond. She extended her hand to meet it. A bored, precocious child, playing out a romantic fantasy.

"Diamond, *no!*"

Diamond snatched her hand back in shocked surprise, but it was too late. Violetta reached her just as the black spot of erasure bloomed in her palm. Over her earbuds, she heard the house's startled report: "I am unable to locate Diamond. She has disappeared from the world."

The nonconscious entity that was the house could no longer identify her, because Diamond had been recruited.

Grief and horror welled in Violetta's heart—and it only got worse when she caught sight of the leering logo of the Professional Revolutionaries on the breast of Diamond's new coverall. "You *volunteered!* Diamond—"

"I was called to serve!"

She darted to one side, trying to cut past Violetta and make a swift escape—as if there was anywhere to run or to hide. Violetta grabbed her arm. Diamond tried to twist away. "No, no! Don't arrest me. Let me go."

"You're not going anywhere. I am locking you up for the rest of your *life!*"

"No, Mom, listen. I'm your daughter. The Revolutionaries erased my identity but I'm still your daughter. Don't arrest me! Don't send me away! Mom! Tell me you remember who I am."

Stillness overcame them both as Violetta looked into her daughter's eyes. She saw fear as Diamond began to understand the enormity of what had happened.

Violetta pulled her close, embraced her, and growled, "Of course I remember you, you idiot. It's your identity that's gone, not my memory. And you are in so much trouble. How long have you been communicating with the Professional Revolutionaries? When did they start working on you?"

"I'm not supposed to say. And anyway, it doesn't matter. They gave me a task."

"They always do." Violetta glanced at her retinal screen, checking on Ash's location. He was still on the commuter stairs, lingering near level five. It was a hunter's duty to arrest all known Revolutionaries. Twelve-year-olds had been recruited before. If Ash discovered what had happened, he would have no choice but to take Diamond into custody, and she would be sent away—unless she carried out her task and won her identity back under the amnesty rule.

"What task did they give you?" Violetta asked, hoping it would be something easy, suitable to a child.

Diamond pouted. "They said it would be fun. That I'd only get in a little trouble."

"What task?" Violetta insisted, as fear's cold fingers touched her heart.

Diamond looked up to the hovering drone. She raised her left hand, exposing the black spot in her palm, a circle so dark it was like a hole to nowhere. The drone dropped the cylinder it carried and she caught it. "I'm supposed to smuggle this to Nexus, where it will be used to destroy Machina Overlord."

Violetta cocked her head, trying desperately to see this as a joke. "Really?"

"Yes."

"Let me see that."

Diamond handed over the cylinder. Violetta didn't trust such easy cooperation, but she said nothing just yet. Using one hand to keep a firm grip on Diamond, she examined the object, finding it strangely light in mass—too light to be a bomb—and slippery in her hand. She realized it was not black. Instead, it was made of a transparent shell at least a centimeter thick. The darkness was contained within. One end of the cylinder was rounded. The other was sealed with a brushed chrome cap that displayed a digital countdown: *3:13:27.*

3:13:26

3:13:25

"It's called a world breaker," Diamond said quietly.

Violetta bit her lip. She'd heard that name before. A world breaker was not an object. It was a theoretical intrusion of another, incompatible, universe. One predicted behavior of such an anomaly was that photons would be unable to react with it, and so they would glide around it in paths that bent along its surface. But that was theory. Speculation. It wasn't real.

And yet, as Violetta gazed at the cylinder, the face she saw reflected in it was not hers. It was her daughter's . . . as if Diamond's image had slid around the darkness contained within the glass.

Ash spoke over her earbuds. "No one on the higher levels saw the drone leave the stairs. I'm coming down."

"No, I'm coming up. I'll meet you on six."

She muted the link and turned back to Diamond, who insisted, "They said it would be easy."

"It's *not* easy."

"The Revolutionaries don't lie!"

"Well, this time they did, because special authorization is required to visit Nexus. The Bullet Transit System would never allow you to—"

Tag. You're it.

Shock rocked her as she grasped the Revolutionaries' scheme. They had not erased her identity, because it was her identity that made her valuable. As a senior hunter, she was one of only a handful of citizens with standing authorization to visit Nexus. If they took her identity, she would lose that authority. So they'd recruited her daughter instead.

Diamond explained it, her voice bitter because she did not believe the scheme could ever work. "You're supposed to help me. That's what it says in the mission plan. They're so stupid they thought you'd help me. But I'm a revolutionary. You're a hunter." Her pout deepened, got lopsided. "That makes us enemies."

"The Revolutionaries aren't stupid, love. Now hurry. We need to get that thing out of Tranquility, and we need to get past Ash. If he finds us, he'll arrest you. He'll arrest me. He has no choice."

Diamond's eyes narrowed in suspicion. "Wait. You're going to help me? But we're not on the same side."

"Diamond, the only way you get your life back is if the task gets done. So I haven't got a choice."

Every world was fitted with emergency escape pods, but those could only be fired into the void at random; they weren't useful for going anywhere. The only effective way out of Tranquility was through the Bullet Transit System. So Violetta told Ash she was coming up the commuter stairs, and then she took Diamond to the emergency chute instead. Ash tracked her position and protested. She didn't answer. "You're compromised, aren't you?" he asked as they stepped through the red door. She bit her lip and kept quiet as the gel curled around them and lofted them to the transit station.

They found police in the concourse, securing the revolutionary, who grinned at Violetta as she swept past. One of the officers called out to her, "Violetta—"

"Sorry! Can't talk. Ash is right behind me, though. He'll help you sort things out!"

Diamond needed no encouragement. What she lacked in judgment, she made up in boldness, darting through the concourse toward the platform. "Mom! You need to get us to the front of the queue."

Violetta was already working on that, muttering to the platform noncon, directing it to summon an emergency bullet.

The noncon argued over the request: "Hunter Gamiao, there is no authorization for an emergency bullet."

She answered as she ran: "I am issuing my own authorization."

Her authority extended that far, though an order out of headquarters could override her.

Ash had reached the plaza. He sounded winded and desperate and furious when he demanded to know, "What are you doing? Where are you going? Why do you need an emergency bullet?"

"I've got this, Ash. You've got to trust me."

Ahead of them, electronic doors observed their approach and opened, admitting them to the transit platform. It was crowded with more than a hundred citizens milling around, waiting for the next long pod.

Violetta gripped Diamond's shoulder. With her other hand she drew her stunner, holding it high where it could be easily seen. And then in an authoritarian voice she said, "Stand aside. There is an emergency in progress. Everyone, move back."

Maybe it was her take-no-prisoners tone, or maybe it was the stunner, but they shrugged and shuffled out of the way. Diamond led; Violetta followed her. A tiny, two-person bullet glided in to meet them at the edge of the platform. The hatch slid open—but across the platform, the electronic doors opened too, admitting Ash. He saw her and shouted, "The revolutionary told me what you're doing! You need to stop. Don't take this any further."

"Get in," Violetta said grimly, gesturing to her daughter. And then she called to Ash, "It's on me! I'm going to make this work."

He wasn't buying it. He raised his stunner, aiming across the crowd. "Everyone down!"

No one went down. Instead, they looked at one another with confused expressions. Wasn't this just a dust-up between hunters? No one wanted to be the first to go down and risk looking like a fool.

Violetta used the moment to follow Diamond through the hatch. She dropped into the rear crash couch. Diamond was strapping in up front.

The hatch slid shut.

"Destination?" the bullet's cheerful noncon asked.

"Nexus!" Diamond yelled.

"That is a restricted destination," the noncon said. "Please stand by while I confirm your authority."

"It's on my authority," Violetta snapped. A series of thuds resounded against the hull. Ash, she presumed, expressing his frustration. "Launch us to Nexus *now*."

"*Open. This. Hatch!*" Ash shouted through her earbuds, each word accompanied by another hard thud.

The assault on its hull did not dampen the bullet's perky tone. "Right away, Hunter Gamiao. Your destination is Nexus. Cleared to launch."

There was a faint vibration, a hint of motion. The hull went quiet as they moved away from the platform. In the sudden silence, Violetta's thoughts turned to Ismo and the twins—and she felt the weight of what she'd just done; she dreaded the consequences. But she'd had no choice. Diamond had been recruited, and Violetta was the only one who could make that right.

Diamond did not share her melancholy. "I can't believe it!" she crowed. "They let us go! Mom, you did it!"

The bullet pod continued to glide, though from within the windowless hull, their motion was hardly perceptible—and it was not fast enough.

Ash would be opening a link to headquarters, begging for an order to stop the launch. But the lightspeed delay would slow his communications.

"Realignment underway," the bullet announced.

Prior to every launch the BTS track had to be realigned and reaimed, its trajectory calculated by a fragment of the mind of Machina Overlord. A minute passed as the machinery reoriented. "I just can't believe it," Diamond said again in quiet excitement. But Violetta listened to the pounding of her heart and wondered, *What have I done?*

"Prepare for launch," the bullet warned.

The launch of a bullet pod was always accompanied by a standard special effect. The transit authority claimed the purpose was to orient the passengers, but everyone knew its real purpose was to make the launch more exciting.

First, the bullet's curved white walls went black. Though Diamond had seen the show before, she gasped at the sudden darkness. Many seconds sifted past and then, as they began to accelerate, a point of white light flared at the front of the pod. The white point expanded into a ring that passed slowly through the darkened walls. Another ring followed it, and another, at ever shorter intervals as their acceleration ramped up, pressing them deep into their seats.

Too late now for anyone to stop them.

The light began to strobe, while Violetta grew so heavy she could not draw a breath. Hard seconds passed under that suffocating pressure— and then it was over. They cleared the track and the pressure was gone.

Zero gravity.

The special effect finished with a burst of slowly swirling colors, an imaginary vision of the mythical realm of hyperspace.

The pod announced, "Glide phase will last two hours, forty-eight minutes, and thirty-two seconds. Deceleration to follow."

Violetta watched the colors fade and the walls return to everyday white. No changing course now. Their path was fixed. No one could interfere. In two hours and forty-eight minutes they would reach Nexus. Ten minutes after that, the countdown running on the world breaker would reach zero.

"Mom?"

"Yes?"

"You know what's crazy about all this?" And then she immediately answered her own question, perhaps fearing what Violetta would say. "I don't think we've ever been on the same side before."

Violetta squeezed her eyes shut and wondered, *Is that what this is about?*

"Mom?"

Violetta looked again, to see Diamond peering at her past the gap beside the seatback.

"*Are* we on the same side?"

"Do you understand what will happen if Machina Overlord is destroyed?"

Only one eye was visible, but that eye narrowed. "It'll be bad."

"Let's talk about the world breaker."

"What about it?" Diamond asked suspiciously. "Because I don't know anything about it. I don't know how it works."

"I'm not asking for the physics of how it works. I just want to know what the mission plan says. How do you use it? How do you set it off?"

"I don't know. The plan says I just need to get it there. Then I get back in the bullet and leave."

"Leave?"

"Yes. *Leave.* Mom, you didn't want to hang around while Nexus blows up?"

"I don't think Nexus is going to blow up. I think it's going to collapse into a parallel universe and pull any surrounding matter with it."

"You mean pull Nexus—and Machina Overlord—with it."

"Yes."

"I don't want to be there when that happens."

"We can't let it happen!" Violetta's temper flared. "What I don't understand is how the Professional Revolutionaries made this thing. They're vandals, troublemakers. They don't have the knowledge to manipulate spacetime."

Diamond's answer came in a subdued voice. "Machina Overlord must have made it. Who else?"

Of course. No one else could have.

The Professional Revolutionaries were obligated to carry out the acts of chaos assigned to them. Violetta had just never guessed the AI might target itself. But it was a machine, after all. No reason to think it would fear death as people did. No reason to think it would try to protect itself. Why should it? Contending against the Professional Revolutionaries was a hunter's job.

It was not Diamond's nature to waste time on guilt. She had made her apology. Now, peering past the seatback, with only minutes left in the transit to Nexus, she reaffirmed her new resolve, insisting again, "I don't want to lose. And I want to make it right. I don't want to be the bad guy anymore."

"I'm glad to hear it," Violetta said.

"So, we need to make a plan."

"I have a plan."

"You do?"

"Yes. When we reach Nexus, your task will be done. I'll take the world breaker. You stay in the bullet pod. As soon as we're sure your black spot has reset, you leave."

"Without you? That's not a plan! I don't want you to die."

"I'm not going to die. I'm going to get rid of the world breaker."

"How?"

"Push it out an airlock."

Diamond's one visible eye shifted to take in the bullet pod's hatch.

"Won't work," Violetta told her. "We can't open the hatch, and even if we could, you don't get your life back until you deliver the world breaker to Nexus."

"But you don't know what will happen. Just because the world breaker is outside the world, that doesn't mean it won't be dangerous when it goes off. It could still suck the station into a spacetime hole."

"You're right," Violetta conceded, "and that's why I need to make sure it's far away from Nexus when it goes off. So I'm going to drop down the emergency chute, find an escape pod, put the world breaker inside it, and use the centripetal force on the rim of the world to fling it far away."

"You think that'll work? You think you'll have time?"

"I think so, but I want you launched and out of there, just in case."

They fell into the maw of Nexus's bullet catcher right on schedule. The gee forces of deceleration were as severe as at launch, but once their momentum was synchronized to Nexus, their pod glided smoothly to the platform. Violetta released her harness. Diamond did too. "Stay in the pod," Violetta warned as the hatch unlocked.

"But you might need my help."

"I won't need your help."

A mechanical tentacle darted in as the hatch slid open. Diamond shrieked in fury as it encircled the world breaker and snatched it from her grip.

The tentacle was attached to the disc-shaped carapace of a maintenance robot that had been waiting on the platform—a compromised robot, infiltrated somehow by the Professional Revolutionaries. Only knee-high, it scuttled away with astonishing speed on its six mechanical spider legs. It kept a second tentacle folded against its carapace as it made for the platform's glass doors.

"Stay in the pod!" Violetta shouted, jumping out after it. It was too fast for her to catch. So she pulled her stunner from its holster and shot it just as the doors opened to allow its escape.

The stunner's net smacked its carapace, delivering a jolt that caused its legs and both its tentacles to spasm. It collapsed, losing its grip on the world breaker, which bounced away into the darkness beyond the doors.

"No!" Diamond shrieked. "We have to find it."

"I'll find it," Violetta told her as she ran across the platform. "You go. Launch the pod."

She jumped over the sprawled robot—and one of its tentacles darted up, wrapping around her ankle. She went down hard on her shoulder, her head bounced against the floor, and she lost her grip on the stunner. Shock drove out pain as she scrambled for the weapon, but the robot dragged her back and she came up short.

"Grab its other tentacle!" Diamond shouted.

Violetta was vexed to see Diamond on the platform, dancing from one foot to another in her eagerness to help.

Diamond said, "If you grab the tentacle, I can get past it and get the stunner."

"No, you're supposed to launch! Time is running out."

"I'm not leaving you, Mom. So *cooperate* and grab the tentacle."

Fear and frustration fought for dominance, but they were useless emotions. There was only one viable option, and that was to do exactly what Diamond had said.

Violetta twisted around and dove for the second appendage. She caught it halfway along its two-meter length. It flailed and wrapped around her arm. She shoved a boot against it—and Diamond was able to jump over the robot unhindered. She scooped up the stunner, turned around, and fired.

Nothing happened.

"It has a biometric lock," Violetta said through gritted teeth. She had one tentacle wrapped around her ankle, one around an arm. But she still had a hand free. "Pass it to me."

Diamond turned it over.

The seconds were ticking past, but Violetta needed to know. "Show me your hand."

"Mom, just shoot it!"

"*Show* me."

Diamond glanced at her palm, then held it up for Violetta to see. The black spot had gone white. "That means I finished the task, right? I'm clear."

Violetta nodded. "That's what it means." By the amnesty rule, Diamond would get her life back—assuming she lived. "Okay. I need to finish *my* task."

"We're doing this together."

"I think we have to. It's already too late for you to launch. Diamond, I'm going to need your help."

She grinned in delight. "Anything."

Ignoring the robot's scrabbling legs, Violetta aimed for its core. "This jolt is going to hit me, too. If I pass out, you need to make sure I wake up *before* this thing does."

She fired.

She didn't pass out. Not quite. But it was two long, agonizing minutes before she could move again. Diamond used the time to find an off switch on the compromised robot, to pry its tentacles off Violetta, and to recover the world breaker from the shadow where it had rolled, on the edge of the inner ring of Machina Overlord's computational strata.

By the time Violetta made it to her feet, the countdown had reached 2:59. She briefly considered putting the world breaker into the bullet and launching it to anywhere—but a launch took time, and there wasn't any.

"Let's get out to the rim and get rid of that thing."

Diamond narrowed her eyes, and nodded. "I already found the red door. Follow me."

They emerged on the rim, in a curving corridor with a narrow, illuminated path down its center. To the right and left, crowding the path on both sides and looming close overhead, was the chaotic black brickwork of Machina Overlord's computational strata. Directly across the corridor was the hatch to an emergency escape pod—only a step away. All that prevented them from reaching it was the maintenance robot—twin to the first—that crouched in front of it.

"How did the Revolutionaries compromise these robots?" Violetta demanded in frustration as she shoved Diamond behind her.

"How should I know! That was someone else's task."

"I meant it as a rhetorical question." She pulled her stunner and fired.

Nothing happened.

"Out of ammo." She dropped the weapon as a tentacle grabbed her by the wrist.

"Mom!"

"Don't worry." Violetta held out her other hand and the robot responded, seizing that wrist with its second tentacle. As soon as it had latched on, she yanked hard and backed away up the corridor, dragging the robot with her. Its spider feet screeched against the glowing path, but she was able to move it half a meter.

"Okay, Diamond. It's up to you. Get the world breaker into the escape pod and then jettison it."

Violetta braced her shoulder against a protruding cluster of black bricks, a tiny part of the brain matter that was Machina Overlord, and she pulled again. But the robot changed its strategy. It released her wrists, leaving her to lunge for its tentacles. She caught them and held on, while Diamond skirted the spider legs and reached the hatch. She worked a red lever and the hatch slid open. On the other side was the round sphere of the escape pod.

"Put the world breaker inside."

Diamond knelt, setting the device gently on the floor. Then she stepped back and closed the hatch.

"Trigger it," Violetta ordered, feeling her heart flutter as the time counted down in her retinal overlay.

00:59

00:58

Diamond opened the translucent box that covered the red trigger switch. She toggled it.

Nothing happened.

She turned mystified eyes on Violetta. "Why isn't it working?" For the first time, she sounded afraid. "Did they compromise the escape pods, too?"

00:52

00:51

Violetta let go of the robot, kicked it hard, and then stepped on it. "You probably don't have the right authorization." The robot tried for her wrists again, but before it could stop her, she jammed two fingers against the toggle.

The machinery responded. Soft electronic motors whirred; the inner hatch closed with a clunk. A hiss and a pop followed—and the robot gave up the fight. It released Violetta and walked away, presumably returning to its regular programming.

"Is the world breaker gone?" Diamond asked.

"I think so."

A monitor was mounted in the hatch, set up to display the feed from an outside camera. Violetta switched it on. It showed them a circle of bright white lights—already distant—that outlined the perimeter of the pod as it receded rapidly into darkness.

They lost sight of it as Nexus rotated. Violetta turned to Diamond. They embraced each other while time wound down—*ten, nine, eight*— not knowing what would happen at zero. She thought again of Ismo and the twins, wanting them to be her last thought if the world breaker was still close enough to pull them in.

Together she and Diamond watched the monitor—and when zero came, the blackness outside awoke. A diaphanous network laddered into their field of view, rainbow-hued, flickering like distant lightning. It raced toward them, and hit. And then it was inside, all around them, flickering threads of color against the black bricks, color in Diamond's face, in her eyes, in Violetta's hands—and she felt as if she was being both crushed and cut apart by those lines.

Then the lines of color retreated. The sensation fled. It was as if time reversed.

Nexus completed a rotation so that on the monitor they could watch as the last glimmerings shrank to a bright point and vanished in the dark.

"Are we still here?" Diamond whispered. "Or are we somewhere else?"

Violetta directed Diamond to look again at the monitor. "Do you see it?"

A tiny object caught and reflected the light of the sun. It was a distant world, one of the Nine Thousand, and as Nexus turned, they spotted another and another, giving Violetta the confidence to say, "Let's go home."

There was a hearing to evaluate Violetta's response to the crisis. Several physicists testified on her behalf, describing to the judicial committee in lurid detail the fatal disaster that would have ensued if Violetta had not promptly removed the world breaker from the vicinity of Tranquility. The revolutionary she'd arrested agreed with their assessment.

Perhaps she had not chosen the most efficient means to rid the Nine Thousand of the world breaker, but the committee agreed that the task had been accomplished without the delay of debate and with no real loss. It was decided that a year's suspension would settle the issue.

Diamond was happy. "We can follow Dad. Travel all together for a year."

"Maybe we will," Violetta conceded as they walked home together.

Diamond looked up at her with a coy gaze. "By the way, the Revolutionaries have been talking to me again. They have new assignments."

This brought Violetta to an abrupt stop. She put her hands on her hips. "Did you know that the amnesty rule only works once? Diamond, I swear, if you—"

"Mom! Take it easy. I told them I resigned. I think now I might want to be a hunter."

Violetta scowled and started again for home. Only after a few steps did she grudgingly admit, "I think you might be a good one."

ABOUT THE AUTHOR

LINDA NAGATA has won both the Nebula and Locus Awards. Her most recent work is the Red trilogy, a series of near-future military thrillers published by Saga Press. The first book in the trilogy, *The Red: First Light*, was a nominee for the Nebula Award and the John W. Campbell Memorial Award and was named a *Publishers Weekly* Best Book of 2015. Book 3, *Going Dark*, was runner-up for the Campbell Award. Linda has lived most of her life in Hawaii, where she's been a writer, a mom, and a programmer of database-driven websites.

She lives with her husband in their long-time home on the island of Maui.

THE CHAMELEON'S GLOVES

YOON HA LEE

Rhehan hated museums, but their partner Liyeusse had done unmentionable things to the ship's stardrive the last time the two of them had fled the authorities, and the repairs had drained their savings. Which was why Rhehan was on a station too close to the more civilized regions of the dustways, flirting with a tall, pale woman decked in jewels while they feigned interest in pre-Devolutionist art.

In spite of themselves, Rhehan was impressed by colonists who had carved pictures into the soles of worn-out space boots: so useless that it had to be art, not that they planned to say that to the woman.

"—wonderful evocation of the Festival of the Vines using that repeated motif," the woman was saying. She brushed a long curl of hair out of her face and toyed with one of her dangling earrings as she looked sideways at Rhehan.

"I was just thinking that myself," Rhehan lied. The Festival of the Vines, with its accompanying cheerful inebriation and sex, would be less agonizing than having to pretend to care about the aesthetics of this piece. Too bad Rhehan and Liyeusse planned to disappear in the next couple hours. The woman was pretty enough, despite her obsession with circuitscapes. Rhehan was of the opinion that if you wanted to look at a circuit, nothing beat the real thing.

A tinny voice said in Rhehan's ear, "Are you on location yet?"

Rhehan faked a cough and subvocalized over the link to Liyeusse. "Been in position for the last half-hour. You sure you didn't screw up the prep?"

She snorted disdainfully. "Just hurry it—"

At last the alarms clanged. The jeweled woman jumped, her astonishing blue eyes going wide. Rhehan put out a steadying arm and, in the process, relieved her of a jade ring, slipping it in their pocket. Not high-value stuff, but no one with sense wore expensive items as removables. They weren't wearing gloves on this outing—had avoided wearing gloves since their exile—but the persistent awareness of their naked hands never faded. At least, small consolation, the added sensation made legerdemain easier, even if they had to endure the distastefulness of skin touching skin.

A loud, staticky voice came over the public address system. "All patrons, please proceed to the nearest exit. There is no need for alarm"— exactly the last thing you wanted to say if you didn't want people to panic, or gossip for that matter—"but due to an incident, the museum needs to close for maintenance."

The woman was saying, with charming anxiety, "We'd better do as they say. I wonder what it is."

Come on, Rhehan thought, *what's the delay?* Had they messed up preparing the explosives?

They had turned to smile and pat the woman's hand reassuringly when the first explosives went off at the end of the hall. Fire flowered, flashed; a boom reverberated through the walls, with an additional hiss of sparks when a security screen went down. Rhehan's ears rang even though they'd been prepared for the noise. Two stands toppled, spilling a ransom's worth of iridescent black quantum-pearl strands inscribed with algorithmic paeans. The sudden chemical reek of the smoke made Rhehan cough, even though you'd think they'd be used to it by now.

Several startled bystanders shrieked and bolted toward the exit.

The woman leapt back and behind a decorative pillar with commendable reflexes. "Over here," she called out to Rhehan, as if she could rescue them. Rhehan feigned befuddlement although they could easily lip-read what she was saying—they could barely hear her past the ringing in their ears—and sidestepped out of her reach, just in case.

A second blast went off, farther down the hall. A thud suggested that something out of sight had fallen down. Rhehan thought snidely that some of the statues they had seen earlier would be improved by a few creative cracks anyway. The sprinklers finally kicked in, and a torrent of water rained down from above, drenching them.

Rhehan left the woman to fend for herself. "Where are you going?" she shouted after Rhehan, loudly enough to be heard despite the damage to their hearing, as they sprinted toward the second explosion.

"I have to save the painting!" Rhehan said over their shoulder.

To Rhehan's dismay, the woman pivoted on her heel and followed. Rhehan turned their head to lip-read their words, almost crashing into a corner in the process: "You shame me," she said as she ran after them. "Your dedication to the arts is greater than mine."

Another explosion. Liyeusse, whose hearing was unaffected, was wheezing into Rhehan's ear. "'Dedication . . . to . . . the . . . arts,'" she said between breaths. "'Dedication.' *You*."

Rhehan didn't have time for Liyeusse's quirky sense of humor. Just because they couldn't tell a color wheel from a flywheel didn't mean they didn't appreciate market value.

They'd just rounded the corner to the relevant gallery and its delicious gear collages when Rhehan was alerted—too late—by the quickened rhythm of the woman's footsteps. They inhaled too sharply, coughed at the smoke, and staggered when she caught them in a chokehold. "What—" Rhehan said, and then no words were possible anymore.

* * * *

　　　　　　　　　　　　　　　COSMIC POWERS

Rhehan woke in a chair, bound. They kept their eyes closed and tested the cords, hoping not to draw attention. The air had a familiar undertone of incense, which was very bad news, but perhaps they were only imagining it. Rhehan had last smelled this particular blend, with its odd metallic top notes, in the ancestral shrines of a childhood home they hadn't returned to in eight years. They stilled their hands from twitching.

Otherwise, the temperature was warmer than they were accustomed to—Liyeusse liked to keep the ship cool—and a faint hissing suggested an air circulation system not kept in as good shape as it could be. Even more faintly, they heard the distinctive, just-out-of-tune humming of a ship's drive. Too bad they lacked Liyeusse's ability to identify the model by listening to the harmonics.

More importantly: how many people were there with them? They didn't hear anything, but that didn't mean—

"You might as well open your eyes, Kel Rhehan," a cool female voice said in a language they had not heard for a long time, confirming Rhehan's earlier suspicions. They had not fooled her.

Rhehan wondered whether their link to Liyeusse was still working, and if she was all right. "Liyeusse?" they subvocalized. No response. Their heart stuttered.

They opened their eyes: might as well assess the situation, since their captor knew they were awake.

"I don't have the right to that name any longer," Rhehan said. They hadn't been part of the Kel people for years. But their hands itched with the memory of the Kel gloves they hadn't worn in eight years, as the Kel reckoned it. Indeed, with their hands exposed like this, they felt shamed and vulnerable in front of one of their people.

The woman before them was solidly built, dark, like the silhouette of a tree, and more somber in mien than the highly ornamented agent who had brought Rhehan in. She wore the black and red of the Kel judiciary. A cursory slip of veil obscured part of her face, its translucence doing little to hide her sharp features. The veil should have scared Rhehan more, as it indicated that the woman was a judge-errant, but her black Kel gloves hurt worse. Rhehan's had been stripped from them and burned when the Kel cast them out.

"I've honored the terms of my exile," Rhehan said desperately. What had they done to deserve the attention of a judge-errant? Granted that they were a thief, but they'd had little choice but to make a living with the skills they had. "What have you done with my partner?"

The judge-errant ignored the question. Nevertheless, the sudden tension around her eyes indicated that she knew *something*. Rhehan had been watching for it. "I am Judge Kel Shiora, and I have been sent because the Kel have need of you," she said.

"Of course," Rhehan said, fighting to hide their bitterness. Eight years of silence and adapting to an un-Kel world, and the moment the Kel had need of them, they were supposed to comply.

Shiora regarded them without malice or opprobrium or anything much resembling feeling. "There are many uses for a jaihanar."

Jaihanar—what non-Kel called, in their various languages, a haptic chameleon. Someone who was not only so good at imitating patterns of movement that they could scam inattentive people, but also able to fool the machines whose security systems depended on identifying their owners' characteristic movements. How you interacted with your gunnery system, or wandered about your apartment, or smiled at the lover you'd known for the last decade. It wasn't magic—a jaihanar needed some minimum of data to work from—but the knack often seemed that way.

The Kel produced few jaihanar, and the special forces snapped up those that emerged from the Kel academies. Rhehan had been the most promising jaihanar in the last few generations before disgracing themselves. The only reason they hadn't been executed was that the Kel government had foreseen that they would someday be of use again.

"Tell me what you want, then," Rhehan said. Anything to keep her talking so that eventually she might be willing to say what she'd done with Liyeusse.

"If I undo your bonds, will you hear me out?"

Getting out of confinement would also be good. Their leg had fallen asleep. "I won't try anything," Rhehan said. They knew better.

Ordinarily, Rhehan would have felt sorry for anyone who trusted a thief's word so readily, except they knew the kind of training a judge-errant underwent. Shiora wasn't the one in danger. They kept silent as she unlocked the restraints.

"I had to be sure," Shiora said.

Rhehan shrugged. "Talk to me."

"General Kavarion has gone rogue. We need someone to infiltrate her ship and retrieve a weapon she has stolen."

"I'm sorry," Rhehan said after a blank pause. "You just said that General Kavarion has gone rogue? Kavarion, the hero of Split Suns? Kavarion, of the Five Splendors? My hearing must be going."

Shiora gave them an unamused look. "Kel Command sent her on contract to guard a weapons research facility," she said. "Kavarion recently attacked the facility and made off with the research and a prototype. The prototype may be armed."

"Surely, you have any number of loyal Kel who'd be happy to go on this assignment," Rhehan said. The Kel took betrayal personally. They knew this well.

"You are the nearest jaihanar in this region of the dustways." Most people reserved the term *dustways* for particularly lawless segments of the spaceways, but the Kel used the term for anywhere that didn't fall under the Kel sphere of influence.

"Also," Shiora added, "few of our jaihanar match your skill. You owe the Kel for your training, if nothing else. Besides, it's not in your interest to live in a world where former Kel are hunted for theft of immensely powerful weapon prototypes."

Rhehan had to admit she had a point.

"They named it the Incendiary Heart," Shiora continued. "It initiates an inflationary expansion like the one at the universe's birth."

Rhehan swore. "Remote detonation?"

"There's a timer. It's up to you to get out of range before it goes off."

"The radius of effect?"

"Thirty thousand light-years, give or take, in a directed cone. That's the only thing that makes it possible to use without blowing up the person setting it off."

Rhehan closed their eyes. That would fry a nontrivial percentage of the galaxy. "And you don't know if it's armed."

"No. The general is running very fast—to what, we don't know. But she has been attempting to hire mercenary jaihanar. We suspect she is looking for a way to control the device—which may buy us time."

"I see." Rhehan rubbed the palm of one hand with the fingers of the other, smile twisting at the judge-errant's momentary look of revulsion at the touch of skin on skin. Which was why they'd done it, of course, petty as it was. "Can you offer me any insight into her goals?"

"If we knew that," the judge-errant said bleakly, "we would know why she turned coat."

Blowing up a region of space, even a very local region of space in galactic terms, would do no one any good. In particular, it would make a continued career in art theft a little difficult. On the other hand, Rhehan was determined to wring some payment out of this, if only so Liyeusse wouldn't lecture them about their lack of mercenary instinct. Their ship wasn't going to fix itself, after all. "I'll do it," they said. "But I'm going to need some resources—"

The judge surprised them by laughing. "You have lived too long in the dustways," she said. "I can offer payment in the only coin that should matter to you—or do you think we haven't been watching you?"

Rhehan should have objected, but they froze up, knowing what was to come.

"Do this for us, and show us the quality of your service," the judge-errant said, "and Kel Command will reinstate you." Very precisely, she peeled the edge of one glove back to expose the dark fine skin of her wrist, signaling her sincerity.

Rhehan stared. "Liyeusse?" they asked again, subvocally. No response. Which meant that Liyeusse probably hadn't heard that damning offer. At least she wasn't there to see Rhehan's reaction. As good as they normally were at controlling their body language, they had not been able to hide that moment's hunger for a home they had thought forever lost to them.

"I will do this," Rhehan said at last. "But not for some bribe; because a weapon like the one you describe is too dangerous for anyone, let alone a rogue, to control." And because they needed to find out what had become of Liyeusse, but Shiora wouldn't understand that.

The woman who escorted Rhehan to their ship, docked on the Kel carrier—Rhehan elected not to ask how this had happened—had a familiar face. "I don't know why *you're* not doing this job," Rhehan said to the pale woman now garbed in Kel uniform, complete with gloves, rather than the jewels and outlandish stationer garb she'd affected in the museum.

The woman unsmiled at Rhehan. "I will be accompanying you," she said in the lingua franca they'd used earlier.

Of course. Shiora had extracted Rhehan's word, but neither would she fail to take precautions. They couldn't blame her.

Kel design sensibilities had not changed much since Rhehan was a cadet. The walls of dark metal were livened by tapestries of wire and faceted beads, polished from battlefield shrapnel: obsolete armor, lens components in laser cannon, spent shells. Rhehan kept from touching the wall superstitiously as they walked by.

"What do I call you?" Rhehan said finally, since the woman seemed disinclined to speak first.

"I am Sergeant Kel Anaz," she said. She stopped before a hatch, and she tapped a panel in full sight of Rhehan, her mouth curling sardonically.

"I'm not stupid enough to try to escape a ship full of Kel," Rhehan said. "I bet you have great aim." Besides, there was Liyeusse's safety to consider.

"You weren't bad at it yourself."

She would have studied their record, yet Rhehan hated how exposed the simple statement made them feel. "I can imitate the stance of a master marksman," Rhehan said dryly. "That doesn't give me the eye, or the reflexes. These past years, I've found safer ways to survive."

Anaz's eyebrows lifted at "safer," but she kept her contempt to herself. After chewing over Anaz's passkey, the hatch opened. A whoosh of cool air floated over Rhehan's face. They stepped through before Anaz could say anything, their eyes drawn immediately to the lone non-Kel ship in the hangar. To their relief, the *Flarecat* didn't look any more disreputable than before.

Rhehan advanced upon the *Flarecat* and entered it, all the while aware of Anaz at their back. Liyeusse was bound to one of the passenger's seats, the side of her face swollen and purpling, her cap of curly hair sticking out in all directions. Liyeusse's eyes widened when she saw the two of them, but she didn't struggle against her bonds. Rhehan swore and went to her side.

"If she's damaged—" Rhehan said in a shaking voice, then froze when Anaz shoved the muzzle of a gun against the back of their head.

"She's ji-Kel," Anaz said in an even voice: *ji-Kel*, not-Kel. "She wasn't even concussed. She'll heal."

"She's my partner," Rhehan said. "We work together."

"If you insist," Anaz said with a distinct air of distaste. The pressure eased, and she cut Liyeusse free herself.

Liyeusse grimaced. "New friend?" she said.

"New job, anyway," Rhehan said. They should have known that Shiora and her people would treat a ji-Kel with little respect.

"We're never going to land another decent art theft," Liyeusse said with strained cheer. "You have no sense of culture."

"This one's more important." Rhehan reinforced their words with a hand signal: *Emergency. New priority.*

"What have the Kel got on you, anyhow?"

Rhehan had done their best to steer Liyeusse away from any dealings with the Kel because of the potential awkwardness. It hadn't been hard. The Kel had a reputation for providing reliable but humorless mercenaries and a distinct lack of appreciation for what Liyeusse called the exigencies of survival in the dustways. More relevantly, while they controlled a fair deal of wealth, they ruthlessly pursued and destroyed those who attempted to relieve them of it. Rhehan had never been tempted to take revenge by stealing from them.

Anaz's head came up. "You never told your partner?"

"Never told me what?" Liyeusse said, starting to sound irritated.

"We'll be traveling with Sergeant Kel Anaz," Rhehan said, hoping to distract Liyeusse.

No luck. Her mouth compressed. *Safe to talk?* she signed at them.

Not really, but Rhehan didn't see that they had many options. "I'm former Kel," Rhehan said. "I was exiled because—because of a training incident." Even now, it was difficult to speak of it. Two of their classmates had died, and an instructor.

Liyeusse laughed incredulously. "You? We've encountered Kel mercenaries before. You don't talk like one. Move like one. Well, except when—" She faltered as it occurred to her that, of the various guises Rhehan had put on for their heists, that one hadn't been a guise at all.

Anaz spoke over Liyeusse. "The sooner we set out, the better. We have word on Kavarion's vector, but we don't know how long our information will be good. You'll have to use your ship since the judge-errant's would draw attention, even if it's faster."

Don't, Rhehan signed to Liyeusse, although she knew better than to spill the *Flarecat*'s modifications to this stranger. "I'll fill you in on the way."

The dustways held many perils for ships: wandering maws, a phenomenon noted for years, and unexplained for just as long; particles traveling at unimaginable speeds, capable of destroying any ship lax in maintaining its shielding; vortices that filtered light even in dreams, causing hallucinations. When Rhehan had been newly exiled, they had convinced Liyeusse of their usefulness because they knew dustway paths new to her. Even if they hadn't been useful for making profit, they had helped in escaping the latest people she'd swindled.

Ships could be tracked by the eddies they left in the dustways. The difficulty was not in finding the traces but in interpreting them. Great houses had risen to prominence through their monopoly over the computational networks that processed and sold this information. Kel Command had paid dearly for such information in its desperation to track down General Kavarion.

Assuming that information was accurate, Kavarion had ensconced herself at the Fortress of Wheels: neutral territory, where people carried out bargains for amounts that could have made Rhehan and Liyeusse comfortable for the rest of their lives.

The journey itself passed in a haze of tension. Liyeusse snapped at Anaz, who bore her jibes with grim patience. Rhehan withdrew, not wanting to make matters worse, which was the wrong thing to do, and they knew it. In particular, Liyeusse had not forgiven them for the secret they had kept from her for so long.

At last, Rhehan slumped into the copilot's seat and spoke to Liyeusse over the newly repaired link to gain some semblance of privacy. As far as they could tell, Anaz hardly slept. Rhehan said, "You must have a lot of questions."

"I knew about the chameleon part," Liyeusse said. Any number of their heists had depended on it. "I hadn't realized that the Kel had their own."

"Usually, they don't," Rhehan said. Liyeusse inhaled slightly at *they*, as if she had expected Rhehan to say *we* instead. "But the Kel rarely let go of the ones they do produce. It's the only reason they didn't execute me."

"What did you do?"

Rhehan's mouth twisted. "The Kel say there are three kinds of people, after a fashion. There are Kel; ji-Kel, or not-Kel, whom they have dealings with sometimes; and those who aren't people at all. Just—disposable."

Liyeusse's momentary silence pricked at Rhehan. "Am I disposable to you?" she said.

"I should think it's the other way around," they said. They wouldn't have survived their first year in the dustways without her protection. "Anyway, there was a training exercise. People-who-are-not-people were used as—" They fumbled for a word in the language they spoke with Liyeusse, rather than the Kel term. "Mannequins. Props in the exercise, to be gunned down or saved or discarded, whatever the trainees decided. I chose the lives of mannequins over the lives of Kel. For this I was stripped of my position and cast out."

"I have always known that the universe is unkind," Liyeusse said, less moved than Rhehan had expected. "I assume that hired killers would have to learn their art somewhere."

"It would have been one thing if I'd thought of myself as a soldier," Rhehan said. "But a good chameleon, or perhaps a failed one, observes the people they imitate. And eventually, a chameleon learns that even mannequins think of themselves as people."

"I'm starting to understand why you've never tried to go back," Liyeusse said.

A sick yearning started up in the pit of Rhehan's stomach. They still hadn't told her about Kel Shiora's offer. Time enough later, if it came to that.

Getting to Kavarion's fleet wasn't the difficult part, although Liyeusse's eyes were bloodshot for the entire approach. The *Flarecat*'s stealth systems kept them undetected, even if mating it to the command ship, like an unwanted tick, was a hair-raising exercise. By then, Rhehan had dressed themselves in a Kel military uniform, complete with gloves. Undeserved, since strictly speaking, they hadn't recovered their honor in the eyes of their people, but they couldn't deny the necessity of the disguise.

Anaz would remain with Liyeusse on the *Flarecat*. She hadn't had to explain the threat: *Do your job, or your partner dies.* Rhehan wasn't concerned for Liyeusse's safety—so long as the two remained on the ship, Liyeusse had access to a number of nasty tricks and had no compunctions about using them—but the mission mattered to them anyway.

Rhehan had spent the journey memorizing all the haptic profiles that Anaz had provided them. In addition, Anaz had taken one look at Rhehan's outdated holographic mask and given them a new one. "If you could have afforded up-to-date equipment, you wouldn't be doing petty art theft," she had said caustically.

The Fortress of Wheels currently hosted several fleets. Tensions ran high, although its customary neutrality had so far prevailed. Who knew how long that would last; Liyeusse, interested as always in gossip, had reported that various buyers for the Incendiary Heart had shown up, and certain warlords wouldn't hesitate to take it by force if necessary.

Security on Kavarion's command ship was tight but had not been designed to stop a jaihanar. Not surprising; the Kel relied on their employers for such measures when they deigned to stop at places like the Fortress. At the moment, Rhehan was disguised as a bland-faced lieutenant.

Rhehan had finessed their way past the fifth lock in a row, losing themselves in the old, bitter pleasure of a job well done. They had always enjoyed this part best: fitting their motions to that of someone who didn't even realize what was going on, so perfectly that machine recognition systems could not tell the difference. But it occurred to them that everything was going too perfectly.

Maybe I'm imagining things, they told themselves without conviction, and hurried on. A corporal passed them by without giving more than a cursory salute, but Rhehan went cold and hastened away from him as soon as they could.

They made it to the doors to the general's quarters. Liyeusse had hacked into the communications systems and was monitoring activity. She'd assured Rhehan that the general was stationside, negotiating with someone. Since neither of them knew how long that would last—

Sweat trickled down Rhehan's back, causing the uniform to cling unpleasantly to their skin. They had some of the general's haptic information as well. Anaz hadn't liked handing it over, but as Rhehan had pointed out, the mission would be impossible without it.

Kavarion of the Five Splendors. One of the most celebrated Kel generals, and a musician besides. Her passcode was based on an extraordinarily difficult passage from a keyboard concerto. Another keyboardist could have played the passage, albeit with difficulty reproducing the nuances of expression. While not precisely a musician, Rhehan had trained in a variety of the arts for occasions such as this. (Liyeusse often remarked it was a shame they had no patience for painting, or they could have had a respectable career forging art.) They got through the passcode. Held their breath. The door began opening—

A fist slammed them in the back of the head.

Rhehan staggered and whirled, barely remaining upright. *If I get a concussion I'm going to charge Kel Command for my medical care*, they thought as the world slowed.

"Finally, someone took the bait," breathed Rhehan's assailant. Kel Kavarion; Rhehan recognized the voice from the news reports they'd watched a lifetime before. "I was starting to think I was going to have to hang out signs or hire a bounty hunter." She did something fast and complicated with her hands, and Rhehan found themselves shoved down against the floor with the muzzle of a gun digging into the back of their neck.

"Sir, I—"

"Save it," General Kavarion said, with dangerous good humor. "Come inside and I'll show you what you're after. Don't fight me. I'm better at it than you are."

Rhehan couldn't argue that.

The general let Rhehan up. The door had closed again, but she executed the passphrase in a blur that made Rhehan think she was wasted on the military. Surely there was an orchestra out there that could use a star keyboardist.

Rhehan made sure to make no threatening moves as they entered, scanning the surroundings. Kavarion had a taste for the grandiloquent. Triumph-plaques of metal and stone and lacquerware covered the walls, forming a mosaic of battles past and comrades lost. The light reflecting from their angled surfaces gave an effect like being trapped in a kaleidoscope of sterilized glory.

Kavarion smiled cuttingly. Rhehan watched her retreating step by step, gun still trained on them. "You don't approve," Kavarion remarked.

Rhehan unmasked since there wasn't any point still pretending to be one of her soldiers. "I'm a thief," they said. "It's all one to me."

"You're lying, but never mind. I'd better make this quick." Kavarion smiled at Rhehan with genuine and worrying delight. "You're the jaihanar we threw out, aren't you? It figures that Kel Command would drag you out of the dustways instead of hiring some ji-Kel."

"*I'm* ji-Kel now, General."

"It's a matter of degrees. It doesn't take much to figure out what Kel Command could offer an exile." She then offered the gun to Rhehan. "Hold that," she said. "I'll get the Incendiary Heart."

"How do you know I won't shoot you?" Rhehan demanded.

"Because right now I'm your best friend," Kavarion said, "and you're mine. If you shoot me, you'll never find out why I'm doing this, and a good chunk of the galaxy is doomed."

Frustrated by the sincerity they read in the set of her shoulders, Rhehan trained the gun on Kavarion's back and admired her sangfroid. She showed no sign of being worried she'd be shot.

Kavarion spoke as she pressed her hand against one of the plaques. "They probably told you I blew the research station up after I stole the Incendiary Heart, which is true." The plaque lifted to reveal a safe. "Did they also mention that someone armed the damned thing before I was able to retrieve it?"

"They weren't absolutely clear on that point."

"Well, I suppose even a judge-errant—I assume they sent a judge-errant—can't get information out of the dead. Anyway, it's a time bomb, presumably to give its user a chance to escape the area of effect."

Rhehan's heart sank. There could only be one reason why Kavarion needed a jaihanar of her own. "It's going to blow?"

"Unless you can disarm it. One of the few researchers with a sense of self-preservation was making an attempt to do so before he got killed by a piece of shrapnel. I have some video, as much of it as I could scrape before the whole place blew, but I don't know if it's enough." Kavarion removed a box that shimmered a disturbing shade of red-gold-bronze.

The original mission was no good; that much was clear. "All right," Rhehan said.

Kavarion played back a video of the researcher's final moments. It looked like it had been recorded by someone involved in a firefight, from the shakiness of the image. Parts of the keycode were obscured by smoke, by flashing lights, by flying shrapnel.

Rhehan made several attempts, then shook their head. "There's just not enough information, even for me, to reconstruct the sequence."

Suddenly Kavarion looked haggard.

"How do you know he was really trying to disarm it?" Rhehan said.

"Because he was my lover," Kavarion said, "and he had asked me for sanctuary. He was the reason I knew exactly how destructive the Incendiary Heart was to begin with."

Scientists shouldn't be allowed near weapons design, Rhehan thought. "How long do we have?"

She told them. They blanched.

"Why did you make off with it in the first place?" Rhehan said. They couldn't help but think that if she'd kept her damn contract, this whole mess could have been avoided in the first place.

"Because the contract-holder was trying to sell the Incendiary Heart to the highest bidder. And at the time I made off with it, the highest bidder looked like it was going to be one of the parties in an extremely messy civil war." Kavarion scowled. "Not only did I suspect that they'd use it at the first opportunity, I had good reason to believe that they had *terrible* security—and I doubted anyone stealing it would have any scruples either. Unfortunately, when I swiped the wretched thing, some genius decided it would be better to set it off and deny it to everyone, never mind the casualties."

Kavarion closed her fist over the Incendiary Heart. It looked like her fist was drenched in a gore of light. "Help me get it out of here, away from where it'll kill billions."

"What makes you so confident that I'm your ally, when Kel Command sent me after you?"

She sighed. "It's true that I can't offer a better reward than if you bring the accursed thing to them. On the other hand, even if you think I'm lying about the countdown, do you really trust Kel Command with dangerous weapons? They'd never let me hand it over to them for safekeeping anyway, not when I broke contract by taking it in the first place."

"No," Rhehan said after a moment. "You're right. That's not a solution either."

Kavarion opened her hand and nodded companionably at Rhehan, as though they'd been comrades for years. "I need you to run away with this and get farther from centers of civilization. I can't do this with a whole fucking Kel fleet. My every movement is being watched, and I'm afraid someone will get us into a fight and stall us in a bad place. But you—a ji-Kel thief, used to darting in and out of the dustways—your chances will be better than mine."

Rhehan's breath caught. "You're already outnumbered," they said. "Sooner or later, they'll catch up to you—the Kel, if not everyone else who wants the weapon they think you have. You don't even have a running start, since you're docked here. They'll incinerate you."

"Well, yes," Kavarion said. "We are Kel. We are the people of fire and ash. It comes with the territory. Are you willing to do this?"

Her equanimity disturbed Rhehan. Clearly, Liyeusse's way of looking at the world had rubbed off on them more than they'd accounted for, these last eight years. "You're gambling a lot on my reliability."

"Am I?" The corners of Kavarion's mouth tilted up: amusement. "You were one of the most promising Kel cadets that year, and you gave it up because you were concerned about the lives of mannequins who didn't even know your name. I'd say I'm making a good choice."

Kavarion pulled her gloves off one by one and held them out to Rhehan. "You are my agent," she said. "Take the gloves, and take the Incendiary Heart with you. A great many lives depend on it."

They knew what the gesture meant: *You hold my honor.* Shaken, they stared at her, stripped of chameleon games. Shiora was unlikely to forgive Rhehan for betraying her to ally with Kavarion. But Kavarion's logic could not be denied.

"Take them," Kavarion said tiredly. "And for love of fire and ash, don't tell me where you're going. I don't want to know."

Rhehan took the gloves and replaced the ones they had been wearing with them. *I'm committed now,* Rhehan thought. They brought their fist up to their chest in the Kel salute, and the general returned it.

Things went wrong almost from the moment Rhehan returned to their ship. They'd refused an escort from Kavarion on the grounds that it would arouse Anaz's suspicions. The general had assured them that no one would interfere with them on the way out, but the sudden blaring of alarms and the scrambling of crew to get to their assigned stations meant that Rhehan had to do a certain amount of dodging. At a guess, the Fortress-imposed cease-fire was no longer in effect. What had triggered hostilities, Rhehan didn't know and didn't particularly care. All that mattered was escaping with the Incendiary Heart.

The *Flarecat* remained shielded from discovery by the stealth device that Liyeusse so loved, even if it had a distressing tendency to blow out the engines exactly when they had to escape sharp-eyed creditors. Rhehan hadn't forgotten its location, however, and—

Anaz ambushed Rhehan before they even reached the *Flarecat*, in the dim hold where they were suiting up to traverse the perilous webbing that connected the *Flarecat* to Kavarion's command ship. Rhehan had seen this coming. Another chameleon might have fought back, and died of it; Shiora had no doubt selected Anaz for her deadliness. But Rhehan triggered the mask into Kavarion's own visage and smiled Kavarion's own smile at Anaz, counting on the reflexive Kel deference to rank. The gesture provoked enough of a hesitation that Rhehan could pull out their own sidearm and put a bullet in the side of her neck. They'd been aiming for her head; no such luck. Still, they'd take what they could.

The bullet didn't stop Anaz. Rhehan hadn't expected it to. But the next two did. The only reason they didn't keep firing was that Rhehan could swear that the Incendiary Heart pulsed hotter with each shot. "Fuck this," they said with feeling, although they couldn't hear themselves past the ringing in their ears, and overrode the hatch to escape to the first of the web-strands without looking back to see whether Anaz was getting back up.

No further attack came, but Anaz might live, might even survive what Kavarion had in mind for her.

Liyeusse wasn't dead. Presumably Anaz had known better than to interfere too permanently with the ship's master. But Liyeusse wasn't in good condition, either. Anaz had left her unconscious and expertly tied up, a lump on the side of her head revealing where Anaz had knocked her out. Blood streaked her face. *So much for no concussions,* Rhehan thought. A careful inspection revealed two broken ribs, although no fingers or arms, small things to be grateful for. Liyeusse had piloted with worse injuries, but it wasn't something either of them wanted to make a habit of.

Rhehan shook with barely quelled rage as they unbound Liyeusse, using the lockpicks that the two of them kept stashed on board. Here, with just the two of them, there was no need to conceal their reaction.

Rhehan took the precaution of injecting her with painkillers first. Then they added a stim, which they would have preferred to avoid. Nevertheless, the two of them would have to work together to escape. It couldn't be helped.

"My head," Liyeusse said in a voice half-groan, stirring. Then she smiled crookedly at Rhehan, grotesque through the dried blood. "Did you give that Kel thug what she wanted? Are we free?"

"Not yet," Rhehan said. "As far as I can tell, Kavarion's gearing up for a firefight and they're bent on blowing each other up over this bauble. Even worse, we have a new mission." They outlined the situation while checking Liyeusse over again to make sure there wasn't any more internal damage. Luckily, Anaz hadn't confiscated their medical kits, so Rhehan retrieved one and cleaned up the head wound, then applied a bandage to Liyeusse's torso.

"Every time I think this can't get worse," Liyeusse said while Rhehan worked, but her heart wasn't in it. "Let's strap ourselves in and get flying."

"What, you don't want to appraise this thing?" They held the Incendiary Heart up. Was it warmer? They couldn't tell.

"I don't love shiny baubles *that* much," she said dryly. She was already preoccupied with the ship's preflight checks, although her grimaces revealed that the painkillers were not as efficacious as they could have been. "I'll be glad when it's gone. You'd better tell me where we're going."

The sensor arrays sputtered with the spark-lights of many ships, distorted by the fact that they were stealthed. "Ask the general to patch us in to her friend-or-foe identification system," Rhehan said when they realized that there were more Kel ships than there should have been. Kel Command must have had a fleet waiting to challenge Kavarion in case Shiora failed her mission. "And ask her not to shoot us down on our way out."

Liyeusse contacted the command ship in the Fortress's imposed lingua.

The connection hissed open. The voice that came back to them over the line sounded harried and spoke accented lingua. "Who the hell are—" Rhehan distinctly heard Kavarion snapping something profane in the Kel language. The voice spoke back, referring to Liyeusse with the particular suffix that meant *coward*, as if that applied to a ji-Kel ship to begin with. Still, Rhehan was glad they didn't have to translate that detail for Liyeusse, although they summarized the exchange for her.

"*Go*," the voice said ungraciously. "I'll keep the gunners off you. I hope you don't crash into anything, foreigner."

"Thank you," Liyeusse said in a voice that suggested that she was thinking about blowing something up on her way out.

"Don't," Rhehan said.

"I wasn't going to—"

"They need this ship to fight with. Which will let us get away from any pursuit."

"As far as I'm concerned, they're all the enemy."

They couldn't blame her, considering what she'd been through.

The scan suite reported on the battle. Rhehan, who had webbed themselves into the copilot's seat, tracked the action with concern. The hostile Kel hadn't bothered to transmit their general's banner, a sign of utter contempt for those they fought. Even ji-Kel received banners, although they weren't expected to appreciate the nuances of Kel heraldry.

The first fighter launched from the hangar below them. "Our turn," Liyeusse said.

The *Flarecat* rocketed away from the command ship and veered abruptly away from the fighter's flight corridor. Liyeusse rechecked stealth. The engine made the familiar dreadful coughing noise in response to the increased power draw, but it held—for now.

A missile streaked through their path, missing them by a margin that Rhehan wished were larger. To their irritation, Liyeusse was whistling as she maneuvered the *Flarecat* through all the grapeshot and missiles and gyring fighters and toward the edge of the battlefield. Liyeusse had never had a healthy sense of fear.

They'd almost made it when the engine coughed again, louder. Rhehan swore in several different languages. "I'd better see to that," they said.

"No," Liyeusse said immediately, "you route the pilot functions to your seat, and I'll see if I can coax it along a little longer."

Rhehan wasn't as good a pilot, but Liyeusse was indisputably better at engineering. They gave way without argument. Liyeusse used the ship's handholds to make her way toward the engine room.

Whatever Liyeusse was doing, it didn't work. The engine hiccoughed, and stealth went down.

A flight of Kel fighters at the periphery noted the *Flarecat*'s attempt to escape and, dismayingly, found it suspicious enough to decide to pursue them. Rhehan wished their training had included faking being an ace pilot. Or actually *being* an ace pilot, for that matter.

The Incendiary Heart continued to glow malevolently. Rhehan shook their head. *It's not personal,* they told themselves. "Liyeusse," they said through the link, "forget stealth. If they decide to come after us, that's fine. It looks like we're not the only small-timers getting out of the line of fire. Can you configure for boosters?"

She understood them. "If they blow us up, a lot of people are dead anyway. Including us. We might as well take the chance."

Part of the *Flarecat*'s problem was that its engine had not been designed for sprinting. Liyeusse's skill at modifications made it possible to run. In return, the *Flarecat* made its displeasure known at inconvenient times.

The gap between the *Flarecat* and the fighters narrowed hair-raisingly as Rhehan waited for Liyeusse to inform them that they could light the hell out of there. The Incendiary Heart's glow distracted them horribly. The fighters continued their pursuit, and while so far none of their fire had connected, Rhehan didn't believe in relying on luck.

"I wish you could use that thing on them," Liyeusse said suddenly.

Yes, and that would leave nothing but the thinnest imaginable haze of particles in a vast expanse of nothing, Rhehan thought. "Are we ready yet?"

"Yes," she said after an aggravating pause.

The *Flarecat* surged forward in response to Rhehan's hands at the controls. They said, "Next thing: prepare a launch capsule for this so we can shoot it ahead of us. Anyone stupid enough to go after it and into its cone of effect—well, we tried."

For the next interval, Rhehan lost themselves in the controls and readouts, the hot immediate need for survival. They stirred when Liyeusse returned.

"I need the Heart," Liyeusse said. "I've rigged a launch capsule for it. It won't have any shielding, but it'll fly as fast and far as I can send it."

Rhehan nodded at where they'd secured it. "Don't drop it."

"You're so funny." She snatched it and vanished again.

Rhehan was starting to wish they'd settled for a nice, quiet, boring life as a Kel special operative when Liyeusse finally returned and slipped into the seat next to theirs. "It's loaded and ready to go. Do you think we're far enough away?"

"Yes," Rhehan hissed through their teeth, achingly aware of the fighters and the latest salvo of missiles.

"Away we go!" Liyeusse said with gruesome cheer.

The capsule launched. Rhehan passed over the controls to Liyeusse so she could get them away before the capsule's contents blew.

The fighters, given a choice between the capsule and the *Flarecat,* split up. Better than nothing. Liyeusse was juggling the power draw of the shields, the stardrive, life-support, and probably other things that Rhehan was happier not knowing about. The *Flarecat* accelerated as hard in the opposite direction as it could without overstressing the people in it.

The fighters took this as a trap and soared away. Rhehan expected they'd come around for another try when they realized it wasn't.

Then between the space of one blink and the next, the capsule simply vanished. The fighters overtook what should have been its position, and vanished as well. That could have been stealth, if Rhehan hadn't known better. They thought to check the sensor readings against their maps of the region: stars upon stars had gone missing, nothing left of them.

Or, they amended to themselves, there had to be some remnant smear of matter, but the *Flarecat*'s instruments wouldn't have the sensitivity to pick them up. They regretted the loss of the people on those fighters; still, better a few deaths than the many that the Incendiary Heart had threatened.

"All right," Liyeusse said, and retriggered stealth. There was no longer any need to hurry, so the system was less likely to choke. They were far enough from the raging battle that they could relax a little. She sagged in her chair. "We're alive."

Rhehan wondered what would become of Kavarion, but that was no longer their concern. "We're still broke," they said, because eventually Liyeusse would remember.

"You didn't wrangle *any* payment out of those damn Kel before we left?" she demanded. "Especially since after they finish frying Kavarion, they'll come toast *us*?"

Rhehan pulled off Kavarion's gloves and set them aside. "Nothing worth anything to either of us," they said. Once, they would have given everything to win their way back into the trust of the Kel. Over the past years, however, they had discovered that other things mattered more to them. "We'll find something else. And anyway, it's not the first time we've been hunted. We'll just have to stay one step ahead of them, the way we always have."

Liyeusse smiled at Rhehan, and they knew they'd made the right choice.

ABOUT THE AUTHOR

YOON HA LEE's work has appeared in the *Magazine of Fantasy & Science Fiction, Clarkesworld,* Tor.com, *Beneath Ceaseless Skies,* and *Lightspeed.* Lee's first novel, *Ninefox Gambit,* came out in 2016 from Solaris Books. Its sequel, *Raven Stratagem,* is forthcoming in June 2017. His stories have also appeared in anthologies such as *The Year's Best SF 18,* ed. David Hartwell; *The Year's Best Science Fiction and Fantasy 2012,* ed. Rich Horton; and *The Year's Best Science Fiction 29,* ed. Gardner Dozois. He lives in Louisiana with his family and an extremely lazy cat, and has not yet been eaten by gators.

THE UNIVERSE, SUNG IN STARS

KAT HOWARD

There is music in the stars. The stars, the planets, the asteroids, the galaxies. Everything that is flung, whirling in orbit through space and time. We dwell inside an enormous, ever-changing symphony, and each of the many universes sings a song of its own.

I replicate them. I make clockwork universes, astraria and orreries, planets and stars and galaxies made microcosm and set ticking in orbit. Gears of bronze and iron and titanium, planets of marble and stars of precious faceted stones, diamonds that twinkle in the light. Each orbit in perfect harmonic distance so that the piece performs the music of the spheres. It's a different kind of beauty from that of the living universes, one artificial and made in miniature, but the songs are no less real for it, and the beauty no less true.

There's a joy, too, in making things precise. The music of a universe, like the music of a symphony, will never be perfect. There will be dropped notes, missed rests, accidental sharps or flats. They are living things, and so they are flawed. Orreries are mechanical. If I do my work properly, there is no unexpected variance in their song.

I had just finished setting a rhodolite in the turning rose of a nebula when Carina walked into my workshop. She had a universe spinning around her as well—stars blinked in the darkness of her hair—but hers was living.

"It's beautiful," I said, picking up my loupe so I could examine it more closely. Pocket universes weren't as rare as they used to be, but I had never seen one in resonance with a guardian before.

I walked an orbit around Carina. A comet flamed through the wildness of her curls, then flashed and died, bright echoes of its passing sparking like inverse shadows in the darkness.

"You should talk to them, Vera," she said. "They're always looking for qualified guardians, and you've kept that star going longer than anyone expected."

My hand went to the nape of my neck, where a white dwarf cooled. I only wore it outside when I was working. Potential customers were fascinated by it.

"I don't think it will last much longer." It was becoming more and more atonal, which was usually an indication of imminent death.

"All the more reason to see if you can be approved for a universe." A galaxy whirled like a halo at the back of Carina's head, and I could hear its resonance. "I'll put in a recommendation for you."

"Thank you," I said.

I unwound the star from my hair when I got home that night, rolling it from palm to palm, watching the pattern of shadows made as its light shone through my skin. The discovery of the pocket universes had proved the Titius-Bode law—all orbital systems of the pocket universes had stable and self-correcting orbital resonances with each other. In those resonances was the music of the spheres, and in those resonances, my calling.

The discovery had been dismissed as ridiculous at first—singing universes were impossible to take seriously as proper science. But then the pocket universes started dying. In some cases, they would collapse in on themselves almost as soon as they were born.

So, the pocket universes, and the salvageable pieces of the dying ones, were assigned guardians. Someone to ground the resonance until they were stable, or to help ease the passing of the dying stars. Someone to play them music until their own songs were known. That last was the key. Without music, the pocket universes could not survive on their own.

I had built a musical universe for my dying star. A rotating cylinder inside a clockwork box that plucked a series of steel teeth I had etched with constellations. I had, as much as I could, calculated backward, based on the white dwarf. I had considered its probable orbit and origins, and designed the music box to play the song of the dying star's universe. Hearing it, I hoped, would make the star less lonely in its passing.

The music box only played when I hung the star inside of it. I closed the mechanical universe around the solitary star and listened as the quiet lullaby began.

Approval, when it came to custody of a universe, didn't mean paperwork and background checks. It meant being walked through a white room, full of universes being born. Tiny explosions of infinity becoming finite. It gave me vertigo.

"Don't worry," the tech said, her hand gentle on my elbow as she led me through the rows. "That happens to most people. The vertigo is actually an indication of who will make a good guardian. If you resonate at the right frequency for one of the universes, it stops."

I nodded once, not trusting myself to speak through the dizziness without vomiting. But then the vertigo cleared. I could hear the beginnings of a song, bits and pieces of it, something that was almost familiar. I leaned closer and stretched my hand out, and the universe in front of me expanded into it. The dying star in its musical cage next to my chest pulsed once, a bass thrum. The young universe wound itself around me, making me a fixed point in its spin.

The song grew louder.

When a universe is being born, it hasn't yet settled into itself. Much like a child learning to speak, there are mistakes. Babbles. So, I didn't pay any special attention to the shift in the music of my universe, the way the song changed from what I had originally heard. Not at first.

Carina's universe had expanded enough that if I stood close to her, I could hear it sing. "I'd like to commission an orrery," she said. "Something that has the same song. Ridiculous to get so attached, I know, but I'm afraid when it's time for this one to leave me, I won't be able to sleep without hearing it."

"Of course." I began taking the necessary measurements, recording orbits, and wavelength, and brightness.

"I'm sorry for the death of your star," Carina said.

The new universe orbiting my head meant that I had stopped wearing the star when I worked. "It hasn't died. I have it right here." I unhung the star from its orrery and held it in my hand.

Carina stepped back. "That can't happen. You could contaminate your universe. You have to get rid of it."

I wasn't about to murder a dying star. "I had it when I went in to the birthing room, and I was wearing it when this universe chose me. The resonance was there, and the songs aren't atonal with each other."

"You're supposed to stabilize your new universe as it's being born, not change it." Carina said.

"I don't think I have."

When she left, I sat down and listened. To the expanding symphony of my borning universe, and the places that echoed the music I had created to make a star feel less alone in its dying. To the fluttering thrum of that star, ringing a counterpoint. It sounded, I thought, less hesitant than it had. Stronger. I removed it from its cage and held it up.

There was a great ringing clang, as if every instrument in an orchestra was dropped mid-note. The star lifted from my hand and then pushed itself in to the universe's orbit.

The song of the universe began again. Changed.

It doesn't happen often, but stars can escape their galaxies. The ones that do are called hypervelocity stars, some large and flung from the center of the galaxy. Some are much smaller, and their escape route remains unknown. All that is certain is that they are gone, crashing out elsewhere into the universe.

That is not their only name, these stars that are flung out of the galaxies they are born in. They are also called outcast stars.

Every so often, these outcast stars make new homes for themselves. They crash into other galaxies. In these explosions, new stars are born.

My original star, the white dwarf, made itself at home in the young universe. I could hear its song getting stronger and integrating itself into the resonances of the new system, and the song of that universe steadied and expanded. It incorporated parts of the dying star's music into its own song, variations on a theme, movements in a minor key.

The new universe flung out stars in a kind of ecstasy of birth. They fell like rain, shedding themselves down my back and into my workroom. They hung themselves in corners, cobweb galaxies, chiming like bells, ringing like cymbals.

Stars sparked from the ends of my fingers as I worked, formed constellations in my orreries, orbiting on wires next to planets made from glass. They added new choruses to older, established songs.

It seemed like chaos, but when I listened, they matched the existing songs in rhythm and tone. When I measured, they fit exactly in the orbits they were predicted to, resonating with the other pieces.

"I've never heard of anything like this happening before," Carina said, as she examined the orrery she had come to pick up. The song of her universe was nearly complete—it would be ready to leave her soon.

"I've measured and checked. All of the new stars obey Titius-Bode. All of them sing in harmony with the music of the spheres." It might not have been usual, but it was possible.

Stars tumbled down my arm, and Carina pulled into herself, her chair scraping backward on the floor. "You've changed things. That isn't what a guardian is supposed to do. You are supposed to keep the new universe safe while it learns how to sing. That's all."

"What better to teach it how to sing than something that already knows?"

She shook her head. "But what happened changed the song."

"Yes," I said. "It did."

I had grown used to the feeling of a universe constructing itself around me, to hearing the music become more assured as the pieces of it settled into stability. But a pocket universe cannot stay anchored to its guardian, and it came time to let it go.

"It may not work, you know," Carina said. Her own universe had been recently released, and she seemed curiously smaller without its singing orbit. "There is always the chance of collapse, and who knows how your superfluity of stars will affect things?"

The white dwarf star still orbited in the young universe, and other, smaller stars still fell like rain from my hair.

The escape of a universe from its guardian is much like the escape of an outcast star. One piece is flung out of resonance with the other. I found and sang a note that was atonal to the music of this universe. It pushed itself up and away from me until I was no longer a part of its orbit. It sang its own song, all of the pieces in harmony.

All of them. Even the dying star.

And then. Outcast once more, it plummeted from where the universe had been, falling to the ground, disintegrating and burning itself up as it fell. But even without that star, the music stayed the same. The song did not falter.

I heard the song still, even as the new universe disappeared from my sight and from what should have been the range of my hearing. The music box orrery was playing. I opened the door. At its heart, spinning, a small white star.

ABOUT THE AUTHOR

KAT HOWARD lives in New Hampshire. Her short fiction has been nominated for the World Fantasy Award, anthologized in year's best and best of collections, and performed on NPR. Her debut novel, *Roses and Rot*, was published in 2016 by Saga Press, with a second novel, *An Unkindness of Magicians*, forthcoming. You can find her on Twitter at @KatWithSword.

WAKENING OUROBOROS

JACK CAMPBELL

He came down from the low red hills, through the ancient ruins of a city that still revealed life in scattered patches of light and the furtive movements of small, silent people, and finally to the low city clustered around the crumbling walls of a canal, where dark women wore tiny bells that chimed wickedly with every movement and grim men lurked amid the gloom of shrines to forgotten gods.

Where had his aimless trek brought him this time? "Locate," Oscar said into the night. A glowing map appeared next to him and background noises dimmed as a voice softly supplied the requested information.

"Mars Two, City of Jekkara, Street of—"

"Enough." Oscar yawned, trying to decide whether to hazard an adventure or just relax.

Not that the choice mattered in the least. He could do something else tomorrow, or the day after, and he had already done everything.

Hadn't he walked through a Mars in the last few millennia? He drew on banked memory, pulling up images of red men and women in flying ships, green monsters with swords, and shining towers. Nine thousand years before? He had been there that recently?

Oscar looked up into the sky, seeing the great bands of light where other portions of the world were experiencing daylight. He remembered when the dark regions had been spangled with the lights of cities and towns millions of kilometers distant. Now they just showed the black of night. The horizon looked absolutely flat, the upward curve of the world being so gradual and so vast that it was not apparent to anyone standing on its surface. A single winking light floated in the vastness between world and sun. "Wasn't I once able to see many orbiting cities out there? What happened to them?"

The question generated an instant reply from the world. "The cities are still in orbit. You can no longer see them because their lights have been turned off."

"Why aren't those places lighted anymore?" Oscar asked the world.

"Energy conservation," the world told him.

Whatever that meant.

Smiling around with the calm assurance and world-weariness of someone who knew nothing could really harm him, Oscar wandered into one of the small, dimly lit bars where the dark women waited. What sort of food did they serve there, anyway?

Before he could voice the unspoken question, the dark women and the grim men in the bar vanished. The lights brightened. Oscar stared around and saw only one figure remained, a woman seated at one of the tables. She gestured to him. "I've been looking for you."

Oscar, intrigued and excited by something different, sat down across from her. "How did you do that? It's easy to mute or freeze the background people, but I didn't think they could be turned off."

"Not by you," the woman said, smiling slightly. "I'm Aiko. You're Oscar. Do you know how many humans used to live in the world? Trillions."

"Used to?" Oscar asked.

"That was a long time ago. A hundred thousand years ago, there were only seven left. Now there are two."

Oscar blinked at her. "But people don't die. Not actual people."

"We've been immortal for a long time," Aiko said. "You can't imagine how long. But people can still die if they choose to, if they become too tired or too bored or simply stop wanting to live. That's been going on for a long time too."

Something about the woman's attitude rankled Oscar. "I've been alive for . . . at least a billion years."

"Pretty close," Aiko agreed. "You were the last human born. Did you know that?"

"How do you know things like that? How can you shut off the background people?"

"Because I was the first, Oscar," she said, her eyes suddenly very hard to look at. There was something inside those eyes that made Oscar flinch. "The first to undergo the eternal-life process." She looked around. "I walked on the real Mars. I lived on a planet that orbited a real star. Eventually, I helped build the world."

"Build?" Oscar stared at her, then at his surroundings. He had simply assumed the world had always been there. "This was built?"

"It's all artificial, Oscar. Humanity didn't want to worry about the random dangers of living on real planets warmed by real suns. The world was based on something called a Dyson sphere, but we wanted it to have a very thick shell, impervious to just about any danger. So, we gathered materials from a dozen star systems and built the world and created a stable sun to light it, and the world has since wandered through space, gathering what it needs to sustain life." She smiled again, this time in fond remembrance. "We had so much room to work with. And so many years to do the work."

"Hold it," Oscar said. "Two of us? Everyone else is background? But I've walked through a lot of places. Cities full of homes and apartments and hotels, and towns, and places in the country. You said trillions? I can believe that. Two?"

"When was the last time you met an actual person?" Aiko asked.

"I don't know." Oscar frowned. "Why isn't the memory bank telling me?"

"The memory must have been purged."

"Purged?" Oscar stared at Aiko again, this time in shock. "Memories are always banked. All memories."

"That hasn't been true for a long time," Aiko said. "Too many people, too many memories. Nobody noticed. After a few million years, most days are pretty much the same." She leaned forward, her arms resting on the table between them. "But the end is coming."

"The end?"

"Of the universe." She waved about. "It takes a long time for infinity to compress back into a singularity, but the world has existed for that long. There's nothing outside now except that singularity. We're orbiting it. And because the singularity has sucked in everything else, there's no longer anything else for the world to draw on for energy."

"That's why the lights in the night areas aren't showing?"

"That's why."

He tried to grasp "the end" and couldn't. "What does that mean?"

"The world runs out of energy, spirals into the singularity, you and I die, and there's nothing left," Aiko said. "Ever."

"That . . . can't happen."

"It will." She smiled again, looking a bit like the wicked, dark women who had formed a background to this place. "But you and I, we can do something about that."

"What?"

"We can fix it."

Oscar slumped in relief. "Fix the world? I thought what you were talking about was real, not a game! You had me going."

"It is real." Her smile was gone. "The option didn't exist for a long, long time. But as the singularity grew and became almost all there was, the laws of the universe itself have altered in significant ways. Enough so that now we can make it happen."

"We?" Oscar spread his hands in confusion. "Why do you need me?"

She smiled, but her eyes still held something odd. "Because doing it will require accessing one of the main control centers below the world surface, and making some . . . significant changes to the world operating systems. The controls were designed so that it requires two people to enter those changes. It can't be done by any other means except two people with their hands on those controls. For safety."

"Safety. Right." Oscar wasn't used to having to think about things that mattered. Nothing could go wrong with the world watching. Even on adventures, the world kept you from actually being hurt. But this sounded important. Like what he decided might mean something. Though he had the odd feeling that Aiko wasn't telling him everything.

She eyed him as he hesitated, then reached out, took one of his hands in hers, and smiled again. "I'm so glad I found you. I've missed being with an actual person."

"Yeah. Me, too," Oscar agreed. Her hands on his felt very good. The world could make physical encounters with backgrounders seem absolutely real, feeding the right stimuli to the brain to provide all the sensations of actual interaction. But some part of the brain always knew it wasn't real, always knew it was a fantasy.

Aiko was real, her body as perpetually young and healthy as his was. And she was gazing at him with wide eyes as her hands tightened on his. "It's been too long."

"Too long," Oscar gasped as they pulled each other close.

The next morning, Aiko led Oscar outside. The backgrounders were still off, leaving the ancient city eerily empty. She noticed Oscar's uneasiness. "Everywhere else is like this, you know. These places used to have a lot of people in them, with the backgrounders for local character. As the number of people dwindled, more backgrounders were created. Eventually, when energy had to be conserved, the backgrounders started being shut down unless an actual was in that area."

"But you said we're the only two actuals left."

"Yes. Since I shut down the backgrounders here, there aren't any running anywhere right now."

Oscar had been wondering whether he should help Aiko. After so many years of whatever he decided to do not mattering, he shied away from the idea of doing something that would make an actual difference. But now he looked up at the vast expanse of sky filled with the world, imagining every place in it exactly like this. An incredibly vast stage built by humanity, but empty of performers. "What we're going to do will fix this, right?"

"It'll fix things," Aiko confirmed cheerfully.

A large sky craft rested in a courtyard where Aiko had landed it the day before. Oscar settled into a comfortable seat as she entered a destination, then sat back as well to watch the terrain of Mars Two dwindle beneath them.

Reaching the proper altitude, the craft shot forward, the land below almost blurring. Oscar saw land he had slowly, aimlessly traversed over thousands and millions of years tear past below, the red of Mars Two giving way to yellowish dunes that transitioned to green fields. Countless cities and towns went by, all perfectly maintained by the world, and all empty of actual inhabitants. The craft barreled through bands of night and day as it crossed vast distances, the dark of the night bands unrelieved by lights.

"We made entire planetary surfaces," Aiko said, her voice distant with memories as she looked down at the landscape. "We had the room. A lot of different Earths, from different real time periods and different imaginary times. That's a reproduction of the surface of Ceta, the first extrasolar world colonized by humans. When we made it, it seemed important to commemorate that, but after a few billion years, nobody really cared."

"How old are you?" Oscar asked.

"I stopped counting." Aiko turned her dark eyes on him. "Since I preexisted the world and helped code it, even the world doesn't know. I made sure of that."

"How far are we going?" he said, anxious to change the subject.

"There's a spot I've visited off and on," she replied, and left it at that.

Eventually, the craft slowed and settled to a stop in a city made of archaic stone buildings. "This is part of a reproduction of an Earth from a time period before mine," Aiko said as they left the craft. "The city is called London. There are a lot of Londons in the world, but this is my favorite."

"The backgrounders are on," Oscar said as the people and animals and wagons and carriages wove around him, Aiko, and the craft without otherwise reacting to their presence.

"I need to talk to one of them," she said, leading Oscar down a nearby street. They stopped at a narrow door with 221B in brass letters above it. Aiko entered without knocking, taking similarly narrow steps up to the second floor.

Oscar followed, finding Aiko standing in a room crowded with odd objects. An angular-faced man, another backgrounder, was sitting in a large chair before a fireplace, his hands steepled together as he eyed Aiko.

"You've returned, Lady Aiko. Another case?"

"No," Aiko said, sounding sad, her gaze roving about the room.

"I deduce that you are in a hurry, and that you will not return."

"That's right. This is goodbye. I'll miss you. I've enjoyed our talks."

The man made a dismissive gesture. "That is unimportant. But the world wonders why you consider this a farewell."

"The world will find out," Aiko said. She turned and walked back down the stairs, Oscar hastening in her wake, until she stopped at the wall on the ground floor. "We put one of the access shafts here as sort of a joke," she told Oscar. "Which comes in handy now. Since I've visited this place before on occasion, my coming here didn't tip off any systems watching me." Tapping a series of figures on the wallpaper, she caused a section to vanish, exposing a manual control panel similar to the virtual ones that Oscar was used to.

"I've never seen one of those," he said.

Aiko ignored him, entered a code, then waited.

"Access denied," a soft voice said.

"Really?" Aiko, her expression hardening, entered another code.

"Priority access denied," the voice said. "Require justification for access."

"Not from me," Aiko said. As she prepared to enter a third code, the sounds of rushing feet came from outside, and a single pair of feet clumped on the stairway from above.

She reached down and hastily activated a device.

Silence fell.

Oscar leaned out far enough to view the now-empty street through a window. "You shut them off?"

"They were tools of the world, which was trying to use them against me. Against us," she corrected quickly. Aiko entered the third code.

"Control level access denied—"

"Maximum Override Omega Nine Nine Nine Alpha," Aiko said angrily.

The wall vanished, revealing the interior of a float shaft. "We use the emergency ladder," Aiko told Oscar, pointing to rungs built into the wall.

"What—What is that?" Oscar asked as something scuttled away down the shaft.

"Maintenance bot," Aiko said. "Everything we built has been kept in repair and physically replaced over and over by automated systems, which have themselves been repaired and physically replaced over and over as time wore them down."

Oscar struggled down the ladder rungs after Aiko, wondering just how deep this shaft was. "Why didn't the world want to let us in? Why can't we use the float shaft?"

"Because the world is worried about what I might do," she called back to him.

"Why would the world be worried? This is going to fix things, you said."

She took a moment to reply. "Yes. That's right. But the world is supposed to keep actual humans safe, and when we go below the surface, we get exposed to hazards, so the world is concerned that we might get hurt."

Something about that didn't sound right, but Oscar's mind fastened on one word that drove other concerns from him. "Hazards? You mean actual hazards?"

"Right. Here's your chance to see what a real adventure is like."

Oscar had never been out of shape. His body maintained itself in peak physical condition no matter how little or how much exercise he did. But he found himself sweating as he followed Aiko down the apparently endless series of rungs, hearing objects scuttling just out of sight. "Aiko? Is there anything else down here? Besides the bots?"

"Good question!" she called back.

The soft voice came again from all around them, but at a louder volume. "Justify your presence in a restricted zone."

"Inspection tour," Aiko replied.

"Invalid response."

"I am Senior Technical Executive Aiko Lys. I have authorized access to all areas above and below the surface."

"Invalid response. Your actions have displayed a pattern which has activated enhanced security protocols. Return to the surface immediately."

Aiko reached a platform and swung off the rungs onto it. "Understood. I will comply." She helped Oscar onto the platform, then urged him down the hallway beyond, lights coming on before them.

"You are not complying with instructions," the voice insisted.

"You did not specify the path to the surface," Aiko said, moving faster.

"Return the way you came."

Aiko paused at a box mounted on the wall and yanked it open, pulling out heavy tools. She held on to a hammer and passed a monkey wrench to Oscar. "This way is shorter," she said.

"Invalid response. Activating level two security protocols."

Something hit the floor behind Oscar. He spun around, seeing something with many legs and glowing red eyes spring toward him.

He had been through this sort of thing many times in adventures on the surface, fighting virtual dangers with virtual weapons. Reflexes honed by those experiences kicked in and Oscar swung the tool he held without thinking. It slammed into the creature as it leapt at him, knocking it against the wall with a muffled metallic sound. It fell to the floor and scrabbled to get up, most of its legs limp. Repulsed by the sight, Oscar swung again and smashed the bot.

He heard a rustling noise behind them.

"Hurry!" Aiko ran down the hall, Oscar right behind, a vague darkness in the hallway revealing a growing mass of bots heading for them.

They passed a heavy door and Aiko yanked him to a stop, then pulled a device from one pocket. She slapped it on the door controls, then tapped rapidly on the device while Oscar debated with himself whether to keep running.

The door slid shut with a *thunk* that sounded comfortingly secure to Oscar.

"That won't hold them forever," Aiko said. She darted down the hall, rounded a corner—

Oscar found her paused on the edge of an abyss. "What is this?"

"It's worse than I thought. The world has already been forced to cannibalize mass from here to feed the mass-energy conversion systems." She pointed. "But it left a ledge to help bots get past. Come on."

"Come on?" Oscar stared down at depths that seemed eager to drag him down.

But Aiko pulled at him, moving with dangerous haste along the narrow pathway that still existed next to one wall.

He tried not to think about what he was doing, and tried to pretend that this was just another adventure on the surface where he couldn't really be hurt, but pretending meant thinking about that huge hole waiting to engulf them, and . . .

He stumbled onto the floor in the intact hallway beyond, breathing heavily. Looking back, Oscar stared. "Why is part of the rock moving?"

"The rock? More bots?" Aiko reached to adjust a lighting control on the wall.

A mass of brown and black bodies, scrambling toward them.

"Rats," Aiko breathed. "That's where they went. Run!"

Down another hall, the lights blinking out partway. But Aiko produced a hand light and they kept going until they reached a massive door. "Maximum Override Omega Nine Nine Nine Alpha!"

"Access denied," the soft voice replied. Oscar wondered whether it was his imagination that gave that voice a smug note.

Aiko paused, angry, then smiled again. "Double Secret Maximum Override Zero Zero Zero."

The door opened.

"How many of those overrides do you have?" Oscar asked as he helped wrestle the door closed again, sealing out the tide of rats.

"Enough," Aiko said. "I hope." She moved to the control panels lining three walls of the room, gazing at them with a wondering expression. "It's been a very long time since I was here. But everything is just as it was. Perfect. Unchanging."

"That's good, right?" Oscar asked, his heart pounding with worry.

"Is it?" She looked at him. "What's the difference between an eternal, unchanging heaven, and a nearly eternal, unchanging prison?"

"Ummm . . . choice?"

"Choice. Free will. We built something so perfect that it meant we never had to make a meaningful choice again." Aiko laughed, moving to one of the panels and entering commands rapidly. "Until now."

A red light began pulsing overhead and an alarm bellowed.

"I need you here, Oscar," Aiko directed. "Stand right here. I have to go over there, make some more modifications, enter some more commands, and then we'll have to confirm the sequence at the same time from both panels."

"All right." Oscar stood where he had been told, the panels before him flashing with streams of data and status reports. He kept seeing the word DANGER appearing, along with frequent glimpses of CRITICAL, UNSTABLE, SEVERE, and IRREVERSIBLE. "Aiko?"

"Wait." She was working with frantic haste. "It can still be stopped."

"But—"

"DANGER! DANGER! DANGER!" screamed the voice of the world.

"Aiko!"

"We're ready," Aiko said. "You see that blank spot? Yes, the clear space. Place one hand flat on that . . . yes, there! Now tap that control that's flashing to the left of it."

Oscar hesitated, his hand on the panel, the red light and roaring alarm filling his head. "Aiko, are you sure?" he cried.

Her head hung low for a moment, then Aiko raised it and looked at him. He flinched away from those eyes again as she answered. "Oscar, I am sure that if we do not do this, then it will all end. But if we do . . . Oscar, what would you give to experience something new? Something you've never seen before? That's like nothing you've ever known?"

"New?" The idea was so alien. And so terrifying.

And so seductive.

How would it feel?

After so many, many years?

"The world can't handle something new, something beyond what it was made for," Aiko said. "All it can do is keep doing what it has been doing, even if that is failing. That's why we have to do this."

Oscar thought of the endless empty cities on the surface of the world, felt Aiko's burning gaze upon him, and slowly reached to touch the flashing control.

The alarms and the flashing red light and the increasingly frantic voice of the world shut off.

A strange humming began to build around him.

"Yes!" Aiko cried exultantly, laughing as she raised her hands upward and looked at the ceiling. "Finally!"

"What—What's going to happen?" Oscar demanded.

"The end of everything," Aiko whispered, sounding almost delirious with joy. "And the beginning of everything."

"You said this was about fixing the world!"

She spun to face him, her smile frightening to see. "No. I said it would fix everything. A singularity is an impossible thing. It's impossible to break an impossible thing. Until the universe is so warped by that singularity that it becomes possible to break the unbreakable. To free everything trapped within it."

"You said the entire universe was in that singularity," Oscar began, fumbling with the words.

"Yes! The entire universe! And the way the universe now works, with space-time stretched to its limit and all matter and energy compressed into that small speck, there is enough potential force in the world if it converts its entire remaining mass to energy to destabilize the singularity!" Aiko rubbed one hand across her face as the humming grew slowly in intensity. "Do you know what we never learned, Oscar? We never learned why. Why did humanity and other sentient species come into existence? Why was the universe predisposed to create us? Did we have a purpose? And now we finally know, Oscar."

She pointed outward. "I'm sorry I misled you. There was no way to fix the world. But the world can fix everything. The universe needs a trigger to restart, and a sentient species can provide that trigger. We're part of the cycle. In a short time, the singularity will destabilize and the universe will be reborn. That's why we're here, Oscar."

"But—" Oscar looked around wildly. "I don't want to be here when the world explodes!"

"We won't be." Aiko hit a control and another door slammed open. She grabbed his hand and yanked Oscar into motion as she ran down hallways that throbbed with the power of the growing vibrations. "There are still ships," she shouted over the noise. "I made sure of that. They haven't been used for more than a billion years, but they've been maintained, rebuilt, and reconstructed! We should have time to reach one and launch it!"

"*Should* have time?" Oscar yelled back. "You're not sure?"

"How does it feel?" she shouted. "To not know what's going to happen? To not know what tomorrow will hold? To not know if there will be a tomorrow? This is what being a god is about, Oscar! Not power and immortality, but the knowledge that life is precious and we face not countless predictable days but countless real choices that will allow us to decide what our tomorrows will be like!"

He had never really been scared before this.

He had never really been happy before this.

They reached a huge open area with great shapes sitting silently, waiting as they had waited for a billion years. One of the shapes glowed with light, an open hatch beckoning.

Oscar didn't have to be pulled along anymore. He ran all out, racing Aiko to reach that hatch as the humming filled the world.

He realized that no one else except for him and Aiko could hear or feel that humming. There was no one else. The world was empty. As frightened as he was, he finally understood a little why Aiko's eyes looked the way they did.

They leaped in, side by side. Aiko slapped a control and the hatch shut, blocking out the still-building vibrations.

By the time they reached the control deck, the ship had taken off, cleared the world, and was accelerating away at inconceivable velocity. Aiko sat down, straps automatically fastening around her. "You should do the same. These ships were designed to endure every imaginable force, but when the singularity explodes, the forces will be unimaginable."

Oscar sat down, feeling the straps wrap about him. The view screen showed the dark mass of the world from the outside, the impossible black of the singularity beyond it, and the completely empty blackness beyond. "We might still die?"

"Maybe." She looked at him, her eyes almost normal but filled with an unholy glee. "Maybe not. We'll find out."

"My choice . . . mattered," Oscar said.

"We mattered."

The image of the world on their view screen vanished and was replaced by a bolt of energy headed toward the singularity.

And there was light.

ABOUT THE AUTHOR

JACK CAMPBELL (John G. Hemry) hopes that someday he'll be able to write space opera even half as well as Leigh Brackett did. He writes the *New York Times* bestselling Lost Fleet series, the Lost Stars series, and the "steampunk with dragons" series The Pillars of Reality. His most recent books are *Lost Stars: Shattered Spear, Beyond the Frontier: Leviathan,* and *The Dragons of Dorcastle*. His short fiction includes time travel, alternate history, space opera, military SF, fantasy, and humor. John is a retired US Navy officer. Being a sailor, he has been known to tell stories about Events Which Really Happened (but cannot be verified by any independent sources). This experience has served him well in writing fiction. He lives in Maryland with his indomitable wife, "S," and three great kids (all three on the autism spectrum).

WARPED PASSAGES

KAMERON HURLEY

My mother left me for the anomaly when I was too young to see over the railing into the tangled gardens at the center of the ship but not yet old enough to climb up onto it and jump into the lake at the garden's heart. The people of the Legion had stopped counting time back in my mother's day, when the anomaly ripped through the fleet and halted us on our two-generation journey to a world that our prophets said would lead to our salvation. Now we were a static fleet, stuck in darkness, drifting nowhere, with uncertainty as to when and how our resources would run out. Would we starve in a generation? Two? Or would we asphyxiate first?

No one was quite certain. It had driven some people mad.

But for those of us who knew nothing else, it just made life that much more worth living. Living is a gift, when you're sure it could end at any minute. And life ended often, in the Legion. Accidents, plague, bad air, support system failures, insurrection, collisions . . . one by one, the ships of the Legion would go dark, and those of us left would cannibalize whatever remained of them.

I suppose that would drive my mother's generation more mad than me, because I had no expectations, not like she did. In school, aboard ship, they were told they would arrive in some brave new world God had chosen for them and the prophets of New Morokov had charted. They were God's chosen people, with a real purpose, a plan. I was just a kid with an uncertain future, drifting through the detritus of the dying.

Everything had gone wrong just halfway into the trip.

The anomaly appeared and passed through the whole fleet, like a great, many-tentacled wave of glutinous energy. It split our ship in two, cutting right through the center of the lake, slicing open the hull in every direction. That should have been the end of us and every ship in the Legion, which were all halted in the same way. We should have been jettisoned into deep space. But though the anomaly breached the hull, the anomaly itself acted as a sort of sealant. There was no breach. But the engines could no longer power us forward. We were stuck in place, having been slowed and eventually rooted to whatever these waves of foreign matter were.

From outside the ship, when I take the long trading walks between our home and those ships aligned with ours, the anomalies look like massive, irregular shimmering discs splitting through all five hundred ships of the Legion. They reflect light, and the ships, and each other, and our tools and clothing, but not our faces. You stare into the flat plain of an anomaly and it's like watching a ghost wearing your clothes. It's like they're eating our souls, my mother used to say, which made her choice to throw herself into one that much stranger. Why would you feed your soul to some alien thing?

My sister Malati says the anomaly is a great manifestation of our own consciousness. Everyone has theories about what they are. All we know is that they don't see our reflections, and that whatever steps into them never comes back out again. The scientists don't think the anomalies are alive, and prophets agree, but the way they act, sometimes, the way they ripple when you talk to them, makes me think otherwise. I spent my childhood throwing junk into those things until my mother caught me and slapped me for being wasteful.

"We need every piece of this ship to survive," she had said. "You don't recycle something, and it's lost forever. Do you understand? You risk your children's lives. You risk our future. Waste is a terrible crime."

I started crying when she yelled at me, because I didn't want to be wasteful. Losing or breaking something was the worst thing anyone could do out here. It meant you would have to trade with another ship, or go on a dangerous scavenging mission to one of the derelicts at the edge of the Legion's gravity well.

When I was old enough to stand up on the rail and jump into the lake with my friends, during the very darkest of the ship's sleeping cycle, I was fascinated by the number of things captured in the shimmering face of the anomaly that bisected the lake. Ropes and chains and plastic tethers that had held instruments and small animals that my grandmother's generation had cast into the thing lay scattered on the banks of the far side of the lake, or tied off to metal balustrades, a record of two generations who had tried and failed to understand the anomaly. It's why jumping into the lake was considered so dangerous. It was easy to float into the anomaly if you weren't careful. And once you threw something in, you couldn't pull it back out. Not the tethers or anything attached to them. No people, either.

There were many theories about the anomaly. Some said it was an interdimensional body, perhaps one that lived in five or six dimensions, and the half-circles of nothingness that split through our ships were simply the manifestation of it that we could perceive in our dimensions. Others thought it was a sentient thing, an unknown being. Some said it was the tears of God, who had wept when we left our home planet, and now punished our arrogance by keeping us here, bound by Her tears.

Me, I had grown up with the anomaly. It was just a part of life. It didn't scare me until my generation hit puberty, and some of us starting giving birth to strange things.

But I'm getting ahead of myself.

I don't know whose idea it was, first, to sever a ship from the anomaly and retrofit it to fly again. It was an old plan, something from my mother's generation, before people gave up hope. Half a dozen ships tried it, cobbling together parts, selecting crews, but they failed every time. I learned about some of those attempts in school, and maybe that's when I came up with my own plan. Maybe that's when I realized what the problem was.

All of these people, they were trying to repair a ship and take other people with them. It was at least another generation more to the planet. Even if they got there and could mount a rescue, it would be another generation back to get us. That's two generations more we'd have to survive out here, and the reality is, we probably weren't going to make it that long. They'd return to a dead husk of ships, all spinning black around the great artificial sun and gravity well that held us together.

It was never the engineers who failed, in retrofitting ships to break free of the anomaly, or at least I didn't think so then. It was the people they involved. People fought about who was going to go, who was going to come back, and the ships were sabotaged long before they could break free. The one to reach as far as the edge of the Legion, the one that got as far as the outer rim of ships, was piloted by a woman named Pavitra Narn and carried just a dozen people. They had kept the whole thing secret right up until the time they opened the fuel tanks to feed the engine.

But Pavitra and her crew were still sabotaged. Probably by one of their own crewmates, or by a lover or a family member left behind.

The remains of that ship still circle the outer rim of the legion, along with the escape pods.

It was after Pavitra's failure that people started using the escape pods. They thought they could escape the gravity well, I guess, though where they thought they'd go after that, I don't know. Maybe they just hoped to cling to a few more cycles of life, to gain themselves more time for a rescue. Maybe the clutch of years they could survive in a pod was more than they expected to live inside the ships.

When my mother had me, after her mother died, there was still some hope in her generation. But that's been gone a long time now. Most old people sit in their quarters, waiting for the end.

I knew, reading about Pavitra, that I was going to learn how to fix ships, and I was going to figure out how to get one out of the Legion. But I was going to do it right. I wouldn't tell anyone but my sister Malati, because though I was becoming a good engineer by then, she was a lot older than me and already an ace pilot. She was allowed to drive our ship's only functioning transport on ship-to-ship runs and salvage missions, one of just a dozen people qualified for it.

Malati and I could do it. If I involved more people than that, it would never work. Someone would get angry. Someone would try and stop us.

Maybe even the anomaly itself.

So, I stopped staying up late jumping into the lake. I didn't go out huffing chemicals with the other kids. I didn't screw around very much, which was a shame, looking back. Maybe I missed out on some things.

But I intended to build something better.

It was out on my third spacewalk, helping a team to gather salvage around a nearby ship now only half-populated, that I saw the ship that I would retrofit.

Pavitra's wreck had collided with another derelict floating at the edge of the Legion. If I told people I was studying systems on the derelict, I could easily get access to Pavitra's old ship and work to retrofit it.

From the derelict I'd also have a long view into the center of the Legion, and the two dozen ships already in the process of being devoured.

We didn't know for sure what had happened on those ships. Rumor had it that the people of our generation were giving birth to strange growing things, like tumors, and they were spreading fast, engulfing ship after ship. But none of those ships it happened to were allied with us, so we had only rumors. We did no trade with them, and many were openly hostile. We offered no aid. The ships that carried the people of the new prophets were only a fraction of the people who made up the Legion. Many followed other gods, or no god at all.

We simply sat in our sector of the Legion, staring at those transforming ships, as I did from the rim of the derelict, wondering when whatever fate had befallen them would reach us.

The engines that powered the ships were all closed organic systems, meant to work in symbiosis with the rest of the ship. It was a concept that worked well as long as nothing happened to any other part of the ship, and maybe that's part of what was wrong with the ships being eaten. That's the theory I had back then. The closed system made the ships harder to retrofit, but I knew Pavitra had already started that process. Though there was little enough left of her ship, getting out there to work on it every day would be easy. I could cover what I was doing by saying I was just studying it and applying what I learned somewhere else, on some other ship—ours.

It was a tricky, two-faced balance. I didn't know if I could pull it off.

I pitched the idea to my engineering instructor not long after puberty, and though much of the class scoffed at the idea of studying another derelict, the professor did not. I spent long cycles in meetings with engineers and scientists, and then I was given permission to go out on my spacewalk. But I wasn't to do it alone, they said. They wanted me to take another student. I convinced them Malati was the best person to accompany me.

And so it started—my attempt to free us all from the death of the Legion.

The various systems of the ship were never meant to work independently, as I said, which is what made it so miraculous that the anomaly hadn't stopped the core life-support functions of the ships. Their influence kept us rooted in space—no matter how much fuel we gave the engines, the ships of the Legions never moved. It was another bit of evidence in support of the interdimensional idea—if the bulk of the anomaly existed in some other dimension, then that's what rooted us here. It was as if some giant beast had thrown out its fingers or tentacles wide, snarled us in them, and fallen back to sleep while we writhed in its grasp.

The stuff that fueled the engines was a complex brew of engineered organisms that excreted a combustible compound. It was pumped into yet another engineered organism at the center of the ship, an organ we simply called the "engine" though it did not at all resemble anything like the early machines that bore that name in my History of Engineering classes. The engine powered all of the ship's systems, not just propulsion; it pumped vital heating and cooling fluid to various parts of the ship and kept the complex algae bath that provided our oxygen at the correct temperature. Ours was not a fully sentient ship but a hybrid of living and dead tissue. When I was younger, I had asked if the ships were alive, but the elders all said the ships were no more alive than an organ grown in a vat, like the time my aunt's heart was replaced by one grown in the medical bay.

"Is your liver a sentient thing?" my teacher asked when I protested. But when you worked on the ships, you couldn't help but think of it like a living thing, a tethered animal.

I spent many cycles working to retrofit Pavitra's ship. Malati thought I was odd, at first. She laughed when I told her my idea. But as the artificial sun went up and down and progress on the engine took shape, she stopped laughing and started helping on our long forays across the tethers that we'd set up between our ship and the derelict.

Finally, the day came when I had the last bit of retrofitted printed parts I needed to fire up Pavitra's old ship.

I sweated heavily in the suit I wore as I went hand over hand out on the tether to the derelict. Malati was already far ahead of me. We'd argued about something petty back on the ship, and she was ignoring me. She seemed much more graceful outside the ship than in it, but I was the opposite. The blackness beyond terrified me. I did every walk like this far too fast, to the point that my instructors often chided me about the need for caution over speed.

So, I don't know why I hesitated that day. You get used to junk flying around the Legion. Our gravity well was still active; it was all that held us together, and we thanked God for that after, but it also meant it was difficult for anything to escape the core. Things could be cast out but never truly discarded.

I saw the piece of junk catch the light from the heart of the Legion before it struck. A sharp glint, nothing more. It zipped by so fast, I barely had time to register it. You forget how fast things are moving around you when you're making the slow, arduous crawl between ships.

The aged piece of dead tech hurtled past me. It snapped the tether. The frayed end of the tether hit me in the face. I let go, grabbing at my face, fearful of a suit breach. I didn't realize I'd slid off the tether until I pulled my hands away, and by then I was already a hundred yards away from Malati, pinwheeling away from her at a constant speed. She had wrapped her hands around the broken tether. I could not see the expression on her face so far away.

I flailed, trying to see where I was headed. A knife of fear cut through my heart. I realized I wasn't spinning toward the Legion but away from it. Reason told me I hadn't been thrown with enough force to escape the Legion's gravity, but reason did not quell my quaking fear as I tumbled between two great ships, signing for help as I careened past them.

They might not get to me in time, but Malati could send a shuttle out after me. If my air didn't run out, if I didn't career into one of the ships, if . . .

And that's when I realized that there was no safe passage between those ships.

Both ships were cut through by the anomaly. It was a broad, disc-shaped plain there, like a bladed saw that split both ships—and I was headed toward the center of it.

I cried out. I came closer and closer, powerless to stop myself. I saw the distorted reflection of my suit in the anomaly's shimmering face. A ghost suit without a body in it. To the anomaly, I was already dead.

Where did we go when we went through the anomaly? Where had my mother gone? Where had all the instruments gone? Where would I go?

"Please help me," I said aloud, and I must have been saying it to God, or maybe the anomaly itself, or maybe both, if they were indeed one and the same. "Please," I said.

I kicked and waved my arms, instinctive, knowing it wasn't going to help, knowing movement meant little in vacuum.

I collided with the anomaly.

Bright white light burst across my vision.

I screamed. I remember screaming.

I wondered if my mother had screamed.

I woke in a warm, pale blue room.

Our medical officer, Jandai, stared down at me from within a heavy medical grade suit.

"Do you know where you are?" she asked.

". . . Jagvani Station?" I said.

"And who are you?" she asked.

"I'm Kariz Bhavaja," I said.

She nodded ever so slightly, lips pressed firm. I tried to figure out what that meant.

"What happened to me?" I said.

"To hear the witnesses on the *Goravna* and *Arashakti* tell it, you passed through the anomaly," she said.

"I'm not . . . this isn't the other side?"

She raised her brows. "It's not the afterlife, if that's what you're asking. But you'll see that soon enough when you're pissing through your catheter," she said.

"But . . . no one comes out the other side of the anomaly alive," I said.

"Some do," she said. "But they . . . bring things with them."

"Is there something wrong with me?"

The pursing of the lips again. Then, "You're under medical watch for a few days."

"Quarantine?"

She nodded.

Quarantine lasted for ten sleep cycles. I asked about Malati, and Jandai said she was shaken but fine. Malati came to visit me early in the quarantine, and we spoke softly through the protective film around my quarters.

"I think we should stop," she said.

"You want to die here, in the Legion?" I said.

She could not answer that.

So, I counted my days in quarantine, which nobody in my generation likes to do, but sometimes you can't help it.

On the tenth one, I already knew something was wrong long before Jandai came back. At night, I had felt something stirring in my chest. And on the tenth morning, when I woke, I had a lump in my chest where one had not been before.

"We've detected something," Jandai said, and I did not let her finish.

"Get it out," I said.

"It's a living thing," she said. "Protocol is not to remove it until we understand what it is."

"Are you insane?" I said. "You *know* what it is! It's one of those things; it's—"

"We can't confirm it's what's been reported on the other ships," Jandai said.

"It's a parasite! It will kill me!"

"We have no evidence of that," she said. "The science council has recommended that we wait and see. We have a very strict policy about how we handle alien life."

"This is insane," I said again, as if by saying it, I could make her understand it. But she was resistant.

"You can't legally keep me in quarantine any longer than ten cycles," I said. "You have to get rid of it or release me. I'll call an advocate."

"I've been given instruction to release you," she said, "but you'll be monitored."

This shocked me. I couldn't understand how they could permit me to leave the medical bay with some alien thing in me, but then I started laughing, because of course the alien things were already here, they were all around us, they had cut into our ships a generation before, and now my mother's generation was just using me as some test tube to see what happened next.

They sent me home with painkillers and anti-inflammatories, and I lay in bed with my hands over my chest. I swore I could feel the thing growing inside of me. I must have dozed, but when I woke, I had terrible heartburn and spent half an hour vomiting bile.

I stumbled out onto the balcony overlooking the great garden at the center of the ship and stared down into the lake, and then up at the shimmering anomaly that bisected it and our ship. I understood my mother's compulsion to jump into it then. I wanted to tear open my chest and get the thing out, but no one wanted to help me.

Was that why she had really jumped into the anomaly? Had it done this to her, too? And if it had, where had she come out again? Had they hidden her from me because she was contaminated afterward like I was? I closed my eyes and imagined those other ships, the half-eaten ruin of them. Rumor had it the first few had removed these organisms, but they clung to the ship instead and ate everything around them, devouring it like some fungus. If it stayed inside of me, it would eat me too, and then the ship. The prophets had to know this. Why were they permitting me to walk around?

It wasn't going to last, I knew. So, I went out to finish what I'd started. I found Malati in our quarters. She had the parts we had carried with us.

"We go again," I said. "We make it work this time. We aren't coming back."

"Are you mad?" she said.

"I know why it won't let us leave," I said, rubbing the thing on my chest. "The engines are alive. It thinks they are, anyway. I think the anomaly sees them as kin of some kind. It thinks we've enslaved them."

"That's a strange stretch," Marita said.

I knew I shouldn't have said it aloud to her. "I don't think it was always us who was sabotaging the ships that tried to get away. I think the anomaly made us do it, the same way it convinced the prophets to let me go from quarantine."

"If all we're doing is what they want, then we have no free will," Marita said. "I don't believe that."

"Some of us do," I said. "I just don't know which."

"Is that why we're going?"

"They'll stop us soon," I said. "This isn't going to last."

We took the shuttle this time, because Malati had access. I would deal with whatever the consequences were. But not Malati. Malati was going to be safe, far away from here.

It took two more sleep cycles to get Pavitra's wreck up and running.

"Why haven't they come for the shuttle?" Malati asked as I powered up the great monster of an engine.

"You should get settled in the back," I said. "I'll deal with them."

"What do you mean?"

"I'm not going with you," I said. "If I go, and that planet's already inhabited by someone who came after us . . . I'll have brought this thing there. I can't let this thing leave the Legion."

"I'm not spending all that time alone! I'll be an old woman when I get there. Don't you dare. I'm not doing it. We didn't go through all this just for you to stay."

"They want me to go," I said.

"What?"

"The prophets. That's why they didn't take it out," I said. "I don't think we have a will of our own anymore, Malati. Not all of us. I think the anomaly is affecting their judgment. It wants me to leave the Legion with this thing."

"That's mad."

"A lot of things are mad," I said. "But you won't have to be alone. I've fitted the rear with escape pods. They'll keep you in stasis for most of the journey. I'll show you how to use them. Switch out once, when the first reaches the end of its cycle, and you'll be there before you know it."

"I can't do this alone," Malati said. "First Mother, then you—"

"You won't be alone," I said. "The fate of the whole Legion goes with you."

She firmed her mouth, then, though unshed tears made her eyes glassy.

I powered up the ship, and I put Malati in deep stasis in one of the escape pods I had hauled off the derelict and fitted into Pavitra's ship. The second waited nearby. I didn't know if she could last the cycles of rest she would have to be awake in between, but if she didn't, then everything that remained of us would die out here. Or maybe, I thought, gazing out the port window at the growing tangles of fibrous matter eating the ships at the core—we would be transformed.

I kicked on the engines and set them on autopilot with a long timer. When I popped free of the ship and into the transport, the growing lump in my chest throbbed. My head ached. I piloted the transport away, quickly, and sat back to watch.

I half expected the ship to explode. I watched it power up and jump forward. It heaved toward the edge of the Legion like a shot. I held my breath as it cleared the gravity well.

Then the blue burn of the cruising thrusters, the intricate combination of organic fuels that burned so hot it powered the ship at near-lightspeed, blazed brightly. I'd only ever seen those thrusters chemically burn in vain, shown to us in recordings of the first few attempts they had made to free the Jagvani, so we'd know what it would look like if it ever worked again. But ours never got us anywhere. We were tethered in place.

Pavitra's ship broke away from the Legion.

I watched it for a long, long time. Long after it was even a speck in my field of vision. Behind me, the artificial sun at the core of the Legion came up and bathed us all in orange light.

When I cycled back into the air lock of the Jagvani, Jandai was waiting for me.

"Come," she said, and I didn't ask what for, not even when she brought me to the medical bay and sedated me.

When I woke, the ever-present lump on my chest was gone. Jandai sat beside me, and behind her, in a large glass cylinder, was a pulsing orb of tissue. It was covered in little tentacles, like cilia, all waving against its glass prison.

"Why won't you kill it?" I said.

"It's been attempted, on other ships," Jandai said. "It . . . fights back. But that's of no concern to us, of course. We have strict protocols about preserving life of any kind, I told you. It goes against everything we believe."

"Why now?" I said. "Because the ship is gone? Because they know I can't get them out?"

"It will serve a different purpose," Jandai said.

"How long have you all known what the anomaly was and what these things are?" I asked. "How long did my mother know?"

"We agreed not to tell the third generation," she said. "It was bad enough for us, living with it. Better for you to believe escape was possible. Better for you to believe you had free will and were not caught in the maw of some monster."

"Is the anomaly God?" I asked.

"It is a sentient being that is beyond our understanding. I suppose that yes, in a way, it is *a* god, if not *our* God."

I stared at the pulsing thing in the cylinder. "Will it eat the ship, like the others?"

She nodded. "In time. But by devouring the ship it will save us, in a way. We'll be transformed."

"It's turning the ships into living things," I said. "Real living things."

"We think it was drawn to them from some . . . other place. It saw them, perhaps, as a species that must be uplifted."

"Then what were we?"

She grimaced. "Parasites."

"Why let us think we had no future? Better to know the truth, so we can fight it."

"Fight a god? No. Your future . . . our future will be in service to these things, as whatever they make us into. People will still live on the ships, but they, too, will become part of it, like any other system on the ship. They can't leave it without the whole system collapsing. We tried it with some of the early ships. If you remove any of the components it grew around and incorporated when it was birthed, it dies, and so does everyone and everything else aboard. We wanted you to get away while you still could."

I tried to sit up, but the drugs from the surgery were wearing off, and my chest throbbed. "Why not take it out, then! I could have gone—"

"No," she said, "Not once you're infected. You're a part of it now."

"Why didn't you tell me all this?"

"Because you were our hope," she said. "If you and the others thought you had no future, you would fight to build one instead of accepting this one. We raised you your whole lives to accept God. How would you have reacted if you thought this was one?"

"Only, Malati got away."

"I know. I guess it doesn't matter. It feels like we're the only human beings in the universe out here, but of course there are many others under many stars. She may arrive to a fully populated world."

"They'll rescue us," I said.

She laughed. "What will they rescue, if we are even still here, once we become like those other sentient ships and putter off to whatever destination they have in store for us? We're linked to these ships; haven't you been listening? We'll become part of these machines, birthing its parts, its organs, like insects. It's best they don't come. I don't want them to see us." She stood. "You should go now."

"Why did you finally tell me about all of this?" I asked.

"Your mother didn't throw herself into the anomaly," she said. "She was pushed on order of the prophets, because she was going to tell you and your sister that the anomaly was God's will and we should not fight it. She was going to ruin the grand experiment. So instead, she became a part of it."

"You kept her from me," I said. "You made her a prisoner. Made her birth one of these things and told me she was dead."

"In the end, the process killed her," Jandai said. "What grew in her did not survive. I'm sorry. But the experiment is over now."

"These things aren't the monsters," I said. "*You* are. All of you."

"Maybe so," she said, and she stood and left the medical bay.

I lay alone in the room with the pulsing alien thing in the jar, the alien that would turn this whole ship into some kind of integrated machine, and I tried to come to grips with the scale of this betrayal. History was a lie. My studies were a lie. My whole life's purpose, all this work, my mother's suicide, all a lie. For what? For science. A grand experiment. A last attempt to save us. Our parents' generation could not live with the truth, so they just never spoke about it.

It had worked, absolutely. Malati was free. But should she be? I didn't know. If we all died here, was it so terrible, in the grand scheme of things? What happens next, when you realize everything is a lie, and life has no purpose?

When I was recovered, I went down to the lake and peered into the anomaly. My mother's generation knew what I did, now, and they had chosen secrecy, and despondency, and suicide. But they had forgotten that we were the same people who had left a blighted, overcrowded planet three generations before to take a risk on a new life among the stars. We were made from stronger stuff than they imagined.

It would take my whole life, I knew, but I would figure out a way to control what we were becoming. If I could not stop it, I could figure out how to influence it. I was an engineer of massive organic systems. I had done what the best of us, Pavitra, had not managed: I had powered a ship away from the Legion. There was nothing I wasn't capable of.

"You cannot break us," I said. "No god ever has."

And I climbed back upstairs to the medical bay and got to work.

ABOUT THE AUTHOR

KAMERON HURLEY is the author of *The Mirror Empire*, *Empire Ascendant*, the *God's War* trilogy, and the forthcoming *The Stars Are Legion*. Hurley has won the Hugo Award, Kitschy Award, and Sydney J. Bounds Award for Best Newcomer; she has also been a finalist for the Arthur C. Clarke Award, Nebula Award, Locus Award, British Fantasy Award, Gemmell Morningstar Award, and the BSFA Award for Best Novel. Her short fiction has appeared in venues such as *Popular Science*, *The Year's Best Science Fiction*, and *Meeting Infinity*. Her nonfiction has been featured in the *Atlantic*, *Bitch* magazine, *Entertainment Weekly*, the *Huffington Post*, *Locus* magazine, and the collection *The Geek Feminist Revolution*.

THE FROST GIANT'S DATA

DAN ABNETT

It was the first time Dwire had been back to Nox since he'd built the place. Built it tight so no one could get in.

Now he was coming back at seventy-three times the speed of light.

"Wake up," he said, and the CLoans woke. He watched them closely, monitoring their startup patterns. They blinked, writhed blindly, and gulped like newborns in their bags as the amnioteks drained out. He'd asked for eight, and the clients had sourced five for him. One of them, an ex-shockwar unit that had probably been sloughed too many times, was having febrile convulsions and its stats were tanking. He shut it down.

Four. He'd have to manage with four.

The CLoans had cost a lot to procure. The CLoans, and the fightware. The ship had cost more. The clients hadn't bought the ship; it was a borrow. But even borrowing an intersystem packet ship had put a dent the size of Mare Imbrium in the mission budget, and bribing an ITA official to certify its eight-parsec detour had cost ten times that.

The detour wasn't much. Just a little wobble in the packet ship's routine monthly mail run. Just a little jink that put it in viable photon-sling range of Nox.

A four-hour range window. Four CLoan tacbodies. Dwire's insider knowledge.

Put together, it might do the trick.

There was a lot riding on it. The clients had been crystal about that.

Dwire flopped into the velocity cot he'd been nesting in since the packet ship launched. Eight days' worth of squeezed-out juice-meals lay scattered on the deck around it. The air smelled of oranges. A twitch of his fingers hapted up a datarray, and he brushed through the images hanging in the air. He knew it all. He knew it backward. He snapped his fingers and centered an image of Nox, enhanced for visual and overlaid with specs: a black orb, a cold, dead heart, out in the middle of nowhere at all, bothering no one. If anyone could crack it open and get at the meat, it was him.

He'd built it.

Not the structure. Indentured Formoid constructors had hollowed out the crust and machine-drilled the subsurface vaults. Some of the stacks were eighteen miles deep. Lucian Vironeers, in cryohazard armor, had installed the immense climate vanes. Nox was stabilized at about nine points off absolute zee. The whole contract had been financed by a property development conglom out of Kuiper City. Dwire had been hired toward the end of the project to design the security package. He'd named his own price and he'd done his best work.

At Dwire's level of the game, you didn't leave back doors. That kind of sentimental disregard for comprehensive security architecture got you fired and never hired again. Just because he'd built it didn't mean he'd left a way in.

Besides, the architecture was fluid. He'd designed it to evolve. By definition, it wasn't the beast he'd created anymore. But he knew how that evolution was supposed to work. That was his edge. That was what the clients were counting on.

On completion, the Nox development had been bought outright by the Frost Giant. Huge payday for the Kuiper boys. The Frost Giant had made Nox one of his primary data claves, a storage facility for the currency that had made him the richest man in the Spiral Arm.

The datarray pinged. The window was about to open. Dwire hoisted himself up.

Time to go.

He ejected from the ship. Just him, riding a thrust-rig. Boosted photon sling, superluminal. He'd routed the datarray feed to retinal display, and it crowded his vision with furious info streams. He couldn't see Nox anyway, only black on black. As expected, the Nox AI had seen the packet ship and queried its close approach. Routine handshakes, clearing codes. The ITA approval seemed like a reasonable excuse. The Intersystem Transit Authority was famously clean.

Dwire was infinitely smaller than the mile-long mass of the packet ship, just a human body, plus the superlight thruster rig, no bigger than an atmospheric drone or a piece of debris. The AI would spot him, but it would dismiss him as dust, or an asteroidal cannoned out by the packet's wake, or an imaging artifact.

He'd jinked his trajectory with a randomizer. The extra distance of the erratic course would eat his time, but the upside was it would take the AI much longer to recognize him as a deliberately approaching contact rather than a speck of crap spinning past.

Photon sling was no way to travel. The vibration was a bitch. His teeth hurt. There was blood in his sinuses. Dwire had borrowed velocity from the packet ship and amped it with thrust from the superlight rig. He had saved reserve energy for course-correction burns plus decel, and hoped it was enough. It would suck to discover it wasn't once he was diving head first toward an artificially cooled rock the size of Mercury.

Eight minutes.

He passed out four times. The derm-sensors monitoring his vitals felt him gray-away each time, and flooded his body with stims that woke him like a slap in the face.

"I'm awake," he growled, tasting bitter metal and chemicals.

He could make out the hard blue shadow of Nox rushing up against the starfield. It was still pretty much nothing in nothing, an eclipsed eclipse, a whisper in a noisy hall. There was a faint halo of luminescence, thin as an arced chalk line, where the light of the starfield bent in Nox's thin atmosphere.

His retinal display flickered. The AI had noticed him and was taking an interest. *Finally, buddy. Took your sweet time.*

Soft-pass scans flooded his way. He was being analyzed. Mass and composition assays. Trajectory analysis. Dwire had about seven seconds before the AI recognized pattern and intention in his randomized course.

He prepared to light the thruster rig for the final burn and dump the fusion mine. It would go off like a small sun. Big, shiny noise. Maximum distraction.

An autosnipe turret on Nox's polar highlands woke up and pinked off a single tachyon hyperkinetic.

Dwire had no time to curse, no time to register disappointment, no time to even feel paternal pride that his AI-governed architecture had evolved so finely, it had cut the target pattern recognition time down to three seconds.

The impact mashed him and the rig into a molecular fog.

The hyperkinetic round touched off the fusion mine. A star winked on and off, hard bright and painful to look at. Nox's perceptor arrays damped protectively, rebooted, and retrained, focusing their attention on the patch of space now occupied by a radioactive heat bloom and a vapor of organic debris.

Dwire watched the distraction with satisfaction. He had expected to have to sacrifice the first CLoan tacbody. He was impressed the AI had caught it so fast. At the moment of body death, the gestalter engine on the packet ship had saved his crashed consciousness and reinstalled it in the skull of the second tacbody, which was now executing a burn-approach on the far side of Nox.

This Combat-Loan tactical body happened to be female. It felt fragile now that he inhabited it, though Dwire knew they were all built to the same level of mil-grade durability. Besides, he was too busy vomiting. Microdrains in his faceplate sucked the fluid out fast. His loaned organs hurt. Point-of-death save-and-installs were high-trauma experiences. Military specialists took a mandatory eight months' leave to recover from emergency gestalter saves in the field.

No such luxury for him. Stims rushed him again, brought him up, made him sharp. This tacbody would be ready for scrap after the stress he was running it through. He had toxins in his muscles and his blood, necrosis, organ damage.

He felt like shit.

His ret-feed updated. More autosnipes were waking up, their matte-gray mushroom domes rising from the powdered dust of the equatorial plains. Dwire had insisted on installing the best: Maxima Grande Gauss Automatic Marksman assemblies, grav-stabilized, mounted with Kemperer Weaponsuites, all slaved to the AI. For a target as close and fast as he was, they would select fluid-dynamic prediction algorithms. That's how he'd programmed them, anyway. Had they evolved? Had they been upgraded or reset?

He was counting on "no." He had switched the drivers of his superlight rig to execute an anti-Mandelbrot recursive descent, embellished with some randomizer jink-turns he'd copied from watching the flight patterns of butcher wasps on Chryse.

The snipes started firing. Hyperkinetics. Jacketed photonics. From somewhere around the curve of the horizon, a spiner cannon started to cut the sky apart with hard-beam ripper shots.

Dwire evaded. The Nox AI hadn't had to ward off this kind of invasive approach much in its lifetime, so it hadn't evolved new ways of doing it. Its targeting protocols were as box-fresh as the day he'd loaded them.

Ret-feed gave him six possible landfalls. He selected the closest. The sky wasn't somewhere you wanted to be any longer than you had to.

He triggered the auto-release that would shed the hard-burning rig and allow him to soar clear. It failed. Fired it again. Fail.

The AI was jamming electronic signals. There was a manual release for the thruster rig, but that fact was moot.

You clever bastard, he thought in the nanosecond before he hit the surface at three times the speed of light.

"You want me to . . . what? Stop the peace accord?" Dwire asked.

"No, no, Mr. Dwire. Not precisely," Oliphant had replied. "We want to . . . inspect the treaty details."

"With a view toward stopping it?"

They had taken a stealth table in a restaurant overlooking the Bay of Naples. The view was magnificent. No one outside even knew they were there.

"Open war could become protracted and cause massive damage to the Sodality's economy."

"Hurting your business," asked Dwire. "Which is . . ."

Oliphant smiled. He was a small man with big ideas and a very patient voice.

"Concerned parties within the Sodality believe the peace accord could have unforeseen consequences. Don't get me wrong. The war would be bad. The war would damage the economy, perhaps beyond the point of recovery. Mr. Dwire, the Sodality is the greatest expression of human civilization, a truly galactic superculture. It behooves us to take its survival very seriously."

"Right." Dwire nodded. "So, stopping a war with the Ushuns seems to be a good idea."

"Indeed." Oliphant raised his wineglass, but did not drink. "A vastly smaller culture than ours. Numerically . . . insignificant."

"But total fuckers when it comes to a fight."

Oliphant shrugged.

"They are tenacious. And ferocious. Their mindset is one of absolutes. They will fight until they die, or until they wound us so badly we bleed out."

"That's been predicted since first contact," said Dwire. "Which is why this chance of a peace agreement is so precious. That the Ushuns even considered negotiation . . ."

"The treaty will be signed in fifty days," said Oliphant. "We want to make sure that what our leaders are signing is actually peace."

"Because?" asked Dwire.

"The treaty is four trillion words long. It has taken nineteen years of negotiation through diplomatic back channels. It was framed to allow for all eventualities and in consideration, at their specific request, of the Ushuns' absolute attention to detail. The complex particulars of the document form the foundation for any hope of lasting peace. Fifty percent of it is written in Ushun."

"Are you suggesting . . . they've slipped something into the fine print?"

"Yes," said Oliphant.

"Shit, I was joking."

"No joke. We welcome peace, but the nuance of the Ushun terms may encode something unacceptable, something that will defeat the Sodality more completely than open military action."

"So, you want to look at the document?"

"We do. It is confidential. We will pay highly for the privilege."

"Where is it?" asked Dwire.

"The only copy is sequestered in a hypersecure data storage clave, watched over by an independent custodian. We have learned the location."

"Who's this custodian?' asked Dwire. He suddenly had a sense of foreboding.

"Deryl Durant," said Oliphant. "The data baron."

"The Frost Giant," said Dwire.

"Yes."

"The treaty . . . it's stored on Nox, isn't it?"

"Yes, Mr. Dwire."

"Now I understand why you're talking to me."

It had not been a clean landing. Dwire had broken some ribs and at least two fingers. The gestalter engine had saved-and-switched him into the third CLoan about thirty seconds after it had made planetfall on Nox.

He got up, unsteady.

Steal a peace treaty from the most secure vault in the Sodality, he thought. *Stop a peace. Start a war.* Not exactly the heroic destiny Dwire had hoped for himself, but Oliphant had been convincing. There were nobility and duty in it. If Oliphant and his fellow clients were right, and Dwire was successful, it would lead to a war that would cost billions of lives.

And that would be preferable. A win.

High cliffs of black rock and blue ice towered over him. He was standing on the lip of one of the thermal canyons. He could see the monumental white phantom shapes of the cryo-vanes. Data was hot. The amount of data stored and protected by the Frost Giant generated enough heat-bleed to stoke a sun. That's why he required specialist holding claves like Nox, sculpted for maximum heat dispersal, cryo-cooled to nigh on absolute zee. The Giant's specialization in ultra-cold storage had earned him his nickname.

Nox was cold as hell and loaded to the brim. Not to mention out of the way, discreet, hard to find or reach, and defended up the ying-yang.

Dwire was the best security architect in the Sodality. He was not a field agent, but he knew Nox like no one else. And he had made it to the surface wearing a synthetically reinforced tacbody that was hardwired with the instincts and reactions of a special forces operative.

Three of four. His margin of error was narrowing; his window was closing.

He set off at a jog. The canyon lip would take him to the base of Vane Seven, and from there he could gain access to the local service shafts. As he ran, he un-sacked his sidearm from the pouch on the front of his suit. Clutching it made him feel more comfortable.

The skeletal service walkways were fitted for heat, motion and vibration. Frost clogged the handrails and the spacer grilles. Dwire wondered if anyone had walked on them since the day he'd finished his work and taken one last look around.

Dwire kept to the rock, though it was sheeted with ice and treacherous. Thermal pads in the soles of his boots thawed each step he took and increased his purchase.

His ribs hurt. The tacbody must have hit the ground damn hard.

There was a supply port in the silo above the service shafts. That was Dwire's entry point of choice. He knew for a fact that there were six autosentry modules in the area. He jogged a route that expertly snaked him between all of their perceptor cones.

He had gotten within sixty meters of the port when the slayborg arrived. The first he saw of it was a howling maw full of stainless steel teeth coming at him like a runaway train.

Dwire had placed slayborgs in the lower levels in his original design, mostly for mechanized patrol and perimeter checks. He hadn't put any on the surface. Was this evolution, or was this the Frost Giant tinkering with the design?

It didn't matter. What mattered was that there was one in his face. What also mattered was that the slayborgs he'd installed down below had been security-grade units, the basic, highly efficient "Supertrooper" model built by Teksimiles out of Lares Hub. He'd bulk-bought ten thousand of them.

This wasn't a Supertrooper with a bland, goofy face and khaki plating.

This was battlefield grade: a Coyne Munitions "Berserker" model, huge and feral.

It lunged at him. Its reach was six times his, and its talons were like sabers.

He let the CLoan body's instincts take over, and evaded hard, puffing up a spray of ice crystals. A nice dodge, but the Berserker was fast. It wheeled and ripped at him. It was trailing loose cables and rubber pipework from its snout, so it looked shaggy, like some emaciated, dreadlocked bear. No eyes. The perceptors were down in its armored chest.

It lashed out. He tucked and rolled. The slayborg's knife-fingers gouged out pack ice and rock like a backhoe. Dwire rolled again, the opposite way. Rime covered his faceplate. His ret-feed was flashing him hazards that he either didn't need to know or were spectacularly obvious. Blades came down at him like icepicks and broke the ground like glass.

He aimed his sidearm. It was a steel frame tactical assault pistol, firing jacketed photonics. A 760 White Liger, manufactured by Coyne Munitions—just like the slayborg. There was some pleasing irony in that. Three rapid shots smacked the charging slayborg onto its ass, as though it had run into a clothesline.

It got up, leaking syrupy fluid from its blast-distorted jawline and cranium. Dwire's ret-feed tight-targeted the rumpled plating above the Berserker's perceptor array, and he put two more rounds into the hole. The slayborg blew out. The power cells in its armored thorax lit off, and its abdomen vanished in a fireball blossom.

The hazards kept flashing. Rising, Dwire saw two more Berserkers bounding over the ice toward him like galloping simians. He stood his ground and put four shots into the nearest one, dropping it in a fountain of fluid while it was still ten meters away. He switched to the second. Three shots didn't stop it. The fourth round dropped it, but it got up again. The fifth and sixth went down its slavering mouth and exploded its spine.

The slayborg Dwire hadn't seen ran him down from behind. He

thought he'd been swiped by a truck. A blade finger stabbed into his back. He felt every centimeter of it go in, felt it slice his liver and shred his intestines. It picked him up like a fish on a skewer and shook him.

Dwire screamed. His faceplate was full of blood. He fired wildly.

The thing dropped him. Dwire flopped over, leaking steam and blood. Trauma was overloading the tacbody's systems. Stim supplies emptied into his bloodstream. The slayborg was on him. It crunched off his left hand and spat it out. Dwire fired point-blank. The pain intensified. It was eating him alive.

Save and switch.

He loaded into the fourth tacbody, bringing the ghost of atrocious pain along with him, a shock so hard, the CLoan staggered and the stims kicked in again. Dwire could barely think. The successive traumas were going to drive him insane.

He'd placed the fourth tacbody last in the running order where he thought he'd need it most. It was a tank form, engineered for frontline duty, the only heavy-grade CLoan in the batch the clients had sourced. It was built like a nose tackle on steroids. Its brute solidity and trauma compensation package soothed him to a whimper and regulated his vitals.

He was standing on the ridge above the supplying port, tears streaming down his face. He had a composite armor exo-suit with a reflective bronze finish, a Bakshine Hypernetic carbine, and an unused fusion mine.

Below him, the crippled slayborg was dismembering his still-screaming former self. Dwire shouldered the carbine, took aim, and put a hyperkinetic round through the head of his previous body. In the pink mist, the slayborg glanced around and saw him.

"And fuck you, too," said Dwire. He fired again and turned the slayborg into a cloud of meat.

Waste of a round, but the satisfaction was worth it.

He started to run, enjoying the increased speed and ground coverage of the new tac. He checked the datarray. One hour left on the range window, and he was down to his last deployable tacbody. That was disappointing. He'd burned through time and resources more quickly than he had anticipated.

The autosentries were whirring around. *Screw them.* Like they didn't know there was an uninvited guest. He lobbed the mine.

It landed smack on the supply port. This tank CLoan had a good arm. The blast took out the armored shutter of the port in a blizzard of metal shards and wrecked the support gantry. It slumped, groaning and creaking.

The autosentries began to fire. Ice flaked and spat at his heels.

Dwire leapt headlong into the flames.

He fell down the service shaft that the blast had uncapped. The walls rushed past. It was a two-mile drop. The tacbody knew how to control itself in freefall. It had made HALO jumps before. The base of the shaft was rushing up at him. He triggered the grav-pod strapped to the small of his back, and floated down the last twenty meters like a feather.

Service hatch. He ripped the plating off with his fingers and stabbed in a datahack. The tool buzzed as it bit into the instructor systems.

Identify: hatch operation functions.
Hatch operation: seal hatch in event of attack.
Reverse instruction.
Confirm instruction.
Verify situation: attack underway.
Initiate function.

The hatch opened. Dwire stepped through. Trick of the trade. He wondered if he would ever have been hired if people realized how simple a walkaround could be. Security architecture was pretty much impossible to break or override. But if you got in underneath, at the instruction level, and simply reversed the instruction order, the system thought it was doing what it was supposed to do and didn't argue back.

The halls were lofty and dim. Frost coated every surface. His footsteps sounded dull and flat. Infilling at Vane Seven put him close to Stack Sixty, so the recovery room there was the nearest.

Hazard flash. Dwire swung up and picked a Supertrooper off one of the overhead walkways before it could tag him. Two more appeared, drawing aim. Scary-fast, he tracked the carbine and punched off their heads, one after the other.

He started active hunting via the carbine's scope as he advanced. Three more slayborgs came into range. He felled them with a burst of rapid, and they sprayed metal and plastic fragments as they shredded. He plugged another through the throat with a single round, and it collapsed, head bowed as if in prayer.

The massive iris hatch of the recovery room was wide open.

The room was vast and domed. Thirty ornate seats were arranged in a circle, like a clock face around a central datarray system. Only one of the positions was active. Data shimmered in the cold, misty air above the station.

"Is this what you're looking for?"

The tacbody was standing near the operational station. It was a heavy-grade CLoan like the one he was wearing, but it was brand-new, and the motile skin armor encasing it was polished chrome, fancy and expensive—this year's model. It made his army surplus cast-off feel shabby and soiled.

"Mr. Durant," said Dwire. "I didn't think you'd be here in person."

"Of course," said the Frost Giant through the tacbody's mouth. "With something this important, I like to mind it myself. My whole business and reputation are based upon my level of service, and this is a very special case."

The tacbody took a step forward.

"Speaking of reputations," it said, "I'm very disappointed in you, Mr. Dwire."

"You know it's me?"

"Of course. Who else could get this far? I recognized you by your approach. And your poor mind's been flying around a lot today from body to body. That's given me plenty of time to process and match your brain patterns.

"I pity you, by the way," the Frost Giant added. "You must be feeling wretched. All that trauma. I doubt you'll ever be quite the same again."

"I'll survive," said Dwire.

"No, you won't, not in any way. I've known you were coming here for weeks. Information, my friend. It's what I do. It's the most powerful commodity there is. I've known about your mission since you were hired. I know who your clients are. I know what their concerns are: the framing of the treaty."

"If," Dwire began, "you knew I was coming, why—"

"It was a wonderful opportunity to run an active test of my security architecture. I've already devised a number of new countermeasures and system evolutions that will make sure this never happens again. So, thank you for that. Good of you to provide aftercare service."

Dwire shrugged. He went to the circle, chose a seat at random, and sat down.

"What happens now?" he asked.

Behind its gleaming visor, the Frost Giant smiled with the face it was using.

"Well," it said, "you've got six minutes before the packet ship moves out of range. After that, it'll be too far away for you to save back to the gestalter engine. Your body will be out there, on a mail boat, and your mind will be stuck here. It will die along with that CLoan you're loaded into."

"Six minutes," said Dwire. "A lot can happen in six minutes."

He snatched up the carbine and fired. The Frost Giant was already moving, a blur. The hyper round clipped it and spanked away into the far wall, but even the glancing impact was enough to spin the hurtling tacbody clean off its feet. It smashed into the station, crumpling a console and wrecking one of the chairs.

Dwire was on his feet. The Frost Giant, a gruesome blister of blackened metal and cooked meat marring the sleek chrome lines of its shoulder armor, tackled him hard. They crashed over together. Another ornate seat was demolished. Dwire punched the Giant in the side of the head and cracked its visor. The Frost Giant rolled clear and delivered a spin kick that carried Dwire clear across the reading station. He bounced off the edge and hit the floor. The Frost Giant kicked the fallen carbine away across the frosty deck, picked up Dwire and slammed him into the chamber wall.

Dwire mashed his elbow into the Giant's face, then punched it in the sternum. He heard bone shear. The Giant fell back. Released, Dwire dropped to the deck. He kicked the Giant off its knees and stood over it.

The Frost Giant looked up at Dwire. Through its broken, blood-flecked faceplate, it smiled.

"Your time is up," it said.

"I know," said Dwire.

"The packet ship has moved out of range."

"I know."

Dwire looked around. The room was slowly and quietly filling with Supertroopers. Their weapons were leveled at him.

"So . . . are they wrong?" Dwire asked. "Oliphant and the others? Are they wrong about the treaty?"

"No," Durant replied. It wrenched off its helmet and spat blood. "The treaty is brilliantly engineered. The Ushuns are very methodical. The peace agreement requires full alliance with the Ushuns, and Ushun participation in the administration of government. If you think they were a military menace, just wait to see how they exert influence and power from within the Sodality legislature. David has killed Goliath. A long and bloody war would have cost the Sodality less."

"You knew this . . . all this, and you protected the information?"

"That's what I do, Mr. Dwire. My reputation depends on it."

"They paid you?"

The Frost Giant shook its head.

"Only in information. In exchange for my services, I become designated custodian of the entire Ushun cultural archive. *Sole custodian.* My claves become true treasure houses. I will possess a data resource unparalleled in human or Ushun space."

"Not just the richest being in the Spiral Arm. The most powerful."

Durant heaved his tacbody to its feet.

"A giant, truly," it smiled.

Dwire shrugged.

"Information is precious," he said. "Durant, what's the active save-and-restore range of a gestalter engine?"

"You know that well enough, Dwire. It is a range your mail boat has long since exceeded."

"But say I ejected an active gestalt base-unit from the packet when I launched my CLoans, it would still be in range, wouldn't it? Easily. And still in range of the ship, too. For another eighteen minutes."

Durant's reply was incoherent. The slayborgs began firing and didn't stop until Dwire's fourth tacbody was a liquefied sludge coating the recovery room's wall.

Dwire opened his eyes. Ret-feed told him he had been down for sixteen hours, and in that time, his heart had stopped on nine separate occasions. The packet ship's medborgs were bending over him.

He'd be sick from the stims for years. The multiple save traumas would probably never leave him. He got up, in his own flesh. The medborgs tried to persuade him to lie back, but he waved them off.

He opened a fast-link messenger blank. It would take two days to reach its destination. It would still arrive before the packet ship.

He selected "Oliphant" from his recipient list with a haptic flick. Then, in the open pane, his fingers touching nothing but light, he began to compose a message telling his client that he'd stopped a peace and started a war, and was now leaving Nox at seventy-three times the speed of light. Somehow, that didn't feel fast enough.

ABOUT THE AUTHOR

DAN ABNETT is a seven-time *New York Times* bestselling author and an award-winning comic book writer. He has written over fifty novels, including the acclaimed Gaunt's Ghosts series, the Eisenhorn and Ravenor trilogies, volumes of the million-selling Horus Heresy series, *The Silent Stars Go By* (Doctor Who), *Rocket Raccoon and Groot: Steal the Galaxy, The Avengers: Everybody Wants to Rule the World, Triumff: Her Majesty's Hero,* and *Embedded,* and with Nik Vincent, *Tomb Raider: The Ten Thousand Immortals* and *Fiefdom.* In comics, he is known for his work for Marvel, DC, Boom!, Dark Horse and 2000AD. His 2008 run on *The Guardians of the Galaxy* for Marvel formed the inspiration for the blockbuster movie. He has also written extensively for the games industry, including *Shadow of Mordor* and *Alien: Isolation.* Dan lives and works in the UK with his wife, Nik Vincent-Abnett, an editor and writer of fiction. Follow him on Twitter @VincentAbnett.

ACKNOWLEDGMENTS

No anthology is made in a vacuum—even when many of the stories take place in one—and thus my most heartfelt thanks and appreciation go out to:

Joe Monti, for acquiring the book, and to the rest of the team at Saga Press. My agent, Seth Fishman, for being awesome and supportive. (Writers: you'd be lucky to have Seth in your corner.) Gordon Van Gelder and Ellen Datlow, for being great mentors and friends. My cosmically wonderful wife, Christie; my stepdaughters Grace and Lotte; my mom, Marianne; and my sister, Becky—for all their love and support. All of the writers who had stories included in this anthology and all of my other projects. And last but not least, to everyone who bought this book, or any of my other anthologies (or subscribed to my magazines *Lightspeed* and *Nightmare*)—you're the ones who it make it all possible.

ABOUT THE EDITOR

JOHN JOSEPH ADAMS is the editor of John Joseph Adams Books, an SF/Fantasy imprint from Houghton Mifflin Harcourt. He is also the series editor of *Best American Science Fiction and Fantasy*, as well as the bestselling editor of many other anthologies, including *Wastelands*, *Brave New Worlds*, and *The Living Dead*. Recent books include *What the #@&%is That?*, *Operation Arcana*, *Press Start to Play*, *Loosed Upon the World*, and The Apocalypse Triptych (consisting of *The End is Nigh*, *The End is Now*, and *The End Has Come*). Called "the reigning king of the anthology world" by Barnes & Noble, John is a two-time winner of the Hugo Award (for which he has been nominated ten times) and is a seven-time World Fantasy Award finalist. John is also the editor and publisher of the digital magazines *Lightspeed* and *Nightmare*, and is a producer for WIRED's *The Geek's Guide to the Galaxy* podcast. He also served as a judge for the 2015 National Book Award. Learn more at johnjosephadams.com, johnjosephadamsbooks.com, and @johnjosephadams.